Weep Tonight

Weep Tonight

Shauna Lee

Editor: Joyce Bellous & Gina Fusco

iUniverse, Inc.
Bloomington

Weep Tonight

This book is based on a true story. All interpretations of events are based on the author's perception and in no way reflect the feelings of any of the characters portrayed in the book.

Hymn "Jesus Lover of My Soul" by Charles Wesley (1707 – 1788) Public Domain

Scripture quotations are from the King James Version, the New International Version or the New Living Translation as noted.

THE HOLY BIBLE, NEW INTERNATIONAL VERSION®, NIV® Copyright © 1973, 1978, 1984, 2011 by Biblica, Inc. ™ Used by permission. All rights reserved worldwide.

Scripture quotations marked (NLT) are taken from the Holy Bible, New Living Translation, copyright © 1996, 2004, 2007 by Tyndale House Foundation. Used by permission of Tyndale House Publishers, Inc., Carol Stream, Illinois 60188. All rights reserved.

iUniverse books may be ordered through booksellers or by contacting:

iUniverse
1663 Liberty Drive
Bloomington, IN 47403
www.iuniverse.com
1-800-Authors (1-800-288-4677)

Because of the dynamic nature of the Internet, any web addresses or links contained in this book may have changed since publication and may no longer be valid. The views expressed in this work are solely those of the author and do not necessarily reflect the views of the publisher, and the publisher hereby disclaims any responsibility for them.

Any people depicted in stock imagery provided by Thinkstock are models, and such images are being used for illustrative purposes only.
Certain stock imagery © Thinkstock.

ISBN: 978-1-4620-2795-8 (sc)

Printed in the United States of America

iUniverse rev. date: 10/12/2011

For Ruth and Waldemar,
who were brave enough to
share their legacy.

There is sacredness in tears. They
are not the marks of weakness, but of power.
They speak more eloquently than ten
thousand tongues. They are the messengers
of overwhelming grief, of deep contradiction,
and of unspeakable love."

-Washington Irving

Acknowledgements

Thank you to my heavenly Father who stirred in me the desire to embark down this road, to capture this story and to share it with others so that they may know His love. Thank you for all of the signposts along the way that led me in the right direction and prodded me forward when I felt like giving up. All of the honor, glory and praise go to You for giving me the words to say.

Thank you to my supportive family who encouraged me along this long journey. To my husband, Matthew, and children, Jacob, Jasper and Jenna, who gave me the time and freedom to work, and especially to Matthew who encouraged me never to give up on this project. May the legacy of Waldemar and Ruth forever touch your lives and the lives of your children.

Thank you to my mom, Marlene, step-dad, Bob, and my sister, Karen, who were my biggest cheerleaders as I wrote and figured out how this idea could become a reality. Thank you for praying for me, reading my chapters and constantly listening to me talk about the story as I figured out how it would unfold.

Thank you to Arlene Lessing for capturing the Lessing family legacy and recording it so that all of the Lessing descendants would know their history. Thank you for sharing with me all of your photos and stories so that I could write about the Lessing family with some degree of knowledge regarding their lives and stories. I am ever appreciative to your gift of genealogy and your passion to discover the past.

Thank you to Catherine Gospodyn who translated and perfected all of the German language in the book. Thank you to my very first reader, Jodi Cobain, who gave me strong words of encouragement.

Finally, thank you to Joyce Bellous who took the time to develop me as a better writer, who turned my story into a novel, who gave me the right feedback to take me from a storyteller to an author. Your contribution is immensely appreciated; because of you I can sit back and be completely satisfied with the finished product. I will always be thankful to you for being such a key part of making this dream a reality.

Shauna Lee

Introduction

His pale, blue eyes danced as he spoke. As I brought the chicken to my mouth, I looked across at him and listened to his story. Every hair on his head was smoothed neatly into place. He was handsome, stunningly so for his age. His back was straight and strong, his weathered hands cutting his meat, his food hanging on his fork, anticipating his next bite while he talked. His deep, melodic voice spoke of a story I had not heard. It was funny. It ran through my imagination like a scene from a movie. Suddenly, I was there with him, running through the fields, feeling the prairie wind in my hair and smelling the morning dew. I could hear his mother calling for him in the distance as he described it. The others at the table listened intently, too, smiling and laughing along with him.

As I chewed and swallowed, I considered the tale. The hum of voices and clink of silverware from the restaurant filled my ears. A wave of emotions swept over me as I realized that when he died, his story would be lost, and . . . so would hers.

Suddenly, I felt a whisper in my heart. It was up to me. I had to be the one to capture it. I had to be the one to tell how it all came to be.

He talked on, speaking of the other children, his parents and the joy he had known. As I ate, I wondered if it was even possible. It was a story of enormous proportions and, as it turned out, I knew so little. Could I even write? Was I a worthy storyteller? Would they tell me the details?

As I looked around the table, I questioned myself. Can you ever really know someone else's life? Is there any way to tell this kind of story accurately?

I took a long drink of water and wondered, Can I do it justice? Can I capture the legacy of their faith, the hardships and the triumphs?

I looked him over as he continued to speak. I fingered the droplets of condensation on my glass. I looked around the table at the wonderful people surrounding me.

I could try. If they were willing, I could try.

*" . . . Today shalt thou be
with me in paradise." Luke
23:43 KJV*

Prologue: Leduc, Alberta
June 11, 1921

Frederick held his wife Pauline's hand as he lay dying. It had been a good life for him. This past month he had felt his days on earth were numbered. He sensed it the day he said goodbye to his young daughter. She had been in the front room, laid out in her black casket, looking so peaceful. She lay surrounded in flowers, a wreath around her head, wearing a white gown her mother had made. Pauline had curled her hair one last time and folded her hands over each other. She tenderly smoothed her gown and carefully placed each flower around her body, tucking her baby girl in for an eternal sleep. As he had looked into her coffin one last time, his grief pressed heavily on his chest, making it hard to breathe. He ached to see her wake up and smile at him, tell him one more story, one more joke, anything. As he and his sons had carried her lifeless body out the front door, he said, "I'll be the next one."

Now he looked out of his bedroom window. He could hear the others speaking in hushed voices outside his room.

He had been a successful farmer for the last eighteen years. Maybe things had been going too well. Perhaps all good things had to end. He had a fancy car, a beautiful home and wonderful children. They had a cow barn to sustain the family and even a rental property in Edmonton. He had good workhorses, a stallion and the newest-model winter sleigh. They even had a telephone, the envy of all the neighbors. He had just made a spectacular purchase of land, 160 acres for $15 an acre. It was a steal considering most land sold for $60 to $100 an acre. He had hired a few men to help him clear his land, but even after nearly one year it was not finished. His heart was not going to let him live to see the project completed.

His daughter, Ruth, and her husband, Herman, had been summoned back from Oregon where they had moved after their wedding. The others had been called, too. Dr. Gold, the family doctor, Dr. Kidd, a local fellow, Dr. Jones a cardiac specialist from Edmonton and his nurse were there to see to his medical needs. All of the other children who still lived close by had come today to say goodbye. His relatives Sam Holland and Paul Marquardt had just been in his room, witnessing him sign the will.

The nurse had given him an injection to help with the pain. Everyone spoke in hushed tones, saying, "The end is near."

His wife sat stroking his hand, tears rolling down her cheeks. He looked over at her, feeling her pain.

"I'm sorry. I'm sorry to leave you with all of the unfinished business."

She looked up at him. "I'll manage."

He panted, "I love you. Always have."

"I love you too."

"I'm going to see our Savior." He smiled and said, "Nothing better than that."

"I know . . . ." Fresh tears ran down her face.

"And," he continued, "I'll see the children again."

Pauline shook her head, crying into her apron. She was a tough woman, but this, this was too much. She wished she could go with him. She wished she could see her daughters and infant son again rather than toil on this wretched prairie without them. Heaven seemed so far away.

Dr. Gold came in the room. "Is everything okay in here?"

Frederick nodded weakly.

"Are you in pain?"

"Well," he gasped, "it's just so hard to breathe . . ."

"Unfortunately, that's normal." He moved to Frederick's bedside and arranged another pillow behind his back. "We'll just try to make you comfortable." Dr. Gold looked at Pauline and sighed. He had been there when her young daughters had died, and he had delivered her last son who never drew his first breath.

"If you'll excuse me, I'll give you some time. If you need more pain medication, please let me know."

"Thank you, Dr. Gold," Pauline said softly. The doctor nodded and left the room.

Frederick thought of all the things he was leaving behind. The farm, the wealth . . . all of that meant very little now. God had blessed his life in Canada. He was happy he would see his Maker very soon, but oh, how he would miss his family.

Frederick spoke in a whisper, "Do you think Ruth will make it before I . . ."

"I hope so." Pauline looked out the window and squeezed his hand. "I hope so."

" . . . I will never leave thee,
nor forsake thee. "
Hebrews 13:5 KJV

December 5, 1921
Leduc, Alberta

"*Bist du bereit?*" Herman Bohlman asked in German. His blue eyes were looking at his expectant bride who was walking alongside him. He was bringing her home from a baby shower she had attended at the church. The night sky above was lit with stars. The moonlight sparkled on the large snow banks lining the road.

"As ready as I can be," answered Ruth in their mother tongue. Her breath formed small clouds in the freezing air as she spoke. "It shouldn't be too much longer," she patted her belly and laughed, "I'm running out of room!"

Herman smiled and asked, "Did you have a good night?"

"Yes, it was lovely. I am so thankful for all of the gifts."

"It seems like you got a lot of things!"

She watched him struggle as he walked with all of the awkward packages. "You'll be thankful too once we get it all home." He carried a basket full of blankets and several bags of baby clothes and diapers. "Can you handle it?" she asked. Her cheeks were pink from the cold. "Can I help you?"

"No, you just watch your footing. I don't want you to slip."

Her eyes danced. "Okay, Hercules."

"Yes I am, thank you," he laughed.

Ruth held firmly to the crook of Herman's arm as they walked. The roads had icy spots, and given her condition she didn't want to fall. She

4

looked down at her three-quarter-length fur-trimmed winter coat. She could only button the top two buttons; the rest was hanging open, leaving only her long wool skirt and sweater to combat the cool night air. The coat buttons around her middle simply wouldn't reach. She was, as best she could figure, at the end of her pregnancy. The baby should be arriving some time before Christmas.

"Are you warm enough?" he questioned.

"I'll be fine. Let's hurry though."

"Easy for you to say," he said jokingly as he adjusted the packages in his arms.

They both fell quiet and were content to listen to the symphony of their boots squeaking against the freshly fallen snow. Herman listened to Ruth's labored breathing as she hurried along next to him.

"You all right?" he asked.

"Just worn out."

The night was calm and quiet. Leduc, Alberta, was a growing town but still small enough that everyone knew one another, and only a handful of people owned a motor car. Most people walked wherever they needed to go and some used horses. In the winter, a horse-drawn cutter was the most popular choice for getting around. As they walked down the road toward their home, they called out warm greetings to the occasional passerby.

Their small wooden-framed home came into view. The modest house was nestled between other houses that were built in a similar style. Drifts of snow capped the rooftop. White clouds emerged from the chimney. The house had a small porch across the front and a frost-covered picture window to the left of the door. On the door was a fresh wreath that Ruth had made from pine boughs and dried berries.

Ruth rubbed her belly with her free hand as the baby turned within. Her pelvis and thighs ached with the pressure.

"We're nearly there," Herman assured her.

Ruth nodded, grimacing from the discomfort.

The couple reached the front steps. Herman gave Ruth a hand through the front door and into their living room. He immediately went to the firebox and stoked the coals to warm up the room. The firebox heater was black and stood on ornate legs in the corner of the room. It had floral detailing on the side, and even though it was a small unit, it heated the whole house. Ruth stood, unbuttoning her coat and laying it on the stuffed armchair.

"Have a seat." Herman gestured toward the striped sofa that sat opposite the heater. She sat down with a sigh.

Knowingly he added, "Put your feet up and I'll help you with your boots." He pulled over a small wooden footstool and Ruth put up both feet. He unlaced her boots and eased them off.

Ruth looked down at her swollen ankles. "Thanks. The thought of unlacing my boots was simply too much. My feet feel like they are on another planet."

He laughed, "You'll be reunited before you know it." He moved back to the firebox to stoke the coals again.

She smiled and laid her head back, looking around the room. Aside from the armchair and sofa, the only other piece of furniture was a curio cabinet with pieces of their wedding china on display. Over the cabinet hung a painting. It was a picture of the rolling prairies. A small farmhouse stood in the distance and tiny cows grazed the fields. It had been a wedding gift. Ruth wondered why anyone would want a view of the prairies when all you had to do was look out the window. Nevertheless, it was something to decorate the walls and Herman seemed to like it. She would have preferred to have a painting of the ocean. They had been in Portland for a short time after they were married. She loved the occasional trip to the ocean they had taken there. She let her thoughts drift to stories that Herman had told her of his journey crossing the Atlantic.

Herman stared into the hot coals. It was hard to believe they were going to have a child of their own. As he was becoming a parent, he thought of his own mother, Juliana Bohlman. He wondered if his mother would ever get to meet their baby. Thoughts of his mother brought a mix of regret and longing. He hadn't heard from his family in so long.

The series of events that brought him to Leduc had started a long time ago, deep in the story of his family history. Although he was born in Tuczn, Russia, in 1894, he considered himself German. His parents were both born in Lodz, Russia. His German roots began when previous generations came from Germany by invitation of Empress Catherine the Great to come and work the Russian soil. His mother had told him the stories of his ancestors, and he imagined he would one day tell his children the same.

Unlike him and Ruth, his mother and his father, Julianna and Frederick Bohlman, had endured many hardships as a young couple. Back in the early 1800s, their ancestors had been welcome in Russia as German immigrants. By the time Frederick and Juliana were married, the tide had changed. The privileges that the German immigrants had originally been offered—religious freedom, exemption from military service and self-administration, were being rescinded by the Russian leader Czar Nicholas II. Frederick and Juliana, their parents and all Germans, were compelled to 'Russiafy' to change their names, their schools and churches, or return to Germany. Their land, where they had once prospered, was taken and they were forced to become tenant farmers. Germans were forced to do share cropping. They often moved around looking for a place where they could once again prosper and live without Russian influence.

In 1890, two years after they were married, Frederick and Juliana had a son named Rudolf who a year later succumbed to scarlet fever. A year after his death, they had a daughter, Lakadia. Herman assumed that, by now, Lakadia might be married and even have children of her own.

Following Lakadia, Herman's parents had three sons and a daughter: Reinhold, Herman, Asalph and Martha. Reinhold, Herman's older brother, had died at the age of seven.

Herman looked over at Ruth.

"Do you want some tea?" he asked her softly.

She nodded, her eyes closed.

"Are you feeling okay?" he asked nervously.

"I'm fine. I'm just uncomfortable." She shifted her weight from one hip to the other and tried to lean back as far as possible on the sofa.

Herman went to the kitchen to prepare some tea for Ruth. She had her hand on her abdomen, feeling the baby move within. She was anxious to see if the baby would be a boy or a girl. She wondered if he or she would have Herman's features or her own, or a lovely mix of both.

A short time later, Herman returned to the living room.

"Here you are, love." Herman passed Ruth a steaming cup of tea.

"Thank you."

She held the cup and saucer in her hands, then closed her eyes again.

"What are you thinking about?" Herman asked.

"Oh, I'm wondering if the baby will have your eyes."

"I should hope not, or how will I see?" Herman laughed.

Ruth laughed and swatted Herman with her free hand, "Very funny."

"What do you think the baby will look like?" he asked.

"I think he will be as handsome as you."

"A boy you think?"

"Maybe." She paused and said, "I can't wait to find out." Ruth sighed, trying to imagine the face of their unborn child.

"Do you think the child will be as stubborn as you?" Herman teased.

"Me? Stubborn?" She faked great surprise at his comment and laughed, "I'm just determined."

"The qualities of a great leader." He smiled at her.

Again he thought of his mother. She had been a great leader. They had faced terrible times in Russia, and yet his mother had persevered. The family had moved from Lodz to the village of Porozov when he was a young boy. Their house had a dirt floor and sparse furnishings. There was no kitchen, just a common oven in the village.

Tragically in 1903, at the age of thirty-nine, Frederick was killed by a horse he was shoeing. The horse ruptured his spleen, leaving Juliana a widow and a single mother to their four remaining children. Her parents helped to support her and the children. No one had money though; they were all in the same struggle for survival. Herman, being the oldest son, left school at the age of nine to help his mother farm their land.

"What are you thinking about?" Ruth asked gently.

"*Mutter.*"

Ruth nodded, sipping her tea.

"I miss my family. I haven't heard from them in so long . . . she used to write." His eyes misted up. "I haven't heard from them in more than five years."

Ruth rubbed his hand. "I'm sorry. I am so sorry. I can't imagine."

"I've sent them enough money by now. I keep thinking that maybe they're on their way here. Maybe they're looking for me. Something tells me . . ."

"They'll find you," she said softly.

When Herman was nineteen, he left Porozov. He and three friends spent three months walking 1,200 kilometers to Antwerp, Belgium. The journey had been grueling. By the time they arrived in Antwerp, they were broke—even more broke than when they left Porozov. The four young men worked until they earned enough for passage on a ship. Eventually, they had enough to travel in steerage across the Atlantic to Quebec. It took thirteen days. They arrived in Quebec City on May 6, 1913.

At that point, Herman left his friends and made his way by train to Cass Lake, Minnesota. He had friends from Russia, the Maskowskis, who lived in Cass Lake. He stayed with them and found work at a local lumberyard. He learned English from the workers there, earning $1.00

per day. The first week, he sent money to his mother, sisters and brother so they could buy their own passage to America.

"I'll never forget the day I left."

"Tell me about it."

"Martha . . ." He buried his face in his hands and sighed. He looked up slowly. "I had said my goodbyes. I was walking down the road, away from the farm. Then I heard her calling my name."

"Martha?"

"Yes. *Herman, Herman, don't leave us—oh, we'll never see you again.* I turned around to wave and saw the tears pouring down her cheeks. She was running toward me, crying and begging me not to leave."

Ruth sat up and put her arm around her husband's shoulders. She gently rubbed his back.

"I'm sorry, I know you're tired . . ." he sniffed.

"Go on—I want to know."

"I said, 'I'll send for you, Martha. I'll see you soon . . . take care of Mother, Lakadia and Asalph for me.' I turned and walked away."

He looked down at his hands. "I believed what I said. I figured it would only take me a few months to earn enough for their passage."

"You did the right thing," she said tenderly.

"She was just a little girl, just ten years old. It must seem like a lifetime to her. I just don't want her to think I've forgotten."

"They know, they know you love them. With the war it's hard to know if mail is getting through. Maybe they have written and their letters haven't made it here."

"I hope so. Sometimes I hear stories from the old country and it worries me. They are Germans in a Russian world."

"They are in God's hands. We all are."

She yawned and stretched.

"You're tired. I'll help you to bed." He rose to his feet, offering to help her up.

Ruth nodded and took his outstretched hand. He pulled her up. She gave him a big hug. "I love you."

"I love you too." He stood with his arms around her. They kissed, "Now to bed with the two of you."

The couple retreated to their room. Herman helped Ruth change and eased her into her place in the bed. The mattress was dimpled where her body lay every night. Herman tucked the warm quilts over her.

"Goodnight, love," he whispered as Ruth dozed off.

Leaving the bedroom, Herman went to the firebox and added more coal. He wanted Ruth to be warm tonight. He picked up her cup and saucer and went into the kitchen. Ruth had filled the metal pail with snow in the morning and had left it on the kitchen stove to melt. He went to work washing Ruth's teacup and saucer in the washbasin. After that, he pulled some bread and butter out of the cabinet and sat at the kitchen table.

He had come so far in the last eight years. Not only in distance, halfway around the globe, but in life experience. He worked in Minnesota four years. At first he received regular letters from his mother, thanking him for the money, and then after the war started in 1914 the letters slowed down. He kept urging her to come but she worried about leaving her parents behind. Eventually in 1916, the letters ceased. He hadn't heard from her since.

By that time he had come to hate his job at the lumberyard. The Englishmen treated him poorly. Tensions from the war carried across the Atlantic, right into the lumberyard. He was the only German working there, and even some of the fellows who had initially been friendly shunned him. During this period he was so conflicted. He wanted to stay in Minnesota to wait for his family but the desire to settle in a German community was strong. After much convincing from some of his friends, he decided to go to Alberta; in particular, to Leduc where other Germans from Russia had settled. His friends promised they would send word if his family ever made it to Minnesota.

He arrived in Leduc by train in November 1917. It was a desolate frontier town. Calling it a town was probably too generous. It was more of a village based on its amenities. Only two streetlights lit the one main street. Surrounding a few shops and houses was farmland, as far as you could see. One look and Herman had been determined to leave the next morning.

For lack of a better place to go and with no funds to travel, he started working at Morris' General Store. He took up residence at the Waldorf Hotel and slowly began to forge relationships with members of the community. Soon he was attending the local church where he met Ruth Lessing.

He had always admired Ruth but it wasn't until 1918 when he became very ill with pneumonia that their relationship first began. The Lessing family took him in. They nursed him back to health. His admiration for Ruth blossomed to love. When she was eighteen, he asked for her hand in marriage and the Lessings were delighted to oblige. The wedding was a quaint ceremony held at First Baptist Church. Ruth's inheritance had left them the means to purchase their small home and start a life of their own. Now here they were, about to welcome their first child. He was thankful that God had brought him to Leduc, to Ruth, and yet he longed for his family to be there with him.

"Wherever they are, Lord . . . bring them safely to me," he prayed.

He put his plate next to the washbasin and then headed to their bedroom. He undressed, pulled on his nightclothes and slipped under the covers next to Ruth. He watched her body rise and fall as she breathed. He slipped his arm around her and rested his hand on her bulging belly. He felt the baby shift.

God had blessed him.

"Goodnight, *Schatzi* . . . goodnight," he whispered to his unborn child.

Herman fell into a fitful sleep, dreaming of little Martha, calling after him.

Suddenly, there was a scream of terror.

*"Every good gift and every
perfect gift is from above,
and cometh down from the
Father of lights, with whom
there is no variableness,
neither shadow of turning."*
James 1:17 KJV

December 6, 1921
Leduc, Alberta

Herman sat up in bed, his heart pounding.

"Herman!" Ruth screamed as pains shot through her back and front.

"What? What's happening?"

"Get . . . the mid-wife," she moaned breathlessly.

"Yes, of course!"

Herman's bare feet hit the wooden floors. He quickly slipped on his trousers and shirt. He fastened his shirt buttons as fast as he could.

She groaned and clutched her abdomen. "The pain . . ."

"Are you going to be okay while I'm gone?"

"Go—go!"

"Okay," he gasped.

His mind was racing. He hastily stoked the heater in the front room. He pulled on his warm boots and coat. He slammed the door behind him and ran down the town's main road to the house of the midwife, Betty Smith. It was a dark night. The street was still and silent.

He knocked loudly on her front door.

"Mrs. Smith," Herman called through the door. "It's Mr. Bohlman! Mrs. Bohlman needs you!"

Herman paced the front porch. He tried to see if there was any sign of life inside the house.

"Mrs. Smith!" He banged again on the front door.

A moment later, the lights came on inside the Smith's home. He could hear someone moving around. Betty opened the front door with her coat on and midwifery bag in hand.

"Hello, Mr. Bohlman," she eyed the frantic young man, "Is it time?"

"Yes! It seems bad—something might be wrong!"

"It's okay," Betty reassured him. She came out of the house and closed the door behind her, "The pain is normal. Having a baby isn't easy."

"Please," he begged, "let's hurry."

"When did it start?" she asked softly as they walked briskly through the snow.

"She just woke up screaming!"

"That's okay," Betty reassured. "You need to be calm for her and . . ." she looked around, " . . . you need to quiet down or you're going to wake the whole street."

He nodded, his brows furrowed. "You're right," he whispered.

"This is a natural process, it takes time and energy."

"Yes," he said quickly.

They were back at the house. Herman took the front steps two at a time. He swung open the front door. He could see through the front room and back into their bedroom. Ruth was kneeling on the floor with her arms on the bed. Her head was resting on her arms.

"Are you alright, *Liebling*?" Herman scrambled to get his boots off.

"It's better when I'm up," she panted.

Betty took over, "Mr. Bohlman, help her to the chair or support her while she stands. Whatever is most comfortable. I need to wash my hands and then I'll see what's happening." She left for the kitchen.

"Do you want to sit?" he asked.

Ruth shook her head, no.

"And get some towels, and some fresh bedding," Betty called from the kitchen.

"Can you hang on to the chair?" he asked.

She nodded and moaned.

"Okay—good."

Herman moved around the room, pulled an extra set of blankets from a basket on top of the wardrobe. He rushed to make the bed. He kept looking at Ruth leaning on the chair. She had her head down, her free hand on her belly. She was panting. She was focused.

Betty returned from the kitchen and helped Herman finish getting the sheets on. She then instructed him to give her a hand with getting Ruth onto the bed. He softly stroked Ruth's head as she leaned back against the pillows.

"Are you okay?"

She smiled half-heartedly. "I'll be fine."

"I'll be right here if you need me," he assured her.

"Mr. Bohlman," Betty said decisively, "go and heat some water on the stove for me. Warm a blanket for the baby when it arrives. Keep the house nice and warm for the baby's arrival."

Herman gave Ruth's hand a squeeze and took one last look at her, propped up in bed.

"I'll be okay," she gasped as another contraction took hold of her.

Betty smiled. "We'll call you in after the baby comes."

He hesitated, then left the room, closing the door behind him.

He paced back and forth in the front room as the sun rose. Ruth's cries filled the house. He could hear Betty's low, calm voice coaching her through the pain. About an hour before, he had gone to the neighbor's house to ask if they could get word to the Lessing farm. Their teenage son had obliged and promised to return shortly with Ruth's mother, Pauline Lessing. He kept checking out the front window to check if he could see them coming.

Finally, he saw Pauline and the neighbor boy coming down the road. He went to the front door to welcome them in.

"Hello, Mother!"

Pauline came up the front steps wearing a scarf over her head and a warm wool coat. "Hello." Behind her the sky was crimson with the sunrise.

"Come in, come in."

"When did it start?" she asked as she stepped into the house.

"In the early morning—she is in incredible pain."

Pauline nodded as she unbuttoned her coat and stomped the snow off her boots. "That's to be expected. I called Mrs. Daum. She should be here soon." She thanked the neighbor boy and sent him on his way.

Herman took Pauline's coat and hung it on a peg behind the door. "Are you going in?"

"Yes, I'll see how she's doing." She looked at Herman and gave him a hug before going into the bedroom. "No need to worry."

Before long, Emma Daum, a close family friend, arrived. She made herself busy in the kitchen making breakfast. Herman tried not to dwell on the cries coming from the bedroom.

Betty emerged from the room, her sleeves rolled up to her elbows. Herman couldn't help but notice the blood on her apron.

"Mr. Bohlman, I'm afraid we need Dr. Gold. It's a big baby; too big."

"Alright."

"Go as quickly as you can."

Ruth was growing weary. Sweat beaded her forehead. No matter how she pushed, she wasn't making any progress. The night seemed endless. This wasn't how she had imagined it would be.

She heard Betty instruct Herman to get Dr. Gold.

"Mother," Ruth gasped, "what's happening?"

"The baby isn't coming down."

"Oh! What can I do?" she asked, trembling.

"You're doing fine. You're doing everything you can. It must be a big baby and you're a petite woman."

"I'm scared."

"I know," she whispered. "We'll get through this, sweetheart. Children are born every day." Pauline quoted a verse from the Bible and in German said, "*Fear thou not; for I am with thee be not dismayed; for I am thy God: I will strengthen thee; yea, I will help thee; I will uphold thee with the right hand of my righteousness.*"

Ruth sank back against her pillows and moaned. Tears streamed down her flushed cheeks.

The house was grand, a large Victorian. Herman could see it in the distance as he ran down the snow-packed road. The siding was white, and the trim and shutters were black. A porch wrapped around the front of the home with large columns supporting the roof overhead. A two-story turret rose grandly on the left-hand side. Dr. Gold ran his practice out of the main floor and lived on the second story.

Herman approached the house. His heart was pounding as he rapped the knocker on the front door. He paced back and forth. It was nine am. The doctor should be up.

Herman rapped the knocker a little harder.

"Dr. Gold!" Herman yelled through the door. Herman hesitantly tried the door. It opened and he stepped into the foyer.

"Dr. Gold?" Herman called out. The house smelled of antiseptic. He walked through the waiting area of the clinic, and after a quick look around the main floor he headed to the grand staircase. The walnut handrail was polished to a shine. It was eerily quiet. "Dr. Gold?" Herman moved softly up the staircase to the second floor.

The floorboards creaked as Herman walked down the upstairs hall. He opened each door slowly, looking into various bedrooms, feeling rather invasive. He thought of Ruth at home and continued. At the end of the hall was the last door, the door to the room in the turret. He knocked on it and waited.

"Dr. Gold?" he called again. He held his breath. His heart was pounding in his ears. He put his hand on the glass knob. He opened the door a crack. The stench was strong of body odor and alcohol. The old man was fully dressed and sprawled across his bed.

"Dr. Gold," Herman said abruptly, "wake up."

The doctor's eyes fluttered open. He groaned.

"Dr. Gold, I need you. Get up!" Understanding slowly dawned on Dr. Gold's face as his eyes opened. He cautiously eased himself from the bed and assessed Herman.

"What'd you need, Bohlman?" Dr. Gold asked in a hoarse voice.

"I need you to come quick! Ruth's having the baby. The midwife's having trouble . . ." Herman's voice cracked with emotion.

Dr. Gold sat up, "Alright then, let's go."

He shuffled over to his doctor's bag and picked it up. His coat and boots were lying on the floor.

"Don't worry, I'm sure it's nothing I can't handle."

Herman picked up the coat and motioned toward the door, "Let's go." His palms were sweating. "Let's go," he repeated. He paced back and forth between the doctor and the bedroom door.

"I'm coming," Dr. Gold grumbled.

Dr. Gold squinted in the morning sun. He rubbed a hand over his stubbled face and cleared his throat. He pushed his hands deeper into his pockets.

Herman and Dr. Gold arrived at the Bohlman's about fifteen minutes later. The tension in the air was mounting. Ruth cried out as each contraction gripped her, her body begging her to push the baby through the birth canal. Dr. Gold removed his coat and boots. His smell lingered in the front room as he went into the bedroom.

"What's going on here?" Dr. Gold asked Betty as he looked at Ruth.

"It's too big," Betty answered. "We're not making any progress. Her membranes ruptured around two am. No mechonium."

"Let's get this done," Dr. Gold gruffly ordered.

He opened his bag. Betty closed the door. Herman saw a glimpse of the tools coming out of the bag.

Herman held on to the back of the armchair and shuddered.

"It's alright, she'll get though this," Mrs. Daum assured him as she came out of the kitchen.

"I know . . ." he breathed.

"Come and have some breakfast." She smiled reassuringly.

"I can't," he sighed. His stomach flipped.

"Sit at the table with me then. Just try to eat something. I'll get you some coffee at the very least."

He turned toward the kitchen. "Fine." He could hear Ruth screaming from the bedroom.

"Oh God . . ." he didn't know what to pray.

Emma patted his hand. "Protect Ruth," she finished for him. She took a long drink of coffee.

Finally, Herman and Emma heard the first cries of life and Pauline exclaim, "It's a girl!"

Emma smiled and squeezed Herman's arm, "Oh that's wonderful!"

He exhaled loudly. Tears rolled down his face as he listened to his new daughter cry. "They're okay," he gasped. He stood up from the kitchen chair, pacing back and forth between the table and the stove.

"Yes," Emma agreed, "yes they are."

It seemed like an eternity before Pauline finally emerged, holding the tightly swaddled baby in her arms.

Herman rushed toward her, "How is Ruth?"

"She's . . ." Pauline paused, "it was a difficult birth."

Herman's face dropped, "But is she . . ."

"Dr. Gold is with her . . . and Mrs. Smith is very skilled."

Emma came up behind Herman. "She'll be okay. Let's take a look at this baby."

Pauline grinned and turned the bundle toward Herman and Emma. "Isn't she something? Here you are, Dad." She passed the baby into his trembling arms.

Herman took his baby daughter and looked into her blinking eyes. "Hello, baby."

"She's beautiful," Emma breathed, "just beautiful."

Herman walked into the front room and sank his tired frame into the armchair. He held his new baby tightly. He watched her eyes, alert, searching around her new environment, taking in her change of scenery. Her little arm struggled out of the swaddled blanket and stretched upwards toward his face. He held his hand flat against her outstretched fingers; they were so small and delicate. He marveled at each tiny fingernail. There, as he admired every detail, he saw something so special. Her pinkie finger was delicately curved, curved toward the rest of her fingers. Ever so slightly, but enough to know that it looked just like her mother's hands. Along the line of the Lessing family, many of their hands held the unique feature of a delicately curved pinkie finger, a sign that you belonged.

A tear rolled down Herman's cheek as he admired his new baby girl. Pauline and Emma chatted softly in the background. Everything else seemed to fade away as he lost himself in this little version of Ruth.

She stared up at his face and her little arm settled with his finger in her grasp.

"I thank the Lord for you, little one, for you are a blessing to me. A joy so deep in my heart, a love I had yet to feel, the love a father holds for his child." Herman continued to let the tears roll down his cheeks. He wasn't sure how he could feel so many things at once. All of his emotions brewed within.

Everything seemed foggy to Ruth. All she could remember was the never-ending pushing and pushing. Finally, Dr. Gold had come and ripped the baby from her womb. Now Ruth felt strangely empty and alone. Every muscle ached from the effort of childbirth. She opened her eyes and realized it was dark. She must have slept the entire day. Her mother was sitting next to Herman's side of the bed in the chair, knitting by the light of an oil lamp.

"Mutter?" Ruth croaked.

"Well hello, child, I thought you'd never wake," answered Pauline in German.

"Where is the baby?" asked Ruth.

"I'll have Herman bring her in. We've given her some sugar water but you had better try to nurse her while you have the strength. She is a mighty big baby, twelve pounds!"

Ruth groaned, "I felt every pound." She smiled at her mother. The two women silently triumphed over Ruth's accomplishment.

Pauline left the room to get Herman and the baby. Herman burst in a moment later.

"Ruth! You're awake!" Herman knelt down next to Ruth's side of the bed. He took her hand in his own, hesitant to embrace her as he wanted to. "I was so worried! Thank God you're alright."

"I'll be fine, Herman, I'm just completely worn out. Childbirth was a lot harder than I expected."

"I'll say." He gave her a gentle hug. "I thought the night would never end."

"Me too." She smiled despite the pain. "Now where is she, this little girl I had to work so hard to get here?"

Pauline stood in the doorway with the baby. She strode forward and placed the baby in Ruth's arms. She took the baby and cradled her against her chest. Herman sat down in the chair next to the bed.

"Amazing," she gasped. "I've been imagining this moment for so long—and now . . ." her voice trailed off as she gazed at the sleeping baby. Ruth stroked the baby's face gently. "She's so soft."

Pauline and Herman both smiled. He said, "Isn't she something?"

The baby stirred and turned her head instinctively toward her mother. The baby's mouth opened wide.

"Should I feed her?" Ruth asked her mother.

"Yes," she answered gently, "that's her way of telling you."

Ruth raised her eyebrows.

"Bring her to your breast; she knows what to do."

Ruth glanced at Herman. "Okay."

She brought the baby to her breast and right away the baby smacked hungrily and sucked heartily. Ruth began to stroke the baby's soft strawberry-blonde hair. While she fed, it gave Ruth the opportunity to study her features.

The baby's eyes were open as she sucked, gazing up at Ruth. They were blue and wide. Her lips were a perfect shade of pink. Her nose rounded to perfection. Her little open hand was resting on the top of Ruth's breast. It was then that Ruth saw the baby's little pinkie finger. It was the same as her own, and her mother's, not straight but curved ever so gently toward the other fingers. Ruth began to cry.

She looked up at Herman. "Did you see?"

He nodded.

God had formed this perfect child in her womb and the enormity of this new life in her arms struck her as she nursed. Ruth's eyes began to grow heavy. She looked over and smiled at Herman.

"We did it, Herman. We're more than just a couple. We're a family."

*"And we know that all
things work together for
good to them that love God,
to them who are called
according to his purpose."
Romans 8:28 KJV*

December 7, 1921
Edmonton, Alberta

The baby's sucking slowed and her eyes shut. She was relaxed and content, snuggled against her mother, hearing her familiar, steady heartbeat. The chaos of the previous night was over. Only the distant sound of Pauline in the kitchen could be heard, and the soft breathing of Herman and Ruth as they admired their baby girl. Ruth's fingers danced over the baby's body, exploring every inch of her new child. Under the blankets, Ruth saw the baby's tiny back, rounded and fuzzy as a peach. Her legs were tucked under her, as though she had not yet discovered that she could stretch without limitation. Her strawberry-blonde hair stuck up on her head in every direction. She was a vision of peace and contentment, and for a minute Herman and Ruth felt the same. As though all of the heartache of the world, death and disease, all of their pain and sorrow could be washed away by the overwhelming love that suddenly consumed them.

Breastfeeding had relaxed Ruth. Her hand slowed its exploration of her child. She had touched every toe, every finger, her back, tummy and each little limb. She had stroked her head and ran her finger along the tender part at the back of her neck. Everything was new and wondrous. Ruth savored the moment.

"Tired?" he asked softly from his place in the chair.

"Oh, very."

"Should I take the baby?"

Ruth closed her eyes, smiled and said, "I need her." She looked at Herman and smiled coyly. "Do you know . . . that if I hold her long enough," she paused for effect, "I can no longer feel where she ends and I begin."

"Really?"

"It's indescribable. You should try it sometime. It's as though God merges you into one being, one mother, one babe, one body."

"Sounds fantastic."

"It is, Hermie. It really is." She closed her eyes.

"Should I take her now?"

She shook her head. "I'm just resting my eyes."

He laughed softly, "If you say so."

Herman moved his chair closer. He could see Ruth slipping into sleep. He put his hand on the baby, as Ruth's hand relaxed. The pair rose and fell with each breath that Ruth took. They were one being, having been temporarily separated, now content to be together and to rest. Herman felt the vitality of the baby. He could see the flicker of her eyes, the twitch of a hand and the wiggle of her bottom as she slept. Ruth looked pale compared to the pink of the baby's complexion. He was relieved that the worst was over.

Pauline returned to the room with a tray of food for Ruth. Once she saw that Ruth was sleeping, she set down the tray on a small night table next to the bed.

"Herman," she paused, her hand on his shoulder, "we should let them rest."

"I'll just stay a minute longer, Mother," Herman replied.

"Fine. Before you go, move the baby to the cradle so that she doesn't fall."

He nodded. "I will."

Pauline left the new Bohlman family to themselves and sank down on the chesterfield. It had been a long night for her as well. An ill feeling lingered as she reflected on the last twenty-four hours. Death had cast a dark shadow over the Lessing family this year. As Dr. Gold had torn the baby from Ruth, she had felt death pulling her daughter away. She had lost too much already. She couldn't let another family member go. Not now . . . not ever, she felt. She had to be the next to go. She could not live to bury another child. This had to be a time of joy, a time of healing.

"I can't bear it, Lord," she whispered, "I need joy. I need this baby to bring our family joy."

The sun rose on December 7th and Ruth still did not wake to feed the baby. Pauline had tended to Ruth through the night, bringing the baby to nurse every few hours as needed. Ruth was so exhausted that Pauline had to lie next to her and watch as the baby fed, making sure it was well latched. She tried to coax Ruth to eat but the young mother was not interested. Pauline's concern increased, as Ruth grew hotter and hotter, sweat dampening her hair around her face.

Dread filled her as she tried to rouse Ruth and she did not respond. She woke Herman who was sleeping on the chesterfield.

"Herman."

"What's wrong?" asked Herman, waking with a start.

"Ruth has a fever. We had better get her to the hospital in Edmonton and see if they can help." Pauline tried to hide the fear in her voice.

"Alright, I'll go get the car from the farm."

The snow was falling lightly. Herman added a warm hat to his coat and boots. He set off for the long walk to the Lessing farm to retrieve the car. Not many people in the area had a car, but the crops had been good to Ruth's father in previous years and he had bought a Buick, his pride and joy. As he stepped out of their house, the cold air stung the tears on his cheeks. He wiped them away with the back of his gloved hand. This was no time for tears. Ruth needed him to be strong. He walked briskly into the wind.

Meanwhile, Pauline tended to Ruth, wiping her brow and caring for the new baby. There were moments where she prayed and others when everything seemed hollow and empty. Her prayers bounced back and forth between being her only source of hope and a futile waste of breath. Her faith was strong. Prayer had accompanied her through many dark valleys, but this year, 1921, was the darkest yet. There were moments since her husband's death where she felt completely forsaken.

She and her husband had been born and raised in Russia, married and had their first son, Rudolf, there. He had been their first source of joy and heartbreak. He died in infancy. Things in Russia had been hard. It was a life that she, Frederick and their parents wanted to escape. Others from their village had gone to North America, following their pastor. They wrote letters back home speaking about incredible opportunities for farming. Their friends talked about religious and political freedoms in North America that they would never be able to experience in Russia.

In May of 1896, Frederick and Pauline—who were expecting their third child—and their ten-month-old daughter, Amelia, boarded the SS Parisian from Liverpool, England. They were joined by Gottlieb and Amelia Schindel, Pauline's parents, and Johann and Anna Lessing, Frederick's parents, along with Frederick's younger brother, Wilhelm, and Pauline's younger sister, Augusta. They all arrived in Montreal, Quebec, ten days later.

The family then traveled to Winnipeg, meeting up with Pauline's sister and family, Samuel and Henrietta Holland. The Hollands had settled there a few years earlier with their children, Rudolf and Emelie. That December, Pauline gave birth to Martha. Frederick took a job cutting wood with Samuel to earn some money before looking for a permanent place to settle. They traveled to Bismark, North Dakota, to find a homestead but were eventually drawn to Alberta where Pastor Mueller had begun a church and where both sets of parents had established a parcel of land and had a home on it.

In 1888, Frederick and Pauline's father, Gottlieb, decided to buy 160 acres from the Canadian Pacific Railway. She, Fred and the girls lived with the Schindels while they developed the land and learned how to farm. In 1899, while living with the Schindels, they had a son who they named Benjamin. In 1901, they welcomed Ruth followed by Robert in 1903. It was then that Frederick decided to build a large home for their growing family and his aging parents.

The house was a work of art. It was finely crafted with logs hauled up from the Coal Lake area. They had set up a sawmill at a friend's property where they processed the logs into usable building material. It was a two-story home with a porch on the front. The front door was in the center of the house with a window flanking each side. There were beautiful double-hung paned windows on all sides of the house allowing ample light into each room. There was a deck on the back of the house. It was painted in a crisp white with dark grey trim.

By 1904, the land was paid for in full. And, by all rights, Fredrick, still a young man, was doing very well for himself. They welcomed more children, Hilda in 1905 and Walter in February 1908. Those were happy years, as Frederick became more and more successful with his farming and his property developed. They were prosperous beyond their wildest dreams.

In 1908, they had their first taste of tragedy in the new country when Martha came down with diphtheria. She died in June, just twelve years old. Pauline was no stranger to losing a child, having lost Rudolf as a baby, but this was even harder. Martha had begged her mother to take away the pain, pleaded for her to make it better, and Pauline was helpless to cure her. It had been agonizing to watch her slip away. Pauline had to carry on with new baby Walter who was demanding her time and attention. It was then that she first felt a longing for death. If only she could lie down with sweet Martha and carry her into the afterlife.

It was five years before another baby came into the family and still the pain of losing Martha did not cease. They named the newest daughter Magdalene. The last Lessing child was born in 1917, a stillborn, God's whisper to Pauline that her childbearing days were over. They buried him alongside Martha in a cemetery near their church.

During these years, the money flowed freely. They added cow barns, cattle, purchased more land, good farming equipment, new sleighs, good work horses and even a stallion. They bought a new car—the Buick—the finest on the market. They even had a telephone installed although hardly another soul had a telephone for them to call. Still it was an impressive bit of technology and Fred embraced it.

The car came in handy in 1919 when a terrible flu epidemic swept through their community. Fred drove the pastor to the members of the congregation who were ill and dying. Fred was happy to share his blessings in this way.

The church was an integral part of their lives. They attended every week. Fred was the Sunday school superintendent and also preached on the odd occasion when the pastor was absent. Faith sustained them through the good times and the bad, and the strength of their church community upheld them through one another's sorrows.

The baby stirred. Pauline picked her up from the cradle and rocked her in her arms, "My love, I hope you never face the sorrow I've endured."

Pauline looked over at Ruth. She slept fitfully.

Pauline continued to reflect. In May of 1921, all the prosperity in the world couldn't conjure happiness for the Lessings. Hilda, one month from sixteen, died of tuberculosis. Pauline's despair reached a new level of intensity only to be compounded by the loss of Frederick in June.

She watched Ruth sleep.

"No, God, no . . . Please," she begged. "Bring healing to my daughter. Surely you have taken enough. 'Oh that my grief were thoroughly weighed and my calamity lay in the balances together! For now it would be heavier than the sand of the sea: therefore my words are swallowed up.'" She prayed as she waited for the men to return.

Before long, there was a knock at the door. Before she could get up, it opened.

"Hi, Mom." Ben came in through the front door, bringing a gust of wind with him.

"Hello." Pauline nodded her head at Herman and said, "Thanks for going."

"No problem. I'm sorry it took so long. The roads were terrible."

"How is she?" Ben asked.

Pauline grimaced, "She has a fever. She isn't feeding the baby. I'm having a hard time keeping her awake."

"Have you called Dr. Gold?" Ben asked.

"No."

"Let's just get her to Edmonton for the best possible care."

"The car is cold, we should heat some hot water bottles," Herman suggested.

"I can do that." Pauline offered the baby to Herman. "Will you hold her while I do that?"

Herman took the baby gingerly into his arms.

"What's her name?" Ben asked.

"I don't know," Herman smiled, his eyes fixed on his daughter. "We haven't had a chance to talk about it. Ruth always said that we'd figure it out once we saw her face . . . perhaps a family name. She said it might be bad luck to choose a name before the baby has arrived safely."

Pauline came from the kitchen. "The water is heating up. It shouldn't be too long."

"I better pack some clothes. I'm going to stay with her."

"Are you sure?" Pauline asked.

"Yes." He looked at Pauline. "Will you take the baby?"

"I can hold her," Ben offered. He took his niece in his arms. He spoke to her tenderly, "Hello, lovely."

Herman went into the bedroom. He stroked Ruth's sweaty hair. "Sweetheart, we're going to get help. You'll be feeling better in no time."

She didn't respond so he opened up his bag and threw in some slacks and sweaters, hardly caring about the contents. He came out of the room a few minutes later.

"Herman, I'll drive and you can sit in the back with Ruth," Ben suggested, "keep her warm."

Pauline said, "Let me see if I can get her to feed the baby one last time before you take her. Ben, can you go to the neighbor's and get me some milk?"

"Sure, Mom." Ben put his coat on and left, quietly shutting the door behind him. Pauline went into the bedroom where she tried to wake Ruth.

"Ruth, sweetheart, wake up."

Ruth moaned, "What is it?"

"You need to feed the baby. Come on now, upright may be easier."

Ruth struggled to sit up.

"Herman," Pauline called.

He rushed into the bedroom, "Yes?"

"Can you help her up? It might help to be sitting up."

Herman came around and lifted Ruth into a sitting position, propping pillows behind her back. Pauline put a pillow on Ruth's lap and lay the baby on it, ready for nursing. Ruth unbuttoned her nightgown and fed the baby who sucked vigorously. Ruth began to awaken as the baby fed, feeling the tingle of the milk letting down in her breasts.

"What is the matter with me?"

"You have a fever," Pauline answered.

"I am so tired." She looked at the concerned faces staring at her and asked, "How is she doing?"

"She is doing well." Pauline took a deep breath, "Herman and Ben are going to take you to Edmonton now. We think you should be cared for there."

"Can't you just call Dr. Gold to come to the house?"

"No." Pauline shook her head. "No, I think the hospital is best."

"What about the baby?"

"She can stay here with me. Ben's gone to get milk. She'll be fine until you're back."

Ruth moaned, tipped her head back against the pillow and closed her eyes. Her hair stuck to her forehead in small sweaty tendrils. "I don't want to."

Pauline took a deep breath and looked at Herman for support, "It's what's best, right Herman?"

"Yes, I think so too." He gently stroked Ruth's hand. "Better safe than sorry."

They dressed Ruth in a simple skirt and blouse. Pauline combed her daughter's hair and packed a few extra skirts and sweaters in a bag.

"I think that should do," Pauline said softly.

"The baby," Ruth said quietly, "I want to hold her again before we go."

Ruth took her daughter into her arms.

Pauline tried to be soothing, "She'll be right here waiting for you when you get back. You just worry about healing and coming back here healthy and strong, alright?"

Ruth said nothing but let the tears fall down her cheeks as she held her daughter in her arms. The baby opened her eyes and looked at her mother, gazing into her face. Ruth smiled at her baby and explained with strained cheerfulness, "*Mutter* is going away for a few days, but I'll be back. I'll be stronger, you'll see. Then I will take you up to Grandma's farm and show you off to all of the family. I can't wait for everyone to meet you." The baby wiggled in her blankets and worked her arms free. Ruth bent her head down and the baby grasped her brown curls in her little baby fists.

"I can't go."

Herman agonized, "You must."

"You don't understand," Ruth said tearfully.

"I can't imagine . . ." Herman said desperately. "We have to get you help so you can take care of her."

"She needs me, here, with her."

"I know. I know she does. I need you too. I need you to get better so that we can be a family."

Ruth kissed the baby's face over and over. She sang softly in German. Ruth studied her daughter's features again, trying to memorize them.

"Herman . . . I-"

He shook his head sadly.

Several minutes passed with only the occasional shuffle of feet.

Finally, Ruth looked up and nodded to Herman. Wordlessly he knew that she was as ready as she would ever be to let go. She cried as Herman passed the baby to Pauline. Ruth rose from the chair with Herman's assistance and hugged her mother and her baby all at once. She touched Baby's brow one last time and said, "For this child I prayed; and the Lord hath given me my petition, which I asked of him: Therefore also I have lent her to the Lord; as long as she liveth she shall be lent to the Lord."

Herman guided Ruth into her coat and boots, and gently laced them for her. He lifted her into his strong arms and carried her through the door into the awaiting car. He covered her with blankets and then sat in the back seat next to her. Ben climbed in the front and started the car down Leduc's main street in the direction of Edmonton.

Pauline closed the door behind them. She rocked the baby gently back and forth. Her grief pressed heavily upon her chest. It threatened to consume her. It was an ugly beast she had battled over the last year; its presence always daring her to give in to the sadness, the madness and the overwhelming fear. She quietly sang her favorite hymn to the baby.

> *"Great is Thy faithfulness,*
> *O God my Father,*
> *There is no shadow of turning with Thee . . ."*

*"The righteous cry out, and
the Lord hears them; he
delivers them from all their
troubles."*
Psalm 34:17 NIV

December 7, 1921
Edmonton, Alberta

They had been driving for three-quarters of an hour. Ben squinted through the snow. It was coming down in fat, lazy flakes. The roads were slick and he was thankful for the Buick that was keeping them safely on the road. Herman stroked Ruth's hair in the back seat. She cried quietly.

They passed by farmhouses and trees laden with the heavy snow. An occasional car, driving in the opposite direction, went by.

"Your mom will take good care of the baby."

"I know. I know that in my mind—but in my heart . . ." Ruth's voice trailed off as she began to cry again.

"How are you feeling? Are you cold?"

"I am cold." She shivered.

"Move closer to me." Herman pulled her toward him.

Ben glanced back at Herman. "It might take awhile . . . the roads—I can't go too fast."

Herman nodded.

"Do you think we can come back tonight?" Ruth asked.

"We'll have to see what they say. The doctors will know what is best. Have you been able to eat anything?"

"A bit."

Finally, country road turned into city streets. Ben navigated his way through the south end of town and to the Misericordia Maternity Hospital run by the Roman Catholic Sisters. It was a four-story Victorian building that stood in the heart of Edmonton.

Ben drove the car to the front entrance. "I'll go wait down the street at the Corona Hotel. I'm going to get some lunch. Can you meet me there?"

"Sure. I'll see you there once Ruth is settled."

Herman jumped out and assisted her. She leaned on him heavily as they went up the stairs to the front doors.

"Should I carry you?"

"I'm okay. I just feel really weak. And the pain . . . oh . . . everything hurts."

Herman pulled open the large wooden door. It was quiet inside. A nun sat at a large desk.

"Good day," the nun called out. "What can I help you with?"

"This is my wife, Ruth Bohlman."

"Hello, Mrs. Bohlman."

Ruth smiled. "Hello. Can I sit?"

"Of course. Let me get a wheelchair." The nun came out from behind her desk and went to a nearby hallway. She came back pushing a wheelchair. "Here we are. Have a seat here." She helped Ruth sit down.

Ruth moaned.

"Did you just have a baby, dear?"

Ruth nodded.

"It was a very big baby," Herman explained. "Twelve pounds."

The nun gasped. "That's something."

"And now she's been feverish. She's very fatigued. She has trouble eating and even feeding the baby." Herman's voice was filled with desperation.

"Where is the baby now?"

"With my mother," Ruth said quietly.

"What is your name, sir?" the nun asked.

"Herman Bohlman."

"I'm Sister Ethel. It's a pleasure to meet you. Now then, let's take Mrs. Bohlman to the postpartum ward and we'll have a doctor see if we can determine what the problem is."

Herman waited in a separate room while the sisters got Ruth into a dressing gown and into a hospital bed. It was nearly an hour before anyone checked in with him.

Finally, Sister Ethel emerged and said, "Here are Mrs. Bohlman's things." She handed Ruth's personal items to him.

"I'll be staying at the Corona, just down the road. If you need me, please send someone for me. If anything changes, I'd like to know right away."

"I understand. Of course we'll be in touch. It looks like an infection. We need to pray that the fever will break and that she'll turn the corner soon."

"She has to," he said despairingly.

"God's peace to you, Mr. Bohlman," said Sister Ethel as she dismissed Herman.

Peace. God's peace. He didn't feel God's peace at all. He felt gut-wrenching fear. Herman walked to the Corona and looked for Ben. He was seated in the restaurant, just finishing his meal. Neither man spoke. It seemed there was no need to state the obvious fears that each man held for Ruth. There was no need for small talk.

"I'll call the farm and let them know we made it safely," Ben suggested.

"That sounds fine."

"Did they say when you could come back?"

"I'll go back in the morning . . . see how she's doing. Then we'll know if we can take her home or if she has to stay."

"I think," Ben said slowly, "that I'll go back tomorrow morning either way. There are things I need to do on the farm and I can always come and get you when you need me."

"That would be fine," Herman said hesitantly.

After lunch, the men retired to their rooms.

Ben patted Herman on the back. He gave him a look of encouragement and added, "She'll be okay. She's a strong girl."

"I know," he sighed. "We're supposed to be celebrating our new family and all I can think of is how much I need her." Herman's eyes welled with tears yet again. He turned down the hall to his room and waved a silent goodbye. Ben ran his hands through his hair and sighed. They all had felt enormous loss this year.

Ruth opened her eyes and looked around. She was feeling better as the nurses forced her to eat and drink. She could still feel her fever raging. Every muscle felt sore. She felt her breasts well up with milk and longed to feed her sweet daughter. She thought of her baby in the arms of her mother and hoped that she was managing on her own. She thought of Herman sick with worry and wished he was here now. She closed her tired eyes and laced her chilled hands together across her chest. Her feet felt cold. Her dreams had been wild. It seemed the fever was bringing the strangest images to her mind while she slept. Ruth saw one of the nuns nearby.

"Sister," she called out.

"Well hello, Mrs. Bohlman."

"Is my husband here?" she asked.

"Your husband is just down the road at the Corona. He'll be by in the morning to see you."

"Oh," she said dejectedly. "Can he come tonight?"

"Visiting hours are over. But not to worry, he'll be back."

Ruth closed her eyes. "I'm so cold."

"I'll get an extra blanket." Sister Etta left Ruth to get another warm blanket. She returned and tucked it in all around her. She prayed silently for healing.

The next morning, December 8, Herman awoke with a start. It took him a moment to register where he was and what was happening. It was the first solid night of sleep he had had in two days. He looked around the cold hotel room. He went to the window and looked outside. Everything was shades of grey. It matched how he was feeling. He dressed quickly and then went to Ben's room. He knocked on the door.

"*Guten Morgen*," answered Ben as he opened the door. "Are you leaving for the hospital?"

"*Ja*," answered Herman, "I'll come back and get you if she's ready to leave."

"That's fine. I'll be here. I think I might go down for breakfast. Have you eaten?"

"I'm not hungry."

"Well, tell Ruth I say hello."

Herman walked quickly back to the hospital, praying for Ruth. He prayed for his mother-in-law and his daughter back in Leduc.

Herman entered Ruth's ward. He saw her across the stark-white room. She was lying very still. She was as white as her sheets. Sister Etta approached Herman as he stood in the doorway.

"Come on in, Mr. Bohlman, you may sit next to her bed. She was asking for you last night."

"Okay." He walked hesitantly toward her.

"The fever is growing worse and she is extremely tired. Sit next to her and speak to her. It will help."

Herman sat down next to Ruth and took her hand. It was cold. Her face, however, was warm. Sweat pooled on the delicate features of her face. Her short hair was cut just as all the girls were wearing it those days. Her soft brown curls framed her face. Her body rose and fell with each labored breath. Herman thought of a calming verse in his mind, *Surely God is my salvation; I will trust and not be afraid. The Lord, the Lord, is my strength and my song; he has become my salvation.*

"Ruth, Ruth, love, can you hear me?"

Ruth's eyes opened slowly. "Hermie . . ."

"How are you?" he asked.

"I'm cold, so cold."

He took her chilly hands in his own.

She spoke hesitantly, afraid to say the words yet afraid to leave them unsaid. "Herman, if something happens promise me you'll always take good care of the baby."

"Don't talk like that . . ." he stroked her hands.

"Don't give her up. Keep her and teach her our faith; keep her close to our family," Ruth's voice cracked with emotion.

"Don't talk like that, love. You'll be fine; you'll go home and hold our precious girl in your arms . . . you'll be fine. You need to rest and, and you'll be fine. I need you, Ruth. You mean everything to me . . . I can't—I can't live without you." Tears were streaming down Herman's cheeks.

"I love you too, Herman. I feel so weak and ill . . . I'm worried."

"Please, I can't stand this, you must stop. You're going to be fine."

"But just in case . . . if something happens I want you to know that I will always be with you. I will watch down from heaven and see our daughter grow into the kind of woman I can be proud of. I'll ask God for a front-seat view of you . . . I'll be there." Ruth paused, her voice growing weak.

"Stop . . . don't . . . please . . ."

"Please, don't forget me . . . think of me when you look into her eyes."

"That's enough." He looked at her adamantly. "Ruth, you don't know . . ."

"It's better for me to say this—I'll feel better knowing that I've told you what's in my heart. I've been thinking about this all night—what I really want you to know . . . what I want *her* to know. I've considered it, I know it sounds dark but please just listen to what I have to say. If I pull through then I'll tell her myself."

"Fine. You will tell her."

"Please, just listen. I've been thinking about this a lot."

"I'm listening," he said softly. He looked into her eyes. They were full of fear.

She continued, her voice shaking, "Tell her I loved her—that she was the world to me—even if only for a day or two. Tell her this wasn't her fault. We each have our time, and this could be mine." Ruth cried freely. "Will you promise me this?"

He nodded. No words came. He lifted her from the bed, blankets and all, and took her onto his lap. He cradled her in his arms, rocking back and forth, kissing her face over and over. She was so young, only twenty years old. She had so much yet to do.

After nearly an hour, Ruth relaxed in his arms, falling asleep. Herman tenderly whispered in Ruth's ear, "Even youths grow tired and weary, and young men stumble and fall, but those who hope in the Lord will renew their strength. They will soar on wings like eagles; they will run and not grow weary; they will walk and not be faint." He cried and cried as he had never cried before. He felt as though he may never be whole again. The hospital carried on as usual around them. The couple was oblivious to everyone else in the ward.

Over the next few days, Ruth slept deeply as her body battled her infection. Herman stayed by her side, only leaving at night to sleep at the Corona. He held her hand and wiped her fevered brow. He whispered prayers and quoted verses of scripture to comfort her.

The nuns suggested to Herman that he gather the family. He sent a telegram to Leduc. Pauline, the baby, Ruth's sister and three brothers came up the next morning.

Ruth had been in and out of consciousness. She had been delirious and confused but this morning she woke with a fresh mind. A renewed energy.

"Why is everyone here?" she asked.

Pauline spoke, "We just want to be with you."

"Is it bad?" She looked at all their teary faces. She looked at her older sister; "You came all the way from Portland? For me?"

Amelia nodded.

Ruth spoke weakly, "I can feel it; the end is near."

Everyone stood still. The baby slept in Pauline's arms, peaceful and quiet.

Ruth looked at Herman. He seemed so broken and afraid. She reached out for his hand. "I'm glad you are here."

Amelia sat opposite Herman and took Ruth's other hand. She wiped the tears falling from her eyes.

"It's alright. I'm not afraid. In fact, in this moment I feel better than I have in days."

"Maybe they're wrong," Walter offered.

No one spoke.

"*Mutter*," Ruth looked at her daughter, "may I?"

Pauline passed the infant to Ruth. Herman supported the baby and laid her against Ruth's bosom. "I suppose," she choked, "I suppose I should say goodbye, while my mind is clear."

"*Nein*," Herman said. His voice was full of anguish.

She looked at her daughter, "I love you." Ruth began to quote her favorite verse, Isaiah 41:10:

"So do not fear for I am with you;

Do not be dismayed for I am your God.

I will strengthen you and help you;

I will uphold you with my righteous right hand."

Ruth stroked the baby's hair as she continued. "Whatever life may bring you, I know you will be strong. I want you to persevere and depend on God to help you through. Your father will guide you but you must always trust your Heavenly Father to get you through life's storms." Ruth stroked the baby's back. "Let God guide you in your life. Live to honor Him alone. God will be your strength no matter what life brings you. He will be there to get you through."

Ruth looked up into the eyes of her beloved husband. "Herman, I love you . . ." the rest of her sentence got caught in her throat. "Remember," she cried, "remember what we talked about."

Herman nodded.

"My precious family, give glory to God. Lead Godly lives and honor Him in all that you do."

Ruth's complexion was very pale now. She said, "I'd like to pray." Everyone nodded.

She bowed her head to pray, "Father, thank you for these special people who surround me now as I come home to be with you. Lord, keep their lives always guided toward you. Let them live to honor you. Take my daughter into your hands, Lord. Help her to know You, to love You and have a personal relationship with You. Take care of Herman, Lord. Bring him peace that only you can give. Help him to be strong and to carry on without me." The circle of family had tears streaming down their cheeks as they listened to Ruth.

Peace, Herman thought, peace was an unlikely companion.

She began to sing. Despite her condition, her beautiful voice rang out strong and clear. She sang the familiar hymn by Charles Wesley.

Jesus, lover of my soul, let me to Thy bosom fly,
While the nearer waters roll, while the tempest still is high.
Hide me, O my Savior, hide, till the storm of life is past;
Safe into the haven guide; O receive my soul at last.

Other refuge have I none, hangs my helpless soul on Thee;
Leave, ah! leave me not alone, still support and comfort me.
All my trust on Thee is stayed, all my help from Thee I bring;
Cover my defenseless head with the shadow of Thy wing.

Wilt Thou not regard my call? Wilt Thou not accept my
prayer?
Lo! I sink, I faint, I fall—Lo! on Thee I cast my care;
Reach me out Thy gracious hand! While I of Thy strength
receive,
Hoping against hope I stand, dying, and behold, I live.

Thou, O Christ, art all I want, more than all in Thee I find;
Raise the fallen, cheer the faint, heal the sick, and lead the
blind.
Just and holy is Thy Name, I am all unrighteousness;
False and full of sin I am; Thou art full of truth and grace.

Plenteous grace with Thee is found, grace to cover all my sin;
Let the healing streams abound; make and keep me pure
within.
Thou of life the fountain art, freely let me take of Thee;
Spring Thou up within my heart; rise to all eternity.

The ward was quiet and still. Baby Bohlman lay against her mother's chest and took comfort in her voice.

Everyone was quiet for the next hour. They watched Ruth struggle between heaven and earth. Finally Ruth uttered, "Hello, Hilda, hello, Father, I'm coming home."

Baby Bohlman listened to her mother's heart beating in her chest no more. Ruth's hand slipped from the baby and came to rest on the bed. On the seventh day after she had created life, Ruth passed from this world into eternity, to be embraced by her Heavenly Father.

"*Nein,*" Herman gasped, "*Nein . . . nein . . .* please," he begged, "*Komm zurück,* come back . . ."

"For me to live is Christ,
and to die is gain."
Philippians 1:21 NIV

December 16, 1921
Leduc, Alberta

It was bitterly cold as family and friends gathered around the graveside of Ruth Lessing Bohlman. People from surrounding communities who knew the Lessing family came out to support and honor Ruth's memory. Snow fell lightly as Pastor Summach delivered the eulogy to the crowd in German. His voice was strong and steady.

"Ruth Bohlman born Ruth Lessing on August 19, 1901, at Leduc, Alberta, died December 13, 1921, from Septicemia. In 1911, she gave her heart to the Lord and was baptized by Pastor Hoffman in August of that year. On October 12, 1920, she married the now grieving Herman Bohlman."

Herman stood in his best black suit and black winter coat, looking at the casket. He could not believe that his whole world had shattered. He could not believe that he wouldn't hear her laugh, wouldn't feel her touch, wouldn't share his days with her ever again. He couldn't believe she had left him alone with their baby daughter. They hadn't even had time to name her.

"They were a happy couple during their short time together. On December 6, she gave birth to a daughter, though it cost her. Ruth was a loving child and a true follower of Christ. She was very talented and was helpful to all. She was indeed a helpmate to her husband in every sense of the word. Her death is a tragedy; her memory is sacred." Pastor Summach paused, feeling the weight of his words on Ruth's family.

"For the dear Lessing family, this is a terrible blow because for the third time this year they stand by the grave of a loved one. On May 16, sixteen-year-old Hilda died, and on June 12 they carried their beloved father to his grave. Ruth leaves behind her loving husband, her infant daughter, her mother, three brothers and two sisters." Several of the Lessing children wept aloud as Pastor Summach carried on.

"Her death was a triumph. Her relatives and dear husband stood at her deathbed and were witness to her glorious home-going. She saw heaven standing open. She saw her relatives that preceded her. With her marvelous singing voice, despite her weak condition, she sang the hymn "Jesus, Lover of My Soul." All present were admonished to lead Godly lives. She prayed for them all. It was an astonishing scene for all that were present at her death. We can be assured they experienced a never-to-be-forgotten scene. Truly that is not death, to go to God in such a way."

Herman felt as though his knees would give out. He felt that he would fall as he stood listening to Pastor Summach's words. He wanted to wake her up, to tell her to stop this madness and to come and be with her new family. He wanted this nightmare to end.

"Christ was her life and death her victory. We can be comforted by the words of Philippians 1:21: 'For me to live is Christ, to die is gain.' Her work in the Sunday school and in other areas was not in vain, because 'Our works will follow us.' Would that God would grant to each of us such a glorious end."

The crowd sang a hymn. Herman stood completely still, listening to the words.

Abide with me: fast falls the eventide;
the darkness deepens; Lord, with me abide:
when other helpers fail and comforts flee,
help of the helpless, O abide with me . . .

Each attendant at the funeral stepped forward to pay their respects and placed Christmas flowers upon the casket. Herman watched as each of the Lessing family members, his only family now, shuffled forward and said goodbye. He watched his church family go by. As they passed, they wished him well. His good friend Emma Daum said nothing as she passed but took his hand and squeezed it gently. Finally, everyone had walked back to their homes or wagons. Herman was left alone with Pastor Summach.

"*Es ist Zeit.* It is time," said Pastor Summach. He nodded at the men who stood by to lower Ruth into her final resting place. Slowly, Herman watched the casket recede into the earth and when his heart felt that it could take no more, it broke—as shovel by shovel they began to cover her with God's earth.

Herman sank to his knees in the snow and bowed his head into his hands. He wept and wept. Time stood still as he listened to the steady thunk, thunk as the dirt hit the casket.

He walked back to his empty home. Pauline was there caring for the baby and yet the house felt so barren. As he stared into their room, he looked at their marriage bed. He went to her side of the bed and lay his weary body down in the dimple in the mattress where she had slept. It was all he had of her now. He let it envelop him as he lay down to sleep.

*

"What now?" she asked softly.

Herman sat in the living room of Pauline's home. He was holding his daughter. He rocked her gently back and forth in his arms. "I don't know," he said. His voice was hollow. His eyes were fixed on his daughter's face.

"Over these last few weeks, with you staying here, the baby—everything . . . I have to make some choices."

He looked up at her and asked, "What kind of choices?"

She stood up and walked to the window. She looked out on the snowy yard. The sunlight made everything sparkle. "I've decided I can't stay here any longer. There is too much—too much grief here."

He was silent as he considered her words. After some time he said, "Where do you go to escape it?"

She sighed. "Nowhere. There is nowhere to escape it." She walked back across the room and ran her finger along the bookshelf, disturbing the dust. "It seeps into everything I do."

He looked at her. "We are a miserable pair."

"Indeed." She pulled a book off the shelf. It was one of Frederick's favorites. "This house," she swept her arm through the air, " . . . everywhere I look I feel like I am missing everything I once loved." She looked at the paintings on the wall, the beautiful rugs, the upholstered chairs and sofa, and the fine china in the cabinet. "All I see is everything I've lost in this home. I need to escape from this cloud of death."

"Well, what are you saying then?"

She set the book down on a side table, stroking the binding. "Amelia has asked me to bring Magda and come and live with her in Portland."

Herman's eyes grew wide. "Portland?"

"I need to start over. I need to be around Amelia. I need Magda to be in a home with some degree of happiness."

"What about me?"

"I don't know. You could come. Start over."

"What about the baby?" He looked at his daughter. "I can't leave my work, the land, the house . . ."

Pauline shrugged. She sat down in the armchair, the weight of the world crashing upon her. "You need to name the baby, Herman."

He shook his head, "I know, I know. Let's deal with Portland first."

"Fine." She surveyed her son-in-law. The pain was evident on his face.

After a few minutes, she said, "I could take the baby. Raise her."

Herman shook his head. "*Nein.*"

"And how do you propose you will care for an infant while you work?"

Herman got up out of his chair, clutching the baby. He walked to the window and looked out, not wanting Pauline to see his tears. "I don't know, Mother."

"I could take her for a time—until you are re-married-"

Herman glared at her. "Re-married?"

Softly she said, "It isn't always about love. Sometimes we must do things for necessity."

He thought about those words. He paced back and forth, his daughter now asleep. How would this work? How could he care for a baby, work at the store and manage his home? He needed Pauline. He needed her to stay.

"Have you considered staying? What about Ben? Walter? What about your parents?"

"The boys can take care of the farm, they are old enough now. My parents are here to help them if need be. And my parents, they will manage without me." She sighed again. "I don't expect you to understand—I need a break. I need to go somewhere warmer, somewhere that doesn't remind me of this."

"I do understand."

They said nothing for several minutes.

"In one week I will go. I will be happy to take the baby with me. I understand that you have commitments here and I don't expect you to come. Amelia and I can care for her until she is older. When she is older perhaps then she can live with you," Pauline paused, "with a nanny."

"I need to think about it."

They sat in silence for a long time. Herman looked out the window at the snow on the trees, the birds moving from branch to branch, searching for winter berries.

"You need to name her. She isn't going away."

He turned around to look at her. Defensively he said, "I don't want her to go away."

"What I should say is that Ruth is not coming back to name her daughter. You must do this on your own."

He turned his back to her again.

The next morning, he went to the postmaster to file a birth certificate for the baby. The bells on the door rang as he went inside.

"*Guten Morgen,* Mr. Bohlman," the postmaster greeted him.

"*Guten Morgen.* I'm here for a birth certificate, for my daughter." The word *daughter* sounded foreign to him.

"Of course." The postmaster shuffled around his desk, bringing out the blue paper he needed to write the certificate. He brought out his logbook to register the information he needed for his records.

"Name, last and first—please include the spelling," the postmaster said.

"My name?"

"Yes, Mr. Bohlman, your name."

"Ah, Herman, H-E-R-M-A-N, Bohlman, B-O-H-L-M-A-N."

"And Ruth's name?"

Herman looked at the postmaster quizzically. "R-U-T-H."

"And the child? What did you name her?"

"We," Herman paused as his voice caught in his throat, "we didn't get the chance to pick a name."

He nodded understandingly, "I see." He looked up from his paper, his pen in mid-air, "I am so sorry for your loss. Nothing more tragic than losing your woman in childbirth."

Herman nodded, not knowing how to reply.

"No name then." He thought about if for a minute. "Then you should call her Ruth Lessing Bohlman, after her mother. That's the only sensible thing to do."

"Ruth." Herman choked back the familiar name.

The postmaster pulled a small red book from his desk. He flipped through it. "Ah ha. Here it is. Did you know it means vision of beauty?"

"Then that's what it shall be."

Herman watched as the postmaster wrote '*verstorben*,' deceased, next to Ruth's name.

Suddenly he said, "Excuse me." He left quickly out the front door and then ran around the back of the building. He felt hot, sweaty and panicked. Suddenly, his breakfast came screaming back up. He emptied its contents into the snow behind the post office. Over and over he heaved. When he was done, he kicked fresh snow over the mess. He walked a few feet away and pulled his handkerchief from his pocket. He wiped his brow. He took a handful of snow and put it in his mouth to soothe the pain.

Deceased. He looked up at the clear blue winter sky. Deceased.

*

They stood at the train station in Edmonton. Pauline wore a black dress. She held Ruth in her arms. Magda stood next to her mother, as quiet as her shadow.

"I will write, Herman. And I can call the farm. We can talk, perhaps weekly, that way you'll know how she is."

"I know."

"And I'll send photos, so you can see how she is growing."

He nodded.

"Herman," Magda said softly as she stepped out from behind her mother, "are you scared?"

Herman bent down on one knee and looked at his young sister-in-law. "Yes, my love, I am. Simply terrified."

"Of what exactly?" she asked innocently.

"Of saying goodbye."

"Me too." Magda wiped a tear from her eye. "Mother says it's not goodbye forever."

"I know." He took her small hands in his own. "You'll be back to visit, and you'll take good care of my baby, won't you?"

"Oh *ja*." Her smile returned, "I love babies."

He pulled her into a hug. "I'm going to miss you too, Maggie. You must promise me you'll teach Ruth everything you know about being a wonderful little girl."

She smiled and said, "Oh, Herman."

He kissed her cheeks and stood up. He put out his arms to take Ruth from Pauline as the departure time drew closer. He kissed his daughter. "*Ich liebe dich*, I love you." She looked up at him with her wide blue eyes. "I am going to miss you . . ."

Pauline patted his arm. "You'll manage. And we'll all have time to heal. It's what's best for all of us." She looked at the train. "We should find our seats."

He gave his daughter one final kiss and then handed her to Pauline. "Goodbye, Mother." He hugged her. "Goodbye, Maggie, say hello to Amelia for me."

Magda clutched her mother's skirt. "I will."

He gave Pauline a hand as she ascended the steps. They disappeared into the car. Herman stepped back and watched them as they sat down. Magda waved out the window. He blew her a kiss.

Finally, the train whistle blew and the conductor yelled out, "All aboard!"

The train wheels began to squeal and grind as they moved forward on the track. Herman continued to wave at Magda and Pauline as the train pulled away. He felt his heart leaving his body and disappearing down the tracks to Portland.

He walked slowly back to the car he had borrowed from Ben. He opened the car door and sat down on the leather seat. It was cold. The day was grey and gloomy. He watched the other people at the station getting into their cars.

"What now?" he asked himself.

He started up the car and steered it through the city streets. The drive back to Leduc was long. He thought about everything he had lost in the last few weeks. His wife, his daughter . . . his will. Over and over he replayed Ruth telling him to keep the baby, to raise her, to stay with the family.

He drove to his house and parked the car on the street out front. He went up the stairs, the snow loudly announcing his every step. He unlocked the front door and walked inside. It was empty. As empty as his broken heart.

" . . . but those who hope in
the Lord will inherit the
land." Psalm 37:9 NIV

June 1922
Lac Du Bonnet, Manitoba

"Pappa," Gustov called from his seat in the empty wagon, "do you think we can get everything in one more load?"

Otto answered as he led the horses, "I should say . . ." He thought about the furniture they had yet to bring to the new house. "We've got the sofa and the chair, the table and the benches, the kitchen cabinet," he paused, "and of course the chickens and the cows."

"And the family," Gustov laughed. "Don't forget about the family!"

Otto smiled, "They can walk!"

"Even Mamma?"

"She doesn't like the bouncing of the wagon at this point anyway; she says it jostles the baby too much."

This morning the pair had taken a load from their home in the town site of Lac Du Bonnet to their new property. On their first trip, they had taken the beds and mattresses along with all the trunks of clothing and personal items. The land was a wooded plot, just two miles out of town in the Riverland Farming Settlement. For the last eight months, they had been building a new house and barn. Now it was time for the entire family to take the walk . . . home.

As Otto rounded the corner, he saw his wife of seventeen years, Alina, standing on the front step. He waved.

"Hello!" she called.

"Hello, love!"

They drove the wagon up to the house. Otto tied the horse's reins around the low fence post in the front yard. "Is everyone ready?" he asked.

"Yes," she answered, "we're all anxious to go. I can't wait to see the new house."

Alina hadn't been out to the property. She was expecting again, her eighth child, and she hadn't wanted to make the long walk in the winter months.

Their eldest child Annie, fifteen, came to the door holding two-year-old Margaret in her arms.

Upon seeing Otto, Margaret wiggled out of Annie's arms and ran to him. "Pappa!"

He picked her up. "Hello, Margie."

She giggled, "New house?"

"Yes, we're ready to go to the new house!"

Alina turned to Annie, "Gather everyone up and make sure they've got their work boots on. The trail appears to be muddy." She pointed at Otto's soiled boots. "I don't need dirty socks upon arrival."

"Yes, Mamma," Annie said as she went back into the house.

Otto put Margaret into the wagon. "You wait here. Gus and I are going to load up the wagon. You and Mamma can keep the horses company."

Margaret clapped. "Okay!"

The warm sun beat down on Alina's shoulders. She grabbed Otto's hand as he walked past her. "Otto, thank you."

He grinned. "It's a good day for us."

A tear came to her eye. "Yes it is."

He pulled her into an embrace. "Now, now. It's a good day. No tears on a good day."

She laughed, "Oh, I know . . . I'm overjoyed!"

He let go of her hand and went inside the house with Gustov. They came back out carrying the kitchen table. They lifted it into the wagon, watching out for Margaret. Next came the chairs, the cabinet, the sofa and the armchair. Victor, their seven-year-old, brought out a crate with two chickens, which were protesting loudly.

"Put that in the wagon, Vic," Otto instructed, "and then we should be nearly ready to go."

"Yes, Pappa."

"Can Victor and Alice ride?" Alina asked.

Otto looked up at the tower of furniture and possessions. "I suppose, as long as they're careful not to disturb anything."

"I can walk," Victor said quietly.

Alina shook her head. "I'd rather he ride." She turned to look at Victor and said, "You should ride."

He sighed.

Waldemar, their four-year-old son, came bouncing out of the house. "I'll ride, Mamma! I want to ride on the wagon!" He ran to Otto who lifted him up.

"Anyone else want to ride?"

The children, Annie, Mary who was twelve, Gustov age eleven, Alice age nine, Victor and Waldemar all stood in a group looking at the overloaded wagon. Alice sighed, "I'll ride, although it doesn't look terribly safe." She cringed as Waldemar climbed to the top of the pile. "Should he be sitting there?"

Otto shook his head. "Hang on tight, Waldy. When the horses start up the whole thing will lurch."

Waldemar nodded. "Okay, Pappa. I will." His fists tightened over the chair he was holding on to.

The family walked through town, Gustov leading the horses and Otto bringing up the cows in the rear. They walked through the wide trails in town and then into the woods. As they walked, the trail grew narrower and narrower, the woods closing in all around them.

"It's beautiful out here," Alina said to Mary.

"Yes, Mamma, it's a pretty spot. You'll love the house."

She ran her hand over her pregnant belly. "I can't wait."

"Is it like the mountains in Sweden?" Alice asked.

Alina laughed. "Well, not exactly."

Annie hiked Margaret higher on her hip as she walked. "Tell us again, Mamma, about how you met Pappa."

Alina beamed at all of her girls walking alongside her. "Well we were both skiing on the mountain. I had come with two of my cousins and he with some friends from church. We were zipping down the hill at the same time. As he passed by he gave me a wink and a wave."

Mary smiled. "How bold!"

"I didn't mind it," Alina admitted. "I thought he was a fine skier. I admired him as he skied down the hill ahead of me."

"And then what?" Alice asked.

"And then when I got to the bottom of the hill, there he was. Waiting with his friends."

"I love the next part," Annie said dreamily.

"He said he hadn't seen many women on that particular hill. He told me that he was impressed by my athleticism."

"Were you very good, Mamma?" Alice asked.

"Oh—I'm not too sure about that. I like to ski, been doing it all my life. I suppose he was just trying to pay me a compliment."

Annie stated, "I'd love to see you ski one day."

Alina laughed. "I'm too old for that now! I was just a young woman then . . . these things are possible when you're young."

"Besides," Mary added, "there's nowhere to ski in Manitoba."

"Indeed," Alina agreed. She swept her arm around them, "But there is beauty all the same."

"Do you miss it?" Alice asked.

"I suppose," Alina said. "The scenery, the people . . . the culture. But Canada . . . in Canada we are free. The land is ours, the money we earn is ours . . . we can choose many things in Canada."

"Does Pappa ever say that he misses it?"

"No . . . we are glad to be here—together."

Gustov finally turned off the narrow path they had been travelling for a long time. "Hang on, Waldy," he called to his youngest brother, up on the top of the wagon.

"Okay, Gus!" The horses turned into thicker woods. The wagon pushed the branches aside as they walked on. Waldemar could hear the sound of water. "Is that a river, Gus?" he asked.

Gus laughed, "No, just a creek. We'll be walking the horses through it but for everyone else there is a small footbridge that Pappa and I built."

"Can we swim in it?"

He laughed again. "I suppose. It's not too deep. But I don't think you'd want to . . . besides, there are too many frogs."

"Frogs?"

The house came into view. Everyone exclaimed as they pulled the wagon right up in front of the house. Gus tied the reins to a tree.

"Oh, Otto!" Alina marveled, "it's beautiful!"

Otto came up from behind, bringing the cows along. "Do you like it?"

The house was large. It had a veranda on the front, several windows and two doors, one to the kitchen and one into the bedroom. The roof was tall and gabled on the right two-thirds of the house, and it was low and sloping on the other third.

He pointed to the left side of the house where the roof was low. "That is the kitchen," he pointed to the other side of the house, "and that is the living room and bedroom."

The horses shifted their feet behind the couple. Otto turned around and smiled widely. "Welcome home, children!"

Everyone began to chatter.

Alina spoke above the voices, "Let's get everyone to unload the wagon. I'll go in and make sure everything ends up in the right place."

Everyone agreed and began to look for something they could carry. Waldemar scrambled down from the wagon. "I can help!"

"Sure you can, Waldy," Annie smiled, "you take this." She passed him a small basket filled with household linens. He took it and ran after his mom.

"Victor," Otto said, "you can take the cows down to the area where the barn is being built. There's a fenced-in area you can keep them in." Otto looked at his oldest son next, "Gus, you go and care for the horses."

"Yes, Pappa," Gus replied. Turning to Victor, he said, "Come on, let's go."

Alina walked up the three front steps onto the veranda. She ran her hand over the smooth rail and smiled. She opened the front door and stepped inside. Waldemar and the others were at her heels.

Mary spoke first, "Oh, Mamma! What a nice kitchen!" The kitchen had two big windows. One faced out the front of the house and one out the back. At the back of the kitchen was a wood stove and a large holding tank for water. Down one wall was a bank of cabinets that Pappa had made. There was a vast counter for preparing food.

Annie ran her hand over the countertop. It was smooth oak. "Isn't this grand? It will make our preparation quite a bit easier." She slid Margaret off her hip and down to the floor.

Margaret went through a large open doorway into the living room. It too had windows facing out both sides of the house. The sunlight shone in. Margaret laughed and ran around the big empty space.

As everyone began to bring in the furniture, Alina directed them as to where to put it. In no time everything was inside. The older girls went to work setting up the beds and putting on the sheets and blankets.

Alina and Alice made lunch for everyone after everything was settled. Alina had made fresh bread early that morning back at the house in town.

Victor, Gus and Otto came in from the barn. Victor was carrying a bucket of warm milk.

"Girls," Alina called, "time for lunch."

Annie and Mary came from the bedroom; Mary was holding Margaret's hand.

Everyone sat down at the large table flanked by two benches. Otto and Alina sat at opposite ends in sturdy wooden kitchen chairs.

"Shall we give thanks?" Otto asked.

Alina surveyed her children, "Wait . . ." she stood up and moved to the doorway into the living room. "Waldemar?" She walked down to the bedroom and looked around. "Waldemar? This isn't funny. Come out from wherever you're hiding. It's lunch time."

There was no answer. Alina's heart began to race. She rushed back to the kitchen. She looked at Otto, "Did he go down to the barn with you?"

Otto got up from the table, his chair scraping against the wooden floorboards. "No, he wasn't there."

Alina rushed outside. "Waldemar?" She called even louder still, "Waldemar?"

Otto was right behind her with Gus at his heels. "We'll walk toward the barn and see if we can find him. Perhaps he got lost on his way to come find us."

Alina clutched her chest. Tears sprang to her eyes. "Otto, you must find him!"

"Of course. We'll find him straight away. He's probably napping in the hay loft, safe and sound."

Fear coursed through Alina, "Go then."

Otto and Gus jogged off in the direction of the barn all the while calling out, "Waldy? Waldemar?"

Alina turned and went back inside the house. She picked up her napkin and pressed it against her face. Annie stood up and put her arm around her mother. "It's okay, Mamma. He'll be fine."

Alina cried into the napkin, "I should have been watching him. I should have talked to him about the animals out here, the creek . . ."

Mary stood up. "Mamma, Annie and I will go down to the creek . . . to the bridge. Perhaps he's there."

"I can watch Margaret," Alice suggested.

"I'll walk around the outside of the house," Alina said quietly, drying her face.

Waldemar loved the sounds of the rushing water. He also liked the noisy birds in the trees. He spotted another frog hopping along the shoreline. He leapt toward it.

"Gotcha!"

The frog wiggled in his hands.

Waldemar spread his fingers to take a look at his captor. "Hello."

The frog let out a loud, "Ribbit."

Waldemar laughed and opened his hands. "Go then!" The frog jumped away and disappeared into the creek. Waldemar stepped down into the current. He felt the cool water run over the top of his boots.

"Uh-oh. Mamma's going to be mad." His mother never liked when he got his wool socks wet. She was forever warning him to stay out of water that went over the top of his boots. He moved back out of the water and sat on a warm boulder. He pulled his boots and socks off.

He really wanted to know where the creek went. He had been walking along it for a long time now but he still hadn't found the river that it came from.

His stomach growled. He was hungry. "Maybe I should go back for lunch," he said out loud. He looked around. He had jumped across the creek so many times that he couldn't remember which way he had come from.

"Hmm."

He heard a loud noise. It was the sound of a woodcutter, chop, chop, chop. Maybe someone was nearby, he thought. He walked away from the creek and into the woods.

"Waldemar!" Otto's feet crashed through the woods. He and Gus had gone in different directions after they had searched the barn. The creek ran along the north side of their property. Otto was searching along it. He prayed that Waldemar had not gone to the other side of the creek. "Waldemar!" The sound of the creek grew louder, drowning out his voice. His voice cracked with desperation, "WALDEMAR!"

Suddenly, he heard the sound of a moose behind him, exhaling loudly. Its massive horns hit the trees, chop, chop, chop, as it came toward him.

Otto held his breath. He slowly turned his head to see if this moose had a calf with her. He knew better than to get between a mother and her calf. He didn't see one as he slowly backed away. His heart was thundering in his ears.

The moose went back to eating.

That's when Otto saw it, a pair of rubber boots and two navy wool socks. He picked up the socks. There was a white 'W' embroidered into the side.

"Waldy," Otto breathed, "where have you gone?"

Waldemar sat down on a log. He was really tired. His feet were hurting. He shouldn't have taken off his boots. He was hungry too. Maybe he shouldn't have come out here by himself.

There was a rustle in the trees behind him. All at once his father appeared. Otto said nothing as he sat down on the log with him, his boots and socks in his hand.

"Hi, Pappa."

Otto looked at his Waldemar sternly. "Hello."

"So you got my boots?"

Otto held them up. "*Ja*, I do."

"My feet are hurting."

"Out for a walk?"

"I was just going to the creek to catch frogs. Gus told me that there are lots of frogs."

"Did you tell Mamma where you were going?"

Waldemar thought about it for a minute. "Ah . . . no."

Otto passed the boots and socks to Waldemar. He stood up. "Let's go." Waldemar slipped his bare feet into his boots. He put his soggy socks over his shoulders.

"Yes, Pappa. Let's go."

The pair walked back to the house in silence. Just before they reached the house, Otto bent down and looked Waldemar in the eyes. "I need you to promise me that the next time you leave the house you'll tell your Mamma. Do you understand?"

Waldemar nodded, his eyes wide. "Yes, Pappa, I do."

Otto exhaled slowly. In his mind he prayed, "Thank you, Lord."

"Thou tellest my wanderings; put thou my tears into thy bottle: are they not in thy book? When I cry unto thee, then shall mine enemies turn back: this I know; for God is for me." Psalm 56:8-9 KJV

June 1922
Leduc, Alberta

She looked at him with her wide beautiful eyes. They were in a rowboat in the middle of a lake. It had been her idea to come for a picnic and a row with the baby. The wind was blowing and the water was choppy.

"We shouldn't have come out today," he said to her.

She was holding the baby tightly.

"It's a bad day to be out. We shouldn't have come."

She hugged the baby for a moment, kissed her head and then passed her to him. She looked at him blankly and then stood up.

"Whoa, whoa, what are you doing? Sit down! It's dangerous! The water is rough! I can't hold the baby and keep the boat steady."

She stood, staring at him, still saying nothing.

"Ruth! Sit down!" he begged her. "You must sit! You could fall!" He tried to hold the baby and keep the boat from capsizing. "Please take the baby back!"

A wave came and jarred the boat. She toppled into the water.

He panicked. "Ruth!"

Her arms flailed, her eyes were wide with terror. She tried to grab at the boat or an oar but she couldn't reach. He quickly set the baby down in the bottom of the boat. She began to cry. He hesitated for a moment, looking at the crying baby, and then jumped into the cold water after Ruth. She had drifted so far away from the boat. How had she got so far? Her head kept slipping under as he swam desperately toward her. Every time she surfaced, her eyes were begging him to help.

"I'm coming!" he yelled as he swam frantically.

Her heavy skirt and sweater pulled her under. He dove under the water, his eyes open. She began to sink, bubbles escaping her lips. He swam and swam, never being able to reach her. Her face turned from terror to peace. In his mind he screamed, *No! No! Try harder! Swim, damn it!*

He tried to grab for her in the inky blackness but she was always just out of reach. Deeper, deeper and deeper she fell. He swam as hard as he could but he could not reach her. He could hear the baby crying at the surface. He felt the pressure of the water all around him as he watched her slip away. He was suffocating.

The baby. The baby would die if he did not row her back to shore.

He took one last look at Ruth, falling away from him, her eyes wide open, her hands relaxed and outstretched. Her face was blank. She was dead. *Verstorben.* Deceased.

He pushed his body in the opposite direction and swam toward the light. He thought his lungs would explode. Finally, the surface was near. He was going to take a breath—

"Ruth!" he called out into the inky night. He sat bolt upright, his body drenched in sweat. He panted as he looked around his bedroom.

It was a dream . . . a terrible nightmare.

He took a deep, shaky breath and looked at the spot in the bed next to him. It was empty. It was always empty. He wiped his face on the sheet and then got up. He lit a lamp and then carried it to the kitchen. He started a fire in the stove and began to make himself a cup of coffee. He checked his watch: four am. He couldn't go back to sleep, his heart was still racing. He walked back and forth across his kitchen and tried to shake the images from his mind.

"I am going crazy," he said to himself. The nightmares had plagued him since Pauline had left for Portland. He picked up his Bible from the kitchen table. He flipped it open, looking for something to ease his mind. The verses swam in front of him.

"God," he prayed, "help me. I don't know what else to say. It is worse than I ever could have imagined. And—and it isn't getting any easier." He ran his hands over the familiar pages of his Bible. "Every day it doesn't get any less painful. I miss her more . . . I just want to see her. Every day that she is with You my longing for her only increases." He wanted to tell God that he should reconsider.

It was all so final. There was nothing he could do to change it. There was nothing he could do to bring her back. There was nothing but a grim future, a life without his wife, stretching out before him. Everything he had been working on now seemed pointless.

He drank coffee until the sun rose.

It was Sunday and he had to shave and get ready for the walk to church. He went to the stove and began to re-heat the water for his face. He pulled out his shaving kit: soap, brush, razor and a small mirror. He remembered how after he shaved, Ruth would come and touch his cheeks, inspecting for the spots he missed. She would proclaim, 'soft as can be,' and then kiss him. His chest tightened. He soaked his washcloth in warm water and then held it to his face.

It had been six months since Ruth died. In some ways it felt like only a moment and in other ways it seemed like an eternity. The grief had not subsided but slowly grown, the sadness eroding him like a river erodes the sides of a canyon.

He pulled out his soap and lathered his face. He looked at his reflection in the mirror. He began to pull the razor carefully across his cheeks. When he was finished, he ran his own hands over his cheeks, looking for any missed hair.

He dressed in his blue suit. He picked up his Bible from the table and walked out the front door.

The birds were singing as he walked down the main street. He could hear people calling to one another and the sound of someone singing drifting from an open window. Life went on.

When he arrived at church, there was a large gathering of people on the front lawn. He looked for Ben and Walter.

"Hello, Mr. Bohlman!" a cheerful voice rang out. It was Gladys Schultz.

He turned in her direction. "Hello, Mrs. Schultz."

She hurried over to him and touched his arm, "Tell me, how are you?"

"I am well."

"*Nein*," she cocked her head, "how are you really?" The expression on her face turned to pity and curiosity all at once.

"Really, I'm fine. The best I can be, given the circumstances."

"So tragic," she moaned, "really. Such a young little thing . . . your Ruth. And then, to top that, you give up your baby. So sad."

Herman's shoulder's tensed. "Actually, I did not give up my baby. She went to be with her grandmother and aunt until I can afford a nanny."

Gladys' eyebrows shot up higher than the bell tower. "A nanny! Whoever heard of a nanny in Leduc?"

"I want to raise my baby."

She scoffed, "A man raise a baby—I say! With a nanny! A single man living with a woman! Shameful, I dare say! Mr. Bohlman . . . be sensible. The baby's been with the Grandma for six months now. The longer you leave it, the harder it will be to take it away."

Herman looked at Ben and Walter. They had their backs to him. Herman waved at them. "Excuse me, Mrs. Schultz. The Lessing brothers are calling me over."

"*Guten Tag,* Mr. Bohlman," she smiled insincerely. "Glad to hear you are well."

He hurried over to Ben and Walter. He could hear Mrs. Schulz clucking to her friends—"A nanny! Whoever heard of such a thing?"

"*Hallo,*" Herman called out as he approached his brothers-in-law.

They turned around, smiling. "*Hallo,* Herman!" Ben extended his hand for a handshake and then pulled Herman into an embrace. "Good to see you. How is everything?"

Herman rubbed his face. "I don't even know if I can answer that."

Walter reached into his shirt pocket. "Mum sent photos for you."

"Oh, that's wonderful!" Herman eagerly took the envelope and carefully opened it. His daughter's big eyes looked out at him from the photograph. His throat constricted. He felt tears rush to his eyes. He cleared his throat. "*Danke.*"

Ben patted his arm. "We understand."

"I know." Herman pulled his handkerchief from his pant pocket. "I'm glad I have you two." Walter looked down at his shoes.

"Come on," Ben said, "let's go find a seat."

After church, the three of them went to a local restaurant for lunch.

Ben pushed his plate back after they had eaten. "I have some news," he said, eyeing Herman.

Herman scowled, "What news?"

"Yesterday, around supper time, Grandma Schindel went home to be with the Lord."

Herman's eyes were wide with disbelief, "What?"

"She was having an afternoon nap and when I went to wake her—she was gone."

"I'm sorry," he said softly.

"It's okay—she has had a long life, seventy-seven we calculated. Now she is at home with Grandpa Schindel."

"What about *Mutter*?" Herman asked.

"I'll telegraph her first thing in the morning, when they open."

Two days later, Herman waited at the train station in Edmonton. Pauline, Charlie, Amelia, Magda and Ruth were due to arrive in the next few minutes. Herman had borrowed the family car and driven up to meet them.

Pauline had been back to Leduc in January when her father, Gottlieb Schindel, had died. Now she was here again, to bury her mother.

Herman could hear the train roaring down the track in the distance. He moved toward the track. The wheels ground to a halt in the station, the train moaning its displeasure at having to stop its forward momentum. Everyone on the platform waited anxiously for their loved ones.

Pauline, dressed in a black travelling skirt and blouse, came off the train with Ruth in her arms and Magda in tow. She smiled at Herman when she saw him.

"*Hallo!*"

"*Mutter!*" he said as he walked up to them. He embraced Pauline and baby Ruth. He turned toward Magda and said cheerily, "Hello, Maggie! How are you?"

"Hello, Herman, I'm fine," Magda replied. "It is such a long train ride."

"I'm sure. Did you see any animals when you went through the mountains?"

"*Ja*," she smiled, "bears and deer along the way."

"Well that's exciting, isn't it!" Herman smiled at his young sister-in-law.

"Hello, Amelia." He hugged her. "And Charlie, good to see you again."

"Indeed," Charlie replied and shook Herman's hand.

"How was the trip?"

Amelia answered, "The train is quite comfortable. It is a shame we couldn't be travelling under happier circumstances."

"I'm glad you're all here, regardless. It's good to be together."

Back at the house, everyone waited in the front yard while Pauline entered the house. It was quiet. She stepped into the front room. There was her mother, laid out in her coffin.

She took a deep breath. She hated this house. She hated this front room—the room where she had said goodbye to so many of her family. It seemed that every time she walked through this door it was because of death. A month after Ruth died, her father passed away. And now, to complete her year of misery, she would bury her mother. She walked slowly over to the coffin.

"*Mutter*," she touched her mother's white sleeve, "*Mutter*, I'm here now." She began to cry. She sat down in the armchair. She looked at her mother who appeared to be sleeping peacefully. She could hear her children outside, talking, and little Ruth, babbling her delightful sounds.

The front door opened slowly. It was Amelia. "Mother," she said softly as she approached Pauline, "are you alright?"

"*Nein.* Maybe I should have stayed here instead of Portland." Pauline cried again. "Nothing is alright anymore."

Amelia took her mother's hand and gripped it tightly. "We'll get through this. Just like we always have—together."

Slowly, the other family members trickled in, coming to offer their support to Pauline and pay respects to Grandmother Schindel. Ruth babbled and cooed, smiling at all of her aunts and uncles.

Pauline took her from Amelia. She snuggled the little girl in her arms and stroked her downy hair. "Here we are, little one, life and death, beginning and end. Each so oblivious of the other."

Later in the afternoon, they took photos in the farmyard. Herman held up his daughter proudly, smiling from ear to ear.

"Looking good, Herman!" Walter called as he looked through his black box camera.

Herman kissed Ruth's cheeks. "I love you!" he proclaimed. She squirmed in his arms and reached out for Pauline who stood near by.

"Daddy's got you," Pauline assured Ruth.

She fussed, reaching out for Pauline again. "I suppose she's just tired," Pauline said quietly.

"I suppose." He reluctantly handed her over. He wished that he knew how to tell when she was tired, or hungry, or anything for that matter.

Amelia and Pauline cooked a large supper in the farmhouse kitchen for all of the family. They talked late into the evening in the front room, remembering their mother and grandmother, Amelia Schindel. Ruth fell asleep in Pauline's arms.

"Would you like to hold her for a while before I lay her down?"

"Yes," he cleared his throat as he looked her, "I'd like that very much."

He held Ruth in his arms and studied her while the conversation carried on around him. He watched her eyelids flutter and her cheeks make a sucking motion while she breathed in and out. In two days, after the services, Pauline would take her back to Portland. He wished he could afford a nanny. He had been racking his brain trying to think of some other way to keep her in Leduc but nothing seemed feasible. Pauline was right—how was a man supposed to work and raise a baby? He was only being selfish. He thought of nosy Mrs. Schultz's words: the longer you leave her, the harder it will be to take her away. She was right. Just since January, Ruth had already formed a strong connection with her Grandma. She didn't know him—didn't recognize him as her dad. The longer she was in Portland, the harder it was going to be to bring her back to Leduc. He looked at Ruth's fists, curled up in front of her. He took his free hand and stroked the back of her hand gently. Her fingers uncurled, showing Herman exactly what he wanted to see. It was her mother's pinkie finger; the top of the finger just slightly curved inward. Some of the Lessing family hated this trait—a funny quirk, they said, but Herman loved it because it was unique. It was not disfiguring—just something you would notice if you really looked. He loved it because it reminded him of his wife. He would tell Ruth that, one day, when she asked. He would tell her that it was something to be proud of. Something to show that you were connected to your mother.

An hour went by, and then two, and Herman held his daughter firmly. His breathing had slowed as he relaxed. He looked down at her again and realized something. Something important. He had been holding her for so long that he could no longer feel where he ended and she began.

*

Pauline and Ruth returned to Portland. Herman continued to work. Spring had turned to summer and summer into fall. Today was December 13th, a cold Wednesday evening. The sun set around four o'clock in the afternoon and now Herman walked in darkness on his errands.

It had been one year since he had said goodbye to his wife. He finished work at the store and was on his way to buy a wreath to take to her graveside. He had seen winter wreaths in the florist's window on his way home from work the day before. He thought, *Ruth would like that.*

He entered the florist's shop, feeling the warm air envelop him.

"*Guten Tag,*" he called out.

"*Guten Tag,* Mr. Bohlman," the florist looked up from his desk where he was busy arranging a garland, stuffing it with berries and cones. "What can I do for you?"

The wonderful fragrance of the small shop filled Herman's nostrils. "Ah, I wanted to get one of the wreaths you have in the window."

"Of course. Good choice. For your front door?"

"Ah—sort of," Herman lied.

The florist went to the window and picked one of the wreaths. It was several pine boughs laced together with an arrangement of colorful red berries and pinecones at the bottom. A large red ribbon was tied around the top.

"This one is a dollar twenty-five," the florist said.

"Okay." Herman reached for his billfold. He pulled out $2.00. "Here you are."

The florist took his money and made change. "Will you be seeing your daughter this Christmas, Mr. Bohlman?"

Herman looked downcast. "No, sadly I won't. It's just not practical to be going back and forth—train tickets . . . well they don't come cheap."

The florist nodded his head. "Agreed. Although," he waved his arm around his shop, "some things are worth spending money on, even if they're not altogether practical."

Herman smiled. "I suppose you're right." He picked the wreath off the counter. "Sometimes you just have to follow your heart."

"Thank you for your business. I suppose I'll see you Sunday at the service."

"Yes, of course. See you." Herman left the store and walked to the post office to see if anything had come from Portland. Pauline had been sending telegraphs saying that Ruth had come down with a terrible infection. Every few days she sent word that the fever wasn't breaking and that her condition was becoming more serious. He kept asking if he should travel out to see her but Pauline insisted that no, it wasn't necessary. He decided that today, if there was another telegram saying that the fever hadn't broken, that he would go anyway. He would see if he could borrow the money from Ben for the train ticket. Like the florist said, you can't always be practical.

"*Guten Tag,*" the postmaster called out as Herman came in.

"*Guten Tag.*"

"How can I help you? Looking for your mail?"

"Any telegraphs from the family?"

"Ah—let me check." The postmaster flipped through his messages. "Yes, there is one." He passed it to Herman.

Herman read the words, "TAKEN A TURN FOR THE WORSE STOP PRAY FOR A MIRACLE STOP WILL KEEP YOU NOTIFIED OF ANY CHANGES STOP."

Herman folded the message and put it in his coat pocket.

The postmaster looked up from his work. "Is your daughter still sick?"

"Ah, yes. Yes she is."

"Well then we should pray for a miracle, just like she said."

It bothered Herman that the postmaster always read the telegraphs. "Yes. Please do."

"It is good that I have been
afflicted; that I might learn
thy statutes." Psalm
119:71 KJV

December 13, 1922
Leduc, Alberta

Herman walked through the dark streets, his hand in his pocket, holding the telegraph. His stomach knotted as he thought of Pauline's words. Surely, the illness was indeed bad for her to say such a thing. She had looked death in the eye too many times to exaggerate Ruth's condition. He had to go to Portland.

As he hurried through town, the wind bit at his nose and ears. He saw the lights on in Pastor Daum's house and decided to see if they were free.

Emma opened the door with a big smile. "Hello, Herman! Come on in, quickly—it's cold!"

Herman came in and shut the door behind him. "Hello, Emma. I was wondering if you and Phillip had a minute."

"Of course! Take your things and hang them on the hook. I'm just cooking supper. Would you like to stay and join us?"

"I don't want to impose." He held the wreath awkwardly in his hands. "I was just on my way to see Ruth when I saw your light on."

"Supper won't take long—just leave that at the front door and come and wash up."

He gratefully agreed, "Okay—I don't suppose it matters to Ruth what time I go." He smiled sadly.

Emma rubbed his arm, "Oh, Herman. It's today, isn't it—a year?"

He nodded, his throat constricted.

A little voice called out a babble and down the hall came Artrude, Emma and Phillip's little girl. She walked unsteadily across the polished wooden floors.

Herman's face lit up. "Hello, Artrude!" He bent down to catch her as she ran toward him. "You're walking!"

"Yes," Emma said. "She just started to get the hang of it this week!"

He hugged the little girl. "It's good to see you." She smiled widely at him.

"Is Ruth walking?" Emma asked.

Herman looked at Artrude in his arms, so comfortable there. "I don't know."

The family sat down at the table and ate. Artrude made a terrible mess—food in her hair, on her face and in a large radius around the bottom of her highchair. Phillip, Emma and Herman talked while they enjoyed their coffee at the end of the meal.

"What's on your mind, Herman?" Phillip asked.

"So many things," he paused, "but this," he reached in his pocket, "this concerns me the most." He laid the telegraph on the table. Emma and Phillip both read the message.

"Oh dear," Emma exclaimed.

"I am sorry," Phillip said. He looked at his daughter, healthy, smiling and laughing.

Herman brought his handkerchief to his eyes, his raw emotions rushing to the surface. "Does God mean for me to lose the only thing I have left of Ruth? Does he plan to take away my daughter?"

"No," Phillip encouraged, "God doesn't take away." He fingered the edge of his coffee cup. "This is a fallen world, with illness, disease, death . . . He upholds us while we face our tragedies. He is there to offer hope for us when we are uncertain of the outcome."

"I feel so alone." Herman looked at his two dear friends. "No one understands me. The people of the church, they talk—they can't understand why I want my daughter. Everyone has an opinion on what I should do . . ."

"But no one is in your shoes," Emma soothed.

"I can't believe that it has been one year. I miss Ruth more and more each day. When will it get easier?"

"It isn't easy," Phillip said softly, "no one said it would be easy. You must bring your broken heart to the Lord."

Herman cleared his throat. "He feels so far away."

"I know," Emma said gently. Artrude hit a metal spoon against her tray. "That is why we have each other. Our church community takes us to the foot of the cross when we are too weak to get there."

Herman buried his face in his hands. "Everything seems so pointless."

Phillip and Emma nodded, each one sending up silent prayers for God to ease the pain of their friend.

After some time, Phillip asked, "Are you going to Portland?"

"I need to. I need to go and be with her. I should have never let her go. If I had known that I would only have a year with my daughter, I wouldn't have wasted it working in Leduc while she was growing up without me."

"She isn't gone yet—Pauline is right," Emma interrupted. "We have hope. We have our Father we can pray to—and we will."

"Yes," Phillip added, "we will bring this to the congregation and we will pray, fervently for Ruth. And," he looked at Emma, "if bringing Ruth back to Leduc is the right thing to do then we will support you with that in whatever way we can."

Herman dried his eyes on his handkerchief. Artrude looked at him and said, "Uh-oh."

Herman laughed. "Uh-oh indeed."

After the dishes were done and Artrude was in bed, the three adults prayed together. They asked God for the wisdom to know what to do about Herman's situation. They asked for healing for Ruth and mostly for peace in whatever Herman would face over the next few weeks.

Now Herman carried on down the lonely, quiet road to the cemetery. It was nearly nine o'clock. He held his wreath in one hand and opened the creaky gate. The moon shone on the snow, allowing him to see where he was heading. He walked across the cemetery to the back, where all the fresh graves were. He saw her stone, reflecting the moonlight. He took the wreath and laid it in front.

"Hello, love," he said into the cool night air. The wind rustled the bare branches of the trees. A dog barked from the neighboring property. He looked around again to ensure he was alone.

He spoke into the darkness, "Ruth is ill. Your mother says it's dire. I am so frightened. I feel . . ." He looked at the headstone of Ruth's father, next to her. "I feel more at home here than in my own house. Nothing is the same without you."

"I know I am missing too much." His words formed clouds in front of his face. "Tonight when I saw Artrude walking I realized how out of touch I am with my own daughter. I don't know what Ruth can say . . . I don't know if she can walk."

He brushed the snow off Ruth's marker.

"I'm going to Portland for a while. I wish you were here so you could tell me what to do."

Ruth's words came back to him from that day in the hospital, *"Don't give her up. Keep her and teach her our faith, keep her close to our family."*

"I haven't given her up—not really. I would do anything to have her here with me. I just don't know what that looks like; I don't know how to be a single father."

"I miss you, Ruth. Incredibly—I don't even have the words to describe. People say it gets easier as time goes on but . . . but I don't feel it."

He bent down and touched the stone. His fingers traced the words,

Ruth Lessing
Beloved Wife of
H. F. Bohlman
Born August 18, 1901
Died December 13, 1921
We will meet again.

The next day, Herman took the train leaving out West. As the next two days of travel went by, he reflected on everything in his life. Not only was he missing his wife and his daughter, but also he had the burden of wondering about his mother, brother and sisters. He continued to send money to Russia but he hadn't heard from them in years. With the war on, he wondered if his mail and his money were even reaching them. He wondered if they were already on their way to North America or if something had happened to them along the journey. The uncertainty was wearing on him.

Charlie greeted him at the station in Portland.

"*Hallo!*" he called out as Herman stepped off the train.

"Hi!" Herman moved through the crowd toward his brother-in-law.

Charlie shook his hand warmly. "I've got the car, is that your only bag?" He pointed at the carpetbag in Herman's hands.

"*Ja*, this is it."

"Let's go then." Charlie moved through the people on the platform and walked toward the gravel parking lot.

They got in the car and headed for Charlie and Amelia's house.

"So," Herman asked, "how bad is it?"

Charlie ran his hands over the wheel, keeping his eyes on the road, "She has an abscess in her hips. The infection is in the bone—quite serious, as you can imagine."

"Oh no."

"The doctors are worried that even if the infection clears she may never be able to walk."

Herman shook his head, "I can't believe this is happening."

"*Mutter* is sick with grief. She prays over that little girl of yours night and day. She really loves her."

Herman looked out his window at the houses going by. "Nice neighborhood."

"*Ja*. Lots of new houses out here. It's a good time to be settling in."

They pulled in front of a large two-storey house with a porch on the front. "Here we are," Charlie announced.

Herman spent weeks tending to his baby daughter. Night after night, he and Pauline took turns at her bedside, keeping her cool and soothing her cries. Soon Ruth began to recognize her dad and find comfort in his arms, just as she did with Pauline.

Herman had never been so happy and yet so devastated at the same time. As each hour went by he realized that losing her would surely destroy him. He prayed without ceasing—every moment of every day that God would let her live.

Eventually the infection began to clear and little Ruth, already a determined soul, came around. She started to perk up slowly and as the days went by she became more and more of her toddler self. She began to bond with Herman. They played endless games of peek-a-boo and tickles. They stacked blocks and rolled a ball back and forth across the living room floor. Magda often joined in the fun as Ruth regained her full health.

Pauline and Amelia were happy to see Herman spending a lot of time with his daughter. When he made his announcement, Pauline was not surprised.

"I'm taking her back with me," Herman announced abruptly one night after supper as the women sat in the living room drinking their evening tea. He sat down in an armchair opposite his mother and sister-in-law on the sofa.

Pauline stared down at her cup. "Really?"

"I'm sorry, Mother."

"You've decided then?"

"I know you want her here but Ruth wanted me to raise her, to be her father." His tone was pleading her to understand.

Pauline said nothing but stared at her cup.

Amelia spoke, "It will be hard, Herman; we've grown to love her as our own. It's been more than a year now that we've had her in our care and, well, we feel like she belongs here."

"I know."

"Perhaps," Amelia suggested, "you could move to Portland so that we can all be together."

"My work, my church community, is in Leduc. And, when my mother and sisters come I don't want to be any further West."

The room was quiet.

Finally, Pauline said quietly, "It's what you need to do, Herman, and we can support that."

Amelia shook her head and with a sense of panic in her voice said, "How can we say goodbye? What will Magda do?"

"It doesn't matter, Amelia, she belongs with Herman. He is her father."

Herman responded, "I wish there was another way. If only we could all live here . . . but my home is in Leduc. I have the prospects of opening my own store someday. George has been showing me the financial sides of the business and in a few years I might be able to open my own hardware store. I have a future in Leduc."

"How will you live, Herman?" Amelia questioned. "She has no mother there—who will care for her while you work? Who will love her as we do?"

Herman sighed. "She is all I have. I don't know how it will be. I have to trust God that it will work out. I have been alone for the last year and I can't carry on this way. I have been sending money to Russia since I came to Canada and I have heard nothing from home. Not one word. Are they are dead or alive? Not one word. Are they coming to join me?" Herman's emotions were raw and the full force of his emptiness spilled out. "Ruth is my family, even if it is just the two of us. She is the only one I even have the possibility of sharing my life with."

The room was quiet and still. Amelia's grandfather clock chimed loudly seven times. Pauline took a long drink from her cup.

"I'm sorry for questioning you," Amelia said quietly. "It will be a difficult adjustment for everyone."

Herman sat with his face in his hands, his body wracked with guilt and fear. Who would care for Ruth? Was she not better with Pauline and Amelia? Were two mothers better than none? Was he just being selfish? What was best for this child? God, why did this have to be so difficult?

Pauline rose from her chair and came to comfort him. She crouched down next to him and looked up into his face. "We don't have the answers, Herman, we just have to do what we think is best. God knows and we have to trust that He will guide us."

"Why *Mutter*?" Herman sobbed, "I don't know if this is the right thing to do—surely I don't . . . but the thought of leaving her again sickens me."

Amelia too had tears running down her face. "I'm sorry if I have put pressure on you to stay. I love her intensely. She is your daughter, and she should be with you." They all sat silently, tears streaming down their cheeks, Amelia on the sofa, Herman in the armchair and Pauline sitting on the floor by Herman's feet.

"We'll have to tell Magda in the morning," Pauline finally said.

Magda was heartbroken. She wailed for Herman to change his mind. She pleaded with the adults to keep Ruth in Portland. Why couldn't Herman stay here? Why did everything always have to change? What would she do without little Ruth?

He made arrangements for Pauline, Ruth and himself to travel back to Leduc where Pauline would have a chance to check on her sons, see how they were managing the farm and to say goodbye to Ruth.

The journey back was long. Ruth occupied herself with looking out the windows and playing games with her grandma. Pauline tried to soak up every last minute with her. She wished she could split her heart in two, one part for Alberta and one part for Oregon. Amelia was expecting and she knew that the new baby would keep her occupied but nothing could replace the bond she had formed with Ruth. She was certain that one day she would return to the farm—permanently—and there she and Ruth could reconnect and Pauline could be the mother that Ruth needed.

After a week on the farm and a tearful goodbye, Pauline returned to Oregon. Emma and Phillip met with the congregation, bringing Herman's problems forward. Several couples in the church had agreed to take Ruth in, taking care of her until she was old enough to live with her father.

Herman was thankful to God for sparing his daughter. He was thankful to his church community for graciously opening their hearts to Ruth. Mostly he was thankful to God for answering his deepest desire—to have his daughter back in Leduc.

*"Silence is no certain token
that no secret grief is there.
Sorrow which is never
spoken is the heaviest load
to bear." Francis Ridley
Havergal*

July 1925
Leduc, Alberta

Herman was on his way to church. It was hot. The mosquitoes whined in his ears. He batted them away. The wind rustled the tall prairie grass. He walked through a beaten-down path, enjoying the warmth of the sun on his back.

It had been three years since Herman brought his daughter back to Leduc. The congregation had been very supportive in his desire to be with his daughter. She had lived with many families of the church, the Daums, the Hendricks and the McKernleys, and now she had spent nearly nine months with the Grinwalds. The Grinwalds were a lovely couple, kind and caring, doting on Ruth endlessly. They had children of their own but all three of them died in infancy. Ruth filled a void for them.

Herman spent time with Ruth on his days off. He took her to the Lessing farm to see her aunts and uncles. He took her to the Daums to play with Artrude and she spent time at his house, playing in the yard and helping him in the garden.

He showered her with anything she wanted: fur coats, fancy shoes and endless toys. People talked. They always talked but he didn't care. He was happy to do it his own way.

Business was good. He continued to work with Mr. Morris at the General Store. Mr. Morris trusted him completely and had given him the lion's share of the work. He put money away on a monthly basis to save up for the purchase of his own building. It seemed unrealizable at this point but it was a goal, nevertheless, and he was working toward it.

He, Walter and Ben had been working for several years on clearing a small plot of land that Ruth had inherited from her father back in 1921. It was heavily wooded and extremely rocky. Farming was impossible at this point but he figured over the next five years that he could make it a place he could call home. He and Ruth had planned to build their home and raise their children there. He was determined to see it through.

The church came into view and he saw all the familiar faces out on the lawn, talking. His eyes searched for Ruth and the Grinwalds.

Mr. Grinwald spotted him first. "Mr. Bohlman!"

"*Hallo!*" he said as he waved and walked toward them.

Ruth came running toward him. "Daddy!"

"*Schatzi!*" He swept her up into his arms and hugged her.

"*Vati,* do you like my dress? Isn't it pretty? I love my dress. And do you see my shiny shoes?"

He laughed. "Yes, love bug, I do! You are stunning!"

She giggled and then buried her face in his shoulder. "I missed you."

Mr. and Mrs. Grinwald came walking over. "*Guten Morgen,* Mr. Bohlman."

"*Guten Morgen.*" He put out his hand and shook each of theirs. "How are you on this warm summer day?"

"We are well." Mr. Grinwald looked at his wife. "We'd like to invite you for lunch after church."

"Why thank you," Herman replied, "that would be delightful. An old bachelor like me always loves a home-cooked meal."

Mrs. Grinwald smiled. "Ruth says you're quite the cook."

"Well I can bake a potato and I've even cooked a bird or two. But if I had it my way I'd eat out every night of the week."

"It sounds like you need to find a suitable wife," Mr. Grinwald said.

Herman laughed. "A wife!"

"Perhaps you're ready for a wife to cook you a meal?" Mrs. Grinwald suggested.

Herman's eyes went wide, realizing that they were serious. He looked at his daughter and then back to the Grinwalds. "Marriage is not in the plans." He laughed uncomfortably. "I have but one love—my Ruth." He tickled his daughter.

The Grinwalds exchanged a nervous glance. "We should find our seats."

"Of course," Herman smiled, "let's go in."

After lunch, Mrs. Grinwald took Ruth outside to cut flowers from the garden. Ruth put the flowers carefully into a large basket.

"She loves the outdoors," Mr. Grinwald said.

"So do I," said Herman, "I like nothing better than to spend the afternoon in my garden."

"I have a serious matter to speak to you about," Mr. Grinwald cleared his throat. "I've been wanting to talk to you about this for quite some time."

"Of course," Herman's brows were knit, "what is it?"

"As you know, the missus and I have been very fortunate to have Ruth in our lives. We've grown to love her as our own over the last nine months."

"I'm so glad." Herman nodded understandingly.

"It's been very difficult for my wife. She's buried three babies in the last five years and," he paused, "it's taken its toll."

"I'm sure."

"We've spoken to many of our fellow congregationers about the matter—it's not something we bring to you lightheartedly . . ."

"What is it?" Herman asked, perplexed.

"We'd like to adopt Ruth."

Herman was stunned. Adopt! He had not expected this.

"I know it must come as a shock to you."

"Why yes."

"With our deepest respect for your situation, I must say that we feel it isn't healthy for Ruth to move from home to home. Such instability surely can't be good for the child. And Mrs. Grinwald, she may not ever have a baby that has a will to live in this world . . ."

"I see . . ." Herman licked his lips, "but . . ."

"Everyone has been waiting for you to get remarried. The talk of the church is that this business with Ruth is temporary—while you get your affairs in order and find a suitable match."

"I—"

"It's been three-and-a-half years now and even just this morning you indicated that remarrying was not on your horizon."

"I know but . . ."

"You must consider what is best for the child . . . what is best for your daughter."

Herman got up and walked to the window. He looked out at Ruth and Mrs. Grinwald cutting flowers. Ruth chatted away while Mrs. Grinwald smiled and listened intently.

Finally, he turned around. "I appreciate your request. I will pray over the matter and give it the attention it deserves."

Mr. Grinwald got up and shook Herman's hand vigorously. "Thank you, Mr. Bohlman. Thank you."

"I'm not making any promises. I have to say that I have never intended to give up my daughter. Quite the contrary in fact. I've worked very hard to be a part of her life. I've never had any intentions to give her care over to anyone else."

"I understand. All I can ask is that you pray on the matter."

Herman went outside and said goodbye to his daughter. "I love you, Ruth."

"Love you, Daddy." She kissed him on the cheek.

"Did you need a ride back into town?" Mr. Grinwald asked.

"No," Herman shook his head, "the walk will serve me well."

Once out of sight of the Grinwald property, he nearly ran to the Daums. Adoption! Adoption! Indeed! He began to sweat in his Sunday suit. He slowed only to remove his coat and loosen his tie. Once he was back in town, he stopped running, so as not to startle the neighbors.

He knocked on the front door of the Daums. Emma opened it.

"Hi, Herman!"

"Hi, Emma. May I come in?"

"Of course. Phillip's just in the backyard with Artrude and Elmer." Emma and Phillip had added a son to their family a year ago.

"I'll walk around then." He went down the porch steps and around the house to the backyard. He called out, "Hello!"

Phillip looked out from where he lay, relaxing on a blanket. "Herman! Nice to see you. What brings you by?"

Herman sat down on the grass next to Phillip. He loosened his tie completely and pulled it off.

"Hi, Mr. Bohlman!" Artrude came up behind Herman and put her arms around his neck.

"Hello, sweetheart. How are you?"

"Where's Ruth?"

"She's at the Grinwalds today."

"Okay." She laughed and then ran away, chasing a butterfly. Elmer sat, propped up against his dad.

"I had lunch with the Grinwalds," Herman began.

"Oh," Phillip smiled, "that's nice."

"After lunch, Mr. Grinwald took me aside and asked me something."

"What's that?"

"He asked me if they could adopt Ruth."

Phillip sat up, nearly toppling over little Elmer. "They did?"

"Yes!"

"Wait a minute. Em!" he called out, "Em, come on out here."

She came through the back screen door and approached the men.

"Tell her," Phillip said.

"The Grinwalds asked if they could adopt Ruth."

"No!"

"Yes!" Herman's eyes were wide. "I was just as surprised as you!"

Emma gave it some thought. "I suppose . . . with all the babies she's had to bury . . . I guess one could come to that conclusion."

"He told me that if I didn't plan on remarrying that it was the only sensible thing to do. They can provide a loving, stable home for Ruth and if I don't have a wife—well, it wouldn't be fair to Ruth to keep uprooting her."

The Daums nodded as they listened. "What will you do?" Phillip asked.

"I don't know. Of course I want to say no. But is that the right thing to do? I told Mr. Grinwald that I would pray on it . . ."

"And you should," Phillip interrupted.

"But I can't ever see myself giving her up."

"No," Emma agreed. "Ruth wouldn't want that."

"If I wasn't going to raise her I would have left her in Portland."

"Of course."

"I don't know what to do. He said that the community has been talking about it, deciding what is best for Ruth, and clearly the opinion is that I make up my mind and remarry or give Ruth up to a loving, Christian home where she can have a mother."

"What a choice . . ." Emma sighed. "I don't know."

"I can't remarry."

"We know." Phillip rubbed his hand across his wife's shoulder. "Your grief is still raw."

"A day," Herman sighed, "a week . . . a year . . . two, three . . . it doesn't matter. I miss her even more."

Herman met with the Grinwalds a week later and let them know that he was not prepared to give Ruth up for adoption, despite their good intentions. He let them know that at the end of the summer he would be moving Ruth to the Daums so that she could spend more time with Artrude. They were devastated.

The church began to talk, everyone deciding on whether or not he had made the right choice. Many sided with the Grinwalds stating that if Herman was not prepared to remarry then he should have given Ruth up. The Daums were ever neutral. Being pastor allowed Phillip to remain that way. The judgment was pressing in on Herman every day, with each interaction in the community. At the store, in the streets, at the post office, it plagued him. People talked in hushed whispers about his decision—questioning him.

He sat on the front porch with Emma one August afternoon while the girls played tea party with Elmer at their feet.

"I can't take it."

"I'm sorry."

"Everyone has a mind to tell me what I should be doing."

"I've heard the talk. Everywhere I go—I can't escape the gossip myself."

Herman ran his hands through his hair. "Agh! What am I to do?" He looked at his daughter, laughing with Artrude.

Emma sat silently for a while, contemplating her idea. Eventually she said, "There is a singles conference in Yorkton next week. Perhaps you should go—entertain the idea."

Herman rolled his eyes. "Not you."

"I know!" She chuckled. "Just hear me out. Perhaps God has plans for you. Perhaps you should open your mind—and your heart."

"I can't."

She looked him in the eyes and grasped his arm. "Maybe, Herman Bohlman, it isn't always about what you want. Maybe you have to do this because it is the right thing to do for her." She looked at Ruth who was busy shoving a teacup toward protesting Elmer.

He shook his head. "I can't, Emma, I can't."

"One never knows what one is capable of until he is forced to choose between what feels good and what is best."

"By the word of the Lord
were the heavens made,
their starry host by the
breath of his mouth."
Psalm 33:6 NIV

May 1925
Lac Du Bonnet, Manitoba

His breathing was steady. Fast and steady. Each time his bare foot hit the ground the impact radiated up his leg. It was dark. All the stars were overhead, winking at him as he ran.

It was four o'clock in the morning and seven-year-old Waldemar was out for his morning run. Each breath he blew out in a loud exhale as he sprinted, farther and farther away from home. Across their eighty acres, onto the neighbor's property and on into the trail through the Riverland woods. The fences, the trees, they all rushed by as he remained focused.

Run, he told himself, run.

He had started the morning in the same way that he always did: quietly. Everyone in the family shared the same bedroom. Each morning he would silently stretch. With his toes he would reach the clothes that had spent the night at the foot of the bed, keeping warm. He changed noiselessly from his pajamas into his shirt and trousers under the covers. His bare feet hit the cold floor and he would make his way to the kitchen to fire up the wood stove.

After lighting the wood stove, he would take a piece of bread that Mamma always left on the kitchen table. And then, then he ran. For nearly an hour as fast and as intensely as possible, he ran.

As the sun began to break through night's darkness, Waldemar changed his direction and headed back to the barn. Once he arrived at the big brown building, he took a deep breath. He turned his arms in circles and stretched.

He entered into the warm barn. He loved its sounds. The animals snorting, calling to one another and stamping their feet. He took the milking stool off its peg on the wall and took it to the first of two cows.

"Good morning," he said softly as he approached her from the rear. He ran his hand along her flank.

She looked at him and mooed.

He set the stool up and put a metal pail underneath her full udder. He ran his hands down the velvety teats, gently squeezing as he went. The milk made a loud sound as it sprayed into the pail. The cow shifted her feet.

"How's that?" he asked. "Shall we continue?"

He carried on milking until the pail was full. She protested as he left the stall. "I'll be back to feed you."

He went to the second cow and repeated the process, filling a second pail. He was happy that spring was finally here. It was still cool in the morning but the days were warmer and the grass had turned green. The snow had disappeared and the walk to school was faster and easier.

In the winter, chores were tedious. In winter, he had to walk the cows all the way down to the river for their water. He had to go out on the ice, cut a hole and then lead them to it to drink. He would have to stand in the cold wind until they were through. Then he would turn them around and follow them back home. It was two miles each way and by the time he returned to the barn, his fingers and toes would be blue.

When he was done the milking, he fed the cows and filled their water trough. He moved onto the horses that needed fresh hay, water and feed. He brushed each one, carefully inspecting their bodies as he went. After that, he went to the chickens. By now he could hear Gus working outside on the wagon.

"I better hurry," he said to himself. He entered into the chicken coop. All the chickens came around his legs, pecking at his bare toes. "Shoo! Shoo!" He pulled open the feed box and began to sprinkle seeds all over the floor. The chickens clucked wildly as they pushed one another out of the way to eat. While they were busy, Waldemar went to the nests and retrieved their eggs. In just a few minutes, he had six eggs in his basket and was ready to go back to the house. He hung the basket over his neck and took a pail of milk in each hand.

"Do you know what time it is?" a voice asked him, startling him, nearly causing him to spill the milk.

Waldemar looked up, "Oh, hello, Pappa."

"Do you?"

"Ah . . . breakfast time?"

Otto glared at him disapprovingly. "Everyone is waiting for you."

"I'm ready." He began to walk through the barn door.

Otto grabbed his arm. He looked him in the eyes as he said, "Did you run this morning?"

Waldemar looked away, pulled out of his father's grasp and started toward the house. "Yes."

"I need you to take care of your responsibilities."

"I do." He lifted the heavy pails in his hands, showing his father his efforts. "See?"

They walked briskly side by side, the house drawing nearer.

"Running serves no purpose, Waldemar. It's a waste of time."

Waldemar shrugged.

"You know that since I injured my back I am counting on you and Gus to manage things on the farm."

"I know." Waldemar paused and asked, "What about Victor? Why do I have to do everything?"

"Victor does his own jobs."

Otto grabbed Waldemar once more. He leaned in close, his musky breath warm on Waldemar's face. "Next time get your chores done a little faster. Do you understand me?" He grabbed the pails from Waldemar's hands.

"Yes, Pappa." Waldemar wriggled free and ran inside the house, the egg basket swinging wildly.

Inside the house, Alina stood at the wood stove. Nearly everyone, aside from Gus, was at the breakfast table, in different stages of eating. Otto set down the milk pails and then sat at the head of the table. Waldemar walked the eggs over to his mother.

She ran her hand over his hair and pulled him in for a hug. "Thank you, Waldy."

"Sorry it took so long."

She smiled at him and bent down to kiss him on the cheek. "It's fine. Are you hungry?"

He smiled. "Oh yes."

"Sit down then."

He sat down at the table next to Singhild, the newest member of the family, now just a few months shy of her third birthday.

"Morning, Sing."

She grinned at him. "Morning."

Four-year-old Margaret piped up from the opposite side of the table. "I wish we were going to school."

"Soon enough," Victor commented. "Not this fall, but next you can walk with Alice, Waldemar and me."

"What about me?" Sing whined.

Waldemar tweaked her on the nose. "It's a long time more for you, Sugar Lump."

She crossed her arms and pouted. "Humph."

Alina brought bowls of steaming porridge to the table for each of the children. "Eat up, you should be leaving right away."

Waldemar shrugged. "We can always run."

Otto scowled as he ate his eggs.

"No," Alina disagreed, "no, you may not run." She looked pointedly at Victor and Alice. "Understand? No running."

Alice sighed, "We know, Mamma."

Alina faced her four other daughters sitting at the table. "And now, Annie and Mary, can you wash the dishes and get the bread baking?"

"Yes, Mamma," they said in unison. They stood up from the table and began to clear the dishes.

"And you," she looked at Margaret and Singhild, "You can help me."

"With what?" Singhild asked.

"We're going to make our plans for the garden today. That way when your father goes into town he can buy the seeds we need."

Margaret jumped out of her seat. "Oh that will be fun!"

Waldemar looked at Singhild. "See, it's not so bad to be home with Mamma."

"Yes," she laughed, "it is fun!"

The two young girls left the table talking about their favorite things to plant.

Alina packed the school children's bags and lined them up at the door. After a quick kiss and a hug, Alice, Victor and Waldemar were on their way to school.

On their way back from school, Waldemar looked at Victor and grinned. "Do you know what day it is?"

Victor shrugged. "What?"

"May 15th."

"So?"

"So it's my day to swim in the river."

Victor's eyebrows furrowed. "You're crazy. It's too cold."

Alice trailed behind. "What are you talking about?" she called out.

The boys slowed to let Alice catch up. Victor said, "Waldy's going to swim in the river."

"Today?"

Waldemar nodded. "Yes. It's May 15th. I always go swimming in the river on May 15th."

Alice looked at him skeptically. "Do you mean always as in starting last year?"

"Well yes. But after last year I decided that May 15th would be my first swim day . . . no matter."

"Well," Alice said disapprovingly, "it's much colder this year. You'll freeze."

They continued to debate the matter until they reached the house. Waldemar went straight to the barn to do his chores. He cleaned out all the stalls, sweeping and shoveling out the dirty hay and manure. He pushed it all out to the manure pile outside the barn. After that, he laid fresh hay, checked on the animals and then went to find Victor.

Victor was in the house, sitting at the table doing schoolwork. Waldemar sat down next to him and said quietly, "Are you coming with me?"

Victor shook his head, "No way. You're crazy. Mamma would be furious."

Waldemar shrugged, "Suit yourself." He called out to his Mamma who was knitting in the living room. "Mamma, I'm going down to the river for some fishing."

She looked up and smiled. "Okay. See you later then."

Waldemar grabbed a bath towel and winked at Victor who continued to shake his head in disgust. Waldemar picked up his fishing rod and bait from the front porch, and started running in the direction of the river.

The river ran all along the east side of Lac Du Bonnet. It was fed by Lake Manitoba. Waldemar and the family had a particular spot they liked to go—it was an inlet where the water was calm and still. It was a great place to wash up at the end of a hard workday or just a refreshing place to swim on a hot day. It was their sanctuary, their undisturbed bit of paradise. They referred to it as the flats.

There was nothing Waldemar liked more than to swim in the river. He was a strong swimmer but Mamma always warned him to stay away from the narrows. The narrows was a spot in the river where the banks came close together and the speed of the current picked up significantly. He secretly wanted to try swimming it this summer. Perhaps he could swim across it faster than it could carry him downstream.

It was wooded the entire way to the river, aside from one farmer's field that had been cleared. As he grew closer to the river's edge, the ground became sandier and the tall trees turned into shrubs and grasses. He jogged the beaten path to his swimming spot. He looked for a place to set down his pole and bait.

He stripped down to his underwear and waded into the water. He gasped as the water hit his knees. It was very cold!

"It's May 15th," he declared and then dove forward into the deeper water. "Oooooo!" he cried out as the cold water enveloped his body. He started to swim quickly out into the deeper water, moving his arms and legs vigorously to try to stay warm. His teeth began to chatter. His entire body was covered in goose bumps but he carried on, swimming swiftly out into the wider part of the river, until his fishing pole was but a tiny dot in the distance.

As his body worked, he warmed up. The cool water had changed from enemy to friend as he went back and forth across the wide river side of the inlet. Finally he decided that he should go back and do some fishing before heading home. As he grew closer to the shoreline, he could see that someone was watching him, someone on a horse. He swam faster now until he could touch the bottom. Then he stood up and walked out of the water, shivering all the way. He went straight to the bush where he had draped his towel and began to rub himself vigorously, all the while eyeing this strange man on the horse.

The man dismounted his horse and approached Waldemar. "Good evening."

Waldemar furiously rubbed his hair and hastily pulled on his trousers and shirt. "Hello."

"You're quite a fine swimmer."

"Ah, thanks." The man was Indian but spoke English with no trace of an accent. He wore traditional Indian clothing. Waldemar had never seen him before.

"What's your name?" the man asked.

"Waldemar . . . Waldemar Pettersson. Otto Pettersson's my father."

"I'm Tom McLeod . . . a neighbor."

Waldemar smiled. "Okay."

Tom smiled, looking at Waldemar's fishing gear. "Is this a good spot to fish?"

"Yes, sir, it is. But I—I haven't been fishing yet."

"I need to catch a fish for supper. How about you?"

Waldemar eyed the sinking sun. "I should but—Mamma will be waiting."

Tom went to his horse and pulled a line from his bag. He tied the horse's reins to a tree and waded out into the water, moccasins and all. He cast the line into the water and in two minutes he had caught a large fish, big enough to feed the whole family. He hit it over the head with a rock and handed it to Waldemar. "Will that do?"

Waldemar grinned, "Yes, sir."

"Would you like some company walking back? I live in your direction, just past your property."

"Sure," Waldemar looked at the man, intrigued. "I suppose."

"You hesitate?"

"Well," Waldemar grinned, "I like to run."

Tom laughed. "I see. Well I will ride and you can run. Give me the fish and I will put it in my bag." Tom wrapped the fish in a handkerchief and put it in his satchel. He mounted his horse with ease and gently kicked it. They began to walk down the trail. Waldemar walked slowly past the horse and then started to run in the direction of home.

Tom had to keep his horse moving quickly to keep up with the young boy. He was surprised at his agility and energy, especially after his cold swim.

In less than fifteen minutes, they were back at the Pettersson property. "A beautiful home," Tom commented as they approached the house.

"Thank you. Why don't you come in and meet my parents?"

"You go in and ask your father, tell him a neighbor wants to meet him." Tom reached in his bag for the fish. "Tell him I've brought a meal."

Waldemar took the fish and ran inside. A moment later, he emerged with Otto.

Otto smiled as he came down the front steps. Tom dismounted his horse.

"Hello," he put out his hand as he approached Tom. "Otto Pettersson. Waldemar says you met down at the river."

Tom shook his hand. "Yes, we did. Pleasure to meet you."

*"For God hath not given us
the spirit of fear; but of
power, and of love, and of a
sound mind."*
2 Timothy 1:7 KJV

October 1925
Leduc, Alberta

It was getting dark. The sun was setting and the sky was lit with hues of pinks and purples, painting the prairie sky. Herman walked to the cemetery alone. It was a place he could go to reflect and try to sort things out.

The singles conference had been enlightening. It was not exactly what Herman had expected. The weekend had been full of visiting and eating. There was a jovial, pleasant mood to the whole affair but beneath the surface was an underlying tension. Spinsters, bachelors and widows eyed one another to see if they could find a suitable match. Every meal was spent asking subtle yet pertinent questions to determine the expectations of the person sitting across from you. In the evenings, there were socials and dances but Herman didn't dance. He was Baptist. He simply watched and drank his coffee.

Once at the cemetery he opened the gate. It creaked at him. He walked the grassy path to the Ruth's marker.

The conference had been held the last weekend in August. He hadn't wanted to go but Emma had convinced him that if he tried it might be enough to soothe the opinions of the church and the community. If he appeared to be trying to find a suitable mate then perhaps . . .

Herman sighed. He touched the cold stone. "*Hallo, Liebe.*"

The leaves that had fallen from the trees rustled back at him as the wind swept them across the grass.

"I need to talk to you." He paused, suddenly feeling ill, "I've met someone."

He dropped to his knees. He felt the cold ground through his trousers. He was quiet for a long time until finally he said, "Her name is Edith. She's from Yorkton. She's a spinster. She says she's fine with the fact that I have a child."

He wiped the tears coming down his cheeks. "I—I don't know what to do. The church, they want me to move on. No one seems to understand the love I hold for you. The love I still do . . ."

The wind blew through the trees. Herman shivered. He pulled his legs out from underneath him and sat with his back against the side of the marker. He pulled the dead grass from the ground absentmindedly as he carried on.

"She seems very practical. She's not terribly outgoing or funny. She is kind though and she's a good Christian woman. She's German mind you but she doesn't speak it very often . . . prefers to be English-speaking. She has family in the area here—a sister—and she says she's willing to relocate. I've tried to see about a nanny but it seems—well I've decided that I'd face even more criticism that way—a single man living with a single woman . . ."

"I need to do what's best for Ruth. As everyone says, I have to make up my mind."

He stopped pulling the grass and folded his hands in his lap. "I never thought I'd be in this situation."

"I want to say that I'm sorry. I don't mean it as a betrayal to you. I want you to know that I love you." He laughed, "Of course you know that . . . nothing has changed since you've gone."

No one answered back. Herman could hear the crickets out in the long grass beyond the cemetery fence.

"Perhaps it is time for me to face what's necessary."

Herman sat in silence. The leaves continued to swirl around him. The sun said its final goodbye before it slipped beneath the horizon. The moon rose. The air grew cold and sharp. Herman closed his eyes to pray.

"Herman," a quiet, far-off voice called to him.

Herman's eyes snapped open. He looked up, his heart racing. He must have fallen asleep. A man stood, leaning against a fence post about twenty feet away. He was a tall man with a strong build. He wore dark-colored trousers, a vest and a long wool coat. Herman clamored to his feet and began to walk toward the man.

The man raised his hand. He looked familiar to Herman but it was so dark.

"They're alright," the man said in German.

Herman recognized the voice. Bewildered he said, "Father?" He looked at the man. It had been twenty-two years since he had seen that face. "*Vater?* Is it you?" Herman had been nine years old when his father had been killed.

The man spoke calmly, "They are with me now."

He stumbled through the cemetery toward the man. "*Vater?*" He tripped in the darkness and when he got to his feet the man was gone. He was sweating all over—his heart was beating in his ears. A vein in his forehead throbbed.

What was going on? He felt chills down his spine. He quickly ran to the exit of the cemetery. He didn't even bother to shut the gate behind him. He ran home. Behind him he could hear the neighbor's dog barking.

A few weeks later, Herman was at work. He was sweeping the floor when the shop bells rang. A man entered the store. He was unfamiliar.

"Good day," Herman greeted him warmly. "Are you from out of town?"

"*Guten Tag.*" The man spoke in German. He asked if he was Mr. Herman Bohlman, son of Frederick and Julianna.

"*Ja.*"

His English was broken, laced with a thick German accent. "We speak in private?"

Herman was perplexed. He leaned the broom against the counter. He turned to Mr. Morris. "Will you excuse us for a moment?"

Mr. Morris nodded. "Please, use my office."

Herman walked the gentleman to the office and shut the door behind him. "What can I do for you?" he asked in German.

"I have traveled for many years now—looking for you. I once lived in your village. You were a young boy then and I an old man. I came to bring you word of your family."

Herman's heart began to race. "Have you seen my mother? Do you know where she is?"

The man nodded.

"Where? I haven't heard from her in years—nearly ten years since I've had a letter. Did they come with you across the Atlantic?"

"No, sir." The man rubbed his stubbled chin. "I left your village in 1919. It has taken me many years to cross this great nation. To find where you had lived and worked. Finally I had word that you had come to the prairies. Now I am here . . . and you are with me."

"Please, tell me what you know of my mother."

"I knew someone who was a political prisoner. He was taken by the Russians and was shipped out to a Siberian labor camp in 1917. The train was cold . . . crowded. Many did not survive. He did. He was able to send word back through the underground."

Herman felt knots forming in his stomach.

"Your mother was on the car with him. She and a young girl. They fought hard . . ."

"No . . ." Herman whispered.

"I am sorry. They froze to death."

He stared at the man in disbelief. They should have been on their way to North America by then.

"I respected your parents deeply. Your mother, she was a good woman. She said that you had gone ahead and that you would send for them as soon as you had work. She treasured the letters you sent. As for the rest of your family—your brother, Asaph—no one knows . . ."

Asaph had been twelve when Herman left for North America. Asaph hadn't wept as Martha had but he had shaken his hand, wishing him God speed.

"He was a young man by then—perhaps he was taken as a political prisoner and shipped somewhere else. Perhaps he survives somewhere—in a labor camp."

Herman felt hot. He pulled his handkerchief from his pocket. "Lakadia?"

"Your sister, Lakadia," the man looked pensive. "Ah, yes. Some said she married and fled to the Black Sea region to escape the war."

"Did they get the money I sent them?" Herman took a deep breath, "I sent them money for years."

The man scoffed, "Dear boy, if we were lucky enough to get a letter—they were censored. And you can bet that if there had been money, sticky greedy fingers would have taken it long before your letter ever reached your mother's hands."

"No . . ." He shook his head in disbelief.

"I am sorry to bring you such news. I know it must come as a great shock."

The room was filled with heavy silence.

Finally, Herman asked, "Are you here to stay?"

"No. I take the train to British Columbia in three days. I have a cousin who settled there and I plan to join him. I wanted to find you—out of respect for your mother and father."

Herman wrung his hands. "Thank you."

"I must go. I'm meeting an old friend for lunch."

The man left the office. Herman sank down in Mr. Morris' leather chair. Had his vision been a dream? Had he seen his father that night in the cemetery? He did not believe in ghosts. Had he had a vision from the Holy Spirit? To comfort him?

The day he left Russia suddenly haunted him even more than it ever had. He promised his sister Martha that he would send for them—rescue them . . . he had left her to die. He imagined his mother and sister, frozen on a horrible cattle car, huddled together, embraced in death.

He cried freely into his handkerchief, sobbing as grief and guilt consumed him. As he cried, a verse from the Book of Revelation came to his mind. "And God shall wipe away all tears from their eyes; and there shall be no more death, neither sorrow, nor crying, neither shall there be any more pain: for the former things are passed away."

*

The following April, Emma Daum sat five-year-old Ruth down to explain what was going to happen.

"Ruth, I am so happy for you," Emma began speaking in German.

"What's happening?" Ruth turned her bright eyes to Mrs. Daum's face.

"Today is a very special day. You'll be getting a new mother! Your daddy has married someone very special and now you will go live in your new home with your daddy."

Ruth grinned. "I hope she is just like you, Mrs. Daum."

Emma hugged Ruth, "Oh thank you. I am sure that she will take good care of you."

"Will we see each other again?" Ruth suddenly looked worried.

"Of course, love, we will be neighbors and you and Artrude will still play. I will always be here for you, honey." Emma enjoyed this time with Ruth in their home.

They spent the evening packing Ruth's things. Emma carefully put all of Ruth's precious toys, and a doll, Rosalie, for which Emma had sewn plenty of clothes, into a large bag. She packed her tea sets and sewing machine, her hats, darling shoes and extravagant dresses.

Ruth lay in bed that night not able to fall asleep. A new mother. She was going to live with her dad. She had always wanted a mother of her own. God had answered her prayers.

The next morning, Herman came to pick up Ruth. Everyone stood in the front hall. The girls hugged goodbye.

"Thanks for everything, Emma." Herman shook Emma's hand. "I really appreciate all of the care you've given to Ruth."

Emma stroked Artrude's hair. "It's been an honor." Artrude wrapped her arms around her mother's skirt. "We love having her. I don't know what Artrude is going to do without her 'sister' under the same roof!"

Herman picked up Ruth. She looked downcast. "It's alright. You'll still be neighbors!"

"But Daddy," she whined, "it's not the same!"

"Come now. We've got lots of things to look forward to. Breakfast with your dad every morning . . . it doesn't get any better than that!"

Ruth smiled. Herman tickled her under the chin. "Chin up. I need a smiling face."

Ruth waved to Artrude reluctantly, "Bye, Arty."

"Farewell, Ruth," Artrude said dramatically.

The adults laughed.

Herman went out the front door, Ruth in one arm and her bag in the other.

They walked down the street. Spring was coming and with it came mud. Endless amounts of mud. Herman walked around the deepest puddles of melting snow to try to avoid soaking his trouser hem. He was happy that Ruth was in his arms and out of the mess. When they reached the house, Herman said softly, "Look, Ruth."

Ruth turned around in her father's arms and looked toward their new house. A woman stood in the doorway. She was still. Her hair was pulled neatly back into a roll at the base of her neck. She wore a navy blue skirt and a cream-colored blouse. She had gold earrings and a simple necklace.

"That's my *Mutter*?"

"*Ja*," he said apprehensively.

They came up the steps. "Hello, Edith."

She smiled. "Hello."

Herman set Ruth down and said, "Ruth, say hello to Mother."

"*Hallo*." Ruth was beaming.

Edith addressed her, "Ruth, nice to meet you." Edith put out her hand and shook Ruth's.

"Let's go inside," Herman cleared his throat, "shall we?"

They took off their coats and went to the living room. Ruth sat down on the chesterfield. The house was nicely decorated and looked formal. There were no things for children, no toys or anything that welcomed her. She tried as hard as she could to remember her manners so that she could impress her new mother.

Edith passed Ruth a cup of tea. "Here you are."

Ruth smiled and took the cup.

"What do you say?"

"Thank you, *Mutter*."

"It is Mother, child. You will speak English to me. After tea you can go to your bedroom," Edith instructed. "You may unpack your things and then I will call you down for lunch."

"We've made you your own room, with plenty of space for your things." Herman shifted uneasily in his seat.

Herman took Ruth upstairs after tea. He sat her on her bed and helped her take off her pretty shoes.

"Do you like your room?"

The room was lovely. It had a large French door window that opened outward. It had a sloped ceiling with a beautiful electric light fixture. There was a bed with an iron frame. It was covered in white linens with a pink pillow that was embroidered. Next to the bed was a small table with an alarm clock on top of it. Beside the night table was a rocking chair. On the opposite side of the room was a large wooden wardrobe. It had a cupboard at the top and a large drawer at the bottom.

Herman nodded toward the wardrobe. "Shall we put your things away?"

After lunch, Herman sat and absorbed the afternoon with his daughter. He carefully hung all of her dresses in the wardrobe and put all of her toys in a chest at the end of her bed. After supper, he helped her into her nightclothes and then the two of them settled into the rocking chair. He told her stories as the sun set. He absorbed the feel of her warm body pressed against him. He took in the smell of her short strawberry blonde hair. He loved her wide eyes looking up into his face as he told her all of the German fairytales he could think of. Finally, when her little eyes began to sag, he carried her to bed and kissed her forehead. He pulled the quilts up to her little chin and tucked her doll in next to her. He knelt by her bedside. As she fell asleep, he prayed for her.

"Thank you, Lord, that you have made it possible for me to have my daughter with me. Thank you for keeping her safe and helping me to create this family for her. Bless her Lord, draw her close to you and hold her in your hand. Thank you, Lord, for her life. Thank you that I can enjoy her. Thank you for blessing me so richly."

Herman placed his hand on the top of Ruth's sleeping body and quoted the bible saying, "For I know the plans I have for you, declares the Lord, plans to prosper you and not to harm you, plans to give you hope and a future. Then you will call upon me and come and pray to me, and I will listen to you. You will seek me with all your heart. I will be found by you, declares the Lord, and will bring you back."

"Thank you, Lord, for bringing her back to me," Herman whispered as he finished his prayer. He stroked her hair and kissed her cheek. With tears in his eyes he said, "You look just like your *Mutter*."

Edith stood in the hallway looking through the crack in the door, unnoticed by Herman.

*"Weeping may endure for a
night, but joy cometh in the
morning."
Psalm 30:5 KJV*

August 1926
Leduc, Alberta

It was a warm August summer night. The wind blew and the skies were turning dark, not with the fall of night but with dark rain clouds. The sound of the coming storm had masked five-year-old Ruth's footsteps on the stairs. She crouched in her nightgown, listening to Edith and Herman arguing downstairs.

Herman sat in the armchair in the living room. "Come now, Edith, she's only a child. She should be able to see her cousins."

She stood in the doorway to the kitchen with her arms crossed over her chest. "I am her family, and you are her family. We need to show her that we are united and you will simply confuse the child by exposing her to these aunts, uncles and cousins."

"She is a part of the Lessing family whether you like it or not. I don't know how it works when you remarry but I never intended to lose that part of our lives when I married you."

"How dare you," she seethed.

"I love you—" he said defensively, "but there is nothing wrong with seeing the Lessings . . . Ruth isn't there anymore—she is dead!"

"I love you—but . . ." Edith mocked. "Is that what we've come to . . . so soon. I love you but I still want everything that feels good for me?"

Herman shook his head. "I do not appreciate your tone."

"And I do not appreciate your words. It's always *I* want this, *I* think this is best. What about what I want Herman? Have you ever stopped to think about what *I* want? I want a family. I want Ruth to be a part of this family—not the Lessings. We are a family now. You and I . . ."

"I know—"

"We are the new Bohlman family. You may have named her Lessing but she is not a Lessing. Her mother is gone. That is my role to fill."

"I understand that." Herman sat quietly, considering his words, "Why can't we have it both ways?"

"I cannot go and socialize with the Lessings without being scrutinized. We are not one big happy family and I'm not going to pretend that we are."

Herman's body tensed, "So what am I to do? Tell them that we're never going to the farm? We're never going to see Mother Lessing? We're going to be a few miles away but Ruth can never see them?"

Edith glared at Herman. "I don't care what you say. Find your way. But I am telling you that you need to choose between her . . ." she pointed menacingly at the stairs, "or me."

Ruth's eyes were wide. She held her breath.

He said at last, "That isn't fair."

"Nothing is fair, Herman. Losing your family, your mother, your siblings, losing your beloved . . . none of that is fair . . . but it happened." She stepped toward him, jabbing her finger toward his face. "And now I am telling you that I am done with worrying about what is fair for you. It's time that you realized that without me there wouldn't be a Ruth," she spit out the name, "under your roof. You need to start realizing how lucky you are that I've put up with your trips to the Lessings for the last year—your trips to the graveside . . ."

"But . . ."

"You think I don't know? You think the neighbors don't talk?" Her tone turned mocking again, "There is poor love sick Mr. Bohlman, off to visit his dead wife." She turned away from him. She turned up the hem of her apron and dabbed her eyes.

Herman sighed, "I'm sorry. I didn't realize." He got up from his chair and went to her. He put his arm around her shoulder. "I didn't know it would hurt you."

She pushed his arm away. "Of course it hurts! Do you love her or do you love me? How can I compete with her? She's just a memory."

"It isn't . . ."

"You say that . . ."

"I mean it. I'm sorry. I am done with the trips to the graveside. You're right. It's not respectful to you."

"And?"

"And everything else. I'll figure it out. I'm sorry."

She turned to him and put her arms around him. She cried on his shoulder. He rubbed her back reassuringly.

They turned toward the steps and at that moment the thunder clapped loudly overhead and the rain began to fall.

"I'll get the windows down here," Edith said. "You go upstairs and make sure the bedroom windows are closed."

Herman took the stairs two at a time. The rain beat against the house powerfully as the lightning lit the night sky. He could hear Edith fastening the windows on the main floor. He raced to their bedroom and shut the windows and then across the hall to Ruth's. Her large window was already closed. He turned around and looked at his daughter, clutching her doll. He leaned in close.

"Are you awake?"

She said nothing.

He sat down in the chair. He let out a deep breath. He looked at his daughter, sleeping so peacefully. What was he going to do?

Ruth's heart beat rapidly as her father sat in her room. What did this all mean? What was going to happen? She loved her Aunt Magda, Uncle Ben and Uncle Walter. She loved her trips to the farm, her grandmother . . . what was going to happen now?

She tried to hold very still as her father studied her.

Ruth awoke to Edith calling her to get up. "Come on, child, out of bed, we haven't got all day now."

"Coming," she called as she sleepily got out of bed.

"Get dressed and get down for breakfast. We've got company coming today. Come now and get on with it."

Ruth dressed quickly not wanting to upset Edith first thing in the morning. She had overheard her mother and dad say that Grandmother Fleck was coming from Yorkton to visit.

Ruth had already met one other Fleck, Aunt Lilly. She and her husband lived nearby. Often Ruth wished that Aunt Lilly had been her mother instead. She would engage Ruth with her dolls and tea sets, and listen carefully as she spoke about what was on her mind.

"Ruth, get down here!" Edith hollered from the bottom of the steps.

"Coming, Mother!" Ruth called back as she tore down the stairs.

"For heaven's sake, child, slow down, a lady doesn't run!" Edith looked sternly at her.

Ruth rolled her eyes as she nodded. Edith took Ruth's chin in her firm grasp. "You will look me in the eyes and say, 'Yes, Mother.' Do you understand?"

"Yes, Mother." She had so many things to say but kept quiet. Her father sat at the breakfast table. Ruth sat down at the table next to him and waited for Edith to serve her breakfast. After they ate, Edith had a long list of chores for Ruth to complete before Grandmother Fleck was due to arrive on the afternoon train.

Ruth started with washing the dishes. The water was warm. She began to scrub the plates and carefully wash the cups. After she washed each dish, she put it in the rinse water and then onto the drying rack.

Edith came by and examined the dishes. She held the plate up in the morning sun. Streaks of grease remained. She looked at Ruth.

"Do you see this? Unacceptable." She plunged the plate back into the dishwater. Next she picked up a cup. It had a bit of lipstick around the rim. "Do you think this is clean?"

Ruth cringed. "No."

"Put some effort into it, child. It's not a race. Do it properly."

Ruth sighed as she scrubbed the offending dishes.

After dishes, Edith and Ruth washed the laundry, hung it to dry, washed the floors and dusted the sitting room. There were pies to make for dinner that night. Ruth rolled out the piecrusts as Edith instructed. At noontime, Herman went to pick up Mrs. Fleck from the train station.

"Be on your best behavior now, Ruth."

"Yes, *Mutter*," replied Ruth as they watched at the window for Herman and Grandmother Fleck to arrive.

"Do not speak unless you are spoken to. Don't ask too many questions and whatever you do," Edith looked pointedly at Ruth, "do not be rude."

"Yes, *Mutter*."

"Mother, child. Call me Mother."

Herman came into sight with Mrs. Fleck at his side. He carried two large bags.

"There they are!" Ruth said excitedly.

Edith smoothed her skirt and walked to the mirror near the front door. She checked her hair. She took a deep breath and opened the front door.

"Hello!"

Ida Fleck waved as she came up the walk. "*Hallo!*" She came up the front steps and embraced Edith. "Good to see you!" She smelled like a sweet familiar mix of flowers and powder.

"Hello, Mother. How was your trip?"

"It was fine, just fine. The train is a marvelous way to travel. It's a beautiful summer day. What more could we ask for?" She kissed Edith on the cheek.

Herman struggled up the stairs behind her with her large bags. Edith motioned to the door. "Come in, come in. We've got everything ready for you."

Everyone came inside. Herman took the bags straight up to their extra bedroom.

"What a beautiful home you have, E! I love everything about it. Such stylish furnishings!"

"Thank you, Mother," Edith said softly, blushing at her nickname.

Ida's eyes fell on the silent little girl seated in the armchair. "And whom do we have here?"

Ruth smiled.

"Say hello," Edith said to Ruth.

"You said not to say anything unless I was spoken to and I thought she was asking you."

Edith flushed and laughed nervously. "Oh Ruth—what a silly child you are. This is Herman's daughter Ruth, of course."

Ida stuck out her hand to Ruth. "Hello, Ruth. I'm Grandma Fleck. It's a pleasure to meet you."

Ruth stood up and took Ida's hand. "Pleasure is mine."

"Isn't she dear?" Ida said as she sat down.

"Would you like some tea?" Edith asked.

"Yes," Ruth answered.

Ida laughed.

"I wasn't talking to you, Ruth." Edith shook her head in disapproval.

"Oh."

"I'd love some tea as well," Ida chimed in. "Nothing better than afternoon tea with a new friend."

Ruth smiled. She was beginning to like Grandmother Fleck already.

The week went by in no time. Grandmother Fleck spent time playing with Ruth every afternoon. They played dolls, tea party and even chased butterflies in the yard. One thing Ruth noticed was that Grandmother Fleck wasn't afraid to laugh. Anytime something bad happened she just opened up her big mouth and laughed. Not a little laugh either. It was the kind of laugh where all your teeth showed. At night, Ruth stood in front of the mirror in her bedroom and silently practiced her own big laugh. She made faces at herself and then pretended to laugh, the big belly laugh that Grandmother had.

One afternoon, Ruth was doing dishes, scrubbing very hard on a persistent bit of food when the plate slid out from her hands and crashed onto the floor.

"Oh no!" she exclaimed.

Edith and Ida sat at the kitchen table. Both jumped to their feet.

"Ruth Bohlman!" Edith said sternly.

Grandmother Fleck began to laugh as tears burst from Ruth's eyes.

"Those plates can be like a big slippery fish! Sometimes they just get away from you, don't they?" She moved toward Ruth as the tears poured down her cheeks. Edith was cross as she went to get the dustbin and broom.

Grandmother Fleck hugged Ruth. "It's okay, love. We all make mistakes, don't we?"

Ruth shrugged as she dried her face on her apron.

"That's how we learn. You're only five years old and already doing the dishes on your own. I'd say that's quite an accomplishment."

"Five-and-a-half," Ruth corrected.

Ida laughed that big belly laugh that Ruth loved, "Of course, five-and-a-half."

Edith came back in the kitchen, scowling. Ida put out her hands and took the broom. "Now you stay right there on the chair while I sweep up the bits. Broken glass is very sharp and I wouldn't want you to get hurt."

"Okay," Ruth said, sniffling.

Later that night, Ida and Edith sat alone in the living room.

"Isn't she such a doll?" Ida gushed.

Edith shook her head, exasperated. "She's been spoiled. She's lived too many years with all of those church families and they did nothing but spoil her. She doesn't work nearly hard enough and . . ."

"She's just a child," Ida said softly.

"And children should know their manners—and respect their mother."

"And does she?"

"What?"

"Respect you?"

Edith thought about it for a minute. "I don't know. I should think she does."

"How do you earn respect, E?"

"I . . ." Edith looked at her mother quizzically, "I don't know. You show them that you are in control. You show them that they need to obey."

Ida studied her daughter for a long time. Finally, she said, "And you show them love."

A week later, there was a large community picnic held after church. The rural church that the Lessing family attended as well as the church in town came together for a big potluck lunch to celebrate the end of summer.

Herman held the picnic blanket under one arm and a large basket of food in the other. "Where shall we sit, Ruthie?"

Ruth pointed toward her aunts and uncles, "There they are! Let's go and sit with them."

Herman looked at Edith nervously. "You know, Ruth, I see the Daums over here," he pointed in the opposite direction. "Why don't we sit with them?"

"Okay." Ruth bounded off toward Artrude.

"Well?" Edith asked once Ruth was out of earshot.

"Well what?"

"Have you spoken to them?"

"Ah—no. Not yet. But I will."

Edith turned her head away from him. "You said that you would."

"I know. I just haven't had the chance. Okay?"

They approached the Daums. "Hello," Edith said cheerfully.

"Hello, Bohlmans," Emma said, smiling.

"What have you brought for lunch?" Edith asked.

The two women compared the contents of their baskets and then spread out the food for everyone to help themselves.

The children chased each other around, laughing. Before long, they ended up at the Lessing picnic blanket.

"Hello, Uncle Ben, Uncle Walter," Ruth said, waving at her uncles.

"Hello, Miss Ruth!" Ben put out his arms for her and said, "Come and give me a hug." She went to him and climbed in his lap, hugging him. "Did you know that fall is coming?"

"Why yes," she responded.

"And there are lots of exciting things happening at the farm. Are you going to come and visit us?"

Ruth nodded vigorously, smiling.

"And you can tell your daddy that *Oma* is coming from Portland at the end of September—before it turns cold. She is really looking forward to seeing you."

"Me too." Ruth grinned. "I love *Oma*."

"And she loves you!"

*"For I was hungry and you
gave me something to eat, I
was thirsty and you gave me
something to drink, I was a
stranger and you invited me
in . . ."*
Matthew 25:35 NIV

December 24, 1926
Lac Du Bonnet, Manitoba

The stove had been busy all day. There was rice porridge in the oven, cakes, cookies and pies all being prepared by Alina, Annie, Mary and Alice. The morning had flown by in a flurry of dough, fruits and vegetables. Lunch dishes had just been washed and now it was time to begin supper preparations for the large family.

"Are you going to get the tree?" Alina asked Otto who was sitting at the kitchen table, reading a store catalogue.

"*Ja*, we can go now. I'll need Victor and Waldemar to come along to carry the tree home." He looked around the kitchen. "Does anyone else want to go?"

"Ooo! I do!" Margaret jumped around wildly. "I want to go!"

Otto laughed and tousled her blonde hair. "You can come. Sing?"

Singhild looked at Otto, "It's too cold!"

"Suit yourself," he replied. He looked at Margaret. "Put your things on then, we'll go down to the barn and get Victor and Waldemar."

Margaret pulled her wool coat off the hook by the door, digging in a large basket for her red mittens and scarf. She pulled on her wool hat, right down to her eyes, and wrapped her scarf tightly around her face. "Ready," she said in a muffled voice.

Otto chuckled, "I'd say." He pulled on his coat, hat and gloves and went to Alina. She turned to him. He kissed her. "I love you."

She grinned. "Love you too."

"Wish us luck!"

Alina pulled Margaret's scarf a little tighter. "Good luck!"

Otto and Margaret left the house and walked hand in hand out to the barn.

"Is Mr. Hansen coming for dinner tonight?" Margaret asked.

"Yes, your Mamma has invited him . . . and Mr. McLeod."

The Pettersson family had acquired a new neighbor this fall, Pete Hansen. He was a young Danish man who had come first from Denmark, then to Eastern Canada, to Winnipeg and had finally settled in Lac Du Bonnet.

Pete had been busy setting up a cabin on his property this past summer. The Pettersson children had spent many afternoons watching Pete saw his logs and put them into place. Waldemar and Otto had a team of horses to haul wagon loads of logs over to his house. The cabin was sixteen feet by twenty-six and was made from birch logs about six to seven inches in diameter. The roof was made from logs and moss, tarpaper and even more moss. The logs were chinked with earth. Pete had recruited the children to push the earth into the cracks in the wall. The floor was simply mud. The shack boasted two windows and one door. The windows were covered with celluloid that you simply took off a roll and nailed into place. It wasn't fancy but it suited the single man until he had the resources to build a better house. Over the door of the cabin, Pete had hung a sign he had made that read 'UTOPIA.'

Alina had taken Pete under her wing by providing a meal or helping him with mending or washing. Tonight he would be joining them at the dinner table.

"I sure do like Mr. Hansen," Margaret said cheerfully.

"Me too." Otto smiled down at his daughter. He pulled open the barn door. The warm air rushed at them. "Go in," he motioned to Margaret.

They found Victor and Waldemar brushing the horses.

"Hello, boys."

Victor looked up at his father. "Oh, hello Pappa."

"Margaret here wants to go and pick the perfect Christmas tree. Could you come along to carry the tree home for us?"

Waldemar grinned. He set down the horse brush. "Of course!"

Otto led the way, axe in hand. Victor, Waldemar and Margaret trudged through the deep snow behind him.

"We've got to find the perfect tree . . ." Margaret looked all around, "not too big and not too small."

"Good thing you're here to pick it for us, Sugar Lump," Waldemar said as he smiled at his little sister.

She scowled back at him. "Don't call me that!"

Victor laughed.

"How far do we have to walk?" she asked, her breath coming in great huffs.

"We'll walk to the river where the smaller trees are," Otto said. "Can you handle it?"

"Sure I can," she said, stumbling as she tried to keep up. "You're just going so fast!"

"It's cold out," Waldemar replied. "We don't want to take too long."

They had walked nearly a mile but there was still another mile to go and two miles to return. "Hey, Sugar Lump," Waldemar stopped and looked at Margaret, flushed and out of breath, "why don't I carry you?"

"Oh would you?"

He bent down and Margaret hopped on his back. Waldemar ran to catch up with Otto and Victor who had carried on. Margaret gripped Waldemar's shoulders tightly.

"Slow down!"

Waldemar laughed. "Just hang on!"

They caught up to Victor. "So, how is your trap line going?" Victor asked.

"Very well!" Waldemar answered.

Tom McLeod had become a mentor to Waldemar over the last year. They had spent the summer out at the river where Tom had taught Waldemar about his Métis heritage. Tom's mother was Métis and his father was Scottish. His hunting and fishing knowledge was extensive and with no children of his own he was honored to pass on his skills to Waldemar. Tom had a flat bottom boat that he allowed Waldemar to take out on the river as often as he liked. He had showed him how to find the best fish and how to use the currents in the river to swim with ease. They had spent many afternoons training Waldemar how to swim the narrows using the pull of the currents.

The best thing that had happened under Tom's mentorship was the trap line. He spent hours and hours showing Waldemar many tricks to having a successful trap line. He showed him how to boil his gloves in Balsam bark to keep his scent off the traps, how to set and maintain his trap line. So far, Waldemar had caught many rabbits, weasels and the occasional fox. He was able to use the meat for his family and sell the skins and furs in town. It was thrilling, at age nine, to have his own source of income. Every day after school, he would put on his warmest socks and boots and walk the line, checking each trap and collecting the dead animals.

Waldemar loved walking his trap line. First he would head up to Pete Hansen's 'UTOPIA' for a visit. His log house was always warm and Pete was always a good host with bread and fruit to offer. Waldemar never had time for supper at home so he was always happy to have a few bites to eat at Pete's. Then he would tell Pete where he was headed so that Pete would know who was on his property and why. Pete had twice as much land as the Pettersson's so there was a lot of ground to cover before he had to be home. Waldemar would follow the fence line through the wooded areas. Where there was a slough or bulrushes he would check his traps that he had placed there. Usually he would find weasels, frozen to death in his traps. Weasels were a real pest. They could kill all the chickens in the hen house in a matter of hours. They didn't even eat the chickens, just sucked their blood and left the carcasses. Waldemar would put the dead weasels or other trapped animals in a bag, throw it over his shoulder and carry on past Pete's farm to the open range for about two to three miles. After that, there were the sand hills where he would check and reset the traps for the next round.

After the sand hills, he would head down to the river to the McLeod cabin to see the family briefly. Tom's mother didn't speak too much English so Waldemar would always just say a quick hello and then head on his way through the thick wooded area down to the river. In the heavily wooded area, there were more mink, which sold for a lot more than weasel skins. The mink liked the creeks and river, and were easier to trap in these areas. From the McLeod cabin it was about two miles into Lac Du Bonnet. He would go about halfway toward the town site and then he'd come back across the open range to their own farmland. Most of his trips were in the black of night with the cold stinging his fingertips and toes.

"I got a fox last night. Did you see the skin hanging behind the barn?"

"Yes," Victor nodded, "quite something."

"Did you want to come with me next time I go?"

"It might be a bit far. But we could go hunting on our property with our slingshots. Perhaps we could get a few grouse."

"That would be fun. We've got a few days off school. Why don't we go the day after Christmas?"

"Sure. Mamma would like to eat fresh grouse."

Waldemar heaved Margaret higher up his back. "Killing animals is so gross," she said.

Waldemar laughed, "If we didn't kill, how would we eat?"

"I know," she sighed, "I just don't like it."

Victor teased, "Do you like when the chickens run around without their heads?" He clucked and waved his arms, sticking out his tongue and rolling his eyes.

She scrunched up her face, "Vic-tor!"

"And how about those fluffy bunnies I skin?"

Margaret swatted Waldemar in the head. "You don't have to enjoy it!"

The boys laughed as Margaret glared at them.

They had arrived at the river's edge where plenty of small trees grew.

"Well, Miss Margaret," Otto asked, ignoring their banter, "which one will it be?"

Margaret got down off Waldemar's back and began to walk around, eyeing each tree carefully. Finally, she settled on a bushy Spruce, just over six feet tall. Otto handed the axe to Waldemar. "Here you are . . ."

Waldemar took the axe and began to swing at the trunk of the tree. Within no time he had knocked it down. He and Victor each took an end.

Otto and Margaret walked ahead, hand in hand, as they turned back home.

"Are you signing up for Boy Scouts?" Victor asked Waldemar as they walked.

"With Sgt. Nicholson?"

"Yes, it sounds fun."

"Well Sunday school has been a lot better since he's been teaching it," Waldemar commented.

"Yes, thank goodness he was stationed here."

"And thank goodness for his daughter," Waldemar began to laugh, "Jenny."

Victor joined in. "All you think about is girls."

"Just the blonde-haired, blue-eyed ones with the pretty smiles."

Victor shook his head. "You're too young to worry about girls. You should be thinking about cows and horses!"

"I'll leave the animals for you to daydream about."

"But seriously, Sgt. Nicholson should be a good scout leader."

"When do you sign up?"

"This Sunday." Victor thought for a moment, "It starts up the first weekend in January and runs until summer. He said that we'll have a campout down at the river."

"A campout?" Waldemar thought about this as he carried the heavy trunk of the tree. "That sounds really fun."

Back at the house, they set up the tree, putting it in a pail with water and stacking heavy stones all around the bottom to hold it upright. Alina brought out sparkling glass decorations—precious treasures that she had brought in her trunk all the way from Sweden. By the time dinner was ready, the tree was filling the room with its splendid fragrance. The candles were all in place, ready to be lit.

There was a knock at the door.

Waldemar jumped up. "I'll get it!" He went to the door and swung it open. Cold air rushed into the kitchen. "Hi, Mr. Hansen!"

Pete came in and closed the door behind him. "Hello, Waldemar! How are you?"

"I'm great."

"Oh, it smells good in here!"

"Can you smell the blueberry pie?" Waldemar asked. "My favorite!"

Pete laughed as he removed his coat and hung it on the hook, "Me too!" He walked over to Alina who was busy at the stove. He put an arm around her shoulder. "How's my favorite neighbor?"

She grinned at him, his light brown hair a mess from his winter cap, his cheeks crimson from the cold. "I'm well, Pete. We're so glad you could come."

"Where's Otto?" he asked as he leaned in the doorframe between the kitchen and the living room.

"He's out at the barn," Waldemar answered, "Did you want to walk down and get him?"

"No, sir," Pete patted Waldemar on the head, "I'm sure he'll be back shortly."

Alina interjected, "He and Gus are down at the barn doing the evening milking."

Pete looked at Waldemar. "And how did you get off the hook?"

Waldemar shrugged. "Pappa said he'd do it for me today."

"Lucky man." Pete turned to Singhild and Margaret, who were reading on the sofa. "Hello, ladies."

They looked up and smiled. "Hello, Mr. Hansen."

"Have you been naughty or nice? Is St. Nicholas bringing you a treat this Christmas?"

They laughed. "We've been nice."

Gus and Otto returned from the barn with Tom McLeod in tow just as dinner was ready to be served. Everyone gathered around the kitchen table that had been covered with a festive red tablecloth.

"This is wonderful, Alina," Otto praised.

"Thank you. And thank you to my lovely girls, Annie, Mary and Alice, who worked endlessly today to make all of this possible."

Everyone nodded. All the dishes were passed around the table. Otto carved the turkey while Alina dished out the rice porridge. Food was eaten until bellies were bursting and belts were loosened. The adults drank coffee and ate desserts as the hours went by. The children played in the living room, some reading and some playing marbles and jacks.

Once the adults had excused themselves from the table, everyone gathered around in the living room.

"Shall we light the candles on the tree?" Alina asked.

The children agreed, "Oh yes!"

She carefully took a candle off the tree and held it to the flame of the lamp. It lit up. She moved around the tree, lighting each candle.

"And now," Annie said, "it's time for Pappa to read the Christmas story," she looked at her tired younger siblings, "before it's time for bed."

Mary went to the bookcase and pulled out the Bible. She brought it to her father. He cleared his throat and began to read, "And it came to pass in those days, that there went out a decree from Caesar Augustus that all the world should be taxed. (And this taxing was first made when Cyrenius was governor of Syria.) And all went to be taxed, every one into his own city. And Joseph also went up from Galilee, out of the city of Nazareth, into Judaea, unto the city of David, which is called Bethlehem; (because he was of the house and lineage of David:) to be taxed with Mary his espoused wife, being great with child. And so it was, that, while they were there, the days were accomplished that she should be delivered. And she brought forth her firstborn son, and wrapped him in swaddling clothes, and laid him in a manger; because there was no room for them in the inn."

His low, melodic voice rang through the room. Everyone listened to the familiar story, each considering it in their own way. "And there were in the same country shepherds abiding in the field, keeping watch over their flock by night. And, lo, the angel of the Lord came upon them, and the glory of the Lord shone round about them: and they were so afraid. And the angel said unto them, Fear not: for, behold, I bring you good tidings of great joy, which shall be to all people. For unto you is born this day in the city of David a Savior, which is Christ the Lord. And this shall be a sign unto you; Ye shall find the babe wrapped in swaddling clothes, lying in a manger. And suddenly there was with the angel a multitude of the heavenly host praising God, and saying, Glory to God in the highest, and on earth peace, good will toward men."

He continued to read until the chapter was finished. As the last word was spoken, he closed the family Bible. Singhild had fallen asleep, leaning against her mother. Everyone else stretched and yawned.

"Say goodnight to our guests," Alina told the children.

A chorus of goodnights went out to Tom and Pete. The children all disappeared into the bedroom.

Pete stood up and stretched. "I suppose I should be on my way."

"And I should too," Tom agreed. "Thank you for your hospitality."

Otto and Alina stood, Alina leaving Singhild sleeping on the sofa. "Thank you for joining us tonight. We're glad to have you both."

Otto shook hands with his neighbors. "*Ja*, thank you for coming."

After Pete and Tom had left, Otto carried Singhild to her bed. Alina gently changed her into a nightgown, tucking her under the heavy blankets. Alina had warmed hot stones on the wood stove. She placed them at the foot of each bed to keep the children warm for the night.

Then she and Otto went into the kitchen where they spread out all of the stockings and gifts on the table. Alina put an apple at the bottom of each stocking followed by an orange and a small bag of peanuts. Otto had purchased candy in town, and a few bits for each child went in next. Finally, Alina put in her knitted items for each of the children. For Gus, Victor and Waldemar there was a pair of dark blue socks. With cream thread she had embroidered their monogram in each sock. For the girls she made bright red mittens. Hours and hours by the candlelight she had knit while the children slept. Every year she made the same things, they just became larger as the children grew.

As they turned in for the night, Otto and Alina hung each stocking on each of the brass bedposts for Annie, Mary, Gus, Alice, Victor, Margaret and Singhild.

Finally, she stood at the foot of the bed where Waldemar slept. "*God Natt.*" She rubbed his feet, tucked under the warm quilts. "Sleep tight."

"For to us a child is born, to us a son is given, and the government will be on his shoulders. And he will be called Wonderful Counsellor, Mighty God, Everlasting Father, Prince of Peace." Isaiah 9:6 NIV

December 24, 1926
Leduc, Alberta

Ruth was waiting for her father to get home. She pressed her nose against the cold living room window. She loved this time of year. The house was decorated with fresh garlands, wreaths and a beautiful tree. Tomorrow was Christmas Day and Ruth's stocking was hung at the foot of her bed, waiting for treasures that St. Nicholas would bring.

Edith hollered from the kitchen, "Ruth! Get your nose off the window!"

"Yes, Mother."

Ruth bounced on the sofa. The springs on the sofa moaned, tattle-tailing her activity to Edith.

"Ruth!" Edith called, "Quit bouncing!"

She stopped bouncing and blew on the cold window, making a foggy patch. She pressed her three fingers into the fog, making a snowman shape.

Edith poked her head into the living room again. "For heavens sake, child! Can't you just sit and wait quietly?"

Ruth sighed and flopped down on the cushion. "*Ach, Mutter!*" she muttered. Edith came tearing in from the kitchen, a wooden spoon clenched tightly in her fist. "What did you say?"

"Nothing."

Edith moved in closer, shaking the spoon at Ruth. "What did you say?"

Ruth crossed her arms and scowled. "I said, yes, Mother."

"You did not. Now I'm not going to listen to another word from you. If you want to be disrespectful to me then you can do it up in your room."

Ruth banged her fist against the arm of the sofa. "Fine!" She stomped up the stairs, Edith glaring after her. Ruth slammed her bedroom door and threw herself on the bed. "Oh, she makes me mad!"

Rosalie sat faithfully on Ruth's pillow, staring at her with her big, innocent dolly eyes. "She's terrible, Rosalie!" Ruth lamented. "Always don't do this and don't do that . . . always, always. I can't do anything without her telling me not to!" Ruth shook the doll. "It's so frustrating!" Rosalie smiled back at Ruth. She hugged the doll and rocked her in her arms. "It's okay, darling, don't cry. Mommy is here." Ruth rubbed the doll's back soothingly. "There, there, you're a good girl."

Downstairs, Edith put the last batch of pies in the oven. As she was taking off her oven mitts, the front door opened.

"I'm home," Herman called out.

Edith came to the door. "Hello!"

Herman put down his bag and went to Edith, hugging her. She held him at arm's length. "I'm covered in flour."

"That's okay," he drew her in, "I don't mind." She reluctantly returned his embrace.

"It's Christmas Eve, the store is closed and now you are home," she said.

"Yes. I'm all yours for the next few days." He took in a deep breath. "It smells wonderful in here."

"Thank you. I've been baking all day."

Herman started to look around at all the treats laid out on the countertops and the table. "What have you got?"

Edith pointed, "Shortbread, gingerbread, tarts, blueberry pie, apple pie, pumpkin pie and roasted nuts."

"Mmmmm," Herman reached for a shortbread cookie, plucking it off the cooling tray. "Don't mind if I do."

"Go ahead." Edith smiled at him. "I made them for you."

He reached out for her hand and squeezed it fondly. "Thanks. I appreciate it."

"How was work today?" she asked.

"There were a few last minute sales. A couple bikes . . ."

"What did Mr. Finn get his wife this year?"

"China. Same as last year," Herman laughed, "and the year before."

Edith chuckled, "What is she going to do with all that china? She never entertains!"

"I know. I tried to give him suggestions of something else he could get her—jewellery or perfume—but no, he had his heart set on another chaffing dish."

Herman popped his third cookie into his mouth. "Delicious!"

"Thanks." Edith sat down in the kitchen chair next to Herman.

He patted her hand. "Where's Ruth?"

Edith turned away and rolled her eyes. "She's upstairs."

"What? What's wrong?"

"Oh nothing."

"Was she causing trouble today?"

Edith shrugged. "Go ask her yourself."

Herman pushed his chair back from the table. "Okay." He walked out of the kitchen and toward the stairs. He took the stairs two at a time up to Ruth's bedroom. He opened the door slowly. "Ruthie?"

Ruth looked up from where she was playing on the bed. "*Vati!*"

He came in and sat down next to her. "How's my favorite girl?"

"Okay," she sighed. "We did lots of baking today."

"I know! I had some shortbread already. It was wonderful!"

Ruth smiled. "It was?"

"Yes. You and Mother did a great job!"

Ruth crawled over to her dad and laid her head in his lap. He stroked her hair. "Did you have a tough day?" he asked gently.

"I can't do anything right. Mother always says, 'Ruth, don't do this, Ruth, don't do that . . . Ruth, Ruth, Ruth.'"

Herman wrinkled his nose. "Oh, *Schatzi*. I'm sure it's not all bad."

Ruth made a grim face. "All."

"Listen," he looked her in the eyes, "you and Mother may not always agree but one thing I do know is that you are an outstanding little girl. I'm proud of you and I love you, no matter what you do."

Ruth sat up and hugged her dad. "Thanks."

"Are you excited for tonight?"

Ruth smiled and said, "Yes. I've got all my poetry memorized and all my carols practiced."

"Good for you. Now, are you going to get your dress on and come down for supper?"

Ruth nodded.

"Very good then. See you soon." Herman left the room, closing the door softly behind him. He took off his glasses and ran his hands over his face. "Oh, Ruth," he said softly. He put his glasses back on and went down the stairs, back to the kitchen.

That night, the three of them walked the short distance to the church. Edith carefully balanced her baked goods in both hands while Herman held Ruth's hand, keeping her from slipping on the icy sidewalks. The night was full of excitement as families arrived at the church.

Philip Daum greeted them as they came through the front doors. "Evening, Bohlman family. Merry Christmas to all of you."

"Merry Christmas," they answered. Herman shook Philip's hand. "Good to see you, Pastor Daum."

"Are you ready to sing, Miss Bohlman?" Philip asked Ruth.

Ruth replied, "Yes, sir. I am."

He tousled her hair. "Good for you."

The Bohlman family entered the church. Edith went to the basement, where refreshments were being prepared. Herman and Ruth went into the sanctuary to look for Mrs. Daum and Artrude.

"There they are!" Ruth exclaimed. "Come on, *Vati!*" She pulled excitedly on Herman's hand, dragging him toward Mrs. Daum.

"Hello," Emma called out as she saw Ruth approaching.

Ruth ran to Mrs. Daum. "Hello!"

Emma gave Ruth a big hug. "How are you, sweetheart?"

"Good."

"Ready to sing tonight?"

Ruth agreed, "Oh yes."

"Wonderful. Find your place with the other children. Your *Vater* will go have a seat in the audience."

Herman kissed Ruth and left to find a place to sit up front. He smiled as he sat down and looked around. The church was beautifully decorated. A large tree was at the front of the church, brightly lit with carefully balanced candles. Large red bows hung at the end of every pew. He listened to the people around him, speaking softly in German as they waited for the Christmas pageant to begin. The organist played familiar carols. Herman hummed along to 'Away in a Manger.' Edith slipped into the pew next to him. He smiled at her. "Hello. Did you get everything where it needed to be?"

"Yes. All the desserts are ready on the tables downstairs."

Herman raised his eyebrows. "My favorite part of Christmas!"

The organ began to pound out the tune 'Silent Night.' Ruth came on stage, in a white gown, with the other children following behind.

She sang alone, "*Stille Nacht! Heil'ge Nacht!*

Alles schläft; einsam wacht

Nur das traute heilige Paar.

Holder Knab' im lockigten Haar."

The other children joined in, "*Schlafe in himmlischer Ruh, Schlafe in himmlischer Ruh.*"

They sang four more carols and then some of the children recited poetry and bible verses. Ruth pulled off her recitation perfectly.

At the end of the service, everyone clapped excitedly. The children on stage beamed at their parents, their pearly teeth lighting up the stage. One little boy on the stage waved wildly to his parents in the audience. His hymnal flew out of his hand and hit the tree. Suddenly, there was a crackle as one of the candles fell and ignited a branch of the Christmas tree. Herman jumped from his seat, rushed up on stage and clapped the fire out with his bare hands. People in the audience screamed as the children all clamored over one another to get away from the tree. Philip steadied the tree to keep it from toppling over. He quickly blew out the other candles on the tree. One of the other church members rushed over with a bucket of cold water for Herman's hands. He plunged his hands into the icy water.

"Oh, that smarts," Herman groaned.

Edith rushed over. "Are you okay?"

"I'll be fine," he winced. "It just stings a little."

Ruth pushed her way through the crowd at the front of the church. "*Vati!* Are you alright?"

He pulled his hands out of the water. Someone passed him a clean towel. He carefully wrapped up the palms of his hands. "Come here, Ruthie."

Ruth approached him cautiously. "Oh, Daddy, you were so brave."

Herman laughed. "Not brave . . . just quick thinking. I'm fine. Let's not spoil the night with this."

Philip went to the front of the church. "Excuse me, everyone! Excuse me! Everyone please have a seat."

Slowly everyone filed back to their spots.

"Let's all praise God for Mr. Bohlman's quick reaction to our fire tonight."

Everyone clapped.

Philip continued, "Thank you too to our fabulous children who did a marvelous job singing and reciting poetry and scripture."

A round of applause went through the church.

"Let's finish our time together with a prayer." Philip prayed for peace and prosperity for everyone present. He blessed the food they were about to share and wished everyone a memorable Christmas.

"Amen," the congregation echoed.

Later that night, Herman went downstairs to the kitchen where Edith was stuffing Ruth's stocking. She placed an apple in the toe, followed by an orange, a bag of nuts and a small bag of candy. At the top of the stocking was a pair of store-bought felt mittens in a beautiful dark green. Edith had previously wrapped two new dresses that Herman had bought for Ruth into boxes and placed them under the tree. There were other gifts too, things that Herman had picked from the store catalogue over the last year.

Herman looked at Edith. "Ready for bed?"

"Yes," she nodded. "What a night! How are your hands?"

"Sore. But I'll be fine."

They headed up to bed. Herman went to their bedroom while Edith tiptoed into Ruth's room and hung her stocking on the bedpost. "Goodnight," Edith whispered. She brushed Ruth's hair from her face. She bent down and kissed her on the forehead.

Well before dawn, Ruth stirred in her bed. She opened her eyes and saw that it was still dark. At the foot of her bed hung her stocking, bulging with goodies. After a quick feel of the stocking, Ruth let her bare feet hit the wood floors and then took a peek out her bedroom door. All was quiet except for the sound of Father's snore. Ruth quietly scampered down the stairs to the living room. There stood the tree in all its grandeur with beautiful red boxes beneath it. Ruth found several boxes with her name and peeked inside. In the largest box was a beautiful Cupie doll and doll carriage; in the next box she found a book of fairytales; in another, china dishes, and in the smallest box an embroidery kit.

Ruth quietly set the boxes the way they were and then padded upstairs and back into her bed.

"Oh, Rosalie, all my gifts are wonderful!"

She fell back to sleep as the sun rose.

*"For men are not cast off
by the Lord forever. Though
he brings grief, he will show
compassion, so great is his
unfailing love. For he does
not willingly bring affliction
or grief to the children of
men." Lamentations 3:31-33 NIV*

August 1927
Lac Du Bonnet, Manitoba

It was the end of August, a few days after Waldemar's tenth birthday. He and Victor were walking into town. The pair was dressed in their Boy Scout uniforms. Their round 'Smokey' Boy Scout hats were pulled down over their eyes to block the midday sun. On their feet they wore sturdy socks and shoes for hiking. In their hands they carried their camping gear.

"This is going to be great!" Waldemar exclaimed.

"I can't wait! I heard Sgt. Nicholson is taking us to Holiday Beach." Victor skipped with excitement.

"Do you think we'll go canoeing?" Waldemar asked.

"I don't know. Do you think we'll have a wiener roast tonight?"

The church came into sight. They could see the boys from town gathered around the parish hall doors. Sgt. Nicholson stood in the middle of the pack of Boy Scouts and motioned for everyone to gather round.

"Come on, Victor, hurry up!" Waldemar began to run toward the group. They joined the other children just as Sgt. Nicholson began.

"Welcome, Scouts! I am glad to have you all here today. Does everyone have their gear? Tents, swim trunks, a change of clothes?"

"Yes, Sgt. Nicholson!" the boys cried out in unison.

"Okay then, let's pack up and start our hike to Holiday Park. We'll be camping near the beach. Everybody ready?"

"Yes, Sgt. Nicholson!" The boys scrambled to line up behind him. The older boys helped the younger boys with their packs.

Before long, they came to a clearing that opened up to a sandy beach with a long narrow dock. A warm breeze blew off the water.

"Alright, young men," Sgt. Nicholson announced loudly, "you can begin by setting up your tents in the clearing here. Find two trees to tie your tents up to."

"Come on!" Victor pointed at a cluster of trees. "Let's set up here!"

"Ya, this looks great!" Waldemar excitedly agreed. They picked a clear area of grass, free from rocks.

The tents were a simple olive green tarp. They hung a rope between two trees and threw the tarp over the rope. The four corners were pegged into the ground and that left just enough room for a single person to sleep. Waldemar and Victor had their tents up in no time. They sat down on the beach with the other boys.

Sgt. Nicholson stood in his Scout leader uniform in front of the boys. "I thought we'd begin with swimming. How does that sound?"

The boys cheered.

"Remember, Scouts, look out for the younger Cubs. Change into your bathing suits and gather down at the dock. After swimming, we'll have our wiener roast. You can work up your appetite while you swim."

Waldemar and Victor scrambled into their bathing suits and raced down to the dock. They were the first in line. Within a few minutes, the rest of the boys had joined them. Sgt. Nicholson had changed into his bathing suit and came down the beach with a towel draped over his shoulder.

"Is everyone ready?" Sgt. Nicholson asked his eager group of swimmers.

"Yes, Sgt. Nicholson!" they cried out.

"Well let's go then!" He let out a whoop, ran down the dock and jumped off the end. Everyone cheered as he surfaced in the water. "Well, what are you waiting for?" he laughed, treading the water as the boys ran down the dock too, let a whoop and jumped.

The afternoon was filled with swimming, diving and laying out on the dock to dry. After swimming, the boys gathered around a campfire on the beach and had a wiener roast. Sgt. Nicholson shared with them the story of David and Goliath while they ate.

"Most of you here have a slingshot, do you not?" he asked.

"Yes," they all agreed as they hungrily devoured their supper.

"And would you say that with your slingshot you are powerful enough to say . . . kill a moose?"

"No," all the boys shook their heads.

"Would you say that you would be well matched against a large bear?"

"No," they all smirked at the thought of facing a large woodland creature armed with only a slingshot.

"Let's think of the young shepherd David from the bible and what he faced when he went into battle with Goliath so many years ago. His brothers doubted him. When faced with the challenge of going into battle against Goliath, they mocked him. They challenged why he had even come to the battle in the first place. Saul, his master, said, *'he's only a boy, how can he defend Israel?'* David spoke of his courage against the lion and the bear while he watched his flock, and he spoke of his God. David said, *'the Lord who delivered me from the paw of the lion and the paw of the bear will deliver me from the hand of this Philistine.'*

The boys sat wide-eyed listening to Sgt. Nicholson bring the bible story to life.

"David tried on Saul's best army equipment, but he said, *'I am not used to these.'* So he went into battle as he was. He took his slingshot and five stones from the riverbed. Most importantly, he took God. Now what do you suppose Goliath said when he saw young little David coming to try to defeat him?"

The boys snickered as they imagined the scene.

"That's right, he laughed! He said, *'Come here, I'll give your flesh to the birds of the air and the beast of the field.'* Do you think David was scared?"

"Yes!" the boys nodded vigorously.

"Do you know what David said? *'You come against me with sword and spear and javelin, but I come against you in the name of the Lord Almighty, the God of the armies of Israel, whom you have defied. This day the Lord will hand you over to me and I'll strike you down and cut off your head. Today I will feed the carcasses of the Philistine army to the birds of the air and the beasts of the earth, and the whole world will know that there is a God in Israel. All those gathered here will know that it is not by sword or spear that the Lord saves; for the battle is the Lord's and he will give all of you into our hands.'"* He paused and looked at the Scouts. "That's a pretty bold statement from a young boy to a towering warrior, isn't it?"

The boys nodded.

"David fitted a stone into his slingshot and hit Goliath in the forehead. He defeated the Philistine army with a single stone and the power of our Almighty God. Let's take a minute and think of what God can do with you. How can God take a single stone in your life and use it for His glory? Remember David when you face challenges. Remember that when God is on your side anything is possible."

"Let's pray," he said. The boys bowed their heads. "Heavenly Father, use these bright young men. Use them for your purpose, in Your battles, Lord. Let their lives bring honor and glory to You in all that they do. Thank you, Lord, for our special time tonight. Please keep us safe from harm. In Your name we pray, Amen."

"Amen," the scouts echoed.

Waldemar and Victor headed off to their tents for the night. They each laid their heads at the door of their tents and looked up at the night sky. The boys listened to the water hitting the shoreline, the other children talking softly in their tents and the hum of the mosquitoes going by as they drifted off to sleep.

*

A year-and-a-half had passed since the night on the beach. It was a few days after Christmas and Tom had come by to visit. He found Waldemar working in the barn, completing his morning chores.

"Hello, Waldemar."

Waldemar looked up at Tom. "Oh hi!"

"How are you?"

"I'm great."

"How is your trap line going?"

"It's going very well. You should see all the animals I have for skinning."

"I'd love to." He paused thoughtfully saying, "I've been thinking about your trap line. How long does it take you to walk it?"

"About an hour, sometimes a little more."

Tom stroked his chin. "That's what I thought. I find my snowshoes help me get around much faster."

"Oh," he said softly, "I don't have snowshoes."

"Would you like some?"

Waldemar cocked his head, "I don't think I've sold enough furs for that—just yet, anyway."

"We don't need to buy them—we can make them," Tom replied.

"Really?"

"Can I show you how?"

"Would you? That would be great!"

"I've brought a deer hide we can use. We can build the frames in your Pappa's wood shop."

They talked to Otto as soon as Waldemar was through with his chores and went into the workshop. Waldemar selected the best pieces of cured wood from the woodpile. He carefully measured the pieces he would need for his snowshoes. He cut them to the length that Tom had instructed. Tom presented the deer hide to Waldemar.

"The first thing we'll do is tear the hide into strips. You start by cutting a small piece of the hide with your blade. As you tear you will notice it will rip in a circular pattern until the hide is gone. Once you have your strips, we will cut them to size and stretch them over the frame. These should last many winters if you care for them."

"I can do that."

Waldemar went to work preparing the hide and building the frame. Several hours later, two frames in a racket shape were formed. He cut the hide to stretch across the shoe in a crisscross pattern. Tom helped Waldemar nail on leather straps that would tie his boots to the snowshoe.

Late in the afternoon, Waldemar held up his completed pair of snowshoes. "These are great!"

"Well done!" Tom said proudly.

Waldemar strapped on the snowshoes at the barn door. He headed out into the deepest areas of snow. He walked gracefully on top of the frozen snow.

Tom watched Waldemar start to run. In an instant, he was on his back, laying in the snow.

"Oh man!" Waldemar laughed. "That wasn't too good!"

"You've got the grace of a grizzly bear!"

Eleven-year-old Waldemar was now in the sixth grade. He sat at the back of the classroom with the other two sixth graders. This morning the bell had rung and he had quickly settled in, pulling out his books. The rest of the school children came in and sat at their desks. Next to Waldemar, Jenny Nicholson's desk sat empty. Margaret, now eight, sat with her girlfriends in the middle of the classroom, and Singhild, now six, sat near the front, in the first grade.

While he waited for school to begin, Waldemar began to think about his family. Victor and Alice were at home working on the farm. Annie and Mary had moved to Winnipeg to work. Gus had gone to pursue an electric welding job.

All summer, Alina, now fifty, had sat in her rocking chair. The children knew that this meant they would soon have a new sibling. There was only one reason why Alina's activities slowed down around the house. Sure enough, on September 25th, Annie ran across the fields to get the midwife. Before long, baby Douglas became the newest Pettersson child.

The teacher, Mrs. Hillson, stood at the front of the room and cleared her throat. "Attention, children, I need you to settle down now."

The room gradually went quiet.

"Welcome back to school. I trust you have had a nice Christmas break." She looked around the room at the smiling faces. "I have some sad news I must tell you before we begin."

A murmur went through the room.

"As you all know, Jenny Nicholson's father, Sgt. Nicholson, is a very dear friend of ours. He has been a leader in our community. He has led many of you in Sunday school over the past three years, and he has led our young men in Boy Scouts."

Waldemar sat with his eyes fixed on Mrs. Hillson, waiting for the big announcement. Suddenly, Jenny's absence seemed significant. Did something happen to Jenny? Was she ill?

Mrs. Hillson took a deep breath and let it out slowly. "On New Years Eve, Sgt. Nicholson was shot and killed in the line of duty." The children's eyes widened. Shocked whispers broke out throughout the room.

Waldemar's stomach lurched. Sgt. Nicholson was dead? How could this be?

"I know you may have questions, but you will need to reserve them until you are able to speak to your parents on this matter. I would like to pray for the Nicholson family now. Bow your heads."

The children prayed for Jenny and her mother. The mood in the classroom was solemn.

"If everyone will please get out their books, we will begin our lessons for the day."

Waldemar walked home slowly, with Margaret and Singhild in step behind. All of the children were silent. It was a cold and miserable day, and it reflected the children's spirits. Alina stood in the kitchen window watching her three children coming down the trail toward the house. Otto had gone to town for supplies today and learned of Sgt. Nicholson's passing.

She looked at Waldemar walking toward the house. Oh, how she loved him. He worked hard and was always challenging himself in every way. He was always trying to find the hardest way to finish his chores. If there was an easy way to do something, it wasn't Waldemar's way. When the boys moved coils of hay, Victor would put his pitchfork into the top of the coil and take small loads onto the hayracks, working his way down until the whole coil was moved. Not Waldemar—he would put his pitchfork into the base of the coil and lift the whole thing at once. He wanted to challenge and build his strength. He broke many pitchfork handles proving it. If Otto and Victor moved bags of flour one at a time, Waldemar would load his arms with three. He always seemed to be in a state of acceleration as he dashed around doing his morning and evening chores. She loved that he worked so hard; it saved Otto from having to do as much. She loved Waldemar's enthusiasm for life, the way he admired Tom, Pete and Sgt. Nicholson, the way he always strived to learn from them. She opened her arms as Waldemar came through the door.

He welcomed her embrace.

"Hello, children." She looked at the girls standing in the doorway, "It's cold, come in and shut the door."

Margaret came inside and began to take off her warm coat, mitts and hat. Singhild followed suit. Waldemar kicked off his boots and sat at the kitchen table. Alina followed him.

"I am sorry." She pulled Waldemar's cap off and rubbed his hair.

"Oh, Mamma," Margaret said quietly, "it is so sad!"

Alina took Singhild and Margaret in her arms and hugged them tight. "Can you go help Alice with baby Douglas? They are in the living room." The girls agreed and left the kitchen.

Waldemar sat silently with his arms across his chest.

"Are you alright?" she asked.

"Yes, Mamma, I am," he said in a monotone voice.

She put her arm around his shoulders. In some ways he was so grown up and in other ways he was still such an innocent child. "I know this is hard for you; he was a dear friend to you."

Waldemar nodded, his eyes welling up with tears.

"God has a plan for us all. Sometimes it is beyond our knowledge why things happen. Sometimes we must trust that God has a heavenly perspective while we have our worldly view."

Waldemar nodded and leaned into his mother. He let himself feel the pain of the loss. Alina gently stroked his hair and hummed a Swedish hymn while the tears rolled down his cheeks.

When Otto came in from chopping wood, he saw Alina and Waldemar at the table.

"Waldemar, I am sorry," Otto said as he sat down at the end of the table.

"Do you know what happened?"

"I have the article from the newspaper—Pete brought it. You may read it if you wish." Otto reached into his breast pocket, removed the article and gently unfolded it.

Local Mounted Policeman Falls in the Line of Duty

On December 31, 1928, Sgt. R. H. Nicholson, in charge of the Lac du Bonnet detachment, was shot and mortally wounded while raiding an illicit still, thereby adding one more to the list of members of the Force who have fallen in the discharge of duty. In the company of the Manitoba Provincial Police, he visited the farm of the suspect and came upon a still in the bush, about a mile-and-a-half from the house. The two approached it from different sides; Sgt. Nicholson, arriving first, found the still in full operation. A rifle was nearby, standing against a tree, and both the suspect and Nicholson

seem to have rushed for it simultaneously.
The rifle discharged, inflicting a terrible
wound in the thigh from which Sgt.
Nicholson died in a few hours. Cst. Watson
arrived about the time the shot was fired and
attended to Sgt. Nicholson, taking off his
own shirt to form a tourniquet and working
in his undershirt though the temperature
was more than 20° below zero (-29°C). His
humane efforts resulted in his contracting a
severe illness.

After reading the article, Waldemar put on his winter coat and hat. He left the house and went down to woodpile. He sat quietly, thinking about everything that he had done with Sgt. Nicholson. The Sergeant had encouraged his running and athleticism. He had never told him that running was a waste of time. He had never said that trying to be strong was pointless. He had known these things were important to Waldemar and he had encouraged him.

Waldemar had built close relationships with a number of men. He was close to Tom McLeod, Pete Hansen and Sgt. Nicholson because they encouraged him in the things that he truly wanted to pursue. He had never given much thought to losing one of them before.

As he sat on the woodpile, a raven came and landed on the ground next to him.

"Hello," he whispered to the raven.

The raven turned his head to the side. His sharp yellow eyes looked at Waldemar. The raven was no stranger to Waldemar. This past summer, he had come to the house many times. Waldemar stuck out his finger. "Come here."

The raven took two steps across the snow toward Waldemar. Waldemar patted the top of his wool cap. "Do you want to sit on my head?" Last summer, he had been able to get the raven to sit on his head, a trick that everyone in the family enjoyed. "It's warm."

The raven flapped his wings and flew up to Waldemar's head. He perched there, his talons grasping Waldemar's hat tightly. "There we are." Waldemar held very still, not wanting to disturb the raven.

"Today was a bad day," he whispered.

The raven shifted his feet.

"My friend died." Unexpected tears sprang to his eyes. "He was killed by someone very bad. It's hard to believe right now. I keep thinking that maybe someone made a mistake."

The raven hopped down off Waldemar's head.

"Are you leaving now?" he asked.

The raven spread his wings and ran, taking flight. Waldemar watched the large black bird soar up into the sky. "Goodbye."

The funeral was massive. People from all of the surrounding towns came to pay their respects. Waldemar sat with his family. His eyes were fixed on the coffin at the front of the church. Draped over it was a Canadian flag. On top of the flag was a photo of Sgt. Nicholson. He had a serious expression in the photo, staring back at everyone who had gathered to say goodbye. His brown, felt Stetson hat was next to the photo. His side arm and belt lay next to the hat. The organist pounded the keys to the tune of 'The Old Rugged Cross.'

A tear came to Waldemar's eye. He wiped it away with the back of his hand.

Alina squeezed Waldemar's hand. "You okay?" she asked in Swedish.

"*Ja,*" Waldemar answered. "*Ja.*" He took in a deep breath and released it slowly.

"Why are thou downcast,
O my soul? And why art
thou disquieted within me?
Hope in God: for I shall
praise Him, who is the
health of my countenance,
and my God."
Psalm 43:5 NIV

July 1929
Leduc, Alberta

Ruth studied her new baby brother. He was lying on a blanket on the living room floor. He kicked his feet and waved his arms. Ruth passed him his rattle.

"Here you are."

He cooed at her, smiling and drooling. He was three months old now and starting to do things like smile, make noise and play a little bit. Ruth liked that.

Edith stood in the dining room holding her heavy iron in front of the ironing board. She finished pressing the last of Ruth's dresses.

"Here, child. Take these to your wardrobe."

Ruth got up and walked to Edith. She stuck out her hand.

Edith pressed the hangers into her palm. "What do you say?"

"Thank you, Mother, for pressing my dresses," Ruth said coolly.

"You are welcome. Now go."

Ruth turned away and went slowly up the stairs.

"We don't have all day!" Edith called after her.

"Don't we?" Ruth muttered to herself.

As she went into her bedroom, she heard someone knocking at the door.

Edith put down the iron and went to the door. She opened it. "Oh, hello."

"Hello, Mrs. Bohlman."

"Mrs. Lessing." Edith opened the door all the way. "Please. Come in."

Pauline walked into the house. She followed Edith into the living room. Edith did not sit down.

"What brings you here today?"

Pauline held up a doll, "I'm here to see Ruth. I have something for her."

"Ruth has plenty of dolls," Edith said flatly.

Pauline stepped toward Edith, smiling politely, determination in her eyes. "I want to see my granddaughter."

"I don't think that's a good idea."

"With the utmost respect, I must say that I don't care if you think it's a good idea. I haven't seen her in years and I am tired of being put off by you and Herman."

Ruth came down the stairs, "Mother—who was . . ." she stopped mid-sentence, her mouth hanging open.

Edith turned around and looked at Ruth who was paused on the landing. "Back to your room," she commanded.

Pauline said, "*Hallo,* Ruth."

"Hello," she answered timidly.

"Do you remember me, sweetheart?"

Ruth nodded, swallowing the big lump that had formed in her throat.

"Come here," Pauline motioned toward her, "come and see me."

Ruth walked down the last two steps. She started toward her grandmother. Edith stepped in front of her. She put her hands tightly on Ruth's shoulders. "Upstairs. Now."

"But, Mother!"

"Mrs. Bohlman," Pauline drilled, "what are your motives here?"

"We'll discuss this later. Ruth—go!"

Ruth sighed and turned away. "*Auf Wiedersehen Oma.*"

The two women watched Ruth climb the stairs, tears brimming in her eyes.

"*Ich liebe dich,*" Pauline said, her hand reaching toward Ruth.

"Stop." Edith glared at Pauline. "Herman is at the store. You can see him there."

"I am not here for Herman. I miss her. I love her. You have no idea what I have been through."

"No, surely I don't. I think it's in Ruth's best interest for you to go."

Pauline scoffed, "You don't know what's best for Ruth."

"I'm asking you kindly to leave."

She pointed at Lorne, lying on the floor, who was unaware of the drama unfolding around him. "Congratulations on the birth of your son. I hope that you and Herman have endless happiness." She set the doll down on the sofa. "I hope you see that Ruth gets her doll."

"I will."

Pauline walked to the door. "Goodbye." She walked through the front door and down the sidewalk. Once at the road, she turned and looked at the house. Ruth sat in her window on the second floor, waving down.

"*Ich liebe dich,*" Pauline called. She could see Ruth's face was wet with sorrow. She blew a kiss to her. She called out, "I'll return. I promise."

"Goodbye, *Oma*," Ruth wiped her tears.

Pauline turned and walked down the street to Bohlman's Hardware. She took a deep breath and tried to steady her nerves.

She marched into Bohlman's Hardware. Bells sounded. The store smelled of oiled hardwood floors and all things new.

Herman had finally bought his own store. He worked just down the road from their home. The new store was made of cement block construction with large plate glass windows on Main Street and smaller windows in the east wall. Large fluorescent fixtures lit up the rest of the store. The walls were painted light green and all the fixtures were in a natural wood finish.

Herman looked up from the store counter and said, "*Mutter!*"

"Herman," she said curtly.

"What a nice surprise? Are you in town for long?"

"For a few weeks, *ja.*"

"It's nice to see you. What brings you here today?"

"We need to speak about a serious matter."

Herman looked around the empty store. "Of course. What's going on?"

"I just came from your house. Your wife was not terribly welcoming."

Herman felt knots forming in his stomach. "Oh?"

"What is going on with you two? I just want to be a part of Ruth's life. I have lost too much to give up on this."

Herman took a deep breath. "Mother, I hate to say this but—you must."

Pauline slammed her hands down on the counter. "Do you know, Herman? Do you know how I felt when you did not come to the services for Amelia? Your sister-in-law dies and you didn't even have the courtesy to call me? Do you have any idea the pain I've been in? Have you ever had to bury a child? Can you imagine? I've buried six and the least I could expect is for the man I once called son to call me when my daughter dies. Now I am caring for Amelia's girls on my own and you don't have the decency to check in and see how things are going?"

"I am sorry. Her death is so tragic. I would have liked to have been there."

"But what—what is it?"

Herman's eyes danced around the store, avoiding his mother-in-law's intense gaze. "It's hard to explain."

"Try me. The boys tell me that you never come round the farm anymore, you never call, you avoid them at church functions . . . what is it, Herman?"

"Ah—well . . ." He put his hands on his hips. "I'm not sure it's best for Ruth to be caught up in the Lessing family."

"What!" Pauline was flabbergasted. "Caught up? Do you mean loved by? We love her. Surely you can understand that. I raised her as my own for a year! You weren't able to let her go? Do you think I am so callous that *I* should just forget her?"

"No," Herman ran his hands over his smooth hair. "Oh . . ." His fingers gripped the store counter. "I don't know what to say."

"I think I've heard enough."

"*Mutter*," Herman pleaded.

"*Nein*. That's fine. If you want to contact us, you know where we are."

"I do. I just . . ."

Pauline turned her back and walked toward the door. She looked back and said pointedly, "Goodbye, Herman. I used to consider you my son." She pushed the door open with such fury the bells fell to the floor in a clatter. She disappeared down the street.

Herman was shaking. He walked to the door and picked up the bells. He flipped the sign on the door from open to closed and locked it shut.

He walked to his office and sat down in his wooden chair. He eyed the invoices spread over his desk. He looked at a framed picture of his daughter and him.

"God," he whispered, "*Was habe ich getan?* What have I done?"

Ruth waited in the window. For hours she sat, hugging her doll, Rosalie. Grandma didn't return. Finally, she got down and went to the mirror. She looked at her reflection. She fingered her strawberry-blonde hair. "Who was my mother?" she wondered out loud.

She had never seen a photo of her mother. Her father and especially not Edith ever talked about her mother. What had her mother looked like? What had she been like? Was she like Mrs. Daum? Caring and thoughtful? Would she have laughed like Grandma Fleck? Did she ever get a chance to know Ruth when she was born or did she die too fast?

Ruth looked at herself again. Did she look like her mother? She went and laid her doll gently on the bed.

"Oh, Rosalie. There are so many things I want to know."

She wondered how her mother had died. Everyone had always said that she had died in childbirth.

"Was it my fault?" she whispered quietly into the silence that was her companion, "Did I kill her?"

Edith never did call her down to supper. Ruth eventually fell asleep on her bed, exhausted from crying. Herman stayed late at the store. When he came home, the house was dark. He went up to Ruth's bedroom and opened the door slowly. It creaked, announcing his presence. Ruth was still in her clothes, atop the covers. Her glasses still sat on her nose. She shuddered as she slept.

He went to the wardrobe and pulled open the bottom drawer. He pulled out a fresh nightgown. He sat on the edge of the bed.

"Ruthie?"

Ruth's swollen eyes opened. "Dad!" She sat up and hugged him.

"Hello, *Schatzi.* You should take your glasses off. Do you want to get into your nightgown?"

Ruth looked out the window. It was dark. "Yes. I do." She began to unbutton her shirt and quickly slipped it off then pulled her nightgown over her head. She slipped her skirt off and left it in a heap on the floor. She crawled under her quilt. She folded her glasses and put them on her night table. She sighed as she laid her head on the pillow.

Herman stroked her hair. He began to sing to her softly in German.

"Sleep, baby, sleep
Thy father tends the sheep
Thy mother shakes the dreamland tree . . .
Sleep, baby, sleep."

He continued, his soft tenor voice filling the bedroom.

"Lu-la-lullaby,
Hush, my babe, and do not cry
In your cradle now you swing,
Until you sleep, I'll softly sing,
Lu-lullaby."

The exchange with her grandmother had given Ruth renewed determination to find out more about her mother. Every day when Edith was busy, she looked in trunks, closets and drawers to see if she could find something. A love letter, a photo, a memento . . . anything.

Every search was fruitless. The house was clean, every drawer, every cupboard was neatly organized. There was only one area that Ruth hadn't checked. The garage. One summer night, Edith and Herman went for a walk down to the lake with Lorne. Ruth said she wasn't feeling well and went up to her room to lie down. Once they were out of sight, she seized the opportunity and slipped out of the house. She took the key from the drawer in the kitchen. She opened the back door, holding her breath. All was quiet.

She tiptoed across the yard and slipped the key into the lock. The door groaned. It was dark inside the garage. Cobwebs were laced across the boxes in the corner. She looked up into the rafters. The setting sun highlighted the dust floating through the air. There were more boxes up there too. She wondered where to start. She went to the boxes in the corner first. She tried to read the faded writing on the side. It was handwritten in German—not a script she recognized. She opened the flaps to find dishes. She moved it aside and opened the next box. Books. The next boxes held more books and some linens, carefully wrapped in tissue. She did her best not to disturb the contents of the boxes.

The boxes didn't seem to contain any photos. She went to the ladder that was leaning against the garage wall. She pulled it apart and carefully set the legs on even ground. She climbed up and reached for one of the boxes in the rafters. It was heavy. It had more dishes and household items. The next box was white with beautiful roses on the side. Perched on top of the ladder she opened it up.

"Wow," she breathed. Inside the dusty box was a gown. A wedding gown. It had layers of chiffon with beautiful swirling embroidery. The neck was U-shaped. There was a long veil and white gloves folded neatly at the top of the box.

"Is this Mother's?" she whispered.

She put the box aside, balancing carefully on the ladder and moved to the next box. Finally. It was a box of albums. She opened the first one carefully and there, looking out at her, was a picture of her father. He wore a dark pin-striped suit, a white shirt and tie, and had a corsage buttoned on his lapel. His hair was smooth and shiny. He looked younger. Next to him, seated in an ornate chair, was a woman. She wore the gown from the box Ruth had just uncovered. She wore the long veil, with flowers woven into it. She had on the white gloves. She wasn't smiling, nor was he. They looked out at Ruth, stony faced, as though they knew what tragedies were around the corner. As if they knew that their first-born daughter would shatter their happiness. Ruth began to cry. She flipped through the album, looking at more photos of her grandmother, aunts, uncles and cousins. She saw pictures of her mother as a young woman, smiling and laughing.

Suddenly, she heard voices. Her heart began to race. She quickly put the albums into the boxes and shut them tight. She tried to arrange them back in the same way she had found them. Her heart pounding, she climbed down the ladder. She quickly collapsed it and leaned it back where it had been. Her eyes went to the boxes in the corner. She considered carefully how they had been and made an adjustment before walking out of the garage. She could hear her father and mother out in the front yard talking to a neighbor. She quickly locked the door and ran inside. She put the key in the drawer just as the front door opened.

Herman and Edith came through the living room and into the kitchen. They found Ruth sitting at the kitchen table drinking a glass of water.

"Hello, love," Herman said, putting Lorne down on the floor. "You feeling better?"

Ruth smiled at him. "Yes, Dad. I am feeling much better."

Edith scowled at Ruth. "Child, how did you get that dirt on your nose?"

*"I will praise you, O Lord,
with all my heart; I will tell
of all your wonders. I will
be glad and rejoice in you; I
will sing praise to your
name, O Most High."*
Psalm 9:1&2 NIV

July 1929
Lac Du Bonnet, Manitoba

It was six o'clock on a warm, foggy July morning. The river was still, aside from the wake of the raft. Waldemar could hear the water lapping against the shoreline. The birds were waking, calling out to one another, as the sun came over the horizon.

Waldemar breathed in deeply. The air was crisp and clean, smelling of pine and wild flowers. It was almost as welcoming as a plate of Mamma's *pepparkakor* cookies at Christmastime.

Davie steered the raft. At their feet were three large baskets full of blueberries.

"It was a good time, eh?" Davie said wistfully.

"Hardly work at all," Waldemar said happily. He reached down, lifted the flour sack cover of one of the baskets and popped a berry in his mouth.

"*Ja*, I've never seen anyone eat as many berries as you."

Waldemar's fingers were stained deep purple. "I never get tired of them!"

Davie Carlson's family had a large farm a few miles up the river from Lac Du Bonnet. Every summer, they hired berry pickers to bring in their blueberry crop. This summer, Otto had sent Waldemar to go to earn some extra money.

Waldemar's days were filled with berry picking and his nights filled with play. Every night he and Davie played leapfrog, tag and kick the can until the sun set at eleven. They slept in the hayloft with the other pickers on the soft thick hay. It was cool and breezy up there. With a pillow and blanket, Waldemar was quite content.

"Are you going into town today?" Waldemar asked Davie.

"*Nej*, I have to get the raft back. Pops has another picker he wants me to take upstream. Can you manage the berries?"

"Sure. I'll go get the stone boat to pull the baskets home."

"Good idea."

The dock came into view. Davie slowed the raft, steering it toward the dock. Waldemar grabbed an oar to help. The raft bumped gently against the side of the dock. Waldemar jumped off and tied the raft's rope around the railing on the dock.

The boys each took a handle of the baskets, groaning as they lifted them onto the dock. They walked up to dry land and found a spot in the trees to set them.

"The covers should keep the birds off while you're gone, but don't leave them too long or some other critter may get into them."

Waldemar pulled the flour sack covers tightly down over the tops of the baskets. "I'll be back in no time."

"Cheers then." Davie stuck out his hand. Waldemar shook it.

"Cheers. It's been fun."

Davie went back down the dock and got onto the raft. He untied his rope and pushed away. He started up the raft's motor, shattering the peaceful morning. He waved as he started back upstream.

Waldemar pulled off his socks and boots, leaving them next to the berries. He hadn't been running in nearly two weeks. He stretched his long arms up to the heavens and down to his toes.

To himself he said, "On your mark, get set . . . go!"

His legs propelled him forward, over the forest floor and down the trail back to the farm. The trees roared past him in a blur of greens and browns. The fresh morning air filled his lungs. It felt exhilarating to run again . . . to be free.

Once back at the barn, he put a bridle on one of the biggest horses, Moonlight, and hitched up the stone boat, a flat four-foot squared piece of lumber that would drag on the ground behind the horse. The black horse nuzzled him as he worked. Waldemar could tell by the clean stall that Victor had already done his morning chores.

"Good to see you too, Moonlight. We've got some work to do this morning. Berries . . . down by the river."

The horse stomped his feet.

"Sound good?"

The horse took some hay in his mouth and began to chew.

"Come on then." Waldemar led the horse out of the barn and up the trail back to the dock.

He could see the family's wagon in front of the house as he was coming back to the house. It was loaded with heaps of laundry, the sheets, the linens and all of their clothing. There were picnic baskets loaded on the wagon too.

"The big wash!" Waldemar exclaimed.

He could hear Margaret and Singhild in the berry patch down the hill from the house. He decided to leave the horse for a minute. He tied the reins to a tree. He patted the horse's velvety nose. "I'll be back in a few minutes . . . just a little something I have to do."

He went around the long way, circling behind the girls, through the trees. He could see them picking and talking. Baby Douglas was propped up against a fallen log, sitting on a blue blanket.

He crouched in the foliage, listening to the thunk of berries as they were thrown into the bucket. Douglas cooed happily, sucking on his fingers.

"Are you going to swim today?" Margaret asked her younger sister.

"I don't know. I was hoping Waldemar would be back to teach me."

"He's such a good swimmer."

"He makes it look easy . . ."

"It's not too bad," Margaret reassured, "once you get the hang of it."

"I suppose."

"Grrrrrr . . ." Waldemar interrupted with his best bear impression.

The girls stopped talking. Finally, Margaret said quietly, her voice shaking, "Did you hear that?"

"Grrrrrrr . . ." Waldemar snarled, snorted and stomped his feet.

The girls dropped their buckets and ran, screaming all the way up to the house. "A BEAR! A BEAR!"

Suddenly, they stopped running. Margaret turned to Singhild, a look of horror on her face.

"BABY DOUGLAS!"

Singhild shrieked and began running back to Douglas. "HE'LL BE EATEN!" She screamed, Margaret running behind, their braids flapping in the wind as they ran. Margaret scooped up Douglas while Waldemar gave one last growl and snarl from the bushes. They screamed all the way back to the house. Alina came out to see what the commotion was all about.

The girls came panting up to her. "Mamma! A bear! There was a bear!"

"And then," Margaret said, "WE FORGOT DOUGLAS!"

Singhild gasped, "He could have been eaten!"

Alina looked down at the berry patch and spotted Waldemar climbing out of the bushes, laughing himself to tears. He grabbed the girls' abandoned berry buckets.

She shook her head as she took Douglas from Margaret's shaking arms. "Now, now girls," she pointed down the hill, "I think I see your bear."

The girls spun around in fear.

Understanding dawned on their faces. "WALDY!" Margaret shouted. She marched toward him. "How dare you!"

Singhild interjected, "You scared us half to death!"

Margaret added, "We thought Douglas was BEAR MEAT!"

He laughed, wiping the tears from his cheeks. "Hi, girls." He gasped for air. "Did you miss me?"

Alina shook her head and pushed back her blonde hair from her eyes. "Enough games, Waldemar. We've got a lot of things to do today."

"The big wash?"

"Yes, we're just loading up the children now. We were waiting for the berries." She took the berries from Waldemar. "I'll wash these and then we can go."

"Oh," he said, "I have some blueberries too. I'll bring them up to the house."

Alina pulled Waldemar in for a hug with her free arm. "Good to have you home." She tousled his hair. "Even if you are scaring your sisters."

Waldemar looked up. "Good to be back, Mamma."

"Now go, get your berries and meet us on the trail."

"Sing," Waldemar offered as they walked the trail to the flats, "today I can teach you how to swim if you want."

"Sure," Singhild answered, "I can try. I've never swam before. Do you think I can?"

"I'll help you."

"Okay." She beamed up at Waldemar. Douglas was in her arms, pulling at her loose hair and chewing on the ends of her braids.

"Ew, Dougy," Singhild chided, "that's gross."

He laughed and smacked his slobbery hand on her cheek.

Once they had arrived at the flats, Alina put the children to work washing their things in the river. The water was clean and pure, and with a bit of soap and scrubbing, all the clothes were laundered in no time. Before lunch, the children had wrung out and spread out the laundry on the Birch trees and Red-osier Dogwood bushes. The sun completed the job by drying everything out.

After lunch, all of the children took turns changing into their swimsuits behind the wagon.

Waldemar took Singhild by the hand. "Ready?"

She nodded apprehensively.

"Don't be scared."

They waded into the cool water. "I think . . ." Singhild swallowed the lump in her throat, "I think I'll just stay here in the shallow part."

Waldemar pulled her in further and further. As the water came up to her chin, she clutched his hand tighter.

"It's too deep!"

"It needs to be a spot where I can reach and you can't."

She shook her head. "I don't think this is a good idea."

Margaret and Alice swam around in circles watching the swimming lesson.

"It's okay, Sing," Alice reassured.

Waldemar took her by the shoulders and looked into her eyes. "Listen to me. Just relax and try to float. I'll hold you." He turned her around and grasped her under the arms. He told her to rest her head on his shoulder. He looked at her hands gripped tightly around his arms and said, "Just relax. Keep your belly button up."

"Are you sure, Waldy?" Singhild looked back hesitantly at her brother.

"Yes, I've got you, now relax and lay back."

Singhild took a deep breath and let go of Waldemar's arm. Suddenly, she started screaming, "Ahhhh! Ahhhh!" She kicked and flailed wildly as Waldemar struggled to maintain his grip on her.

"SING! What are you doing? Relax!"

"Ahhhh! I'm going to drown!"

"Stop it!" Waldemar grabbed Singhild under the arms and turned her facing toward him in the water. He had his feet firmly planted in the sand in the river. Singhild was in over her head. "Focus. If you want to learn how to swim you need to calm down."

"Okay, I will." Singhild looked at Waldemar seriously. "I want to learn. I'm just a little nervous."

"Alright. Let's try again." Waldemar turned his sister away from him again. He tried to get her to relax and float.

Singhild spread out like a starfish, her arms and legs stuck out to the side. At that moment, a wave of water came over her face. Again she started shrieking. "Ahhh! Save me!" Her arms and legs flailed wildly. Waldemar whipped her around and gripped her arms.

"Sing!" Waldemar was getting exasperated with his little sister.

Alice and Margaret laughed.

"I know, I know," Singhild laughed nervously, "relax, right?"

Margaret glided by, swimming with ease. "You can do it, Sing."

"Let's forget floating and try swimming. How about that?"

"Okay."

"When you swim, keep your head up, move your arms and legs and don't swallow the water. Got it?"

Singhild nodded. "Let's try again."

Waldemar held her under the arms, facing him, and encouraged her to kick her legs while he held her up. Again a tiny wave came up to her face. She screamed, swallowing the river water. Her arms and legs flailed as she coughed and sputtered.

Tears sprung from her eyes, mixing with the river water. "I'm never going to get it. NEVER!" She gripped Waldemar tightly, crying loudly in his ear. Exasperated, he grabbed her around the waist and tossed her away from him into the deep waters of the river.

Singhild thrashed madly in the water. The other Pettersson children watched anxiously as Singhild struggled to keep herself above the water. "HELP!" she screamed. "Help me, Waldy!"

"Kick, Sing! Kick your legs!" Waldemar yelled. "I'm right here. Swim to me!"

Singhild focused on her body. She kicked her legs and moved her arms as Waldemar had showed her. Waldemar stretched his arms toward her. "Come here, swim to me." His eyes sparkled as she moved toward him, keeping her head up. "You're doing it!"

She gasped and struggled her way toward her big brother. "I'm swimming!"

"Yes you are!"

"Good job, Sing!" Margaret encouraged as she swam nearby.

Waldemar grabbed Singhild's outstretched arms and pulled her toward him. "You did it! Now you know, right?"

Singhild laughed nervously. "I guess I do. You scared me!"

"Sometimes you just have to go for it, you little sugar lump. I knew you could do it." Waldemar dove under the water and disappeared. He swam around looking for fish, feeling satisfied with his swimming lesson.

The children swam in the calm waters all afternoon. After they were all worn out, they helped Alina fold the laundry and load it back into the wagon. On the way home, Alina sat in the wagon with everyone except Waldemar. He led the horses, walking in his bare feet and whistling a tune.

" . . . For in you my soul
takes refuge. I will take
refuge in the shadow of your
wings until the disaster has
passed." Psalm 57:1 NIV

April 1930
Leduc, Alberta

Eight-year-old Ruth rolled over in her bed. She could hear Lorne crying again. Night after night he had been awake, coughing and crying. Mother was getting more and more concerned that he wasn't getting any better. Ruth sighed and stared up at the ceiling. She could hear Mother and Dad talking. Her alarm clock read 3:45. It was a school day. She was still very tired.

The next time she woke, she heard Edith yelling frantically, "Herman! Herman! Get in here!"

She heard her father's footsteps lumbering from his bedroom to Lorne's. She heard him exclaim and then hurry down the stairs. Ruth threw the covers off and tucked her feet into her slippers. It was still dark out.

She opened her bedroom door hesitantly. "Mother?" She looked into Lorne's bedroom that was kitty corner to her own.

Edith was crying over Lorne who was flopping around in her arms.

"What's wrong?" Ruth asked, fear creeping into her voice.

"He's having convulsions! Your dad has gone to get the doctor!"

Ruth went up to her baby brother and touched his sweaty head. He relaxed in Edith's arms. His eyes shut. Each breath rattled as he took air in and out. "Is he going to be okay?" she asked.

Edith dabbed her face with her sleeve. "I don't know."

Ruth looked at her mother—suddenly fragile and scared. "It's okay. I know he will be. I'll pray for him."

Edith smiled at her.

Ruth walked out of his bedroom and back to her bed. She knelt down at her bedside. "Dear God, please heal my baby brother. He's only just one and he hasn't had enough time. Please take away his cough and make him better. Amen."

She went to the window to watch for her father coming back. Within a half-hour, she could see him and the town doctor coming down the road.

Ruth crouched at the top of the stairs, eavesdropping, as the doctor examined Lorne downstairs in the living room.

"I'm afraid he has whooping cough," the doctor said gravely.

"Oh no," Edith gasped.

"What do we do?" Herman asked.

"Does Ruth have any signs of illness?" the doctor asked.

"No," Herman looked at Edith, "no she doesn't."

"You must remove Ruth from the home and quarantine yourselves here with him."

"We can do that." Herman looked up at the staircase. He could see Ruth's fingers curled around the top rail. "Ruth, you can come down."

Ruth came down from her hiding spot. "Yes, Dad?"

"You need to pack your things. After school I'm driving you out to Aunt Lilly and Uncle Fred's."

Ruth's eyes widened. "For how long?"

The doctor answered, "As long as it takes for your brother here to get better."

Ruth stood, frozen on the bottom step. "Okay."

Edith looked at her. "Now go. Go and pack your things."

Ruth turned and went back up the stairs to her bedroom. She pulled a large bag from her closet and began to take her clothes from her wardrobe. She packed them carefully along with Rosalie, her favorite books and a tea set that she knew Aunt Lilly would enjoy.

She dressed in her navy wool skirt and white blouse for school. She pulled on her long blue socks. She combed her hair and cleaned her glasses and then headed downstairs for breakfast. She made her own oatmeal and toast, as everyone else was preoccupied with Lorne. She sat at the table alone, contemplating what was going to happen after school. Herman came into the kitchen.

"Hi, Dad."

"Hi, love." He tousled her hair. "Are you okay?"

"Oh sure. I'm fine."

"You'll have a good time at the farm. Sort of a vacation for you."

"So I'll be missing school?"

He put the coffee on. "I'm afraid so. You're a smart girl, you can catch up. You must ask your teacher for some extra work today. Something you can work on with Aunt Lilly."

Ruth's eyes went down to her oatmeal. Gloomily she said, "Okay."

Herman sighed, "I know you love school, and being with Artrude, but this is what's best. We don't want you to get sick too. Whooping cough is very serious."

"*Ja*, I know." Ruth thought of a little boy in their church who had died of whooping cough last winter. "I just hope Lorne is okay."

"He will be," Herman reassured her. "We will pray for him. He's a strong little boy."

"But he's only one. He's still a baby."

"When you get back he'll be laughing and running around, full speed as usual."

Ruth smiled, "Okay, Dad."

The coffee was done. He poured it into a cup for the doctor. "Now finish getting ready for school. You need to be on your way shortly. When you get home, I'll drive you to the farm. Don't dawdle after school either."

"I won't." Ruth watched Herman walking out of the kitchen. "And, Dad?"

He looked back. "What is it?"

"I love you."

He smiled, "I love you too, Ruthie."

Ruth was in the third grade. She did very well in all of her subjects but especially math. She was always the leader at school. The girls would follow whatever games she came up with when they all played on the school ground. Artrude was still her closest friend. The two were inseparable. They spent hours after school and on weekends playing make-believe, playing dress-up with Mrs. Daum's old clothes and jewelry, and having tea parties with their dolls. As she walked to school, she thought of everything she would be missing out on.

She entered the schoolyard. April mornings were still quite chilly and all the children huddled together by the door. Ruth found Artrude.

"Hi," she said grimly.

"Hi, Ruth! What's the matter?"

"Lorne has whooping cough."

"Oh no! Is he okay?"

"He had convulsions this morning. Everyone is frightened. The doctor put a quarantine on the house. I'm going to Aunt Lilly's after school today."

"Oh no! For how long?" Artrude grabbed her friend's arm.

"For a long, long, long time."

Artrude's eyes began to well up with tears. "What will I do without you at school? And to play after school?"

Ruth felt teary also. "I don't know."

The bell rang and all the children filed inside.

All morning, when the teacher turned her back to the board, Artrude and Ruth exchanged whispered conversation. Knowing that they wouldn't see each other for quite some time had added an air of desperation to the day.

After lunch, Ruth approached the teacher for some extra work to take along with her to the farm. "Excuse me, Mrs. Freisson."

The teacher smiled at Ruth, "Yes, Miss Bohlman."

"My brother is ill and my parents are sending me away for a while. I was hoping that you could arrange some work for me to take along with me."

The teacher frowned, "Miss Bohlman, how long have you known about this?"

"Just since this morning, ma'am."

"And why didn't you come to me in the morning so that I would have some time to get some work organized? Perhaps I could have got it together over the lunch hour."

Ruth shrugged, "I don't know."

"Next time I will trust that you will let me know these important matters first thing in the morning."

Ruth nodded. She turned away. Looking at Artrude she mumbled, "Oh brother."

The teacher tensed. "Excuse me, Miss Bohlman?"

Ruth turned around, flushing. "Nothing, ma'am."

"You will not be cheeky to me. You have just earned yourself detention."

Ruth's shoulders sagged and she looked up at the ceiling. "Oh, Mrs. Freisson! I can't! I have to get straight home."

"I'm sorry, young lady. If you can't be courteous of my time then I'm afraid that I can't be courteous of yours. Now find your seat. We're about to begin our spelling test."

Ruth sat at her desk and pulled out her chalkboard. Detention. Just wonderful. Father would not be happy when she didn't get home until five o'clock.

"The first word is courteous. Please write the spelling on your boards."

After school, Ruth spent an hour writing on the chalkboard 'I will be respectful to my teacher' one hundred times. Her arm ached and her sweater was covered with white chalk dust.

After she wrote the last sentence, she looked at her teacher. "Am I done then?"

"Yes, Miss Bohlman, you are. She passed her a parcel of books and papers. Here is your work. You can study the spelling words, complete these math sheets and practice your cursive writing."

"Yes, ma'am." Ruth picked up the parcel and bolted out the door. She ran the entire way home, angry that she hadn't been able to play with or even speak to Artrude after school.

When she came through the front door, she found her father, sitting in the armchair reading the paper. He looked at his watch.

"Hello, Ruth."

"Hi, Dad."

"Where have you been?"

"Ah . . ." Ruth looked at him, "ah, I had detention."

Herman shook his head. "I've been waiting for you."

"Yes, sir."

He got up from his chair. "Let's go. Out the back door, your bag is already in the garage."

Ruth slipped her shoes off and carried them to the back door. She put them back on and went out to the garage. She eyed the boxes in the rafters. What she wouldn't give to be able to slip a box into the trunk of the car. Imagine if she had unlimited time to look through them.

Herman looked at her, looking up. "Let's go, Ruth," he said sternly.

Ruth got in the car and shut the door behind her.

Herman was one of the few people in Leduc to own a car. He often was summoned when women of the town were in labor. He was happy to drive them up to the hospital to give birth. Every time he drove a nervous couple up to Edmonton, he thought of his wife Ruth and how things might have been different for them if he had driven her up to Edmonton that night.

Lilly and Fred were delighted to take Ruth under their roof while Lorne was sick. Lilly spoiled Ruth with endless hugs and kisses, and plenty of playtime. Uncle Fred showed Ruth how to feed the baby lambs with a bottle and let her ride the horses around the paddock. Ruth missed school desperately and her schoolmates, but her dad had been right—it was sort of like a vacation. It had been three weeks already—time was flying by.

Every Saturday, Herman drove out to the farm to pick Ruth up for the day. She was able to come back to the house for supper and to see her family.

One Saturday afternoon, Herman asked Ruth how she was doing.

"I'm doing well." Ruth looked at him and smiled. "I really like all the animals."

"Good. It sounds fun."

"And Aunt Lilly is so nice to me. She likes to play. She lets me help out a lot but she always tells me that I am a really big help. She never tells me I'm doing it wrong, she just shows me how to do it her way." Ruth paused, watching the fields go past the car window. "I like that."

Herman responded, "That's good. How is your school work going?"

"Oh I finished it ages ago. It was easy."

"Do you need me to get some more work for you?"

Ruth shrugged. "I suppose. How much longer until Lorne is better?"

"He's on the mend now. We've hired a nurse to care for him over the last week and through next week."

"A nurse?"

"Yes. Mother is exhausted and Lorne needs care all though the night. I was able to take a bit of time away from the store but I've had to return to take care of some business matters. The nurse is very helpful."

"Wow."

The fields turned into town streets. Herman turned a few times until they were driving down their street. He pulled around into the alley and took the car into the garage. Before Ruth got out, he put a hand on her arm. "Now listen to me. Your mother has had a tough few weeks. I want you to be on your best behavior tonight. You be sure to help with the meal, clean up—and don't chatter too much about the farm. It will only bother your mother."

Ruth scowled. "Fine."

Herman sighed, "Thank you, Ruth."

The pair entered the house through the back door. A woman was in the kitchen, making a bottle.

"*Guten Tag.*"

"Hi," Ruth's eyes lit up.

"I'm Helen Dupont."

Helen wore her white nurse's uniform with bib and tucker over her long dress. She had a crisp white nurse's cap that she wore on her neatly pinned hair.

"Hello, Miss Dupont."

Helen put out her hand. "Pleasure to meet you, Miss Bohlman."

Ruth smiled and shook her hand. "The pleasure is mine."

After supper, Nurse Dupont took Lorne up to his room. Ruth waited for a while to see if she would come back down to visit but she didn't return.

"Dad?"

"Yes, Ruth?"

"I need to get one more thing from my room before we go back to the farm . . . a book I've forgotten."

"That's fine. Miss Dupont has been staying in your room so don't disturb any of her belongings."

"And," Edith added, "don't disturb the nurse. She is taking care of Lorne."

"I understand." Ruth quickly ran up the stairs and peeked into Lorne's room. The nurse was standing over the crib, brushing Lorne's hair off his forehead.

Ruth went into her room and looked around at Miss Dupont's suitcase and personal items around the room. On her dressing table sat a genuine nurse's cap, and Ruth could not help herself from trying it on. She slipped it over her short hair and smiled at herself in the mirror.

"Hello, I'm Nurse Bohlman. I will make you better." She made a dramatic, sympathetic face in the mirror at her make-believe patient. "I'm afraid we almost lost you but I am here now. I'll nurse you back to health.

148

I am the most wonderful nurse in town." Outside the door she heard footsteps so she quickly placed the cap on the dressing table and went to the wardrobe to retrieve the book she was looking for.

"Knock, knock." Helen opened the door a crack. "Well hello there."

Ruth smiled her most charming smile. "Hello."

"You have such a wonderful room. Thank you for sharing it with me."

"You're welcome." Ruth was awestruck at this beautiful nurse who spoke to her, as though she were the queen of England. "How is Lorne?"

"He is sleeping right now. He is getting stronger every day."

"So, how long have you been a nurse for?"

"A few years now. I work with families who have sick children. It helps them get through these difficult times."

Ruth went on to ask Helen a hundred more questions. Helen patiently answered them all. Ruth was so amazed at this grown up who took the time to talk to her and who treated her as if she too was all grown up.

Finally, she was summoned by her dad. It was time to go. That night at the farm as Ruth was trying to fall asleep, she hugged Rosalie and told her all about Nurse Dupont.

"Rosalie, one day I'm going to be a nurse just like she is."

"You will go out in joy and
be led forth in peace; the
mountains and hills will
burst into song before you,
and all the trees of the field
will clap their hands."
Isaiah 55:12 NIV

June 1932
Lac Du Bonnet, Manitoba

Waldemar and Victor were hunting in the woods. The chores had
been completed hours ago. The day was theirs to enjoy. Waldemar, now
fifteen, was at the end of the ninth grade. There were only four more days
left before the end of the school year. Everyone was looking forward to
Canada Day, the first of July.

As they crept through the woods, looking for game, he thought
about his baseball practice later that night. He had spent the winter
playing hockey and curling but now that summer was here, he immersed
himself in baseball. He was good, the best on his team. Everyone in the
Riverland farming district knew his name. Baseball was the best thing in
his life right now.

Times were hard in Manitoba. The weather was dry and crops were
failing. Many people in town were out of jobs and several businesses had
closed down. Life on the farm was mostly self-sustaining. Despite the
weather and the failing crops, the Pettersson vegetable garden had done
well for the past few summers. The milk cows were still producing.

"I'm tired of hunting," Victor sighed, swatting away the mosquito that was humming near his face.

"Ya," Waldemar agreed. "There's nothing out right now. It's too hot."

Victor pointed to the north. "We're nearly at Mr. Hansen's place. Why don't we go and say hi to him?"

Waldemar pulled up his shirt and wiped his forehead. "That sounds good. Maybe he has something to drink."

The young men found their way to the trail that led to Pete Hansen's land. They put their slingshots in their back pockets.

"How's business?" Victor asked.

Waldemar had spent the spring selling cards and flowers door to door. "Pretty good. I've made three dollars over the last two months."

"That's really good!" Victor climbed over a fallen log. "What are you going to buy?"

"Oh, I just give the money to Mamma. She can get the things we need at the store. You know, coats, boots, clothing . . ."

"Our crops don't look too good." He pointed to the underbrush. "It's so dry. If only it would rain some more."

"If Mamma wasn't hauling well water and dumping it in the garden, I don't think our vegetables would be doing as well as they are."

"I've heard," Victor said, looking sullen, "that there are fires everywhere. The underbrush is burning. It won't be long before it gets to us."

"I heard Pappa talking about cutting down sections of wood to make a fire stop."

"Yes, and he was thinking that we might need to dig culverts and pull up any vegetation. It would prevent fire from reaching the house."

On windy days, the smell of the fires reached the Pettersson farm. The underbrush was burning slowly and steadily. Depending on which way the wind blew, their property could be at risk.

"Are you going to be picking again at the Carlson farm this summer?" Victor asked.

"Yes, for a few weeks. It's the best way to get our berries for free. I'm not sure if he'll be able to pay us this year, but the berries are worth the effort."

Victor laughed, "Sure, Waldy, we know you couldn't survive the winter without your blueberry pie."

They came into an open clearing. Pete's house came into view. Pete was at the side of the house. He was about four feet in the ground, focused, digging and throwing the dirt behind him into a large pile.

"Hello, Mr. Hansen!" Waldemar called out.

He looked up. "Hello, boys! What brings you by today?"

Victor answered, "We were hunting but we couldn't find anything."

Waldemar added, "We were getting hot and thirsty so we decided to see if you were home."

Pete smiled. "I'm thirsty too, and tired of walking to the river for my water." He leaned on his shovel and wiped the sweat from his brow. "Can you guess what I'm digging for?"

Waldemar looked around the yard at several holes Pete had started. "Water?"

Pete laughed, "You got it, boy! Water indeed! I started digging here," he pointed to another hole, "there, and there . . . and I wasn't feeling lucky. Now I think I've got the spot."

"How do you know?" Victor asked.

"I don't! Just a prayer and a bit of luck. After about six feet of digging, then I can tell if I'm going to get lucky by the type of soil I'm hitting."

"Do you need us to fill the other holes back up?" Waldemar asked.

"That would be great." Pete looked at Victor. "Why don't you go inside and get us some lunch? Waldemar can fill the holes."

Victor shrugged. "Sure thing." He went into Pete's cabin.

Waldemar picked up a spare shovel and began to move the dirt back into the empty holes. Pete continued to dig. After fifteen minutes, Victor emerged from the cabin with three sandwiches on a butcher-block cutting board. He placed it down on a tree stump.

"I need to grab some mugs," Victor said as he went back inside the house.

Pete brushed off his hands on his pants. "Come on, Waldemar, take a break."

Waldemar set his shovel down and went to a bucket where Pete was rinsing his hands. "Your cabin is looking good, Mr. Hansen."

Victor came out of the cabin with three glass mugs in his hands. "Yes, I like the windows!"

"Real glass," Pete said, "a big improvement over celluloid sheets I had."

"And a new roof," Waldemar added.

"Yes," Pete nodded, "no more thatch for me. I've got proper shingles this year."

Victor took a large bite of his sandwich. "Are you coming over next Friday for your annual picture?"

Pete took a drink of water and set his mug down. "Oh yes, my boy!"

Waldemar started to laugh. "It wouldn't be Canada Day without a picture of Mr. Hansen in his uniform."

Pete was a W.W.I veteran in the Danish army. He had a long-standing tradition of dressing up in his blue uniform and posing with one of the Pettersson's finest-looking horses.

"Is your Mamma entering the pie contest?" Pete asked.

Victor and Waldemar both nodded. "Of course!"

After a few minutes, all three had finished their sandwiches. "Shall we get back to digging?" Pete asked.

Waldemar returned to filling holes while Pete continued to dig. Victor sat in the shade watching them work. The pile of dirt next to Pete got larger and larger until finally he was in over his head. Then he started filling pails of dirt that Victor hauled up and dumped on the pile. The day was beginning to cool off. It was nearly six o'clock.

"How far are you now?" Waldemar asked as he came over to peer down the hole.

Pete looked up. "I'd say eleven feet."

"How far will you dig?" Victor questioned.

Defeated, Pete leaned on his shovel and sighed. "I'm tired. I think I'll call it quits for the day." He jammed his shovel down into the dirt and looked up. Waldemar and Victor's eyes were wide. "What?" Suddenly he felt ice cold water rushing around his feet. "HOLY SMOKES!"

Victor and Waldemar jumped up and down at the top of the well. "You did it!" they cried. "You hit a spring!"

Pete let out a loud whoop as he began to shimmy up the sides of the well. They all watched the water bubbling up out of the earth and filling up the bottom of the pit.

The following Friday, the family was in the wagon on their way into town. It was Canada Day, the sun was shining and everyone was smiling. Alina carefully balanced an apple pie on her lap.

Otto smiled at her, "Award-winning?"

She moved closer to him on the wagon seat. "I'd say." She kissed his cheek.

"Do I get a taste?" he asked, an eyebrow raised.

"Not unless you're judging the contest."

"I wonder how a fellow gets that job . . ." he smirked.

Alina laughed. "I think the pastor gets the job. He is a bachelor after all."

They pulled up to the large clearing near the river's edge. A young man stood at the side of the road directing wagons and horses into a wooded area. There was a paddock for the horses complete with water and hay. Otto drove the wagon in, pulled up next to another wagon and climbed down. Waldemar leapt from the back of the wagon and began to unhitch the horses.

"Take the horses to the shelter, Waldemar," Otto instructed, "and see that there is water."

"I know, Pappa," Waldemar said as he clucked at the horses. He began to lead them away from the wagon. Everyone else climbed down off the wagon and began to talk about where they wanted to go first.

A dirt road led them into the heart of the festivities. The riverfront hummed with excitement. A band was playing, children were laughing and the sound of people swimming in the river carried up onto the beachfront. On the right side of the road, near the river, a midway had been set up with a variety of games. In front of the midway, on the beach, was a large area with picnic tables. Alina and Otto headed to a big tent where the pie contest was being held. The children carried on down the road. On the left side of the road was a Ferris wheel, turning around and around. At its base people, were setting up a table and an ice cream grinder.

Four-year-old Douglas said wistfully, "I love ice cream."

Everyone agreed.

Alice answered softly, "It's too much if we all want it."

Waldemar shook his head. "I wish I was rich. Then I'd buy an ice cream for everyone."

"Well you're not," Victor said practically. "None of us are. But there are lots of other ways for us to have fun today." He turned to Margaret and Singhild. "What are you two sugar lumps going to do today?"

Margaret responded, scowling at Victor, "We," she said, pointing at herself, Douglas, Singhild and Alice, "are going to join Mamma at the pie contest. Then we'll watch the races. How about you fellows?"

Waldemar smiled confidently. "I am going to do everything . . . the hog wrestle, the midway games, the swimming races . . . anything and everything I can."

"Why don't we see if there are any swimming races for you, Waldy?" Victor suggested.

"That would be good." He pointed to the satchel over his shoulder. "I've got my swim suit and towel."

The children parted company, the girls and Douglas going back to find Alina while Victor and Waldemar carried on to waterfront.

Waldemar went into a cabana to put on his swimsuit. Once down on the dock, they found a contest underway. Next to the dock were two very large logs in the water. A man sat on each log, holding a pillow. When the whistle blew, they proceeded to whack one another until someone ended up in the river.

"That looks like fun," Waldemar said.

"No thanks," Victor shook his head, "not for me."

They continued to watch for a while as time after time men slipped and fell into the water.

"I think I've got it," Waldemar said as he stepped forward, picked up a soggy pillow and announced boldly, "I'll take on a challenger."

One of his schoolmates, Fred, stepped up. "I'll take you on."

They both proceeded out onto the logs, trying to keep steady until they could sit down. They both paddled with their hands until they were close enough to hit each other. Fred landed a few good blows to Waldemar's torso. He held steady, winding up for a clear hit to knock Fred over. Finally, as Fred raised his arms to swing the pillow, Waldemar used all his strength to hit Fred in the side. Fred toppled into the river. Everyone cheered as he came sputtering to the surface, laughing.

Fred raised his hand up to Waldemar. "Good game!"

Waldemar shook his hand, "Thanks!"

Challenger after challenger stepped up and tried to knock Waldemar from his perch but his legs held tight while he waited for his opponent to lose focus. His long, muscular arms were so powerful that with one blow, his opponent was in the water. Victor watched from the dock, laughing and cheering each time Waldemar won another round.

After at least a dozen opponents, a young, strong-looking man stepped forward. He was wearing a suit and tie. He had light brown hair, smoothed neatly into place.

"I'll take you on," he announced.

Waldemar looked at the man. "Go get your swim suit on then."

The man laughed. "I don't need a swim suit. I'm confident that I won't be going for a swim today."

Waldemar smirked. "Alright then. Mount your log."

The man pulled off his shoes and socks, and rolled his trousers up to his knees. He pulled off his suit jacket and tie, and passed them to a friend of his. He stepped gingerly onto the log, nearly losing his balance. He laughed, "No worries . . . I've got this."

He sat down, reached up to the dock for someone to hand him a pillow. Once he had his pillow, the man paddled toward Waldemar.

Waldemar took the first swing. He landed the pillow squarely on the man's arm. The man held steady. He flung his pillow at Waldemar. Waldemar quickly paddled to the side, moving out of the way. They hit one another back and forth, the man putting up a good fight. Finally, Waldemar brought a crashing blow into the man's left side. He toppled into the water, suit and all.

Waldemar raised his arms in victory and let out a whoop.

Victor cheered madly, "You did it!"

The other man paddled back to the dock where his friends pulled him up. The man turned toward Waldemar, still seated on his log; "Good game, my friend. You were a worthy opponent! I thought you'd be worn out by now—an easy target, but, you proved me wrong."

"Thank you," Waldemar said as he paddled back to the dock. "I will end on that note. It was a good match."

Waldemar went back to the cabana to change into his shorts and shirt.

"Why don't we go to the race track?" Victor asked when Waldemar was done changing. He pointed a little further down the road where there was a large track set up for field games. "The big race is about to start."

Fallen logs were lined up as benches all around the track. The finish line was marked with bright red flags. An officiate stood up on a podium. The runners stood near the starting line, stretching. Some were tightening their leather running shoes while others straightened out their racing uniforms. There was a huge crowd of people, all finding a place to watch the big race. They spotted Otto sitting with some friends of theirs from church.

As they made their way toward their father, Victor asked, "Why don't you race Waldy?"

"I don't think so . . . Pappa wouldn't—"

"Never mind Pappa. You should race. You're the fastest guy I know. There's a big prize for this race."

"I can't run in my boots," Waldemar protested, looking down at his heavy leather work boots.

"Take them off," Victor suggested, smiling at his brother. "Come on, I know you want to!"

Waldemar thought about it for a minute. "Okay, why not?" He laughed as he took off his boots. He looked down at his stocking feet, smirked and approached the race official at the podium.

"Sir, I'd like to race," Waldemar announced.

The race official laughed. "Well, boy," he looked down at his socks, "you don't look ready for a race, but we could use the entertainment. Off you go to the start line there, twice around the half-mile track to the finish. First place wins a cash prize."

Waldemar looked back at his brother sitting with his father at the sidelines. Victor had a big grin on his face. Waldemar knew that he looked ridiculous in his farm clothes and socks next to these trained athletes in their uniforms and leather running shoes. "What have I gotten into?" he muttered to himself as he approached the starting line.

"ON YOUR MARK, GET SET, GO!" The official blew an air horn. The runners took off around the track.

Waldemar could hear the crowd cheering. He started off as fast as he could. He tucked his elbows in and focused on passing every runner in the race. His sun-bleached hair flew back as he ran. Each time his foot hit the track, he would use every muscle to propel himself farther and farther ahead of the pack.

After the first lap, the crowd began to cheer him on. Waldemar's school friends and Victor were yelling wildly from the sidelines.

"GO, PETTERSSON!"

Waldemar could feel his heart pounding in his chest as he looked toward the finish line. *Run, run, run*, he told himself. The other runners were a distant memory behind him. He felt a huge rush of excitement as he burst through the bright red ribbon at the finish line.

Victor rushed over, laughing and cheering, "THAT WAS GREAT!" Everyone came around, clapping him on the back and shaking his hand in congratulations.

The official came toward him smiling. "Well done, farm boy. You sure showed those city racers a thing or two. What's your name?"

"Waldemar Pettersson."

The official stuck out his hand with an envelope. "It's all yours, five dollars to the winner." He grabbed Waldemar's wrist and thrust his arm up in the air, "THE WINNER, WALDEMAR PETTERSSON!"

Everyone cheered and whistled. Waldemar looked for his father in the crowd. He couldn't see him. Waldemar took the envelope and beamed at Victor. "This is great!"

They replayed the race again and again as they walked back up the road to the midway area where the other kids were.

The other Pettersson children were trying a game, desperately attempting to knock over milk bottles with a baseball. Waldemar came up behind them.

"Feeling lucky?"

The girls jumped. "Oh hi, Waldy." Singhild threw her hands up in the air. "We're terrible at this."

Victor was grinning like a Cheshire cat.

"What's going on?" Margaret asked.

"I was thinking about how much Douglas wanted ice cream." Waldemar bent down and looked his youngest brother in the eyes. "Do you want an ice cream, buddy?"

Douglas smiled, his eyes wide and bright.

Alice chided, "You don't have any money for that. Don't tease him."

Waldemar took Douglas' hand. "Let's go and find that ice cream man. Shall we?"

The girls followed reluctantly as Victor and Waldemar led Douglas back to the table where a man was making ice cream.

Waldemar smiled at the man. "We'd like six ice creams please."

Alice, Singhild and Margaret all gasped. They all began to protest at once.

Waldemar held up his hand and pulled the envelope from his pocket. "Allow me."

The ice cream man smiled. "So you're the young fellow that won the big race. I hear you did it in your stocking feet!"

Waldemar laughed, exchanging a look with Victor. "Yes, sir."

"For now we see through a glass, darkly; but then face to face: now I know in part; but then shall I know even as also I am known." 1 Corinthians 13:12 NIV

July 1936
Leduc, Alberta

Ruth, now fifteen years old, walked with William Heinz down Leduc's main street. They were off to the movie theatre. Herman had allowed his daughter to go on a date tonight, much to Ruth's surprise. She wasn't terribly interested in William anyhow; his brother Matthew was the one she had her eye on. The chance at a free show couldn't be refused though, so Ruth had been happy to take William up on his offer.

The movie was 'Rose Marie,' starring Jeanette MacDonald and Nelson Eddy. It was a romance about an opera star and a Mountie, and Ruth was looking forward to it. William had kindly paid her ticket and the two shared popcorn during the show. The Heinz brothers were farm boys. Ruth had long ago determined that she would never be a farmer's wife. She had higher aspirations. She wanted to be a lawyer. She had told Artrude who had burst out laughing.

"Ruth, German Baptist girls from Leduc don't go to university. We get married and have children. That is the sensible thing to do."

"Not this girl," Ruth had replied. *"I'm destined for adventure. If I can't be a lawyer I'm going to go to be a nurse. You'll see!"*

William and Ruth walked to a local ice cream shop for a treat after the movie. The pair chatted about the youth group at church that Ruth organized, the drama club that they were a part of and subjects at school that they were enjoying.

When Ruth got home that night, Herman greeted her from his favorite chair where he was reading his newspaper.

"Good Evening, Ruth," he spoke in German.

"*Gute Abend, Vati.*" She sat down on the sofa and looked at her father.

"How was your evening?"

"It was fine. The movie was great."

"Which one did you see?"

"'Rose Marie' . . . about a opera star and a Mountie . . ." she sighed dreamily.

Herman's eyebrows rose. "Really?" He started to chuckle.

Ruth laughed, "Oh, Father!"

"Be quiet when you go upstairs; Lorne and Mother are sleeping."

"I will." Ruth kissed her father on the cheek and then quietly went to the kitchen to fix herself a snack. After some cookies and milk, she softly stepped up the stairs to her bedroom.

Herman folded the newspaper. He picked up a stack of envelopes off the table. He followed Ruth up to her room. He knocked softly on the door.

"Ruthie?" he whispered.

Ruth opened the door. "Hi. Come in."

Herman walked in and shut the door behind him. He sat down in the rocking chair.

"I was speaking to Mrs. Daum today."

"Oh?"

"The family is travelling to Oregon and has invited you along."

"Really!" Her face lit up. "Can I?"

"*Ja.* You may." He was calm, withholding something.

"What is it?"

"Ah," Herman hesitated and then waved the envelopes in the air. "These are for you."

Ruth came to him and took the envelopes from his hand. She sat down on the bed. They had all been opened. The same neat writing was on the outside of each one. They were all addressed to the store.

"What are these?" She studied him, looking at his stoic face.

"Letters . . . from your grandmother."

Ruth was puzzled. "Grandma Fleck?"

"No." Herman leaned forward in the chair, his face tense, his hands gripping the armrests. "Grandmother Lessing."

Ruth's mouth hung open. "Really?"

"Listen, don't open them now. I just wanted to tell you that you might have the opportunity to see your grandmother while you are in Oregon. Mrs. Daum is trying to arrange it."

"She is?" Ruth was completely surprised.

"Your grandmother . . ." Herman leaned back in the chair and began to rock. "She . . . she helped me a lot when I was young. She took me in as a part of their family. She," his voice cracked with emotion, "she loved me."

Ruth's eyes began to well up with tears.

"She also loved you." Herman took a deep breath. His eyes were fixed on the wardrobe doors, his gaze avoiding Ruth. "After your . . . your mother died, she took you to Portland. She and your Aunt Amelia raised you until you were one. Then you were very ill and—" he paused.

Ruth held her breath. She waited patiently for him to continue.

"I thought I might lose you. So I had you come back to Leduc." He looked at his daughter. "I don't know if it was the right choice but I couldn't risk losing you again. You see, when your Grandfather Lessing died . . . your mother and I—we were in Oregon. He waited by the window for us to return home on the train . . . we didn't make it in time. He died, waiting for us. I knew first hand how far away Portland was if something were to happen to you." He sniffed.

"It's okay, Dad."

"She—your grandmother—was heartbroken . . . missing you. She visited a lot in the early years and then once I married your mother. Well . . ." his voice dropped to a whisper, "things changed."

Tears came to his eyes and Ruth felt emotion rising up in her. Like a tidal wave it threatened to drown her. She looked away from him.

"She's wanted to see you for years now and well . . . you are growing up. I think it may be the right time."

"That would be wonderful," Ruth breathed, barely able to believe she was having this conversation.

"Pack your things then. You'll be leaving the day after tomorrow. And please," he looked her in the eyes, "let's not speak of this with your mother."

"That's fine."

"And the letters," he added, "are a private correspondence between she and I. I trust you will respect that."

"I understand."

Herman gave his daughter a hug and left the room. Once Ruth heard his bedroom door close, she opened the letters.

Dearest Herman,

I am sorry about our conversation in the store. I was out of line. I know we each grieve in our own way. I want to see the child. I miss her and I want her to know me. I love her dearly and want nothing other than to sit and talk with her, to share my story with her. I want to share my faith, the lessons I have learned. A grandmother is a rare treasure to a young girl—especially a girl who has lost her mother. Please accept my apologies and call me. Send me a letter or a telegram. Please, let's arrange a date. She could come to Portland and stay with me for the summers. I could come to Leduc. I am willing.

Sincerely, Mother

The other letters were virtually the same. Every year she had sent one, begging Herman to allow contact.

Why? Why had he not allowed it? She fingered the delicate script, if only . . .

The drive to Oregon was long. She and Artrude talked about the youth group they hosted and the drama club they participated in. Ruth loved acting. When she was on stage she could be anyone . . . escape everything. The prairie fields turned into rolling hills and then, hours later, into looming mountains. They stayed the first night in a beautiful hotel in Banff.

The next day they went through the mountains, south to Spokane and then east to Portland. As they drove, Ruth reflected on her life in

Leduc. Lorne was seven now and certainly the apple of Mother's eye. He could do no wrong. It annoyed Ruth to some degree but she and Lorne got along all the same. Since he was considerably younger, their worlds did not often collide.

The exception to that was, of course, piano lessons. Lorne was being taught weekly. Ruth was very jealous. She had always wanted to have piano lessons but Mother had determined that girls did not need to play the piano. Whenever the piano teacher came, Ruth would lie on her belly on the landing and listen to the teacher's instructions, hoping that she might catch on. Edith insisted that Ruth help Lorne with his practicing but it was so tedious. He wasn't terribly interested in his scales and while he plunked away, he would kick her in the shins as she sat next to him. One time Ruth had decided she'd had enough and gave him a good solid kick back in his shins. He hollered so loud and long she thought that Father would hear him at the store! Edith had chewed Ruth out for nearly an hour over that one.

As they neared Portland, Ruth began to wonder what it would have been like to grow up here.

"Are you nervous?" Artrude asked, interrupting her thoughts.

"A little," she admitted.

"What are you going to say?"

"I don't know. I guess we're just going to have lunch together."

"Are you going to ask her?"

"About my mother?"

"Yes . . ." Artrude looked at her friend. "Don't you think she would tell you?"

Emma Daum listened from the front seat. "What do you want to know about your mother, Ruth?" She twisted around in her seat and looked at the young girl.

"Um," Ruth looked out the window, her eyes suddenly feeling misty. "I'm not sure. I guess I'd like to know what she was like."

"Do you know that your mother and I were friends?" Emma asked softly.

"I guess I've never thought about it," Ruth said quietly.

"I was there, the night you were born. Your mother and I were very close."

Ruth felt the hot, salty tears escape her eyes and torrent down her cheeks. "What was she like?"

"She was funny. She loved to laugh. She loved the Lord. She was dedicated to the church. She was a good woman . . . just like you."

"I don't know . . ."

"Yes, Ruth. You are."

Ruth looked out the window.

The following day, the Daums took Ruth to the Lessing home. It was a big, white, two-storey house in the heart of town. It was grand, but needed some care. The paint was peeling on the front porch and the screen door sagged. It looked lonely and sad.

Ruth walked up the front steps on her own. She rapped the doorknocker. She waited, holding her breath.

"*Hallo*," an old woman opened the door.

"Hello. I'm Ruth."

"Of course you are." Pauline smiled. "Please, come in."

Ruth turned around and waved to the Daums. Emma called out, "We'll be back at two o'clock to pick you up!"

"Okay," Ruth called back. She walked inside the house. It was dark.

"I keep the shades pulled in the summertime," Pauline explained. "Then it doesn't get so hot in here."

It was warm, Ruth thought. The air was muggy and the house smelled damp.

"Please," Pauline motioned to the sofa, "have a seat." Pauline had long grey hair that was pulled back into a bun. She had many, many wrinkles on her face. She had big, haunted eyes and a chiseled jaw line. She seemed tough, and yet fragile all at the same time. She walked toward a doorway that led to the kitchen.

"May I get you some tea?"

"Please," Ruth answered, "I'd like that." She could hear Pauline in the kitchen, picking up the kettle, pouring it into tea cups and the clink of the cups rocking on the saucers as she brought them back out. She passed a cup to Ruth. "Careful, it's hot."

"Thank you." Ruth didn't know if she should call her Grandma or Mrs. Lessing so she omitted her name.

"And finally," she sighed, "you are here. For a short time, but we will treasure it anyhow."

Ruth nodded, "Yes. It's nice to be here."

Pauline cleared her throat. Silence fell heavily between the two women. Finally, Pauline said, "Tell me, Ruth, have you had a happy childhood?"

"Ah," Ruth lied, "yes, I suppose."

"Did your mother treat you well?"

How could Ruth explain the complex relationship between Edith and her? "Fairly, I suppose."

"Has your father told you very much about your real mother?"

Ruth's stomach flipped, "No, ma'am. Not much at all."

Pauline let out her breath, sighing. "Do you have a photo of her?"

"*Nein*," Ruth answered. Pauline looked disappointed. Ruth quickly added, "But I've seen one . . . once."

"And why didn't you get to keep it?" she asked.

"I found it," she fudged, "by accident. When I went back for it a few months later, someone had taken all the photos of my mother out of the album. I don't know why."

Pauline wrung her hands. She put her teacup down on a side table. She pushed herself out of the armchair and went to a drawer. She pulled out a cardboard picture frame. It was dark brown with golden trim. She passed it to Ruth. Ruth opened it up and inside was a picture of her mother and father, on their wedding day, just as she had seen in the garage that day.

"You can have that one. Every girl should at least have a photo of her mother."

Ruth felt all kinds of emotions crashing in on her. "Thank you."

"Now tell me all about yourself." Pauline settled back into her chair. Ruth spoke for quite some time about school, church, friends and family. As time went on, she felt more and more comfortable with Pauline. She had a knack for listening. Finally, it was Pauline's turn to talk.

"Will you tell me about my aunts and uncles?" Ruth asked timidly.

"Of course. My husband and I married in Russia in 1893. His name was Ferdinand, although everyone in Canada called him Fred. He and I had ten children together. Rudolf . . . he died when he was a baby, Amelia, Martha, Ben, Ruth, Robert, Hilda, Walter, Magda and one more son."

"Oh?"

"He died at birth. We never did name him. He's buried in the Fredericksheim Cemetery. Near your mother. Martha's there too, Hilda and of course Fred." She looked at Ruth, "Have you seen them when you visit your mother?"

"Ah . . . no. I haven't . . . I mean to say I've never been."

"Your father used to go nearly every day after your mother died. I used to tell him that the dead have moved on . . . he ought to as well. Probably better that you don't go. It doesn't bring them back."

Ruth felt her chest getting tight. She hadn't ever considered where her mother was buried. She fingered the picture in her lap. The grandfather clock rang a quarter to two. "Thank you for the photo."

"You know, Ruth. Your grandfather and I, we had everything we could have wanted when we immigrated to Canada. We had successful crops, a growing family and a good church where we could worship freely. We had reached the promised land. But it wasn't enough. Soon our fortune turned. People in our family got sick. Everyone began to die and there is nothing you can do about that."

Ruth looked at this old woman, who was pensive and sad.

"But I had you," Pauline looked Ruth in the eyes, "and you made life better for a while. You gave me hope when I had none. There are times when life gets so hard, you can't even pray. But you were my light, a baby who needed me—and oh, love, I needed you."

"I see."

"It's been my greatest heartache, Ruth . . . losing touch with you. I hope you can forgive me for not trying harder."

Ruth wanted to get up and go to her. "It's okay. I know there is more to it than meets the eye."

Pauline nodded, folded her hands in her lap and looked down. "Yes. Life is complex. I am glad," she looked up, "glad for today."

"So am I." Ruth agreed.

"This is the day that the Lord has made. Let us rejoice and be glad in it."

"Whether you turn to the right or to the left, your ears will hear a voice behind you, saying, 'This is the way; walk in it.'" Isaiah 30:21 NIV

July 1936
Lac Du Bonnet, Manitoba

Waldemar had spent the wee hours of the morning running through the Riverland Farming district trying to round up the family cows. He still knew them all by name, even though he hadn't lived at home for the last two years. There was Daisy, Molly, Sweetie, Sugar Plum, Betsy, Glenda and Bertha . . . all lovingly named by Margaret and Singhild over the years. The cows wandered adjacent properties day and night. They were in search of fresh grass, which was sparse. The underbrush was still burning. The muskeg and peat moss had continued to smoke even through the winters. This spring, the fires had burned down all the trees between the Pettersson farm and Pete Hansen's property. Waldemar and Victor dug furrows to keep the fire from spreading to the house and the barn.

Waldemar spent the last two years since graduation working odd jobs—anything he could find. He had cleared bush on the power lines, worked as a delivery driver, a pipe fitter, trench digger and had done just about anything else he could to earn a living. After graduation, Otto ordered the college books that Waldemar needed to become a teacher. Waldemar had taken one look at the teacher's salary and decided that it wasn't worth his while.

Now he pushed open the big barn door, the last cow in tow.

"Vic?"

"Hey, Waldy," Victor called out from the milking pen, "over here."

Waldemar brought his cow to join them. He shut the gate behind her.

"Find all the cows?"

"Yep," Waldemar answered, "this is the last one."

"That's good."

Waldemar sat down on the milking stool and began to pull his cow's udder, releasing the warm milk into the bucket. "So, what's the plan for today?"

"I don't know . . . are you almost done the porch?"

Waldemar was working on screening in the front porch. He no longer liked to share the family bedroom. He was often coming and going at late hours.

"I'm nearly done. Just the screening to tack up. I completed the framing last night."

"Mamma has a cot you can use to sleep out there."

"I saw that." He leaned his forehead against the warm side of his cow. "What do you need help with over the next few days?"

"I don't know. Whatever you think needs to be done. You've always been better at that than me."

"You're twenty-one now, Vic." Waldemar laughed, "You should have this figured out by now."

"Oh shut up."

Suddenly, an arc of milk came from under his cow and hit Waldemar square in the chest.

Waldemar promptly squeezed the udder of his cow and shot back, hitting Victor, who was peeking under his cow, right in the face.

Victor laughed. "Hey!"

The two continued to aim at each other until they were both dripping with milk. Their laughter got louder and louder. The cows began to protest, stamping their feet.

Wiping his face, Victor cried, "Truce! Truce!"

Otto, now sixty-five, came limping into the barn. "What's all the commotion about?" he growled.

Waldemar wiped his face on his shirt. "Nothing, Pappa. We're just milking the cows."

Otto looked around the milking pen at all of the milk dripping from the walls. "Don't waste the milk." He walked slowly on to the horse section of the barn.

"What's his problem?" Waldemar hissed at Victor once Otto was out of earshot.

Victor cocked his head to the side. "Don't give him a hard time. His back is in really bad shape. He's dependent on me for everything . . ." he paused thoughtfully, "you're not always around . . . there's a lot of pressure on us to keep things productive here."

"We're doing fine," Waldemar scoffed. "A lot of farmers have had to sell their land and move to the city. He's lucky that our farm has the creek and such good soil. Besides, I'm always here when you need me."

"I know," Victor sighed. "We still shouldn't be wasteful. Lots of folks are going hungry these days. We've no right to waste milk."

Waldemar rolled his eyes. "You sound like Pappa."

"We've got a busy day ahead of us; it's almost six o'clock. We need to get our haying done before it gets too hot."

Waldemar stood up with his bucket full of milk. "Let's go then."

He went out into the pastureland and looked for two horses that would serve as his morning mowing team. He led each one back to the barn where he hitched them up to the equipment.

Victor and Waldemar drove the horses out into the hay meadows and began the tedious job of cutting. Waldemar drove the horses in circles, cutting a four-foot swath as he went. Victor worked along the fence line with a scythe, cutting the areas that were hard for Waldemar to get to with the horses. The sun rose steadily as they worked. By ten o'clock, it was beginning to get too warm. Waldemar brought the horses back to the barn to feed and rest while the sun was at its hottest.

In the midday heat, while the horses had a break, Waldemar decided to take the children's berries into town. All the raspberries and strawberries that had been picked could be sold at the general store, or bartered for goods. There were two large baskets full in the icehouse.

He found Victor in the summer kitchen with Mamma, Alice and Douglas. In the summer, they had a simple outdoor shelter where Mamma and the girls could cook. Alina and Alice were busy making bread in the wood fire stove. Douglas sat with Victor who was eating a late breakfast.

"Good morning, Waldemar," Alina said.

"Morning, Mamma." He went to her and gave her a kiss on the cheek. "How are you?"

"Just fine. Did you want some breakfast?"

"Maybe just a sandwich to take with me. I'm going into town to sell the berries."

"There's milk you can take to the creamery too," Victor added.

"How many urns?" Waldemar asked.

"Two."

"I can take those too."

Alina shook her head. "You won't be able to take two urns and two large baskets of berries. You'll need to take the wagon . . . I don' t think it's available. Your Pappa is fixing the axle."

"I'll just take two trips."

"You won't have time," Alice protested. "You need to be back to help Victor with the haying once it cools off a bit."

Waldemar looked around at his family, all eager to give their opinion. "I can handle it . . . I'll run."

He took the sandwich that his Mamma had made, kissed her again and headed off to the icehouse. He grabbed the berries first and started his jog into town.

"I'll give you one dollar for each basket," the grocer offered.

"A dollar twenty-five," Waldemar said firmly. "These are the juiciest berries in the district."

"Fine," the grocer sighed, "a dollar twenty-five." He pointed to the door behind him. "Go and put them in the ice-house."

After dropping off the berries, Waldemar came to the counter for his payment. The grocer's wife stood next to him.

"So," the grocer punched some buttons on his cash register, "how's the family?"

"Pretty good."

"What is Gus doing now?" the grocer's wife asked.

"He's up at Gunner Mine."

"And Annie? Mary?"

"They're married now. Annie is married to a fellow named Gus Westburg, and Mary is married to a fellow named Stanley Strome."

The grocer's wife looked at him quizzically, "Have *you* found romance?"

Waldemar laughed. "Only girls I spend time with are the cows. No prospects for a wife just yet."

She tapped her fingers on the counter. "Our daughter Anika is graduating high school this year. It's always nice to find a Swede to marry."

The grocer shushed his wife. "Now, now. No need to rush the boy. I think all she's trying to say is that it's always good to keep your eyes open."

"Oh my eyes are wide open." Waldemar winked at the grocer. He had many good girlfriends during high school. His good looks brought him no shortage of attention. He didn't need any encouragement to keep his eyes on the girls.

The grocer put the money on the counter. "There you are. Wish your Mamma and Pappa a good day from us."

"I will." Waldemar picked up the money and shoved it in his pocket. "See you then."

He left the store and started back toward the house. Once he was off the town streets, he began to run. He pushed himself as hard as he could. Within ten minutes, he had covered the two miles between town and home. He went to the icehouse, grabbed the two urns and began to jog to the creamery. He sold the milk at the creamery for a fair price and ran back home, just in time to meet Victor in the fields. Victor already had the horse team hitched up.

They worked for four more hours until every last piece of hay had been cut down. They stood back to survey their work.

"We did it," Victor sighed, leaning on his scythe.

"Looks like we'll have enough for the season."

"I thought we might have to use the public land this year . . ."

"I guess we can leave it for someone else, someone who comes up short."

The public land was fair game for anyone who chose to cut it, stack it and gather it. Every season over the last five years, since the weather had been so dry, the land had been claimed by a farmer who didn't get enough hay off his own property.

Victor wiped his brow. "Are you coming in for supper?"

Waldemar looked at the height of the sun in the sky. "Maybe. I'd like to catch a ball game in town tonight."

Victor shook his head. "Aren't you tired?"

"No. I'm okay."

"I'll take the horses then so you can get on your way. Tell Mamma I'll be in shortly for my dinner."

Waldemar slapped Victor on the shoulder. "Thanks, Vic."

It was dark and the day was done. Waldemar walked swiftly back to the farmhouse. Now, he *was* tired. He had joined a baseball game out near the airfield. Some of his old schoolmates had also come to town to help with haying season. After the game, a few of his friends had gone into town to receive the daily mail. Every night at 7:30, the bus came in from Winnipeg. The postmaster took nearly an hour to sort it. Waldemar caught up with his friends while they waited. Now it was nearly nine o'clock.

By the time the farmhouse was in sight, Waldemar could see that everyone had already gone to bed for the night. He walked out to the barn and began his chores. In the summer, most of the horses and cows roamed the pastureland but a few had made it back to the barn on their own. All the stalls needed to be clean and ready for the next day.

Once the animals were taken care of, Waldemar knew he had just one more thing to do before heading to bed himself. He quietly crept into the house to avoid waking Alice, Mamma and Pappa. He went to the kitchen breadbox where Mamma's fresh baked bread was wrapped up tightly in a moist tea towel. Waldemar grabbed the rest of the loaf, a tin cup and tiptoed out to the well that was about ten feet from the house. He silently lifted the wooden lid that covered the well and began to pull a large can of cream to the surface of the chilly water. He carefully opened the lid of the cream can, and poured himself a cup into his tin mug. He tore off large chunks of soft fresh bread and dipped it into the cream. By now it was completely dark and only the moonlight and twinkling stars filled the night sky. He listened to the sound of the creek trickling by, the animals moving in the barn, the wind blowing against the house. It was peaceful here. He took a deep breath and sighed.

He whispered into the night, "Where is my life going? Is this it? Lac Du Bonnet? Working one day to the next?" He laid back and tried to count the stars.

Soon his eyes grew heavy. He closed the cream can lid carefully and lowered the cream can into the cool well water. He closed the well lid. He walked back to the barn in the darkness and climbed the ladder into the hayloft, joining his sleeping siblings. He pulled a blanket around him and listened to the loud breathing of the animals below.

Four weeks had passed. Waldemar had been out working on other farms in the area, making a few dollars by helping with their haying. This morning he was going to help Victor with the stacking. He had returned the night before, sleeping in the loft with his siblings.

"Morning, Waldy," Victor greeted his brother as they lay in the hay.

"Mornin'. Shall we get started?" Waldemar stretched his long arms and legs. He pulled bits of hay from his blonde wavy hair.

"Yes. Can you go get the team to hook up to the hay racks?"

"All right." Waldemar descended the ladder into the barn and went out to the pastureland to gather two suitable horses for the job.

Two weeks ago, Victor had raked the hay into wind rows and then coiled the hay to cure it further. Now the coils were ready to be thrown onto the hayrack and taken to make haystacks next to the barn. Victor would stand on the top of the hayrack using his pitch fork to keep the rack balanced and keep the horses moving while Waldemar would throw the coils of hay up to him.

The two men worked in the hot sun with their shirts off and trousers rolled up. They each wore a hat to keep the sun off their heads. Waldemar moved the entire coil at once onto the hayrack. His muscles flexed as he dug in his pitchfork to the bottom of the coil. He heaved the coil up to his brother. They worked all morning moving coil after coil until the hayrack was full.

They unloaded the rack at the barn every time it was full. They built large haystacks about ten feet wide and twenty feet across. Before the hay was moved to the haystack, they stopped in a large dirt clearing near the barn. Victor had to pick out all the weeds, sticks and other foliage that might be caught up in the hay. He dumped the waste into a separate pile.

They stopped with their final load of hay. Victor pulled out the last of the weeds. "I think I've got all the weeds separated," Victor called out to Waldemar who was holding the horses steady.

"Okay," he answered, "just say the word when you're ready for me to walk us over the haystacks."

"Just wait. I see a bit more." Victor ran his hands through the hay and pulled out a few more weeds. Waldemar stood, stroking Moonlight's side. He looked up at the sun. It was nearly suppertime.

After Victor finished getting the last of the weeds off, he jumped off the hayrack. He stood, looking at his pile. To himself, he said, "I should burn this so that these weeds don't spread." He pulled a match from his pocket and dropped it onto the weed pile.

The weeds snapped and hissed, burning up instantly. The fire grew quickly. The wind picked up. It blew an ember from the weed pile onto the remaining hay in the hayrack. Once the ember hit the hay on the hayrack, it turned into an inferno. The hay crackled and spit as it burned. The horses reared up. Waldemar tried to hold them steady.

"WALDY! GET SOME WATER!" Victor screamed to his brother, realizing what he had done.

Waldemar could no longer hold the rearing horses. They ripped the reins from his grasp. He desperately tried to run alongside them with the hopes of releasing their harness. Even his top speed did not match the fear that propelled them forward. The horses ran through the pastureland with the entire hayrack burning. All of the burning hay flew out the back.

"YOU IDIOT!" Waldemar screamed at his brother. He ran toward the water trough and began grabbing buckets of water to fling onto the burning weed pile.

"PAPPA! PAPPA!" Victor screamed. Otto came rushing out of the barn.

"WHAT HAVE YOU DONE?" Otto yelled as he began to beat the flames of burning hay out with empty burlap sacks. "Go after the horses, Waldy! Save the horses! Forget the weeds!"

Waldemar ran as fast as he could in the direction the horses had gone. It was not easy to miss as they had left a trail of burning hay in their wake. Thankfully, the pastureland was mostly dirt and didn't have any plant life to ignite. Waldemar could hear Victor and Pappa in the distance madly pouring water on the weed pile and trying to smother the small fires throughout the property. Waldemar ran and ran until he found the horses. They were out of breath and frothing at the mouth. Moonlight had a large bleeding cut across his chest. They had come to a halt against a barbed-wire fence.

Waldemar shook his head. The hayrack was burnt. All the hay was gone and the entire structure of the hayrack disappeared. The only thing left was the metal of the wheel rims, the harness to the horses and the steel bolts that had held the rack together.

"Easy there, Moonlight," Waldemar called out as he approached.

The horses whinnied, looking panicked as he came close. They pranced on the spot nervously.

"Shhh, shhhh, it's okay. Nice and easy now." Waldemar put out a hand as he came along side the distraught horses. "It's okay, I'll get you unhitched now, just calm down, and we'll get you out of this."

The metal frame of the harness was hot as Waldemar eased the two nervous horses out of it. Once the horses were free, Waldemar led them back to the barn holding their bridles and reassuring them.

Otto and Victor had extinguished the last of the fires and stood in the barnyard looking angry.

"What is the matter with you, boy?" Otto seethed at Waldemar as he approached.

"Me?" Waldemar was aghast.

"Yes, you! What in the hell are you thinking setting a fire so close to the hay rack?" Otto roared.

Victor stood with his head hung down. Waldemar glared at his older brother. "I didn't set the fire, Pappa."

"I don't want to hear it," Otto interrupted, "you can bet that you'll be busy rebuilding that hayrack and finding hay to replace the load we lost! You can pay for your carelessness. You could have burnt down the whole barn! You could have killed the horses!" Otto took Moonlight and Pepper from Waldemar so that he could tend to Moonlight's chest. He stormed off into the barn.

"What is the matter with you?" Waldemar glared at Victor.

"What?" Victor looked at Waldemar. "You should have moved the hayrack up before I set the fire."

"You didn't tell me you were setting the fire, you idiot!" Waldemar roared.

"Well you should have known!" Victor leaned into Waldemar, jutting his chin forward stubbornly.

"This is unbelievable." Waldemar turned away from his brother and ran off in the direction of the river. He had to get away. Anger pulsed through his body. He ran through the fields, hopping fences with ease. He kept running right through the wooded area near the river, even as the trees scratched his bare chest. His heart pounded in his ears. His breath came quickly. He ran into the water and began to swim vigorously through the waves and currents. He swam to drown his anger.

After nearly an hour of swimming against the currents, Waldemar had worn out his frustration. He sat perched on a rock near the water's edge drying off. He listened to the noise of the woods. He had cleared his head while he swam and now he had a plan. He would go home and make amends. He would rebuild the hayrack and help Victor finish out the season. Then he would leave and start his own life as a man. He would find his way in the world on his own—now was the time.

" . . . Oh, that I had the
wings of a dove! I would fly
away and be at rest—"
Psalm 55:6 NIV

July 1936
Leduc, Alberta

It had been a week since Ruth came back from Portland. She had been consumed with household chores upon her return. This morning, she stretched and grasped her headboard while her toes pushed against the end of the bed. The bed moaned in protest. Her window was open and she could hear the birds outside, singing to her. What a beautiful day.

She dressed and went downstairs. Edith was in the kitchen cooking eggs.

"Morning, Mother."

"*Good* morning, Ruth. We say g*ood* morning. Are you so lazy that you can't say *good* morning?"

"*Good* morning then, Mother." She pulled out a chair at the table and sat down. Sarcastically she said, "Or perhaps it's not?"

Edith turned around from the frying pan and glared at her. "Don't be smart. We have a lot to do today. I have things on my mind. We can't all be on vacation all summer." Edith turned back to flip the eggs.

Ruth rolled her eyes. "Of course. And what exactly is on the agenda today?"

"Floors. You can wash the floors. And . . . I did your laundry. Do you think I'm going to sit and stare at your bag for the rest of my life?"

"Sor-ry. I was going to get to it."

Edith dished up the eggs onto a plate and shoved it in front of Ruth. "'Going to get to it' isn't good enough for me. One either gets to it right away—or they don't. And you, child—you didn't."

Ruth took a bite of eggs. Edith crashed a cup of orange juice down on the table. It splashed its contents in a tiny radius around the cup. Ruth looked up at Edith, her eyebrows furrowed. "I said I was sorry."

Edith dished her own eggs, poured some coffee and sat at the table with her stepdaughter. They ate in silence. Ruth listened to the sound of Edith pulverizing her eggs with her teeth.

After breakfast, Ruth washed the dishes. Edith excused herself to her bedroom. Lorne sauntered down.

"Hi, buddy."

"Hi, Ruth."

"Want some breakfast?" There was a plate that Edith had made up sitting on the counter.

"Sure." He sat in the chair at the table. "Can you get me some juice?"

Ruth smiled at him. "Sure I can." She went to the icebox and pulled out an orange. She rolled it back and forth on the kitchen counter to get the juices flowing. "What are you doing today?" she asked.

"I dunno. Maybe I'll go to Billy's house. We might go down to the lake and play around."

"That sounds fun."

"Are you working with Mother?"

Ruth smiled coyly, squeezing the orange as hard as possible into the cup, "Yes, we can't all be on vacation all summer, now can we?"

Lorne shrugged and took a bite of his eggs. Ruth finished the dishes, dried them and put them back in the cupboards.

Edith left the house and went out. She met with a group of ladies from the church that got together once a week to pray—and, Ruth figured, to gossip. She spent the morning and part of the afternoon washing every floor in the house, sweeping and beating the rugs and polishing every spindle on the stairway. Once finished, she went to the yard to collect her laundry. It was drying on the line. She saw her bag near the wash basin. As she worked, she replayed the visit with her Grandma over and over in her mind.

Suddenly, she felt a knot in her stomach. She rushed over to the bag and opened the small pocket on the side. It was gone! The picture was gone!

"How dare she!" Ruth seethed.

She pulled each skirt, each blouse and each pair of underwear off the line. She folded them and made a pile on the lawn chair. This—this was by far the lowest of the low. Had Edith taken the picture intentionally? Had she hidden it? Destroyed it? Ruth stopped folding. She looked around her dad's beautiful garden. Perhaps she had missed it. She went back to the bag and flipped it inside out. She ran her hand in and out of the pocket again and again. No, it was definitely gone. Ruth exhaled loudly and put her hands on her hips. *Just wait 'til she gets home . . .*

She folded the sheets and the remaining clothes with incredible fury. When they were done, she carried her clothes up to her room. Once upstairs, she began to look around her room. Perhaps Edith had brought the photo up to her room for safekeeping. She tried to think positively. She opened her wardrobe and pushed the clothes aside to see if it lay on the bottom of the cupboard. Nothing. She opened the drawer and leafed through her underclothes. Nothing. She went to her bedside table and looked under the books and in the drawer. Nothing. She even looked under her pillow and mattress to see if it had been hidden there. Nothing. She put away the rest of her clothes and then went onto the upstairs landing. Lorne's door was to the left. The family bathroom to the right and her parent's bedroom was straight across the hall. Should she go in and look? She never went in their bedroom. It was hard to imagine going in and actually looking through drawers and cupboards. She stood there, frozen, trying to decide.

The front door creaked open. Ruth took a deep breath and came down the stairs.

"Hello, *Mutter*," she said icily.

Edith looked up, startled. "Oh, hello. I thought you were in the yard."

"Yes. I was."

She looked around. "The floors look okay . . . did you scrub on hands and knees?"

Ruth crossed her arms across her chest. "Yes."

Edith put her handbag on the bench near the door. "Did you get everything else done that I asked you?"

"*Ja.*"

She walked through the living room and into the kitchen. She pulled a glass from the cupboard and filled it with water from the tap. She took a long drink. "Well thank you then."

"I even folded the laundry."

"Oh. That's good."

"And put it away."

Edith looked puzzled. "That's fine, child."

"And," she hesitated before completing her sentence, "it seems that you may have misplaced something that belongs to me."

Edith stared into her cup. "Oh?"

Ruth stepped forward, shaking her fist. "Don't 'oh' at me, Mother! You know perfectly well what I'm talking about!"

Edith was astounded. "Child! You don't shake your fist at me. I am your mother! Show some respect!"

Ruth snapped back, "You weren't always my mother!"

Edith slammed the glass down on the counter. "Watch yourself."

Ruth's arms were straight at her sides, her fists clenched. Her jaw was tight and anger pulsed through her, spilling out into the space between her and her stepmother. "That was a gift. A gift from *my* Grandma. You had no right to take it."

She was silent for a while, her hands firmly planted on her hips. "I don't know what you're talking about."

Ruth shook her head, tears starting to flow. "She gave me a picture. The only picture I've ever had!"

"Hmmm."

Ruth was outraged. "Hmmm?" She turned on her heel and left the kitchen. She wiped her tears away. "Argh!" She stomped up the stairs, slamming each foot down on every tread. "I," slam, "hate," slam, "you!" She crashed her bedroom door shut. "Oh," she seethed, "I hate you!"

She paced back and forth across her room, fuming. *How dare she! How dare she take that photo! And what has she done with it?* "I am so angry!" she proclaimed to her four walls. "I cannot believe I didn't think to unpack my bag myself! How could I have been so careless? Of course she's going to nab the photo . . . she's done something with all of the photos in the garage. Who else would have pulled the photos out of the albums? Father?" She sat down on her bed and tried to breathe deeply. "In and out," she coaxed herself. "Calm down. Think rationally. How can I get it back from her?"

She sat for nearly an hour, tracing her finger over the stitches on her quilt, mentally rehearsing her next move with Edith. Finally, she went downstairs. She looked through the kitchen window. Edith was in the backyard pulling the clothespins off the line and putting them in a small silver pail.

Ruth braced herself and opened the back door. She walked outside slowly and as calmly as she could. Edith looked up at her and said nothing. Ruth sat down in the lawn chair. She stared at Edith—boring holes in her with her intensity of emotion. Edith carried on removing the clothespins. When each and every one had found its way into the pail, Edith took it inside and placed it inside the back door. She came back out and wound up the laundry line. She hung it on a peg in the garage.

The silence was as deep and wide as the ocean.

Finally, Ruth said, "Why is this such a forbidden topic?"

"What?"

"My mother."

"I never said that it was." Edith shrugged, "It just has ended up that way."

"Really?" Ruth said, skepticism lacing her voice. "I mean, really? You've never suggested that it was too hard for you to talk about? I find that hard to believe."

Edith rolled her eyes. "Honestly, the way you talk . . ."

"Truthfully?"

Edith turned to her stepdaughter, her hands on her hips. "Rudely."

"How did she die?"

"You already know this . . . in childbirth."

"Yes," Ruth was exasperated, "but how?"

"I don't know."

"Rubbish," Ruth muttered. "Why can't I have a photo of her, a memento? Surely, Dad kept something of hers. Why can't it be mine?"

"Material things don't replace a person who has died."

"I'm not saying that it does . . . but it can help someone grieve."

Edith shook her head and spat out the words, "You don't need to grieve, you never knew the woman. It's like saying that *I* need to grieve. One only needs to grieve a relationship one has lost."

"I have lost a relationship," Ruth said quietly, "I've lost a chance to know my mother."

"I am your mother."

"I mean my *real* mother." Ruth's words stung Edith.

Edith turned away and grabbed a broom that was leaning against the garage. She began to sweep the path with a vengeance. "You've made this all into such a fantasy, Ruth—you read too much. It's not all romance and heartache. You need to realize that you never knew your mother and you should be grateful for what you have."

Ruth stood up. "I'm not! I just want to know who she was! What was she like?"

"What difference does it make?" Edith asked, her voice raising its pitch.

"It makes a difference to me! Why am I the way I am? What are my aunts and uncles like? My cousins? Everyone else I know has a big extended family—people they can count on, grandparents!"

"You have your Aunt Lilly," she retorted.

"And I love her dearly, but I want more."

Edith looked her square in the eyes. "That's the problem with you, Ruth. You're never satisfied. You always want more. Stop worrying about a woman who died fifteen years ago. Stop thinking about this remarkable family you've lost and start realizing that it's all just rubbish! You have a family—me, your father, Lorne! You have everything you need right here—and more! Stop daydreaming about how it could have been if your mother had lived and start living in reality!" Edith shook the broom as she made her point.

Ruth inhaled through clenched teeth, "Oh! You'll never understand! Just tell me, where is the picture?"

"I can't say that I know."

"Argh!" Ruth kicked over the lawn chair in a rage. "I can't stand you! You say you want to be my mother and yet all you ever do is tell me what I'm doing wrong! You've always said that I'm not good enough! Just give me the picture!"

"I'm done." Edith set the broom down and walked inside. She shut the door behind her.

Ruth took a few deep breaths, tried to calm herself and then followed her. She opened the back door. Edith was standing at the sink, looking out at the yard.

"I am going to rip this house apart and find it," Ruth threatened.

Edith whirled around. "Oh no you're not, young lady. And I've had just about enough from you."

"And I've had enough from you!"

Edith slammed her hand down on the counter. "That's enough! One more word from you and you can bet that you will be off to reform school before you can utter the word 'Mother' one more time."

"Argh!" Ruth ran out the front door. She slammed it as hard as she could behind her. It was hopeless. She took off running down the road, over the railroad tracks and on to the lake. She cried as she ran. She let the tears roll freely over her cheeks.

As she ran, she moaned, "God, why does this have to be so difficult? I just want a sense of my history! I just want to know my Lessing family!"

With a sob she asked, "Why does Edith hate me?"

The lake came into view. The water lapped the shoreline calmly, softly in contrast to her inner turbulence. Ruth felt so alone, so broken. She felt no quiet whisper from her heavenly father as she had in the past. She felt no comfort, no peace. She only felt loss. Enormous loss at what she had never known. All she wanted was to grieve for her mother. She wanted a sense of belonging, a sense of identity. She felt nothing, only emptiness.

"Where are you?" Ruth asked as she looked up at the sky, sobbing. "And who am I?"

*"Do not boast about
tomorrow for you do not
know what a day may
bring forth."*
Proverbs 27: 1 NAS

October 1939
Gunner Mine, Manitoba

"How are my two favorite Swedes?"

Waldemar and Gus looked up from their dinner plates. "Oh hello, Mr. Magnusson."

"How's the meal today?" Mr. Magnusson plopped his tray down on the table and sat down across from them. "Good as always?"

Waldemar smiled, "Yes, sir. Always fresh and tasty."

"They treat us like kings here," Gus laughed, "as if they need us to stay!"

"Well," Mr. Magnusson said as he began to shovel his food into his mouth, "well not only do we find gold, we power most of northern Manitoba! I'd say we're pretty useful."

Waldemar had taken a job at Gunner Mine a little over a year ago. After the incident with the fire, he had made amends with Victor. He stayed to sort out the affairs on the farm and rebuild the hayrack. Following that, he had gone to work for a contractor. A month later, Waldemar insisted on his pay at which point the contractor admitted he never intended to pay him. He had already spent the pay. Waldemar was furious. He wrote a letter to Gus explaining his situation. Gus invited him to come to the mine, promising that he would find him something to do.

It was a long, three-day walk to get there. Waldemar and a good friend, Ray, traveled together. They walked under the power lines where the bush was cleared. It made for easy travel. Alina had packed plenty of sandwiches for the trip, however, all of them had disappeared within the first two days. At night, he and Ray ate porridge and hot tea to keep away the chill. They slept in the open night air using their packs as pillows.

It had been bittersweet to leave. This time, now that he was twenty-one, he knew that he wouldn't be returning. His mamma cried as he left, saying that life on the farm wouldn't be the same without his smiling face. He assured her that he and Gus would come and visit as often as they could. All the same, everyone knew that this time he was leaving for good.

Waldemar worked alongside Gus doing various plumbing jobs until he eventually was given a spot in the boiler room. The boiler was the size of a train's steam engine. In the boiler room, attached to the wall were all of the mechanisms that ran with steam. Waldemar needed to maintain the pressure gauges. The steam travelled to the nearest town site, providing power. He worked the night shift and quickly got the hang of how to clean the ashes from the boiler while keeping the pressure steady.

"How's Houston's daughters?" Mr. Magnusson asked, snapping Waldemar out of his thoughts.

Waldemar laughed, "They're good."

Mr. Magnusson winked, "You keepin' them good company, *ja*?"

"We made our last trip out to the island about a month ago. Now it's getting too cold to socialize. I'll have to wait until next summer."

Gus slapped Waldemar on the shoulder. "Always a ladies' man, this *bror* of mine."

Waldemar rolled his eyes. "That is not true."

"Tell me then," Gus teased, "how many girlfriends have you had?"

"Wait," Mr. Magnusson interrupted, "let me guess." He surveyed Waldemar. "Tall, blonde hair . . . nice-looking Swede . . . I'd say at least a dozen."

Waldemar shook his head and took a bite of his supper.

"More!" Gus prodded Waldemar. "How many do you have right now? Waiting for you? Two? Three?"

Waldemar shrugged. "I didn't make any promises. Lorraine sends me letters and photos every month but it's not serious. I love a good game of baseball more than I love her."

Mr. Magnusson patted Waldemar's arm from across the table. "Just giving you a hard time. You and Gus here are the only single fellows at the mine. We've got to hear all about the girlfriends you've got. Us married men don't have too much excitement. We eat, sleep and breathe gold. We've got to have some entertainment. Bettin' on which of you is going to marry a Houston girl—that's a gamble I'm willing to wager."

Waldemar shook his head again. "I'm not planning to marry any time soon."

"And why is that?" Gus asked. "There's plenty of girls chasing after you. Even up here at the mine. The only two single girls that come to visit are both after you."

"First of all," Waldemar leaned back in his chair and pushed his meal tray aside, "the girls are the boss' daughters. I am simply a good host, but I do not want to marry either one of them. The girls at home . . . they think that I'm interested, but the first weekend that I ditch them for a good ball game or curling tournament . . . well then they're on to someone else. I like the kind of girls who know that my love of sports comes first, someone who can keep up with me swimming in the river. Someone who likes to have a good time but who isn't too wrapped up in the idea of marriage."

"He's been looking in Pinawa Bay," Gus added. "Nearly every weekend he walks into town to find a girl to take for dinner and a dance."

"Well," Waldemar said defensively, "it's better than sitting around here wasting my time on booze and gambling."

Mr. Magnusson whispered across the table, "I've been a miner for a long, long time, Waldemar. I've seen a lot of things." He tapped his temple. "I know a lot of things. One day you'll be looking for a girl to settle down with."

"Well that isn't now." Waldemar stood up from the table. "Besides, Houston's daughters won't be back until next summer so we don't need to be worrying about this."

Gus chuckled, "All in good fun, Waldy."

Waldemar walked away. "See you in the barracks."

He dumped his tray and dishes into a bin that was headed for the kitchen. He pushed open the dining hall door and walked through the night back to the bunkhouses. They were large, military-style buildings full of rows and rows of bunks. The unmarried men and the married men whose wives lived offsite all slept here. He and Gus slept opposite one another.

Waldemar sat down on his bunk. He sighed. There wasn't much to do in the evenings other than drink with the other miners. He thought of his family. He wondered how Victor was managing with all of his fall duties. Harvest was a busy time. He never had been as good as Waldemar at negotiating livestock and grain. Waldemar hoped that he had received a fair price for his goods. He pulled out a pen and pencil from under his pillow. With all these things on his mind, he began to write.

October 13, 1939
Dearest Mamma,

> *How are you? I am doing well. Work is steady. I continue to work nights in the boiler room. It is a strange existence, working all night, sleeping through the morning and into the afternoon. Gus and I always share our evening meal—breakfast for me and dinner for him.*
>
> *The food here is good, there is always an endless choice of delicious pies and tasty food, but nothing beats your cooking. I miss eating your fresh bread late at night by the well.*
>
> *How was your harvest this year? How are things on the farm? How are Victor and Pappa managing? Have you sold any livestock this year? How are Mr. McLeod and Mr. Hansen? Tell them I said hello. I hope that they are helping you with your maintenance needs around the farm. Tell Mr. McLeod he owes me a game of checkers when I'm home.*
>
> *Have many of the young men in Lac Du Bonnet signed up to go overseas? Are you frightened of the war? I hear we may have rations soon. I hope the farm will sustain you. I imagine there will be more jobs as our local men go overseas. It's hard to believe there is a war going on when we are so secluded in the bush out here. We are in our own little world here, living and breathing Gold.*
>
> *Gus and I are thinking of coming home for Christmas. Houston says I've been here long enough to take a break over the holidays. We might be able to be home for a day or two depending on the weather. We may be able to hire some horses in town and ride down. It will be interesting to see the changes at the farm and in the town since I've been gone.*

I hope the children are well, I am sending $10 for you to purchase the things you need for Christmastime. Tell Sing, Marg and Doug I said hello and give my regards to Pappa and Victor.

Love to you, Waldemar

He folded up the letter and put it in an envelope. He sealed it shut and addressed the outside. After changing into his work clothes, he walked to the mailbox. He dropped the letter in.

"And now," he said to himself, "it's time to work."

He went to the boiler room and spoke to the fellow who was coming off the day shift. Then he checked all the pressure gauges on the wall. A few were low. He loaded wood into the fire to raise the temperature. All night he kept his vigil of the pressure versus the heat of the fire. Logs went in and ashes came out. Finally, the sun rose and the day shift fellow returned, accompanied by a supervisor.

"Good morning, Mr. Pettersson."

"Good morning."

The supervisor nodded at the day shift worker who began to take over for Waldemar.

"I'd like to take a walk with you."

Waldemar shrugged. "That would be fine."

The two men walked away from the boiler and down the path to the bunkhouses.

"I've noticed that we never have any pressure issues on the boiler when you're on duty," the supervisor began.

"Yes, sir."

"I'm impressed," he said.

"Thank you."

"You've only been here for a short time," he paused, looking at Waldemar, "and you've never been licensed, but I'm ready to promote you to the crusher."

Waldemar stopped walking and turned to the supervisor. "Really?"

"Yes. The pay is better—and the working conditions are a little easier. No night shifts."

"Oh, that would be great."

"Well then," the supervisor put out his hand, "I think we have a new crusher employee."

Waldemar shook his hand. "Thank you very much."

They continued to walk toward the bunkhouses. "Take today off. Rest and recover from your night shift. Tomorrow morning report to the crusher for your training."

"Yes, sir. I'll do that, sir."

The supervisor patted Waldemar on the back. "You and your brother are an asset to the mine. Good, hard-working men. I like that about you."

"Thank you, sir. I won't let you down."

*

Five months later, Waldemar's crusher job had become as easy as breathing. Bins of ore came from underground. Waldemar loaded them into the crusher. From the crusher he moved the ore onto a conveyer belt that carried it into the mill to be refined. He worked the day shift during the week and around the clock on weekends. This allowed his married co-worker to go into town and see his wife.

After his shift, he went to the dining hall to meet Gus for the evening meal.

Gus sat with Mr. Magnusson. They were already eating. Waldemar waved at them, grabbed a tray of food and sat down to join them.

"How's my favorite Swede?" Waldemar asked jokingly to Mr. Magnusson.

Mr. Magnusson looked up, his eyes watering. His face was pale grey. "Not too well."

Waldemar's eyebrows knitted together. "What's wrong?"

"I'm not feeling well."

Gus added, "He's been sick for some time but this morning he woke up feeling worse than before."

"It's the cough," Mr. Magnusson started to say just before he broke into a fit of coughing. He took a drink of water and exhaled slowly. "I'm telling you. It's the life of a miner."

"I'm sure it will pass," Waldemar said reassuringly.

Mr. Magnusson began another fit of coughing.

Gus and Waldemar ate their supper in silence. Mr. Magnusson closed his eyes and covered his face with his hands.

"I knew this would happen one day," he wheezed.

"What?" Gus said quietly.

"I started as a miner . . . a long time ago. Good money. Better than anything else you can do. That way you can have a better life for your wife . . . your children."

He went silent for a few minutes. Waldemar and Gus just watched him, his eyes welling up with tears.

"The mineral dust, the cyanide, it'll get into your lungs and it'll kill you. Mark my words. It may seem like good money now but all the money in the world won't bring you back from the grave."

Gus and Waldemar both shook their heads. "I'm sure you'll be fine," Gus soothed.

"It's probably just a cold," Waldemar added. "You'll be feeling better in a few days."

Mr. Magnusson looked at both of them. "Listen to me, Petterssons. I want you to get out of here. I've grown to like you fellows. I don't want you to be in my shoes in twenty-five years. *Ja*, you think this is a good life . . . but it won't last. I've seen it before. Lots of the miners die from this . . . their lungs go bad. I don't want that to happen to you two."

Gus and Waldemar finished up their supper in silence while Mr. Magnusson breathed heavily on the opposite side of the table.

He spoke in Swedish, "*Tack,* please. Listen to me. I want you to leave the mine."

They pushed back their trays. They looked at their good friend. "Okay . . . we'll think about it."

"If I die," Mr. Magnusson began another fit of coughing, "will you go? Will that convince you?"

The walk back to the bunkhouses was quiet. Both Waldemar and Gus were thinking about what Mr. Magnusson had said. The problem was that there weren't any other jobs that paid as well. With Germany's invasion of Poland, there had been a slight increase in teaching and other city jobs but they didn't pay anything close to what they made at the mine.

"Maybe we could join the army," Gus said at last.

"We could."

"I'm tired of the mine anyway. I've been here for a long time. I'm ready for a change."

"I suppose."

"I know this is good money . . . but . . ."

"I know," Waldemar agreed to his brother's unspoken words. "It's not the first time we've heard of a miner getting a sickness in his lungs."

Gus put his hand to his chest. "We need to start our lives. I'm a lot older than you. It's time I start looking for a wife . . . a career . . . a family."

*"For I know the plans I
have for you," declares the
Lord, "plans to prosper you
and not to harm you, plans
to give you hope and a
future. Then you will call
upon me and come and pray
to me, and I will listen to
you." Jeremiah 29: 11 &
12 NIV*

April 1940
Winnipeg, Manitoba

Waldemar sat on the plane with Carl, a friend from the mine, and Gus on the way to Winnipeg. Carl and Gus had decided to check out the possibility of enlisting in the Air Force. Waldemar had spent the last few months corresponding with the RCMP. Inspired by his boyhood dream of being a Mountie, he had decided to take the step and apply. It would be a cut in pay from mining and require some serious sacrifices over the next few years, but Waldemar felt a deep sense that the RCMP was where his future lay.

Mr. Magnusson had indeed grown sicker. He left the mine a few weeks after he had developed his cough. Friends of his had reported that his condition was serious. With Mr. Magnusson's warning in mind, Waldemar had decided to write the letter to Winnipeg and express his interest in enlisting in the RCMP. He had given Gunner Gold Mine one-month's notice and then Gus, Carl and he boarded the plane to Winnipeg.

He read over the letter he had received from the RCMP as they made the trip. It was on official letterhead. It read:

Ottawa, March 27, 1940
Canada

Mr. Waldemar W. Peterson,
Beresford Lake, Man.

Dear Sir:

1. *With reference to recent correspondence in connection with your application to join this Force on the understanding that you will volunteer for service with the No. 1 Provost Company presently in England with the First Division, if you are still desirous of engaging under these conditions, you should report at your own risk and expense to the RCM Police offices at WINNIPEG. Should you fail to pass the medical examination or not prove suitable, it will be necessary for you to pay your own return transportation, as this Department cannot accept any responsibility in the case of applicants who are rejected. The period of engagement is for five years.*

2. *You will understand that your medical examination will include an X-ray examination of your chest, which, if you pass successfully, will both qualify you for service with this Force and the Provost Company.*

3. *Your engagement can only be made provided you are still a single man. If you are now married, please advise this office accordingly. In connection with marriage, it is pointed out that should you be engaged in the Force you will be unable to obtain permission to marry until you have completed seven years' service, and this must be clearly understood. Should you marry after your transfer to the Provost Company of the Canadian Active Service Forces, upon your return to Canada you will not be continued in the RCMP. Your discharge from the RCMP would also follow if you transfer from the Provost Company during your service with the CASF.*

4. *An application form for engagement is attached in order that you may be aware of the rates of pay. Your engagement, provided of course you are accepted, will be in the capacity of a Third Class Constable at a salary of $1.50 per diem, which is subject to 5% deduction to be applied toward a Pension Fund for widows and dependants.*

5. *It is the Commissioner's intention that all applicants who are given the opportunity of engaging in this Force with the proviso that they join the Provost Company will, so far as possible, receive their Recruits' Training in Regina, which is looked upon as a six-months probationary period to determine their suitability for the Force.*

6. *The general policy in peace time concerning those engaged in the Force is to transfer them after they have completed their period of training to whatever point their services may be required, but never to their home Provinces.*

7. *Please advise this office and the RCM Police office at WINNIPEG by return mail if it is your intention to present yourself. If no reply is received from you within a reasonable time, it will be presumed that you are no longer desirous of engaging and another selection will be made.*

8. *The undermentioned documents are required to complete your file, and must be taken with you when reporting for engagement: birth Certificate, two references and proof as to vaccination.*

Yours truly,
FA Blake A/Supt. Adjutant.

Waldemar read the greeting on the letter: Waldemar Peterson. They copied his name off his birth certificate as Peterson, rather than Pettersson. When Otto and Alina had immigrated, their names had been written down as Peterson. Since they didn't speak a word of English, the error had gone unnoticed. Waldemar had meant to correct his birth certificate but it was a long, involved process that he had never got around to doing.

Oh well, he thought, *I suppose it makes little difference now.* Waldemar looked over the letter and thought about what all this would mean—the

Provost Company. The Provost Company did military-style policing overseas. He looked over the pay guide and shook his head.

The plane jolted as it hit the runway. Waldemar momentarily gripped the armrests of the seat. They came to a stop on the runway and after a few minutes, the pilot came out and opened the steps down to the tarmac.

"Safe travels, gentlemen," the pilot said to his passengers as they disembarked.

"Thank you," Waldemar responded to the pilot. He looked up at the clear blue sky and stretched. "Back to the real world!"

Gus turned to Carl as they waited to get their bags off the plane, "We're going to Mary's. I'll speak to you in a couple days, then we'll go down to the drafting office and see what we can find out about the Air Force."

"That sounds good," Carl answered. "I'm looking forward to seeing Clara and Missy again." Carl had a wife and daughter waiting for him in Saint Bonaface, just outside of Winnipeg.

"Say hi to your family for me." Gus shook Carl's hand. The Pettersson brothers parted ways with Carl.

Waldemar turned to Gus. "You know the way to Mary's?"

Mary, the second-eldest Pettersson child, ran a boarding house in Winnipeg.

"Yes. We'll get a taxi—once we drop our bags off we can go out and celebrate our freedom from the mine."

"That sounds great." Waldemar looked happily at his older brother, "Do you think Mary will be happy to see us?"

"I'm sure!" Gus laughed. "She's always got a cot for her brothers."

Mary was indeed happy to see her younger brothers. She set up cots in her basement and told them that they could stay as long as they needed. After several days of celebrating at pool halls, and undergoing some vaccinations, medical checkups and entrance exams that were required, Waldemar met up with a girlfriend. Over the last few days she had joined him in his celebrations.

He and Lorraine had known each other from Lac Du Bonnet. She had written him while he was up at the mine and frequently sent photos of herself that he could hang on his bunk. Lorraine was hopeful that Waldemar was ready to commit to more, now that he was done working at the mine. Her father was an RCMP officer and she knew that Waldemar had six months to change his mind about enlistment. She hoped that she could be the one waiting when he decided it wasn't for him.

This morning, Waldemar received a call at Mary's telling him to come down to the RCMP office so they could finish processing his application. He quickly phoned Lorraine and asked her to meet him at a local restaurant for lunch. He spotted her leaning against the building, waiting for him.

"Hello!" he called.

"Hi, Waldemar!" She grinned and waved excitedly.

He hugged her. The two went in and sat down to lunch together. He studied her across the table. She was beautiful. She had a fair complexion, brown hair and brown eyes, a few freckles on her nose and a great smile.

After some small talk, Waldemar cleared his throat and began in on the reason he had arranged this meeting: "I'm going in to finish enlistment today so I wanted to say goodbye."

Waldemar smiled at Lorraine, reached across the table and took her hands in his own.

"You know you have six months to change your mind and bow out, right?"

"I know, but I'm leaving to Regina next week and I'm afraid that will be the end of 'us.'"

"This doesn't have to be goodbye, we can stay in touch. Just like we did while you were at the mine." She paused, looking into his eyes. "Maybe you'll change your mind about the RCMP."

"You're looking for a husband and I'm not going to be him. You know the Force doesn't allow you to marry for seven years. I don't want you to wait for me, it isn't fair to you."

She smiled coyly. "You're worth waiting for."

"We can keep in touch," he sighed, "but I want to be clear that I don't have marriage on my mind right now. I care about you. I might be a different man in seven years. I could be anywhere at that time. I don't want to leave any false promises."

"I know, Waldy. You're a free spirit." She let go of his hands and brushed her brown curls from her face. "We'll keep in touch and see what happens." She straightened up matter-of-factly and began to eat.

After they had finished lunch, Waldemar embraced her and kissed her on the cheek. They walked out of the restaurant hand in hand.

He looked into her eyes. "It's been fun, Lorraine, really, and I've had a great time re-connecting with you this week."

"You too, Waldy," she looked up at him, "I'll write to you in Regina and when you make up your mind I'll be here."

"I guess," he brushed her hair away from her face, cupping her chin in his hand, "we can be friends, right?"

"Sure. Goodbye then, friend." She gave him one last kiss, and walked down the street in the opposite direction. She didn't turn around but gave one last wave as she walked. Her hips swayed side to side in her trendy skirt.

"Jeez." Waldemar shook his head and ran his hands through his hair. Lorraine was sweet but he knew this wasn't the time in his life for a woman. Women were complicated and he was not. Like she had said, he was a free spirit.

He headed down to the RCMP office to check on the status of his enlistment. He entered Headquarters and asked for the recruitment officer. Waldemar expected to talk more about the recruitment process but instead he found himself being sworn in, taking the oath as a new officer.

"I, Waldemar Peterson, solemnly swear that I will faithfully, diligently and impartially execute and perform the duties required of me as a member of the Royal Canadian Mounted Police, and will well and truly obey and perform all lawful orders and instructions that I receive as such, without fear, favor or affection of or toward any person. So help me God."

The Officer shook Waldemar's hand. "It's official. You're going to be Third Class Constable Peterson. Welcome to the Royal Canadian Mounted Police."

"Thank you," Waldemar said, astounded. "It's my honor."

"I've got your tickets here for the train tomorrow, late afternoon. You'll be off to Regina for training. You'll hear about your posting to the Provost Company. Do you have any questions?"

"No, sir. I just need to go home and get my things together."

"Good luck then."

"Yes, sir." Waldemar left the office and took a taxi back to Mary's. He had no idea that things were going to move so quickly. He expected to have a few weeks before training began. As he sat in the back of the taxi, he thought about the next few days. He'd have to write Mamma and tell her that he was leaving the province.

The taxi pulled up in front of Mary's boarding house. Waldemar stepped out.

"That'll be three bits," the taxi driver spoke.

"Thank you." Waldemar paid the taxi driver and turned toward the house. Mary was waiting on the front step.

"Hello," she called.

"Hi, Mary!" Waldemar came up next to her with a big smile on his face. "You'll never guess who's a Third Class Constable."

"You? You're official?"

"Yes, they swore me in this afternoon. I have a train ticket for tomorrow at 4:30 to Regina!"

"You're kidding! Well won't Mamma and Pappa be thrilled to hear!"

"Speaking of Mamma, I need to write the family on the farm and let them know."

"You had better get organized if you're going to make your train tomorrow. I'll go get your laundry from the yard."

"Thanks, Mary!"

Mary helped Waldemar pack his things. The next day, Waldemar took his suitcases and headed out the door. He hailed a taxi to the train station.

Once on the train, Waldemar looked out the window at the Manitoba landscape. This was the beginning of a whole new chapter.

*

Waldemar stepped off the train in Regina. He was met by an officer who took him by car to the RCMP Training Headquarters where he needed to check in. Training would be in Regina from April until August followed by practical working experience and then further training.

The officer who greeted him took him to the main reception office. The officer said, "This is Waldemar Peterson reporting for training."

"Welcome, Peterson," the other officer spoke to Waldemar. "Let me see here," he looked down a long list of recruits that were arriving. "Says here you're going to be part of the Provost Company. You'll be on the third floor of the barracks. I've got another recruit here. The two of you can go down to the Quartermaster and get your supplies. Once you have your supplies, go up to your barracks. Most of the recruits will be checking in on Monday so you and the other recruit will have some of your own time on the weekend. Understood?"

"Yes, sir." Waldemar turned around and saw the other recruit sitting on a bench. He had a stunned expression on his face. Waldemar walked up and stuck out his hand. "Hi there, I'm Waldemar Peterson."

"Jimmy Wright, pleasure to meet you."

"Do you know where the Quartermaster is?"

"No, but let's take a walk and we can see if we can find it."

The two young men walked around the training facility. It didn't take long to find the Quartermaster, situated in one of the only buildings that were open. There was also a swimming pool, a mess hall, a chapel and stables.

The Quartermaster methodically pulled out all of the supplies that were to be issued to Jimmy and Waldemar. He threw them at their feet as they waited. The men received all of the uniforms and clothing that they would wear during training, as well as toothbrushes, toiletries, socks, shoes and a bedroll. Everything was standard issue and came with a large duffel bag to stuff it all into.

"Excuse me," Jimmy asked the Quartermaster, "can you point us in the direction of the barracks?"

"Ronald will show you around," the Quartermaster answered. "Ronald!"

A young boy, no more than sixteen, came out of the back room and assessed the new recruits. He had a camera around his neck.

"Howdy," he said.

"Hi there," Jimmy and Waldemar answered.

"I'm Ron. I'm the official trumpeter in the band. I'll show you around."

"Thanks," Waldemar said.

Jimmy and Waldemar packed up all of their new belongings, took their suitcases from home and followed Ronald to their barracks. It was a three-storey brick building that matched the other buildings on the property. Ronald showed Jimmy and Waldemar up to the third floor. He opened a big metal door and waved his arm at the large, empty room.

"Here it is, fellas, not too much but you can make yourselves comfortable."

"Thanks."

Jimmy looked around and scowled.

Waldemar was quiet, taking it all in. The room was cavernous. There were rows and rows of white, metal spring beds. Waldemar noticed that there was no shortage of roaches scuttling about.

"Not too fancy," Ronald interrupted Waldemar's thoughts, "but it'll feel like home soon enough."

Waldemar and Jimmy laid out their bedrolls and set out some of their clothes and personal items. Above each bed there was a shelf and some pegs to hang their clothes. Waldemar placed his tall boots, Serge and hat on the shelf. Jimmy stretched out on his new bed. Waldemar sat down.

"Here, say cheese!" Ronald held up his camera. He took a photo of the two newest RCMP recruits. "I'll make you a copy so you can remember this great day."

"Thanks," Waldemar smiled. The springs on the bed creaked with his every movement. "Hey, where can we eat?"

"Everything is closed until Monday on the base here but you can head into the city. There are some good restaurants where you can get a bite to eat."

"All right then, let's go." Jimmy rose from his squeaky, uncomfortable bed and the three men headed out for supper.

Waldemar took the streetcar with Jimmy and Ron into town. He thought about what he had got himself into. There was a six-month probation period where he could bow out if it wasn't what he wanted. He knew he always had a job at Gunner Gold Mine. Houston had told him as much when he left. There was always the army or the Air Force too. He wanted to give this a fair try. He had always seen himself in the scarlet serge, the blue serge breeches, the long boots, jack spurs and the brown gauntlets. Now here he was. Ready to begin. He thought of Sgt. Nicholson for a moment and gave a little smile.

"My soul is in anguish.
How long, O Lord, how
long?" Psalm 6:3 NIV

March 1941
Leduc, Alberta

It was a mild winter day. The sun shone through the window. Ruth
stood in her childhood bedroom packing her clothing and personal items.
She looked around once more, taking a deep breath and processing the
moment. It was finally time. She was leaving home and starting the spring
session of nursing school. She had spent the last year-and-a-half since
graduation waiting for this moment.

It had certainly been a year of mixed emotions. Because of the war,
things were hard for everyone. The depression was over but life hadn't got
any easier. Many of her young schoolmates had gone off to war. Some had
even been killed. The community was in fear of who might enlist next.

Tension ran high between different immigrant groups. Germans, like
herself, were ostracized from the community. Because of this, they stuck
together in social and religious groups. Ruth could never figure out what
people thought she had to do with Hitler, but people were fearful and
fear made people think stupid things. Artrude had moved to Winnipeg.
She missed her confidant. Artrude was practically a sister. She had other
good friends through school and church social circles but none as dear as
Artrude.

The dating scene was sparse. There weren't as many young men to
choose from. Ruth, however, had met a nice young man from Edmonton,
Nick Schellenburg, and the two were seeing each other casually. He had

come down from Edmonton on occasion with friends. They had all gone to movies together in order to escape thoughts of the war. Father and Mother approved of Nick because they were friends with the Schellenburgs, a nice German Baptist family.

Ruth had taken voice lessons with Mrs. Carmichael for the last year, once a week. Every Tuesday after supper, she took the bus to Edmonton and then had an hour of lessons before meeting up with friends from Central Baptist Church. Mrs. Carmichael said that Ruth had a voice of an angel and was determined to get her into the Chicago Opera. Ruth had seriously considered this but the thought of being so far away from home and the lifestyle of an opera star were less than desirable to her. She had wanted to attend university. She had asked Father but he had said no, that young women did not attend university, especially during a war. Nursing seemed to be the most practical option. And so for the last six months, Ruth had worked on the application process. She had been interviewed by her doctor, to see if she had the potential to be a nurse. Ruth had chosen a family doctor, Dr. Shumaker, from Edmonton who would sponsor her throughout her residency. Herman and Edith had to drive up to Edmonton to be interviewed by the nursing school as well, which they had gladly done. After letters of reference from high school, the final request was fulfilled and Ruth was accepted into the Miseracordia School of Nursing under probationary terms for the first nine months.

Ruth had also filled her last year since high school graduation doing music theory, teaching Sunday school, acting as the president of the Young Peoples Group and spending time finding ways to help others in her community. She was never idle and avoided being at home as much as possible.

She looked around her room once more. Her childhood doll Rosalie sat on her dressing table.

"Well, this is it, Rosalie, I'm finally leaving." Ruth picked up the well-loved doll and held her close for a moment. "I'll come back and tell you all of the exciting things I've done." Ruth smiled at the doll and placed her gently back down on the dressing table. "So long, dear friend."

There were a few things she would miss. This—her childhood refuge, her room and her rocking chair where she had sat with her father on so many occasions—this is what she would miss.

She shut the door gently behind her and went downstairs where her father was waiting.

"Hello, *Vati*." Ruth smiled at her father.

"Hello, Ruth, are you ready?" he asked in German.

"I think so. I've got all my things." Her eyes swept around the living room. "It's hard to believe the day is finally here. It's exciting, isn't it?"

"Exciting and sad for this old man I'm afraid." He smiled at her. "I'll miss you."

"I'll miss you too. I will still see you once a week and I'll call the store if I can."

Herman looked at his daughter. So much had happened in their lives in the last nineteen years. She was a woman now, close to the same age as his Ruth had been when she died. It seemed like a lifetime ago. He could picture his wife when he looked at his daughter now. Now he would be driving her to Edmonton, her new home for the next three years. He would be handing her over to the world. It was almost harder than if she were marrying, at least then she would be under the care of another man, but with this, she was on her own.

"You're beautiful," he said softly. "All grown up."

She smiled at him. "Oh, Dad."

"I'll get your bags." Herman picked up Ruth's suitcases, "let's load up the car."

"Where's Lorne?" Ruth asked.

"He's upstairs," Herman gestured toward the staircase, "go ahead, take a minute and say goodbye."

"I'll be quick." Ruth went upstairs and knocked on Lorne's door. "Lorne?"

"Yes?" Her younger brother called out as he opened the door.

"I'm leaving now, for Edmonton." She smiled at him.

"Okay then, safe travels."

"See you around."

"See you." Lorne watched his sister turn and go back down the stairs.

Ruth went out to the car and sat in the front seat with her father.

"Ready to go?" he asked.

"As ready as I'll ever be. Say goodbye to Mother for me, will you?"

"I will." Herman nodded. Edith had decided to spend the afternoon with some ladies from the church while Herman took the drive.

Herman and Ruth drove the snow-covered highway into Edmonton.

"So," Ruth asked, "how are things at the store?"

Herman cleared his throat and answered, "Good. Busy. I've always got a lot of things to do. Business has really picked up in the last couple years as folks are working again."

"That's good." She looked out the window at the familiar scenery. The same old houses, barns and cows went by.

"If you need anything while you're away, you can always call me at the store. I can bring it up on Wednesdays when I come to do my purchasing."

"Okay. I can't think of anything I'd need . . ."

"I know," he interrupted, "but just in case you do."

Ruth reached out for his hand, looking at the profile of the man she loved so dearly. "I'll be alright, Dad."

"I know you will." He looked straight ahead, his eyes fixed on the road.

Before long, the hospital came into view. Ruth held her breath as her dad drove up. He put the car into park.

"Ready?"

Ruth opened her car door. "Let's go."

Herman went around to the trunk and unloaded Ruth's things. They went inside the hospital's main doors. A kindly nun sent them down the hall to the office of a nun named Sister Saint Christine, the head of year-one residents.

Ruth knocked on the open door of the office, a bag in her other hand. "Hello?"

A young lady with blonde hair pulled tightly into a bun looked up from her desk. She wore a long blue-grey habit. She smiled broadly. "Hello." She stood up from her desk and moved around toward them. She put out her hand. "I'm Sister Saint Christine."

Ruth returned the handshake and said, "Ruth Bohlman and this is my father, Herman."

"Pleasure, Mr. Bohlman, Miss Bohlman. Lovely to have you. Welcome to the Miseracordia School of Nursing. Miss Bohlman, I trust you have your uniforms and are ready to begin your learning."

"Yes, Sister, I am."

She looked at Herman's hands, full of luggage. "I'll take you to the residence where you can unpack your things."

"Thank you." Ruth clasped her bag tightly. "Shall we then?"

The three of them walked to the nurses' residence, a small brick building behind the hospital. Once inside, they walked up the stairs to the second floor. They went through a common room, past the women's facilities, and then they faced four bedroom doors.

"This is your home for the next three years," Sister Saint Christine said warmly pointing to one of the rooms on the left. "You'll be sharing a room with another first-year student."

"Thank you." Ruth smiled at Sister Saint Christine and her father.

"Well," Sister said, "I'll excuse you now. I'll expect to see you in the morning for your first class in the training room. There is a map of the hospital in the welcome package on your desk. I'll be in charge of first years so we'll be seeing a lot of each other."

"I'll look forward to that," Ruth replied.

Sister Saint Christine left, her habit flowing behind her. Herman and Ruth went inside the room. It was small with two single beds and a desk in between. A radiator was under the desk and a window was above it. Near the door there was a closet for each student.

Herman sat down at the desk chair and began to flip through the welcome package.

"Why don't you read it to me while I hang up my clothes in the closet?" she suggested.

"Sure. Says here that the cafeteria is in the main part of the hospital . . . ah, on the main floor."

"I suppose that's most important," she laughed.

He went on to read everything she needed to know about the first year of nursing school. She carefully arranged all of her clothes and personal items in the closet. At last, she looked around satisfied that everything was in its place. She tucked her luggage beneath her bed.

"Well, sweetie, I guess this is it," Herman sighed, speaking in German, "I should be getting back to Leduc before nightfall."

"I guess."

He was reluctant to leave.

"I'll miss you." Ruth took her father's hand.

Herman pulled her close and hugged her, "Goodbye, Ruthie." A tear rolled down his cheek. He quickly wiped it away and pulled away from her. "I just can't believe you're all grown up." He sniffed and blew his nose into his handkerchief. He hesitated, thinking of all the words that her mother had told him to pass on to her. Was now the time? Did she know that this was the hospital where her mother had cradled her against her bosom for the last time? Where she had taken her last breath? Would Ruth walk the ward where her mother had lain? *Oh God, what should I do?* He bowed his head.

She sensed his thoughts were far away, but where? "Chin up, Dad. I'll visit. You won't miss me too much."

"Ah, but that's where you're wrong." Another tear rolled down his cheek as he looked her in the eyes. "I'll miss you for certain."

Ruth hugged her father and then walked him back to the car. The cold March wind whipped at their faces.

"Try to stay out of trouble."

"Trouble?" Ruth laughed, "Never."

Herman chuckled and kissed her cheek. "I love you."

"I love you too. Safe travels."

"Goodbye, *Schatzi*."

Ruth watched him get into the car and start the ignition. He reached for his handkerchief and blew his nose again. He smiled half-heartedly and waved. The car pulled away, the snow moaning as the tires drove over it. Ruth watched him until he was out of sight. She hugged herself. The cold seeped into her bones.

She thought of her father driving back alone. He was such an interesting, complex man, and oh, how she loved him.

Night was falling quickly. As the highway stretched before him, he felt a weight as heavy as steel in the pit of his stomach. This had been his chance to set things straight with his daughter and he had missed the opportunity. He sighed.

"Are you watching Ruth?" he spoke aloud to his first wife. "Do you see her now? Oh what a day . . . so many emotions."

"Our baby girl is all grown up. Nineteen. Can you believe it? Nineteen years since you've been gone. And," he choked out the words, "I miss you even more than ever. As each milestone passes, I long for you to be here to share it with me even more."

The sky was lit with hues of purples and pinks. He thought about that hour he had spent in the residence with his daughter. All the silence he could have filled with stories. Stories of his love, stories of the past . . . everything that her mother had said.

He swore under his breath and pounded his hands against the steering wheel. "This is hard, Ruth, much harder than I thought. I'm so sorry."

"I know what you asked me, I haven't forgotten. I remember your words. I'll never forget the promises I made to you." He thought of his daughter. Her smile, her laugh, the way she moved and talked, little characteristics of her mother.

Night had fallen by the time Herman drove past the town site of Leduc and on to the Fredericksheim Cemetery.

"It's been a long time," he said to himself.

He turned out his headlights to avoid being seen. He parked about 300 yards away. The wind had died down and now snow was softly falling. It was dark out in the country. Only the moonlight lit his way. He came around the backside of the church and came up the slope to the spot where she lay. He brushed the snow off the grey stone. He read the inscription he had chosen so many years ago.

Ruth Lessing
Beloved Wife of
H. F. Bohlman
Born August 18, 1901
Died December 13, 1921
We will meet again.

Herman was on his knees in the snow, no longer the young man he had been in 1921, yet oblivious to the cold. He fingered the letters that were etched into the stone.

"It feels good to be here again. Just to talk . . . to you."

He looked around the cemetery, eyeing the neighbor's house in the distance. Its nosy windows were looking down on him. They were dark.

He touched the headstone. "I'm sorry it's been so long. I've got a lot to say." A tear slipped down his cheek. "I promised you I wouldn't give her up. I didn't. I kept her. I raised her. It wasn't easy. Everyone told me that a single man couldn't raise a little girl. God helped me find a way. I taught her our faith but," he hesitated, "I haven't kept my other promises. I couldn't keep her close to the Lessings."

He stroked the headstone.

"I'm sure I let you down. But the—the worst thing Ruth is that I—I didn't tell her about you." He cried freely now.

"It's complicated," he continued, "but with Edith, I just can't. I'm so sorry. I've never told Ruth how much fun you and I had together, how you made me laugh every day. I've never told her about your smile that lit up the room. I haven't told her our love story."

"Worst of all I've never told her about your faith and your love for her." Herman wiped the tears away but more kept pouring down, chilling his cheeks.

"I haven't given her your wedding ring. I haven't passed on our wedding gifts and your favorite things. She doesn't know how you held her. She doesn't know how you loved her and she doesn't know that you didn't blame her." His voice cracked, "I am so sorry, Ruth."

His legs were going numb against the cold, snowy ground. His fingers ached from the cold. He stood up and pushed his hands into his pockets.

He prayed quietly, "Heavenly Father, thank you for your grace. Thank you that no matter how I may make the wrong choices here, you forgive me. Tell Ruth I'm sorry. Tell her that I'm doing the best I know how." He kissed the tombstone.

In German, he uttered, "What will you say when we meet again?"

*"Whatever you do, work at
it with all your heart, as
working for the Lord, not
for men."*
Colossians 3:23 NIV

March 1941
Peace River, Alberta

Waldemar sat in the Peace River detachment looking over a report he was working on. He had completed his first four months of training in Regina and for the last seven months had been working in Peace River doing practical training. His corporal, Michael Taylor, was helping him phrase things correctly in the report, before they sent it to the readers in Edmonton. The readers would check the report before it was filed in Ottawa.

His practical training had been interesting. It was not exactly what he had expected but it was working out well. Michael Taylor had been a great corporal to learn from. On Waldemar's first day, Taylor had driven him around town and shown him the areas they would be working. He then gave Waldemar a few small files to work on and investigate. Taylor had gradually worked Waldemar up to more complicated cases that he could handle.

Waldemar had grown to like the small town of Peace River and had come to know the residents well. His charming grin and commanding physical presence made it hard for the townspeople to forget this newest RCMP recruit.

He leaned back in his chair, twirled his pen around his fingers and thought about one resident in particular that he had his eye on Marie

Brown. She was something else. She had shoulder-length brown hair, piercing green eyes and a smile from ear to ear. Waldemar and Marie had met at the local curling rink. She had been there with friends learning how to curl. Waldemar had been curling since he was a young boy so he decided he could offer them some assistance. He smiled as he remembered the day they had met.

"Hi there, can I offer you some advice?" Waldemar crossed the curling rink.

"Sure, handsome, what's your name?" one of the girls asked.

"Waldemar Peterson, my friends call me Waldy."

"I'll call him whatever he wants!" one girl whispered to another. Waldemar cringed.

"I'm Marie." One of the young girls stepped forward confidently and stuck her hand out to Waldemar, "Marie Brown. It's nice to meet you, Waldemar. We'd be delighted if you'd join our game and help us out." She turned to glare at her friends behind her.

Waldemar relaxed and shook Marie's hand. "Nice to meet you, Marie. Let me show you some techniques that might help your game."

Marie's friends giggled as Waldemar showed her how to toss the rock in the right form. They played for nearly an hour. After the game, Waldemar asked Marie if he could buy her a drink at the rink soda fountain.

She bade her friends goodbye and sat down for a drink at the cozy table. "So tell me about yourself, Waldemar, I know that you're a constable because I've seen you around town but where are you from?"

Waldemar smiled warmly at Marie. "I'm from Lac Du Bonnet, Manitoba. I grew up on a farm there."

"Farm boy, huh?" She stirred her soda with her straw and took a sip.

"Yep, the genuine article. I worked all over, including mining in Manitoba and then I joined the Force. I'm training now and once I'm finished I'll be sent overseas with the Provost Company. How about you, where are you from?"

"I'm from here. My mother works at a local drug store and I work at the telephone office."

"I've met your mother, she's very nice." Waldemar gazed at Marie.

"Tell me about your training . . . how long are you in Peace River for?"

He responded, "I'm not sure. It's just one day at a time with the RCMP. When they want us to move they give us a notice. I imagine I'll be here until I'm shipped overseas."

"I've got a man overseas myself," her eyes twinkled at Waldemar.

"You're married?" He took a large drink from his cup.

"No, just a high school sweetheart I made a promise to."

"I see."

"And you, Constable Peterson? Are you engaged?"

"No, not me. The Force doesn't allow marriage for seven years after enlistment."

"I see." She looked into his pale blue eyes.

"I should be getting home." Marie finished her drink and pushed her glass aside. "Thanks for the drink. I'll be seeing you."

"You're welcome. I'll look forward to seeing you again." Waldemar rose as Marie stood up from the table and walked her to the door of the rink.

Since then, he had formed a friendship with Marie's sister and mother. She invited Waldemar over for Sunday dinners on a regular basis. After supper, Marie and Waldemar would stand next to each other at the wash basin and chat while they worked. Waldemar respected Marie. She was the first girl that he could actually carry on a conversation with. She was mature for her age. Although she was five years younger, he hardly felt the difference.

"Hey, Peterson," Michael called out, "you day dreaming again? Wake up and finish your report."

Waldemar snapped upright in his chair and stopped twirling his pen in his fingers. "Yes, sir."

"Are you dreaming about that Brown girl?" he said with a smile.

"No, sir." Waldemar wiped the goofy grin off his face and looked as serious as he could.

"Get to work then," Michael chuckled.

"Yes, sir. I will, sir." Waldemar leaned over his page and wrote about some immigrants they had found in Peace River country that had not filed. His mind wandered back to thoughts of training.

The lifestyle of RCMP training had suited him well. It was a rigorous schedule but in some ways it was easier than farm life. All of the recruits woke up and ate breakfast at seven o'clock. After breakfast was physical training and then study time in the classroom. At noon they had had fifteen minutes to run and get their boots and breeches then get back down to the Parade Square for foot drills. There was endless exercise and study, caring for the horses and riding practice. Waldemar always felt right at home in the RCMP barn, shoveling out stalls and putting down fresh hay. The smell of the fresh hay always reminded him of life in Lac

Du Bonnet. His growing up years, filled with running, swimming and athletics, had prepared him physically for RCMP training. There wasn't a muscle in his body that wasn't prepared for anything that the sergeants had to challenge him with.

Waldemar wondered what it would be like once he was sent overseas. The war raged on in Europe. The British had just advanced into Northern Africa to try to defeat the Italians. The Germans had rung in the New Year with an air raid on London. Jewish people were being rounded up and persecuted for their faith. It was a terrible time. Waldemar wondered what it would be like to be policing there in the midst of it all. In the fall of next year, they would be called to Rockcliffe, Ontario, for their final training before being sent overseas.

Waldemar completed his report and handed it to Taylor.

"I'm finished."

Taylor looked it over. "Good job, Peterson." His eyes rose from the report. "I want to discuss something with you."

Waldemar looked at Taylor with curiosity. "What's that?"

"You've been doing well here. Subdivision headquarters wants to send you out to the detachment in Slave Lake to cover for a senior constable while he is away. Do you think you can manage your own detachment?"

"Yes, sir," Waldemar said eagerly.

"I have to let you know that this detachment isn't exactly glamorous. If you need help with anything, you'll need to go down to the rail lines to call. There isn't a phone in the detachment."

"Yes, sir."

"You'll be heading out in two days," Taylor said, "and one more thing, it'll do you good to get to know the district nurse. She'll come in handy with a lot of the situations that may arise. She'll be a valuable asset to you, Peterson. Make sure you get close to her." Taylor smirked. "But not too close!"

Waldemar laughed, "Yes, sir. I understand, sir."

The bells on the door rang as Waldemar entered the telephone office. A rush of cold March air followed in behind him.

"Miss Brown?" Waldemar greeted Marie who had her back to him. Her red dress clung to her curves as she reached over her head to flip a switch.

She whirled around. "Hello, Constable Peterson." She grinned at him. "What brings you by the telephone office today?" She winked as she said, "An important investigation?"

"Not today," Waldemar grinned from ear to ear. "I'm looking for an invite to supper."

"Ah, I see. Why don't you come by then, I'm sure Mother won't have a problem with that; she loves having a man in uniform at the table."

Waldemar chuckled, "Alright. I'll see you later."

"Sounds good." The telephones began to ring. "Duty calls!"

Waldemar gave Marie a silent wave as she picked up the line and connected the incoming calls. She winked at him as he walked out the door into the winter sunshine.

Waldemar walked down the snowy Peace River street. He enjoyed Marie's company. She had her commitment to her man overseas. He had his commitment to the RCMP. It helped to keep things fun and not get too serious.

Waldemar sat at the Brown supper table. He had the attention of all three Brown women, Mrs. Brown, Marie and her sister, as he talked about days on the farm and his adventures in the woodlands.

"Sounds like you were quite the explorer, Constable," Marie's sister commented.

"Well I found out today I'll be exploring a little more." Waldemar looked at Marie for her reaction. "I'm being sent to Slave Lake for six weeks."

Marie looked up from her plate. "Oh really?"

"Yes I leave the day after tomorrow; I'll be covering for a senior constable."

"Well good for you, rookie." Marie winked at Waldemar. "I'm sure you'll be just fine."

Later, Waldemar and Marie stood in their familiar spot in the kitchen, washing the supper dishes.

"Do you think you'll be okay out there all on your own?" Marie looked up to Waldemar, a head taller than her.

"Of course. I'll be staying at a hotel there. The detachment is just a small cabin, complete with an outhouse. No water, no phones, it's just me out in the bush."

"Sounds like fun. Where is the nearest phone?"

"Don't you know, Miss Operator?"

"I'll find out and I'll call you from the office. We can keep in touch. I might be your only friend out there."

"Taylor told me that there is always a district nurse out there too. He said it's best to be on her good side."

"I'll only be a phone call away." Marie bumped Waldemar with her hip.

"I know," he smiled, "I know."

A week later, Waldemar sat in his new post. It was everything Taylor had promised. It was cold—only a wood stove heated the small cabin. He had connected with the district nurse but she was busy and only came by for company about once a week. It was lonely. Most days he struggled to find something to do. He was just putting out the fire in the stove for the day when there was a knock at the door.

"Constable Peterson?"

Waldemar jumped up and opened the door, "Yes?"

A young man dressed in a Northern Alberta Railway (NAR) uniform stood at the door, shivering. "There's a phone call for you down at the rail yard."

"Oh great!" Waldemar grabbed his warm RCMP coat and quickly jammed his feet into his boots. "Let's go!"

Waldemar walked through the cold, crisp air with the fellow from NAR. They talked while they walked.

"I'm Graham. I've heard of you, Constable, it's nice to meet you."

"Nice to meet you too, Graham."

"How do you like it here?"

"I'm enjoying the post. Not too much to do but it's only for five more weeks. Then I'll be heading back to Peace River."

"Is it your sweetheart calling?" Graham asked as his breath puffed in clouds in front of his nose.

Waldemar smiled. "No, just a good friend."

Graham winked at Waldemar. "Ah, I see."

The two talked about Graham's job at NAR while they walked to the rail yard.

Once they arrived, Graham showed Waldemar to the phone. Sure enough, there was Marie on the other end of the line, waiting patiently. Waldemar sat on top of an old shipping crate. He talked for over an hour with Marie about Slave Lake. She told Waldemar about things back in Peace River and they both talked about their families for some time.

That night as he fell asleep, he looked at her picture. He had placed it on his bedside table. The picture frame had been a gift from his former crush, Lorraine. She had given him *her* photo in the frame. He had changed out the photo as his interests shifted from girl to girl. There had been several pretty faces in the frame over the last year, but Waldemar wondered if Marie's pretty face would stay for a while.

*

Waldemar sat in the cutter behind the driver and team of horses as the cold winter wind whipped all around him. The bells on the horses jingled as they trotted across the frozen lake. He was on his way to Wabasa, an Indian Reserve. The residents there worried that a mentally disabled man might hurt himself or someone else. Waldemar had been warned that this young man was dangerous and unpredictable. He needed to be taken to a mental hospital in Edmonton. The instructions on getting to Wabasa, by themselves, were interesting enough. He had to cross Slave Lake, over the ice with a team of horses and then take a winter road up to the reserve. His hands were cold, even inside his winter gloves. He pulled his fur cap lower over his brow and rubbed his hands together vigorously to create some circulation and warmth.

Waldemar was relieved when he arrived at the Catholic mission three days after he left Slave Lake. They had a warm place to stay with a wonderful dining room that served delicious hot meals. After staying one night in the mission, he went to the home of the man he was going to escort. He spoke to the young man's mother.

"I worry about son," the Native woman, Mrs. Bearhead, said in halting English, wringing her hands. "He is angry, you help?"

"Yes, ma'am. I'll take him to Edmonton for treatment. They can help him there."

Mrs. Bearhead showed Waldemar to her son, John's room, where he was sleeping. "I made him strong tea to help sleep," she whispered at the door to his room.

"Alright, ma'am, let's get him to sit up and I'll speak to him about our journey."

"He may anger at you." Mrs. Bearhead's forehead wrinkled in concern.

"It's alright, I can handle him." He put his hand on her shoulder.

"Okay."

Mrs. Bearhead went to her son's bedside and woke him. He was groggy at first and then looked scared as he saw Waldemar's tall frame filling in the doorway.

"Who's that?" he asked in his native tongue.

His mother explained that the constable would be taking him to the city, and that he needed to listen to this man who would be taking him.

Waldemar and John had a relatively easy trip despite the warnings that John was prone to violence and unpredictable behavior. Waldemar had a cool head and a calm demeanor. John seemed to be at ease in his company.

As they crossed Slave Lake, Waldemar patiently pointed out the different animals that they saw. John was quiet and absorbed in everything Waldemar showed him. John had never been off the reserve before and everything he saw was new and interesting, especially when they arrived in the Slave Lake town site. John was amazed by all of the buildings, horses, sleighs, cutters and people bustling around the town.

The two boarded the train to Edmonton. Waldemar asked John to carry both their bags and John was quick to oblige. He sat quietly next to Waldemar on the train. Waldemar talked softly to John, showing him the various sights out the train window.

"Where we going?" John asked Waldemar.

"We're going to Edmonton, to see some people who want to help you. How does that sound?"

"Good." John beamed at Waldemar. "Mama coming?"

Waldemar shook his head. "No. You'll see your Mama soon though, okay?"

"Okay."

When the pair arrived in Edmonton, they met another RCMP officer who drove them to the Edmonton hospital.

John looked at Waldemar with wide eyes and asked, "You come with me?"

"No John, I'm going to be leaving you here but they'll take good care of you, okay?"

John looked scared and nervous as he looked out the cruiser window. "Mama come soon?"

"Yes, your mama will come soon, don't worry." Waldemar reached over and patted John's hand that was resting on the seat between them. "You're going to be fine."

Waldemar bade John goodbye at the hospital and reassured him again that he would be all right.

The other agent, Spencer, commented on Waldemar's calm handling of John, "Shucks, seems like he hardly needs the mental hospital after spending a few days with you."

Waldemar laughed, "I guess I have that therapeutic effect."

"I've heard he's violent and hard to handle."

"Nah, he was so overwhelmed and frightened by all of the sights of the city, he didn't have time to be angry. He stuck to me like glue, heck I even had him carry my bags at the train station!"

Spencer laughed, "Maybe you're in the wrong line of work!"

*"Blessed be God, even the
Father of our Lord Jesus
Christ, the Father of
mercies, and the God of all
comfort; Who comforteth us
in all our tribulation, that
we may be able to comfort
them which are in any
trouble, by the comfort
where with we ourselves are
comforted of God." 2
Corinthians 1: 3 & 4 KJV*

August 1942
Edmonton, Alberta

Ruth had been scrubbing for hours. Each white metal bed frame
had to be thoroughly scrubbed every day. The thin mattresses had to
be washed after every patient and the linens sent to the laundry. It was
a never-ending job, the cleaning, the sanitizing and the washing. If she
had thought that cleaning on her hands and knees for Edith was bad, it
was nothing compared to the cleaning in training. Sister Saint Christine
would inspect with her white-gloved hand after the students were done,
and heaven help them all if there was a speck of anything to be found. As
her hands plunged into the bucket of Lysol and water, Ruth thought of
her life now.

Nursing school had been an amazing experience so far. She was in her
second year and she had grown in many ways. School had its challenges

for sure, but they were good challenges that were helping her mature. Ruth had classes to attend and needed to study to prepare for exams. There was the work on the ward, learning 'hands on' as you went. A third-year student would lead the less experienced and would train them in each situation as it arose.

Ruth met some wonderful friends as well. There was Evelyn and Rachel, fellow students who turned out to be kindred spirits right from the moment they all met. They made the hard days at school bearable and the good days even better. Things at home were relatively good too. Ruth enjoyed her weekly visits to Leduc to see her father and mother. Mother even seemed proud of what Ruth was accomplishing at school. It was just the right dose of Mother. Once a week was enough to keep things positive and to keep the discontent at bay.

Ruth was still dating Nick. He had completed his training as a medic last year and had been sent to a Canadian military hospital in the Maritimes. They corresponded by letter. He came back to Edmonton on leave from time to time and the two would always get together for a date. Ruth was glad that neither one of them was in the position to marry, however, because she still felt like something was missing. Perhaps in time it would come but for now she was happy to let things be as they were.

Ruth was growing spiritually too. There were so many moments in the day when she would send a prayer upward for comfort or strength to complete what needed to be done, or for a patient she was caring for. Here she faced life and death, joy and sorrow. At times, the intensity of pain, a family for a dying child or a husband for his wife was more than she could bear on her own. At these times, she called on her Heavenly Father for the strength to care for the families left behind, or for the bodies of the deceased.

It had been a strange adjustment being in a Catholic school. Students were told when they first signed up that there would be no pressure to convert, but after a few months that didn't seem to be the case. For the first six months, Ruth had sung at morning prayers and then finally felt that she couldn't be true to *her* beliefs and continue on. As a young probational nurse, a 'proby,' she had felt somewhat intimidated but knew it was a matter she must talk about with Sister. As she scrubbed, she remembered how she had sat down with Sister Saint Christine one afternoon.

"I can't do it." Ruth said abruptly as she sat facing Sister Saint Christine in her office.

"What is it, lady? What is the trouble?" Sister Saint Christine sat with her hands neatly folded on her desk, taking in this striking young woman before her.

"I just cannot participate in morning prayers any longer." Ruth looked Sister in the eyes.

"And why not?" She smoothed her already neat blonde hair.

"Well, I don't believe in the words I am singing. Singing to Mary. Yes she was an important role in Jesus' life but I won't worship her. There is only One who I will worship, and that is my Heavenly Father."

"I see," she said at last. She tapped her fingers on the desk.

"I am sorry if this offends you, Sister, but there is nothing you can do to change my mind. I have decided."

"I see, Miss Bohlman." Sister Saint Christine closed her eyes and thought of what to say.

Ruth waited anxiously to be reprimanded and sat with an arsenal of reasons as to why she felt the way she did.

Sister was silent for a while longer. "Young lady," she paused to look Ruth in the eyes, "I admire your moxy. I knew that when you came in under my care I would have my hands full. I understand and respect your decision, even if I do not agree with it."

Ruth relaxed a bit in her seat.

"I thought that you might feel this way and I wondered how long it would take you to approach me. Young lady, you do not do anything by halves and I admire your conviction. I would hope that all of my young nurses would have the same faith and conviction that you have."

"Thank you, Sister." Ruth sat quietly, thanking God for the tone of the conversation thus far.

"You may go now, Miss Bohlman. Thank you for coming to speak to me."

"Thank you." Ruth rose from her chair and left the office. "Thank you, Lord," she breathed as she turned down the hall and headed back to her residence.

"Ruth, are you finished?" Rachel stuck her head into the ward where Ruth was cleaning.

"Hi, Rachel!" Ruth picked up her bucket and rags. "I'm through here."

"You look deep in thought, are you okay?"

"Oh yes, just daydreaming while I work."

"Thinking of Nick?" Rachel asked in a teasing tone.

Ruth laughed, thinking of how far off the mark Rachel was. "No, Sister Saint Christine!"

"Well that's not much to dream about!" Rachel laughed.

After Ruth put her things away, the two girls went to see if there was any mail for either of them. Rachel and Ruth were roommates this year and always did everything together. Rachel had a few letters from friends and family, and Ruth had two letters of her own in her mailbox.

"What did you get?" Rachel asked as she ripped open her letters.

"Ah," Ruth looked over the addresses on the outside of the envelopes, "one from Nick and one from Dad. That's strange that Dad would write."

"Let's go back to residence so we can read."

"Sounds good, let's go." Ruth clutched the letters tightly in her hand as the two friends walked silently back to residence.

The girls settled in their room and lay back on their beds to read. Ruth tore open the letter from Nick and began to read his familiar scrawl.

Dearest Ruth,

How are you? I am well and am happy to say that I will be in Edmonton the last week of August. I will call you at the residence to arrange a time to come and see you before I go back overseas. I am greatly looking forward to holding you in my arms once again.

Love, Nick

Ruth folded up the letter and placed it beside her. It was most likely to be any day now that he would call, she thought. She looked over at Rachel and smiled as Rachel sat grinning, fully engrossed in her own letters. Ruth pulled her father's letter out of the envelope. She wondered why her father would be writing when he would be seeing her this week. It was written in German, short and to the point.

Dearest Ruth,

*How are things at school? Unfortunately, I am writing with
sad news. Your Grandmother Lessing has passed away. I wanted
to tell you before you hear from someone else. I look forward to
seeing you this week.*

Love Father

Ruth sat frozen with the letter in her hand. Grandma Lessing was
gone. Her maternal grandmother was gone. She thought of that day
back in 1936 when she had sat with Pauline in her home and felt such
unconditional love. Even though the two of them had not shared a lifetime
together, Ruth felt such a sense of family, of history and connection to her
lost mother. Clearly, her father had not wanted to discuss the news in
front of Mother on their next weekly visit.

Rachel sat reading her letter and laughed out loud. "You'll never
believe this, Ruth." She stopped and looked over at her friend. Ruth's
color had drained from her face.

"What's the matter?" She came over to Ruth's bed and took the letter
from her shaking hand. "What does it say?"

Ruth explained the contents of the letter. She buried her face in her
hands and cried.

"Oh, Ruth, I'm so sorry. Are you alright?"

Ruth brushed her tears aside with her sleeve and looked up at her
friend. "I know I hardly knew her but it feels like such a tremendous loss
all the same."

"Oh but it is. She was the closest thing to your mother, your history."
Rachel knew all about Ruth's difficult past. Late-night conversations had
left Rachel an expert on how Ruth felt about her family history.

"It's true. I feel like it is so ridiculous and maddening that I should be
kept from these people. They are so close to me. They live right there in
Leduc and yet they may as well be on the other side of the moon. I can't
dare contact them for fear of word getting back to Mother."

"Is there any other family in Oregon?"

"Yes, Uncle Charlie, Myrtle and Marion, and my Aunt Magda and
her husband Hans."

"Why don't you try to get in touch with them?" Rachel asked.

"Oh, Mother would have a fit if she knew." Ruth's eyes were wide at the prospect.

Rachel smiled. "She doesn't have to know, does she? You're a grown woman now, you mustn't let her control you so."

Ruth sniffed and dried her eyes. "You're right, Rachel, I need to get in touch with the Lessings. I will write to Aunt Magda. I will ask her the things I want to know before I lose another Lessing." Ruth hugged Rachel. The two sat quietly thinking of the questions that needed to be answered.

*

Rachel and Ruth sat in the new obstetrics wing that night stretching long, narrow bandages. Supplies were limited because of the war. Stretching bandages was a good lesson in conservation but a tedious chore. They washed bandages in hot water and bleach. After they were washed, the nurses stretched them out and rolled them back up.

The phone rang and Ruth rushed to answer it. "Hello?" Ruth paused as she listened, "Hi, Nick!" She paused again. "Tomorrow night would be great. Meet me at 10:30 outside the southeast door. I have a break between 10:30 and two o'clock. We can talk outside the hospital." Ruth smiled as she listened, "See you then."

"Do you think Sister will approve of your late-night visitor?" Rachel asked.

"Do you think she needs to know?" Ruth winked at Rachel and went back to stretching bandages.

Rachel laughed, "Only you." She changed the subject. "Do you think Dr. Warner will be back tonight?"

"I don't know. He has such an ego; someone needs to knock him off his high horse." Ruth shook her head and thought about Sam Warner.

The interns' residence was on the ground floor, beneath the new obstetrics wing. Every night the interns would wander through the ward and stop at the nurse's station. They could have gone around the long way but instead they insisted on stopping by to 'chew the rag' with the nurses. Rachel, Ruth and any other nurses who were working would have snacks and hot chocolate for themselves to sustain their energy through the shift. The interns would come and eat their snacks and drink the hot chocolate, and were even quite demanding about it, as though it were their personal coffee shop. Sam Warner in particular was the worst, always demanding that his cookies should be fresh and his hot chocolate piping. It drove the nurses crazy. They grumbled about Warner any chance they had.

"Wouldn't you just love to tell him to take a hike?" Rachel asked.

"No," Ruth was deep in thought, "I'd like to do better than that."

"What are you thinking, Bohlman?" Rachel grinned, knowing the way her friend's mind worked.

Ruth smiled. "I'll tell you my idea, as long as you promise to help."

The two friends smiled at each other and laughed as Ruth leaned over and whispered her plan to Rachel.

"Brilliant, just brilliant!" Rachel grinned from ear to ear.

"Yoo hoo," Sam Warner called out loudly at the empty nurses' station, "where is everyone?"

"Oh hi, Warner!" Rachel beamed as she came around the corner from the obstetrics kitchen followed by Ruth and two other nurses.

"Hi, Warner!" Ruth smiled sweetly as she brought out a tray of cookies and a warm mug of hot chocolate. "I have your drink ready!"

Sam looked at Rachel, Ruth and a few other nurses sitting behind them at the station. He had nothing to complain about this evening. It seemed they had finally understood that he wanted his snack ready and waiting when he came through. "Well thank you." He picked up the warm mug and took a drink. It was sweet, rich and delicious. He took a bite of cookie and washed it down with another mouthful of hot chocolate. "This is superb."

The nurses all smiled sweetly at him as he polished off every crumb of cookie and drop of hot chocolate.

Ruth smiled and leaned over the counter of the nurses' station, her chin resting in her hand, her eyelashes batting. "You've had a kind of drink that you haven't had in a long time."

"What?" Sam looked perplexed as all of the nurses started to snicker.

Ruth smiled mischievously at Warner, trying not to burst out laughing. "Good, wasn't it?"

"WHAT?" Sam started to look panicked, "What is going on here?"

"It's a special formula we use here, extremely healthy, straight from the obstetrics patients." Ruth faked a serious face at Sam.

"WHAT? BREASTMILK?" Sam turned green and began to heave. He burst through the laughing nurses into the kitchen and threw up in the sink. He heaved over and over, swearing between rounds of vomiting.

Rachel beamed. Ruth laughed out loud as they listened to Sam.

Sam came out of the kitchen wiping his mouth on his sleeve. "Bohlman, you have a serious problem! What the hell is the matter with you?"

"When can we expect you back?" Ruth asked sweetly.

"NEVER!" Sam stomped out of the nurses' station and down to his residence.

All of the girls keeled over laughing uncontrollably.

"Rejoice in the Lord
always; and again I say,
rejoice."
Philippians 4:4 NIV

August 1942
Edmonton, Alberta

The next afternoon, after sleeping through the morning, Ruth sat at her desk. Instead of opening her books to study, she took a pen and paper and began to write to her Aunt Magda in Oregon. She asked Magda about Grandmother's passing and how Marion and Myrtle were coping. She closed up the letter, addressed it and pressed a stamp to the top.

This afternoon, she planned a meeting with some of the other student nurses to discuss working conditions. She went to the lounge of the residents' hall and met some friends there. Once the young ladies had gathered, she clapped her hands to get everyone's attention.

"Thank you for coming today." Ruth smiled confidently around the room. "I appreciate you taking your time to come here today. We will try to move quickly through the meeting to avoid undue negative attention, and to get you all back to your studies and rest time as quickly as possible."

A murmur went around the room. Heads nodded in agreement.

"I'd like to begin by saying that this will not be our only meeting of this nature. I'd like you to tell your schoolmates about the meeting and encourage them to attend our next meeting as well. We will be informally calling this the organization of student nurses. I will be your leader and your voice to the administration of the hospital. Let's begin with your greatest sources of concern and your ideas for improvement on working conditions."

"What makes you think you can change things, Bohlman?" One of the third-year nurses spoke out skeptically.

"I don't know that I can. However, I do know that nothing changes without someone speaking out and questioning the way things are done. I will use my leadership skills to invoke changes for the good of all of us and our patients."

Someone said, "Let's begin."

"Okay," Ruth smiled reassuringly. "What are our greatest concerns?"

"Shift length," one of the students said.

"Yes," another agreed, "there's no time to rest, therefore, we're making errors, putting patients at risk."

"True," a quiet young lady added. "It would be fine to work twelve-hour shifts if all we were doing was nursing, but we've also got classes and homework."

"Very good," Ruth said, writing down the comments. "I think that this is a very valid concern."

"Another thing," a red-headed girl in the corner said, "is the way the interns treat us. There's no respect."

Agreement rippled through the group.

"Sometimes I feel like we're the slaves of the hospital," a first year said timidly. "No one realizes the immense responsibilities that are placed on us—aside from patient care."

"And we," Ruth agreed, "want to give patient care our full attention. We want to be able to say that we are giving our undivided attention to the people on our ward."

"Why should we be making coffee for the interns?" Rachel asked.

"Or hot chocolate," Evelyn laughed.

Others chimed in, laughing, retelling Ruth's story with Dr. Wagner to the ones who hadn't heard it yet.

They talked on for nearly an hour until Ruth wrapped things up.

"Thank you, everyone, for coming today. I look forward to bringing our thoughts to the administration. Hopefully, we will see some positive change."

Ruth's good friend Evelyn congratulated Ruth after the meeting, "Well done, Ruth, I think you really got some good feedback. I am looking forward to the next meeting."

"Thank you. I think this will serve us well in the long run."

"When are you going to talk to Sister Saint Christine about our ideas?" Evelyn asked.

"Next week, once I prepare the meeting notes into presentable ideas."

Evelyn looked at her watch. "I better go. We should meet up on one of our nights off."

"Definitely. Come by our room when you're free."

"I will. See you!" Evelyn gave Ruth a quick pat on the shoulder and headed off to work.

Ruth felt a deep satisfaction after the meeting. Almost all of the students came to thank her personally for her strength and courage as their ambassador in the hope of improving working conditions for the good of all the students and the patients.

On the way to her evening shift, she dropped Aunt Magda's letter in the post box, hoping for a quick reply. As she walked to the obstetrics ward, she heard a familiar voice call out to her from down the hall.

"Miss Bohlman?"

Ruth turned around and saw Sister Saint Christine sticking her head out of her office. "Yes?" she answered.

"May I see you for a minute?"

Ruth walked back toward Sister's office wondering what this could be about. Had someone complained about the meeting already? Probably Marilyn, she was the only student who was a nun and the Sisters favored her above all others. She probably went to complain to cozy up to the Sisters even further.

"Have a seat, lady."

Ruth sat in the familiar chair across from Sister Saint Christine. Sister shut the office door and then went around and sat in her chair.

"How can I help you, Sister?" Ruth asked tentatively.

"I had a chat with an intern this morning, Sam Warner. Do you know such a fellow?" Sister Saint Christine looked at Ruth and saw her smile.

"Why yes I do. He often visits the obstetrics ward after his shifts."

"Miss Bohlman, let's get to the point. Your stunt last night is not appreciated by the administration of the hospital. If things like this continue, I may have to call your father."

"You are welcome to call my father, Sister; he would probably have a good laugh."

Sister rose from her chair and turned her back to Ruth, an indication that she was really angry. "You may go, Miss Bohlman, I don't want to hear about these types of things ever again. Do you understand?"

Ruth tried to be serious as she thought of the look on Sam's face last night. "Yes, Sister." She rose from her chair, looked at the angry backside of Sister Saint Christine and then hightailed it out of the office and off to her shift. She giggled to herself as she went.

That night, Ruth took her break at 10:30. She was sent by Sister Saint Christine to the residence to rest. Instead of doing that, however, she sneaked out the southeast door of one of the wards. She propped it open to ensure her admittance back into the building. At night, only the main doors remained unlocked and it would be very conspicuous for Ruth to be coming in through them after hours. Nick waited in the shadows of the building. He was happy to see Ruth emerge from the side door as promised.

She rushed forward into his arms. He hugged her fiercely. "Ruth, I'm so happy to see you." He took in the smell of her hair and the feel of her crisp white uniform against his body.

"Hi, Nick! It's so nice to see you!" She took his hands in her own and led him to some steps along the outside of the building. It was a warm summer night and the pair sat down and caught up on the details of their lives. They held hands as they talked.

"How are things at school?" Nick asked.

"Good, challenging of course, but I've started a student union of sorts and I'm working to make some really important changes."

"Wow, sounds like you haven't wasted any time getting your opinion to count."

"No, I feel like God brought me here for a reason and if I can change things for the better then I think that's what He wants me to do."

"Well good for you. How's your family?"

"They are well, how about yours? How is your mother?"

"She's good; they are always so happy to have me home. It's strange though to go from the military hospital to here. It is so different there, you really wouldn't understand unless you've been. And even if you have been, I think most days it's beyond understanding. There is staggering loss. Such a waste of life. It's sad." Nick looked down at his hands. Ruth wrapped her arms around him in a warm embrace.

"I'm sorry. It must be hard for you."

The summer sun set just before midnight while Nick and Ruth talked about life, love and family.

"When this is all over, we can finally be together." He squeezed her hand. "When my service is through, we can settle down in Edmonton . . . together."

"Only God knows what the future holds, Nick." Ruth was hesitant to offer up a long-term commitment. "But we'll all be happier when the war is over."

Nick leaned over and kissed Ruth tenderly. "I love you, Ruth."

Suddenly the door banged shut behind them. Ruth's plan to sneak back into the building was foiled.

"What in the . . . ?" Ruth looked at the door.

"Was it the wind?" Nick asked.

"There's no wind." Ruth was worried. "I better go. I have to get back soon anyway. It was good to see you, Nick. Keep writing. I love your letters."

Ruth and Nick hugged one last time and then Nick disappeared into the darkness. Ruth approached the door that had shut and tried to pry it open. No luck. Suddenly, it came swinging open toward her, nearly knocking her down.

"Hello, Miss Bohlman." Ruth was startled as Sister Saint Christine stood there glaring, holding the door.

"Hello, Sister."

"I've been waiting for you."

"Oh?" Ruth raised her eyebrows and smiled, wondering what Sister was about to say.

"Do you think, young lady, that it is appropriate to be fraternizing with young men in the shadows of the hospital after hours?" Her brows nearly touched one another.

"He is my boyfriend, Sister, and I haven't seen him in over a year." Ruth crossed her arms across her chest defensively.

"I don't care who he is. You don't go out in your uniform and meet with young men in the middle of the night. Do I need to call your father?"

"My father is quite fond of Mr. Schellenburg. I'm certain he wouldn't object."

"Young lady, I've had enough of your disrespect. Get to work!"

Ruth turned and walked away, heading up to obstetrics. After she arrived, she told Rachel and Evelyn about her visit with Nick, and his words of commitment and promises for the future.

They laughed when she recounted how Sister had caught her. "Did you know she used to be a ballet dancer?" Rachel asked.

"Yes," Evelyn remarked. "I'd heard that. I also heard that she was quite good, professional even."

"And," Ruth added, "I've heard she was engaged to be married."

"Boy," Evelyn laughed, "some man must have crossed her to make her turn to being a nun!"

The three of them laughed.

"So, he said he loved you?" Evelyn asked Ruth.

"Yes, I'm just not sure if I feel the spark? You know?"

"It's probably just because you haven't been together in so long," Rachel assured her friend.

"Maybe."

A week later, Rachel and Ruth awoke after a long night shift. After returning to residence just after seven o'clock, the girls slept until after lunch and then got up to study for their upcoming Registered Nurse exams. After a few hours of reading, Rachel stretched and said, "I'm going to get the mail, do you want to come?"

"No I had better stay," Ruth answered, "will you get mine?"

"No problem. See you in a bit." Rachel left the room and Ruth was alone. She poured over her books and tried to memorize every bit of information. She prided herself on her academic achievement. So far she had been at the top of her class.

Rachel returned about fifteen minutes later with envelopes in her hand.

"Mail for you!" she said in a singsong voice.

Ruth looked up from her books and smiled, "Great, who's it from?"

"Artrude and AUNT MAGDA!"

"Oooo! Great! Pass them to me!" Rachel put the letters in Ruth's hand. She ripped open the one from Magda. It was written in familiar German script.

Dearest Ruth,

Thank you for your correspondence. It was lovely to hear from you. Thank you for your kind words about Mother; it has been a most trying time since her passing. My health is poor now as I am suffering from tuberculosis. Your letter brought me much joy. The photo you sent was stunning; you are a spitting image of your mother. It was glorious to see your mother's eyes looking at me from the photo. You and I have a family resemblance as well; I would love to see you in person again one day.

My dearest husband Hans has been worried sick over my health. We have no children and I am his whole world. He is such a wonderful, faithful man who has been at my side praying for my recovery.

I am thrilled to hear of your accomplishments vocally and in nursing school. I too am a singer and it would be quite something for you and I to sing together one day. I understand your need to put the pieces of the puzzle together regarding your mother. She was a wonderful older sister, although you must remember I was quite young when she died. I have many fond memories of you, however. You were like a china doll of the very best kind. I was nine when you came into our lives. After Father, Hilda and your mother died, your grandmother was devastated. I remember being sad to leave my brothers and the farm and all that I had known. I felt so sad to leave five of my immediate family members in the Fredericksheim Cemetery and go to a new country and home. It was a trying time for all of us.

You were such a wonderful distraction for Mother and me. I cared for you every day, feeding, changing and rocking you to sleep. You were such a dear baby. I remember the day your father came to take you back to Alberta. I thought I would die inside. Life moved on, however, as it always does. Amelia had her girls and we all adjusted to life without you. It is hard for me to write too much but I will continue to correspond as my health holds on.

*I've enclosed a photograph of myself at the sanatorium. I am
of course much thinner than usual because of the tuberculosis.
Anyhow, it's better than nothing!*

Love, Magda

Ruth closed the letter and let out a deep breath. She studied the picture
of her young aunt. Wow. This was actually happening for her. Away from
Edith she was able to reach out to a Lessing family member and she was
reaching back. Magda seemed to be genuinely happy to hear from her.

Rachel was bursting at the seams to hear the contents of the letter.

"What? What does it say?" Rachel asked.

Ruth looked at her friend and smiled. "It's good. She's talking about
the beginning, when I was born. She talked about when I lived with her,
until I was a year old. She also said I look like my mother."

"Wow. That is amazing. I knew it was a good idea to send your
photo."

"I'm so glad you suggested that." Ruth rose from her desk and walked
to the small mirror that hung by the door. She looked in the mirror and
studied her own reflection. "She said I am a spitting image." Ruth paused
and felt lost in so many thoughts and emotions. "Can you believe she died
here? In the very wards we work every day?" It was the first time she had
said it out loud. She thought about it every day but to say it out loud to
Rachel, to have someone else consider the situation, made it even more
real.

Rachel sat quietly looking at her good friend as she stared into the
mirror, searching for so many things. She was searching for a family lost
to secrecy, searching for her past, searching for her future and searching
for herself.

"God is our refuge and strength, an ever-present help in trouble. Therefore we will not fear, though the earth give way and the mountains fall into the heart of the sea."
Psalm 46:1 & 2 NIV

February 1943
Dawson Creek, British Columbia

Waldemar got off the train and stood in the aftermath of the explosion. The smell was sickening. The sky was black and the air was thick with smoke. He had been posted in Beaverlodge, Alberta, when the call had come in. There had been a huge explosion and fire in Dawson Creek two nights ago. He was being sent to investigate the cause of the explosion and to support the existing police presence. The damage was extensive, to say the least. An entire city block had been leveled.

An American soldier moved through the crowd of people getting off the train. He walked up to Waldemar and stuck out his hand. "Hello, Constable Peterson. I'm Corporal Wickerson. Thank you for coming to give us a hand."

Waldemar shook the man's hand. "Hello, pleasure to meet you."

"Come with me back to our temporary headquarters and we can talk about what we know and what we still need to learn." Wickerson led Waldemar through the crowded train platform. "There are a lot of people arriving yesterday and today. Reporters, family, all sorts who want to get an eye full of the damages here. We've had reporters arriving here all the way from New York."

"Really?" Waldemar looked around at the people bustling through the area. "Looks like we'll have enough work to keep us busy for a while."

Wickerson nodded his head in agreement. "You can say that again. There are plenty of people leaving too. Some are looking for medical care themselves. There are also people who came looking for relatives but now they've realized they've been flown out to Edmonton." Wickerson waved his arm around, gesturing at the platform and station. "They've set up this temporary platform here until the inspectors get here to take a look at the foundation of the station. Take a look at it. We're a half a block away from the blast, and the whole thing up and moved two feet off its original location."

Waldemar could hardly believe it as he looked at the foundation of the train station. It *had* been lifted several feet off its foundation and shifted to the north. "Unbelievable."

"That's the least of it; you should hear the stories of survival. Some people were blown hundreds of feet and lived to tell. As you'll soon see, others were not so fortunate."

"Well I'm anxious to get started."

They walked up to the temporary headquarters the army had set up. There Waldemar was introduced to FBI agents, military officers and local RCMP. He listened to the details of the recovery effort.

Afterwards, Wickerson asked, "Are you ready to go to the blast site now?"

"Of course," Waldemar answered.

"The truck is over here." Wickerson pointed to the east of the headquarters. "Let's go."

The M35 two-and-a-half-ton truck, commonly known as a Deuce and a Half, was parked near Headquarters. Wickerson drove the large truck cautiously through what was left of Dawson Creek. People were still milling about, bloodied and injured, looking for family members and belongings. Nothing was left standing but a few odd chimneystacks and the old Co-op Union store, which had been looted and vandalized. Small fires burned all over. It was like a war zone. Waldemar sat in the passenger seat of the M35, wide-eyed, taking it all in. Every window was broken. Every door twisted and mangled. All the buildings were in smoldering ruin.

"I'm sure you have some knowledge of Dawson Creek but I'll give you some background anyhow," Wickerson broke in. "As you know, Dawson Creek's population is huge, full of truck drivers, construction personnel and military men. This is the base of the Alaskan Highway project and we've got our American military here, working their way north so they can set up defenses in Alaska. The population is largely transient, so to figure out who was actually lost in the explosion will be a difficult task."

"I see," Waldemar nodded as he listened.

Wickerson parked the truck, turned to Waldemar and said, "Crime here is rampant, as you can tell by the looting. We've had complaints before this even started of arson, theft, sex crimes. With the population constantly moving through here and the foreigners coming and going, it has been a real challenge policing this community."

"I can't imagine." Waldemar was thankful this wasn't his post.

"This is not a good time for us either with the war. We don't have access to water. There is no fresh water for the residents. We have no springs or wells in town; all our water is brought in by horse power and wagon tanks. Also, we never have enough ration books because the population is expanding faster than we can get ration books sent from Edmonton."

"What do we know about the fire?" Waldemar asked.

"The building was an old livery barn, crammed full of supplies for the northern expansion. It was a large building, more than 100 feet in length and half the width, full of supplies from different contractors. Things such as tools, kegs of nails, bolts, cables, copper wire, telephone wire, tires and other building supplies needed for this project. There were chemicals as well, batteries, all mixed together with dynamite."

"Good grief."

"It was a recipe for disaster. There was no way to fight the fire with the lack of water here. We just stood by and watched the building burn. It was in the center of the town. There was a massive crowd gathering to watch the building burn. Because there wasn't any water to fight the fire, the nearby business owners tried to protect their buildings by soaking burlap sacks and putting out the offshoots of fire that were coming off the old livery. Our soldiers had their weapons out to press back the crowd. There were moviegoers, local residents and business owners, and to add to the problem, a train had just come in with all the passengers at close range, taking in the sight of the burning building. We were concerned and yelling at everyone to leave and take cover, but nobody believed it was going to blow sky high. They all just stood there gawking until they were all blasted off their feet."

Waldemar and Wickerson got out of the truck to take a look around. There were American soldiers milling about, guarding the site, as well as two other provincial police officers. The smell was sickening. It was the smell of burnt flesh, burnt chemicals and smoldering metals all mixed together.

"Hello," a soldier called to Wickerson, "you two can come over here."

Waldemar carefully walked on a thin path through the rubble toward the man. Wickerson followed right behind.

"You two here to work?" the soldier asked.

"Yes, sir," Waldemar answered.

"Okay. So we're going through the rubble. We'll assign you an area of the grid that you can work in. We're looking for valuables, remains and anything that might give us a clue to what happened here."

"What do we do with the items we find?" Waldemar asked as he sifted through the rubble.

Wickerson answered, "There's metal bins we are putting the bones into. If you find a body—say at least 50 percent of a body—or a skull . . . call over the photographer to come and take a picture. If it's only bones or fragments, then throw it in the bin."

Waldemar took a deep breath. The stench permeated his nose. "Fine then."

The soldier added, "Any valuables we find we are going to make an effort to match them up to the rightful owners."

Wickerson continued to talk to Waldemar as they walked closer to the remains of the old livery building where the ashes still smoldered. "The people, they just fell like dominos in concentric circles, one after the next as the blast radiated out from the warehouse. We had one American soldier who was struck by a keg of nails exploding and then, even worse, he was run over by a truck while he fled the area. Poor fellow died in the operating room in the hospital that night. It's been horror after horror hearing the stories of those who were near the blast. Many have been sent to nearby Pouce Coupe for treatment as well. The Sisters at our hospital are completely overrun."

"What other police details have there been aside from the recovery effort?" Waldemar asked.

"We've got police in the community. There has been a shortage of ration coupons. The lady who looks after that has written into Edmonton requesting more but everything seems to be taking its time. The Co-op has been looted, all the food stolen and Marshall Law has taken over. We're trying to get things back under control and into a state of order."

Waldemar shook his head. "Ah, I've found something."

Wickerson came over. They looked at Waldemar's discovery. A delicate left hand stuck out, fingers curled. It was charred black. A gold wedding band sat on the slim ring finger.

"Ugh," Wickerson turned away. "I hate this part. Let's get a photographer in case there is a body under here." He pointed at the rubble covering where the woman presumably was lying.

Waldemar hollered for a photographer. He was a young fellow with light brown hair and a long pointy nose. He came over.

"What have you got?" he asked.

"We don't know," Wickerson answered. "Did you want to take a picture of the arm before we move the rubble?"

The photographer nudged the arm with his toe. Waldemar's stomach lurched.

Wickerson pointed at a large piece of wood that covered the body. "Peterson, you grab that end. I'll get this side. On the count of three we'll lift."

Waldemar took a deep breath. Again the smell made him gag.

"One, two, three." They lifted the wood and debris up and out of the way.

"Oh God," the photographer moaned, "this is terrible."

"Wow," Wickerson exhaled loudly. "Never get used to this."

Waldemar's stomach lurched again. He set the piece of wood aside. "Excuse me please." He walked away. The image was burning into his mind. He wanted to shake it out. He tried to think of something else but the sight he had just witnessed clung to his mind like a leech. He walked as far away as he could until Wickerson and the photographer were spots in the distance.

"Oh God . . ." he prayed. "Oh God . . ."

A Red Cross nurse approached him. "Are you all right, Officer?"

Waldemar nodded slowly. "I'm fine."

"You look a little pale. Would you like to sit down for a minute?"

"No, I'm fine."

She touched his arm softly. "Are you working on the recovery effort?"

He looked at her. She had blonde hair and sparkling blue eyes. The feel of her hand on his arm was comforting. "Yes . . . yes I am."

She put out her hand. "I'm Nora. Red Cross."

"Waldemar Peterson. Third Class Constable with the RCMP."

"Did you just arrive?"

"Ah," he said distractedly, "yes, I did . . . just today."

She took his hand in her own and patted it soothingly. "It's hard. There is a lot of devastation. I've just come back from overseas and it's not much different there. My husband is a doctor. We were on our way back to the West Coast when we heard about the disaster here. We've been working here the last two days, trying to help with all the surgeries, the triage."

He stepped back from her, pulling his hand from her grasp. "Thank you, Miss Nora. Thank you for your conversation. I should get back to work."

She smiled kindly. "Well, if you need anything. You just ask."

"Yes, ma'am. I will." He gave a little wave and walked back to Wickerson.

Waldemar worked wordlessly alongside Wickerson for the next few hours. He saw something in amongst the ashes. He bent down to take a closer look. It was a pocket watch. He used his gloved hand to pick it up and brush it off. The inscription on the back read, *'Forever yours, Love Nelly.'*

Not anymore, thought Waldemar as he slipped it in his pocket. Perhaps he could find this Nelly and return this remembrance of love.

The afternoon continued on in this way, looking for bodies, finding remains of the dead and tokens of humanity. The people who had been closest to the blast site had been burned so badly that little remained of their bodies; their bones were charred beyond recognition of sex or age.

Back at the hotel that night, he was given his ration of water from the army. One quart to wash up and a bar of soap. He went into the bathroom and meticulously scrubbed himself from head to toe, careful not to waste a precious drop of water. He washed his hair, scrubbing it until his scalp ached. He used a facecloth to scour his body, trying to wash away the smell of the day. By the end his skin was burning, yet still the memories of the day had not washed away.

Two weeks later, Waldemar had a few minutes on the phone line at the hotel. The first place he called was Peace River. The operator picked up the phone.

"Peace River, to whom can I connect your call?"

Her voice was pure sunshine. "Hi, Marie," he said.

"Hey, Peterson! How are you?" she asked.

"I'm okay. It's busy here."

"I've heard! The papers say it's as though a bomb was dropped."

"Yes. There's a lot of devastation."

"How long are you going to be there for?"

"I don't know," he sighed, "until we figure out who is responsible."

"Are you close to knowing that? Have you figured out what happened?"

"We're getting there; let's just say when you mix dynamite, fire and percussion caps, and hundreds of people standing around watching, it's a mess." He sighed. "Everyone wants someone to blame—but the truth of the matter is it might not be that simple."

"That sounds intense."

"Ah, it's okay. You should hear some of the stories the people here have to tell. It's extraordinary. One man told me he was across the street from the warehouse that exploded, in his barn, about sixty feet away, and he ended up in his stocking feet on the other side of some boxcars at the rail yard. He went back for his shoes and rubbers that were right in the middle of where his barn used to be! He was blown up right out of his shoes! He just slipped them back on and walked away!"

Marie gasped, "You're kidding!"

"There are more, you wouldn't even believe but I'll save that for another day."

"I hope you're coming home soon. I miss having you around."

"Soon . . . I'm sure it will be soon. I think we have about three more weeks here to get things under control and wrap up the investigation. What are we going to do when I get back?"

"There is a dance next month at the Trion in Edmonton; hopefully you'll be back so you can take me."

"I'll try. Nothing sounds better than that. I better go . . . there's lots of people waiting for the phone. I'll be in touch when I'm back in town."

"Sounds good Pete. See you then!"

"Bye, Marie." Waldemar hung up the phone and smiled for the first time in the last two weeks.

*

A month later, after concluding the investigation in Dawson Creek, Waldemar made good on his promise. He stood swaying back and forth to the music with Marie in his arms. They had taken the train from Peace River to Edmonton that morning. They stood on the Trion dance floor dancing to the last few songs of the night. Waldemar's good friend from the Force, Tim Armstrong, was there with his girlfriend.

"I'm so glad you're back." Marie looked up at Waldemar and smiled.

"Me too; I'd be happy never to see Dawson Creek again."

"What was the worst part?"

"Not one part in particular but you know what bothered me was the business owners trying to commit frauds against the insurance company. The American military has to pay for everything that was leveled so of course we had a lot of shop owners who hid their merchandise that wasn't damaged. I'm telling you, everyone in town was wearing a fur coat. The merchant of the fur coat shop swore that every coat he had was burned up in the fire."

"People are awful, aren't they?"

"Indeed."

She traced a finger over his chest. "But not you. You're one of a kind."

He smirked, "So are you."

He bent down for a kiss. She obliged. She sighed and laid her head on his chest as they danced.

"Are you going to be in Peace River for a while now?" she asked softly.

"I hope so, but you never know with the Force."

"True."

"At least I'm not going overseas."

A few months ago, Waldemar had heard that the Canadian government had decided not to send anymore members of the Force to war. They had been told that there were too many casualties in the Provost Company. Waldemar had his suspicions that they were simply running out of members to police the home country. He wasn't as disappointed as some of the other recruits had been. One of his fellow members had been so upset he had filed a complaint with the government. Waldemar wondered why he didn't just enlist in the army. He didn't really care where he was, as long as he was working.

"Pete," Marie leaned in closer to Waldemar, "I love being here in your arms." She listened to his heart beating strongly in his chest.

Waldemar bent down and kissed Marie again. "I love being here with you too."

"Will you always save the last dance for me?"

Marie was referring to the last dance of the night, which was always saved for your true love, the one you intended to marry.

"I will . . . but what about you?" He looked her in the eyes and asked, "What about your sweetheart?"

She cocked her head to the side and shrugged. "It was a promise I made a long time ago. I didn't know then the things I know now." She batted her eyelashes. "Things change."

He leaned in for one more kiss.

"Do not be anxious about anything, but in everything, by prayer and petition, with thanksgiving, present your requests to God. And the peace of God, which transcends all understanding, will guard your hearts and your minds in Christ Jesus."
Philippians 4: 6 & 7
NIV

August 1943
Leduc, Alberta

Ruth stared up at the ceiling of her childhood bedroom. She never thought she'd spend this much time here again. Her father had been caring for her for the last six weeks because she was recovering from hepatitis. She had contracted it while working at the hospital and then went from being the nurse to being the patient. She was kept in isolation there for six weeks and then sent home for six weeks to recover. It had been a long and tedious recovery. She had wanted to get back to school and to her studies, but her body had not cooperated. She was so dreadfully tired, feverish and had terrible vomiting. The last few weeks had been better. Sister Saint Christine was allowing her to come back next Monday.

Ruth lay in bed thinking of how hard she was going to have to work in order to catch up to her classmates. She left as head of the class but knew it would be hard to maintain the academic standards she had set for herself. She thought of all she had accomplished so far. Last year, because of her work with the group of student nurses that she rallied, Ruth had managed to change their work schedule to eight-hour shifts with one afternoon off every week. After she had had several meetings with her classmates, she went to Sister Saint Christine and discussed better working conditions for the students. She pointed out that more mistakes were made in the last four hours of each shift. While they were students, they needed to be able to balance practical training and book learning. She had even helped other student nurses in other cities. After they had heard about her success at the Miseracordia, they asked for her guidance in forming their own student groups.

When she got back to school, she would do a rotation in surgery. Pediatrics was her favorite rotation so far. She thought of the weeks before she had contracted hepatitis. Her patient had been a six-year-old girl who had been battling pneumonia for over a week. Ruth was relieved when her fever finally broke after two days of being dangerously high. She had learned that if a fever over 104F held on for three or more days, death was imminent.

In this, her third and final year of nursing, she learned that death was something she had no control over. Her role was simply to make the patient as comfortable as possible. She remembered when she was six years old and had scarlet fever. Her poor father had been terrified for her life. She knew the anguish in the parents' faces as they kept vigil by their little one.

A week later, Ruth was back at school and getting her mind back on nursing. This year she had gone to Sister Saint Christine and asked for a room of her own for her final term. Even though she loved Rachel and the other roommates she lived with, it was nice to have her own space to study and rest.

"Hi, Ruth!" Evelyn came into Ruth's bedroom in her white uniform with her nurse's cap slightly askew on her head.

"Hello, how was your shift?" Ruth asked. This was Evelyn's first day in the ward for the dying and she had promised Ruth she would stop by for a visit so that they could catch up when she was through.

"It was alright, just getting to know the patients, the ward."

"How did you find the atmosphere?"

"It's so different . . . there is such a sense of sadness."

"I know."

"The hardest is to see those without faith." She paused, removing her cap and flopping down on the bed. "What do you do when you have nothing to look forward to?"

"Death has a whole new meaning without the promise of eternity."

"I just tried to keep quiet today and really focus on the needs of the patients."

"That's good."

"Some are definitely more talkative than others."

"Did you meet anyone interesting?"

"A few." Evelyn nodded.

"I found," Ruth said, "when I was doing it, that people wanted to tell you why their lives had meaning. And some," she paused, "to say what they regretted most. As though they could save you from experiencing those same regrets yourself."

"I guess looking death in the face gives you a fresh perspective."

"We'll all be there one day."

Evelyn smoothed her skirt. "I suppose."

Ruth looked back at her books, thinking about the conversation.

"Oh," Evelyn said suddenly, "there was a patient of mine who asked about you. He wanted to speak to you."

"Who is that?" Ruth looked perplexed, wondering if it was one of her former patients.

"An older fellow . . . um, Gold. He says you'll know him from Leduc."

Ruth looked at her friend, her eyes wide and her mouth gaping.

"Are you okay?" Evelyn asked.

"Yes, I'm okay. Do you know who he is?"

"Who?" Evelyn had a puzzled look on her face.

"He," she said slowly, "is the doctor who delivered me."

Understanding dawned on Evelyn's face. "Oh dear. Why do you suppose he wants to speak to you?"

"I guess I'm going to find out."

"Are you actually going to see him?"

"I am sure that God brought him here for a reason. I guess I am going to find out why."

The next day, Ruth entered Gold's private hospital room with trepidation. With butterflies in her stomach, she walked over to his bedside. She studied him. He looked old. He had white hair, a thin grey face and a frail body.

"Who's there?" his voice rasped as his eyes slowly opened.

"Ah, hello." Ruth shuffled her feet and looked around, not wanting to look this man in the eyes. *Lord give me strength,* she prayed silently as she felt sadness, anger and resentment build up all at once.

His words dropped like a stone in the silence, "You must be Miss Bohlman."

Her heart thudding, at last she said, "Yes."

The room hummed with the sound of electric lights. The sound of his labored breathing filled the air between them. As though each breath was fighting its way in and out, over and over.

"Miss Bohlman, I have so many things to say to you," he paused, lost in his memories. "It is hard to know where to start."

She felt unease seep through her. Maybe she should just leave.

He drew in air sharply. His hand went to his chest. His face lit up with pain. "It was a long time ago," he began, "and yet it feels like yesterday."

She looked at him penetratingly.

"You know the story I am sure, but I have to say that I am sorry. God, I am so sorry."

She crossed her arms over her chest. No, she did not know the whole story. All she knew were fragments of the past she had woven together on her own. Her mother had died as a result of childbirth, and Gold, being a drunk, had not helped the situation but had somehow caused it to be fatal for her mother. All she knew was that her father had deep resentment against this man who had taken his true love. All she knew was that because of him, her life had been hard, much harder than it should have been.

He continued, shifting his weight in the bed. "It affected my life you know. Everyone in town knew what I had done."

She gazed past him indifferently.

"They held it against me for the rest of my career."

He had a fit of coughing. Finally he sighed, his eyes closed. Then he opened them, searching her face.

"We've all made bad choices, but my lifetime of bad choices led up to her death, and for that I am truly sorry."

"It makes little difference now." Ruth looked at her hands, avoiding his eyes.

"You're right," Gold nodded in agreement, "it does make little difference now. I just wanted to let you know. I wanted to ask for your forgiveness."

Ruth sat quietly thinking of what this meant. She longed to hear the details of the day, but not this way. She didn't want to find out what happened from this man. She wanted to hear it from her father. God had brought her here to forgive but she did not feel ready. God brought Gold to her for a reason, which was forgiveness, and that's what she was supposed to do.

"I forgive you," Ruth finally said, more to ease Gold's conscience than for her own benefit. She could feel Gold's eyes fixed on her. She was sure that she didn't mean the words. She still was deeply troubled by everything that had happened.

Ruth stood to leave, feeling that there was nothing else to say. "If you'll excuse me, I must get back to work."

The silence was so absolute that Ruth barely dared to breathe.

"Thank you for coming to see me."

"You're welcome." Ruth turned to walk away.

She did not hear Gold mutter, "You look so much like her . . . it haunts me."

"What was that?" Ruth turned around and looked at Gold.

"Nothing. Nothing at all." Gold closed his eyes.

She took one last glance at him. He looked so frail and broken, as though life had got the better of him.

Ruth let out a deep breath and headed off to the operating room for her shift.

As she entered its doors, she tried to put aside all of the thoughts and emotions swirling inside her.

"Nurse Bohlman," Dr. Frederick greeted her.

"Good day." Ruth looked at Dr. Frederick, the surgeon she would be working with. He appeared agitated. Ruth was filled with apprehension. "What are we doing?"

"Tonsillectomy."

"Alright." Ruth started to prepare the instruments they would need. She lined them up on the surgical tray and looked at Dr. Fredrick.

"Tell them we're ready for the patient." He pointed toward the hall.

Ruth went outside of the operating room and said to the other nurse who was waiting with the patient, "We're ready."

The other nurse wheeled the patient in. After introductions between the patient, Ruth and Dr. Fredrick, the anaesthetic was administered.

Dr. Fredrick began to look inside the patient's mouth. "Nurse, you're not shining the light correctly. Get it right."

Ruth tensed at his tone. "Yes, Doctor." He was such a jerk.

He studied the tonsils for some time. Sweat ran down his temple. He turned to the tray of instruments and growled, "Where is the snare?"

"Right there, Doctor, second from the right."

"Next time put it where I can see it, Nurse," he growled.

"Yes, Doctor." Ruth would have liked to tell him to just open his eyes and pay attention but she held her tongue. He placed the snare inside the patient's mouth and began the procedure to dissect and snare the tonsils. Ruth shone the light on his shaking hand. His hand jerked slightly and blood spurted up from the patient.

"Damn it!" Dr. Fredrick had miscalculated the placement of the snare. "Nurse! Damn it! Watch what you're doing! I couldn't see with you shining the light in the wrong place!" The two of them worked frantically to control the bleeding while being doused in blood.

"I was shining the light in the right place, Doctor. You should watch what you're doing!"

"Damn it, Nurse! You're such an idiot! Why the hell do I have to work with idiots like you?"

Ruth looked Dr. Fredrick straight in the eye and stripped off her rubber gloves. "I will not be blamed for your miscalculation, Doctor. YOU ARE ON YOUR OWN!" Ruth threw her gloves to the floor with a dramatic splat. With that, she turned on her heel and left Dr. Fredrick there all alone with his bleeding patient.

Ruth stormed down the hall toward the exit to the residence. "What is his problem?" Ruth muttered to herself as she walked. "I will not be spoken to that way. I will be treated with respect!" She slammed the residence door behind her as she came in. All the nurses' heads turned as a blood-spattered Ruth stormed through.

"What now?" they commented.

Hearing this she angrily turned back toward the nurses' lounge. She addressed the ladies sitting there.

"Dr. Fredrick. That's my problem. You should have heard the way he spoke to me after HE was the idiot who mishandled the patient!" The nurses cringed as Ruth turned her back on them and went into the washroom.

Less than an hour later, there was a knock on her bedroom door. A young first-year nurse stood there, looking scared. "Sister Saint Christine would like to see you in her office."

"Thanks." Ruth's shoulders drooped. "I'll go right now."

"Lady, this type of behavior is not acceptable. This hospital will not allow you to simply up and walk out of a surgery when things get difficult."

"Sister, I did not walk out because things were difficult." Ruth struggled to keep from shouting at Sister Saint Christine. "I walked out because I will not be yelled at for his incompetence. *He* miscalculated the placement of the snare and he turned his self-fury on me. I do not need to be sworn at and yelled at because he is upset with his own mistakes."

"Lady, I will need to call your father and tell him about your unacceptable behavior today."

"I don't care, call my father. It makes no difference to me."

"You should care. Now get out of my office and start thinking of your apology to Dr. Fredrick."

That night Ruth was on her rounds. She was working in the ward for the mentally ill. She went into a private room of a male patient. He lay still in the bed, his hands folded over the blanket. He opened his eyes and looked at her. He was new to the ward.

"Hello," Ruth acknowledged as she snapped on her rubber gloves.

His fingers began to move across the blanket, clenching its folds.

Ruth went to the instrument tray. She began to disinfect each gleaming silver tool. She had a small bucket with soapy, bleach-filled water. The water was scalding and it warmed her hands through her rubber gloves. The bleach smell singed her nostril hairs.

When she was done, she arranged each instrument on the enamel tray and placed it on a rolling cart between his bed and the door.

He studied her as she worked. When she was done with the tray, she moved around his bed, readjusting the blankets and carefully tucking them in.

"How are you doing?" she asked.

He didn't answer. His eyes flashed at her.

"Are you feeling alright? Can I get you anything?"

He still said nothing. He breathed loudly through his nose.

"Water? Would you like a glass of water to drink?"

He nodded slowly. She went to the table next to his bed and poured some ice water from the pitcher there. She turned around to hand it to him.

"Here you are."

He waved his hands and shook his head no.

Ruth's eyebrows shot up. "No? No water? Okay. Well I'm going to check your temperature and maybe have a listen." She pointed to the stethoscope around her neck. "Would that be okay?"

He said nothing.

"Alright then." She shook the glass thermometer. She began to hum, soothingly. "Let's put this under your tongue then. Can you say ah?"

Before she knew what was happening, he lunged at her, his meaty hands wrapping around her neck. The thermometer clattered to the ground. Ruth's hands went to his arms and desperately tried to pull them away. She could feel him pressing harder and harder on her vulnerable windpipe. She couldn't utter a sound as he squeezed. He was looking her right in the eyes as she wordlessly begged for mercy. He smiled at her as he choked the life out of her.

I'm going to die, she thought. *Here and now.*

"Yea, though I walk
through the valley of the
shadow of death, I will fear
no evil: for thou art with
me; thy rod and thy staff
they comfort me."
Psalm 23:4 KJV

August 1943
Edmonton, Alberta

She struggled, her whole body flailing against the man. He now had his legs off the bed and was beginning to stand. She pulled away, walking backwards toward the door but he jerked her forward. He continued to smile as he tightened his grip.

Suddenly, she twisted to the right, kicking out her right leg as hard as possible. She kicked the table over that held the tray with all of its instruments. It sent a deafening clatter through the room as it hit the door. Ruth continued to twist left and right, trying to get out of his grasp.

The door flew open and several nurses came in and yelled, "SOMEONE GET HELP!"

The women valiantly pulled the man's arms back while a doctor shot the man with a sedative. He staggered and then finally collapsed on the bed.

Ruth gasped for air. She sank to the floor, shaking, her hands going instinctively to her neck.

"Ruth," one of the other nurses said, "are you okay?" She helped Ruth to her feet. "Let's get you out of here."

Numbly, she staggered out into the hall. Someone got her a chair. She sat down in it and began to cry. Several people came around her, offering their kindness and sympathy. She didn't want to talk to anyone. After a glass of water, someone checked her airway. Then she slowly walked back to the residence. On her way out of the hospital, she stopped at the public telephone. She picked it up and dialed. It was the middle of the night but she didn't care. She dialed a familiar number . . . home.

It rang.

"Hello?" his voice was filled with sleep.

"*Vater?*"

"*Hallo?* Ruth? *Ist alles in Ordnung?*"

She began to cry, "*Nein.*"

Three days later, Ruth heard a soft knock on her dorm room door.

"Ruth?" Evelyn called.

"Come in." Ruth looked up from her books toward the door. There stood Evelyn in her uniform, looking solemn. "What's wrong, Evelyn?"

"I wanted to tell you something."

Ruth wondered what was bothering her friend. "What is it?"

"Gold died today."

Ruth sat quietly, taking in the news.

"I thought you'd want to know." Evelyn took Ruth's hands in her own. "Are you alright? You've had a tough week."

"Yes, I am fine." She was silent for a while. "It makes no difference to me. We've had our words."

"You are so strong, Ruth. I'm not sure how I'd handle this."

"God helps me . . ." She hoped that very soon she would get the opportunity to hear the story from her father so that she too would know what had happened that day. She was glad for the opportunity to offer forgiveness to Gold before he died . . . if only she could mean it in her heart.

*

"I can't believe this class," one of Ruth's classmates grumbled as they walked from the old general hospital location back to the Miseracordia.

"I know—just because we're Protestants in a Catholic school doesn't mean we should have to suffer," another nurse complained.

"Every time *they* have a religion class, we have to work twice as hard to cover their shifts and then we have to suffer through this awful ethics class that is really a conversion class!" Evelyn was fuming.

Rachel burst in, "You know we were told when we signed up that we were not going to be pressured to convert, and yet the Catholic girls get favored and we end up in this ridiculous class with the Archbishop."

Ruth had been walking quietly along listening to the conversation. Her mind had been going a mile a minute thinking of a resolution. The student nurses' group she ran had been working hard to improve working conditions, but this was a bit out of the usual scope of problems. She couldn't help listening though and realizing that rather than just complain they needed to think of something to do to fix the problem.

"Ladies," Ruth spoke up and interrupted the griping, "I have an idea. Let's take the bull by the horns and address the real issue." All the girls went quiet and stopped on the sidewalk to listen to what Ruth had to say.

"I don't want to be overheard so why don't you all come down to my room tonight and I'll tell you what I'm thinking." The student nurses agreed and planned on a time to come by Ruth's dorm room.

They came in small groups throughout the night to avoid suspicion. Ruth proposed that in their next class they could make a statement. All the girls would need to be on the same page. She made them all swear that they would not speak a word of this even to their closest fellow nurses who were Catholic.

The next day in class, the Archbishop stood at the front of the room and began his ethics lesson. As he turned his back to write on the chalkboard, Ruth stood up from her chair with confidence. The chair scraped across the floor and interrupted the Archbishop's words. She wordlessly gathered her books and walked out of the room. Chairs scraped in a harmony of subtle rebellion against the floor, as wordlessly, all of the other girls in her class followed behind. Ruth looked back briefly and saw the Archbishop standing with his mouth open, frozen in place, with the chalk in his hand.

Point taken, Ruth thought as she led the line of students down the sidewalk back to their residence. They all said nothing, simply going to their respective rooms and shutting their doors. Ruth wondered how long it would be before Sister Saint Christine would be coming to call.

"Lady! I am outraged! I am appalled!" Sister paced back and forth behind her desk, shouting. "I am furious with you! You have crossed the line and have finally managed to pull a stunt to have you thrown from this school!"

Ruth cringed as Sister Saint Christine flung her anger at her.

"I have never been so embarrassed by any of my students in all my years! I could not believe when the Archbishop came here to tell me what happened!" Sister's face was flushed as she yelled. Her finger waved at Ruth. "How dare you? How dare you insult the school and the church this way? Who do you think you are?"

"I have my faith and I will stand by it! I do not need this hospital telling me how to run my spiritual life!"

Sister turned her back to Ruth. "Get out of my office," she hissed, "get out now before I say something I regret. You will be meeting the Archbishop at his residence after supper. I suggest you prepare your humblest apology. It will be your last apology at this school." She turned around to face Ruth and looked her in the eyes. "Ruth Bohlman, you are finished with the Miseracordia."

Ruth walked back to her dorm room and considered Sister's words. So she had finally done it. Sister had been threatening to send her home for the last three years and finally, it seemed, she had pushed poor Sister to her breaking point. Ruth wondered what her father would think when he got the phone call. She was sure he wouldn't be terribly surprised. She had certainly not been free from conflict these last three years.

As she entered the nurses' lounge at the residence, all of the nurses greeted her warmly.

"What did she say?" Rachel asked.

"Well," Ruth paused, thinking of how to phrase this, "she seemed to understand the point. I think she understands that we aren't impressed by our ethics class."

"Really?" Evelyn looked at Ruth, "and what else?"

"She wants me to go and see the Archbishop tonight, at his home."

All of the girls murmured.

"Are you going?" Rachel asked.

"Why of course," Ruth faked confidence and boldly stated, "well, I better go get ready." With that, she gave a little wave and went to her room. As she shut her door, she knew one thing: she was committed to her faith and she knew God would stand by her, even if it meant leaving nursing school.

"Young lady, I have to admit I was surprised when you left my class today." The Archbishop laced his fingers and placed them on his lap.

Ruth sat in an armchair across from him, in his home. "Yes, I know. I wanted to make a memorable point."

"Hmmm, memorable indeed." He sat examining her, looking deeply in her eyes.

He pointed to the tea on the tray on the table between them.

"Please, help yourself, Miss Bohlman."

"Thank you." She leaned forward and poured herself a cup. She mixed a bit of sugar into her cup. The spoon sang loudly as it tapped against the side of her teacup. She looked up at the Archbishop. "And you? Can I pour some for you?"

"Thank you, that would be kind." She poured him a cup and rose to hand it to him.

"So," he said, bringing the cup to his lips and taking a drink, "you wanted to make a memorable point."

She looked back at him with confidence. "I was told when I began nursing school that we would not be pressured to convert to Catholicism. I feel that your class contradicts that notion."

"I see. And what is your spiritual stance?"

"I believe that God is my personal Lord and Savior. I believe that Jesus Christ died for my sins on the cross. I believe that I can come to God in prayer, on my own behalf, and that he will hear me."

He looked away from her, toward the window. She watched him thinking things over.

"Thank you, Miss Bohlman, for taking the time to bring your feelings to my attention."

"I am sorry if I offended you, Archbishop, but I stand firm in my own beliefs. I do not feel that you and I are spiritually so far off base that we cannot agree to disagree."

Looking her in the eyes he said, "Thank you, Miss Bohlman. I admire your convictions." He set down his empty cup. "You know, to be that committed to your faith is something I don't see very often. Go now back to your dormitory. Sister Saint Christine will be in touch with you."

"Thank you." Ruth left the room with mixed emotions. The Archbishop had been kind. She couldn't believe that this was the end of her time at the Miseracordia. She walked back to her room so that she could pack her things.

"Miss Bohlman," Sister knocked on Ruth's door.

"Yes?" Ruth went to the door and opened it.

The pair looked at one another. Ruth wondered what more Sister had to say. Sister looked at Ruth's bags, full of neatly folded clothing. The hangers in the closet were empty.

"I have come to tell you that after speaking with the Archbishop, I have been convinced to give you another opportunity to attend our school. It goes against my better judgment, but we have agreed that your conviction to your faith is not something that you should be punished for. I would also like to tell you that your ethics class will be ceasing." Ruth smiled and said nothing but simply nodded and watched Sister Saint Christine walk away down the hall, graceful as ever.

*

A few months, later Ruth was working in the kitchen. Each RN had to take time in the diet kitchen to learn how to care for their patients with the right types of foods that would be suitable for their illnesses. The hospital provided good, healthy food for the patients. Every morning when Ruth cooked bacon, she longed to have a little taste. This was a luxury that was not served to the residents. Some of the students had been talking about how if they had their way, they would help themselves to the delicious food in the hospital kitchen.

Tonight some of the third-year nurses were meeting in the river valley for a campfire and some singing. Soldiers who were on leave would be meeting them there for the party and it was sure to be a good time. As the bacon sizzled on the grill, Ruth thought about how much the other nurses would love to eat bacon grilled on the campfire.

The smells came off the grill and permeated her senses. The idea began to grow in her mind, and as it did, it seemed to merit action. Ruth decided that she would take two packages of bacon from the kitchen cooler and bring them to the party. She wondered how she could do this without anyone noticing.

"Has everyone got their breakfast trays ready?" Sister Saint Agnes called out to the students working on their meals. "Everyone take them over to the trolleys and then we'll begin preparing our lunch service. Everyone on the left side of the room will take wards one through four. Everyone on the right will take wards five through eight." Sister Saint Agnes clapped her hands. "Let's begin, ladies!"

Ruth carried her breakfast tray over to the trolley and began to make her lunch trays. Afterwards, she cleaned up her dishes from her preparations. She carried the butter back to the cooler. As she found herself alone in the cooler, she realized that this was the best opportunity to snag the bacon. Before anyone else came into the cooler, she stuffed two packages of bacon into the wide belt around her waist. She held one hand on her waist to keep the bacon in place as she walked out the door.

"Goodbye, Miss Bohlman. Good work today." Sister Saint Agnes smiled at Ruth as she left the kitchen.

"Good day, Sister," Ruth replied to Sister Saint Agnes as she left, already tasting the bacon that they would feast on tonight.

Ruth walked down the hall briskly with her head down. She was only a few feet away from the door that led outside to the residents' hall when Sister Saint Christine bumped into her.

"Hello, lady," Sister Saint Christine looked at Ruth curiously.

Ruth tried to look natural as she held her waist. "Hello, Sister."

"Are you feeling all right?" Sister couldn't pinpoint what was not quite right with Ruth.

"I'm fine, thank you." Ruth wanted to get away. "I better be going."

"Good day, lady." Sister stuck out her hand to shake hands before they parted.

Ruth stuck out her right hand instinctively and as she did the bacon dropped to her feet. She gasped, "Oh no!"

Sister looked down on the floor at the bacon. "What on earth? Where did you get that?"

"From the diet kitchen."

"Well," she paused completely flabbergasted, "at least you told me the truth." She shook her head in disbelief.

"Yes, Sister, we're having an open fire down in the river valley tonight, down the hill. The night nurses and I. We're going to enjoy it thoroughly."

Sister said nothing and walked away, shaking her head all the way down the hall. Ruth quickly bent down, scooped up the bacon and ran the whole way back to the nurses' lounge. As she entered, she held up the bacon in triumphant victory and announced, "I've got bacon!"

Cheers went up around the room as Ruth recounted her story.

*

It was the end of her third year. Ruth had written her exams and completed all of her practical training. It was finally time to leave the hospital and strike out on her own. She needed to make one more stop before she left the Miseracordia Hospital.

"Come in," Sister called from behind the door.

Ruth opened the door. "Hello! I've come to say goodbye."

"Oh, Miss Bohlman, I'm so glad you took a minute to see me. Have a seat; we'll talk before you go."

This was a familiar spot for Ruth. She settled in the hard wooden chair and sat facing Sister Saint Christine.

"I wanted to congratulate you on coming in second place for top marks. You'd have been head of the class if not for your episode with your illness."

"Thank you, Sister."

"You're an excellent student, Ruth; you should be very proud of your accomplishments. You did incredibly on your RN exams. I am quite proud of you."

"Thank you." Ruth beamed at the praise.

"Where are you planning to go now? Private nursing?" Sister asked. "Or . . . I'd be happy to have you here as a clinical supervisor."

"Thank you but I've heard about nurses working on the reserves. It appeals to me as something I might try."

"Hmmm," Sister considered, "it can be challenging work on the reserves, but if anyone can do it, it's you."

Ruth smiled. "Thank you."

"You know, lady, you challenged me for sure." Sister folded her hands on her desk and looked Ruth in the eyes.

"Well, if you see it that way." Ruth knew she had indeed challenged poor Sister over the last three years. Neither had any hard feelings. "I've learned a lot from you, Sister, and I thank you for that."

Sister smiled. "I know you are destined for great things. Remember to *listen* from time to time. You will find that there are others in this world with things to offer who may just know a little more than you."

"I'll keep that in mind." Ruth smiled and rose from the chair. "I better be going. Father should be here any time now to pick me up."

"Goodbye, Miss Bohlman." Sister Saint Christine came around her desk and embraced Ruth with a warm hug. "Come back and say hello from time to time, alright?"

"I will." Ruth hugged her back. "Goodbye, Sister."

Ruth walked out of the office and down the halls one last time. She walked outside to the car where her father was waiting. He rushed out to greet her, "Ruth!" Herman hugged her fiercely and kissed her cheek. "It is wonderful to see you!"

"Hello, *Vati*," Ruth beamed at her dad, "I'm Nurse Bohlman! I did it!"

"I had no doubts, *Schatzi*, no doubts at all."

Ruth smiled and looked out the window as they drove away. She watched the hospital fade from view. This phase of her life was over. A new chapter was just beginning. Ruth was now a graduate nurse, the class of 1944, of the Miseracordia Hospital.

*"Repent, then, and turn to
God, so that your sins may
be wiped out . . ."*
Acts 3:19 NIV

February 1944
Slave Lake, Alberta

Jessie, the district nurse, came into the detachment and shut the door behind her. "Oooo, it's cold out today." She put her bag down just inside the door.

"Oh, hi, Jessie." Waldemar looked up from the papers on his desk.

"Brrr, brrrr, brrrr! I am frozen!" She pointed out the window, "It must be nearly twenty below."

Waldemar stood up. "Let me take your coat. Come and sit by the stove to warm up." He eased her coat off her shoulders and hung it on a peg near the door. He pulled a chair up right next to the wood stove and gestured toward it.

She laughed and pushed her blonde hair away from her face. "Oh, Pete. You're too kind, such a gentleman."

"So," he asked, "what brings you by today?"

She rubbed her hands together and held them next to the stove. "I don't know. I've only got one case that I need your help with. Mainly, I just couldn't stand the thought of sitting in my cottage all day with no one to talk to."

"Did you leave a note on the door?"

"Yes, pegged up there myself. Two nails, in fact, so it won't blow away in the wind. I said I'd be down at the RCMP office for most of the day."

"Well then," he smiled as he leaned against his desk, "I guess I have company for the day."

"I have good news . . ."

"What's that?"

"I brought lunch."

"Oh, that is good news. What is it?"

"Beef stew. We just need to warm it on the stove."

"That sounds delicious." He sat back down in his chair. "Thanks."

"So, Constable Peterson. I always talk about myself when we're together. This time it's your turn. Tell me more about yourself."

"What do you want to know?"

"Well," she grinned, "where were you working before you moved here?"

"First of all, I haven't moved here. I'm just covering for Constable Drake while he is away."

"Oh yes."

"And I came from Peace River. I've been there since the fall of 1940."

"That's a long time. Do you like it there?"

He paused for a minute, considering the question. "Well . . . I don't know. There are some good things and some not so good things."

"Like what?"

"The people there . . . the community. They are really warm and friendly. I also am part of the RCMP curling team there. It's been a great season for us so far. We've got a Bonspiel coming up this Friday."

"Oh, are you going?"

"I'm not sure."

Waldemar thought about the circumstances that had led up to this point. The honeymoon was over in Peace River. The first year had been good but then, as he came to understand the politics in the RCMP, his opinion had changed. Not everyone or everything was as it seemed. There was competition to get ahead and no one wanted to take responsibility for anything. If something went wrong, it was always someone else's fault.

The whole reason he was in Slave Lake was because he had ticked off his superiors. He was in charge of the record keeping for the Force gas pump. The pump was old fashioned and not terribly accurate. Every month when he measured how much gas he had versus how much had been used, he always came up short. At first it was just a small discrepancy. Then every month the difference grew. The problem was that there was no accountability. Officers were required to record their gas every time they filled up their patrol cars, but the key to the pump was in the office and anyone in the Force could use it when they needed it. No one monitored the usage.

The day before he came out to Slave Lake he had been pulled aside by his superior and questioned regarding the shortages.

"It's simple," he had explained, "Someone is taking the gas and filling up their own car."

His superior had growled, "That's not possible."

"Sure it's possible," Waldemar had argued. "It's not ethical, but it's possible."

The two had argued that if it was Waldemar's responsibility to keep track of the gas then ultimately he was responsible for the shortages. After that, his superior had told him that he was going to be spending the next six weeks in Slave Lake.

"But what about the RCMP bonspiel?" Waldemar had asked.

"Listen, Peterson. I like curling . . . I do. But the fact of the matter is that your detachment comes first. You'll have to find someone to fill in for you."

"Yes," he answered Jessie's question, "I'm going."

"But who will cover the detachment?"

"It will be fine," he said coolly, "It's only for a night. What can go wrong?"

Jessie shrugged. "I suppose it'll be fine."

"So," he asked, changing the subject, "where do we need to go today? Who are you going to see?"

"Mrs. McKinley. She's a widow in the community. She has a grown son—he's a drunk. The neighbors say he's been terrorizing her. She's had a terrible cough for months now but he won't bring her out to my cottage or get her any medical attention. I was hoping we could go out together so that I can check on her."

"And you didn't want to run into the drunk son?"

"Well," she winked, "I can handle most men, but I would like the company."

He chuckled, "I can come along. It will give me something to do. I've been here four days and I haven't had much to write in my police diary."

"Ya, not much going on out here is there?"

"That's probably for the best," he replied. "But at least I'll feel useful if I come with you."

She rubbed his arm affectionately. "Let's go then. Then we can have our stew when we get back."

He took her hand and pulled her to her feet. He grabbed her coat off the peg. "Here you are."

She slipped her arms in and did up the buttons while he reached for his fur cap and warm wool coat. He opened the door. She picked up her bag and walked out into the snow. He offered his arm, which she grasped tightly as they walked to the car.

Once on the road, Waldemar asked, "So how is nursing out here?"

"It's pretty good. Not too busy but just enough to keep things interesting."

"Are there any doctors in this area?"

"No, Peace River and Athabasca don't have a doctor. I do all the deliveries and emergencies . . . regular care and that sort of thing. Anything serious goes to Edmonton on the train."

"Where did you go to school?"

"The Miseracordia in Edmonton," she said. "It's a good school. I graduated in '41. How about you? How many years since you've signed up?" She started to laugh. "I guess what I want to know is how many years until you're eligible?"

Waldemar laughed uncomfortably. "Ah—three more years."

"Oh, too bad." She patted his arm as he drove. "I'm not necessarily asking for me . . ." She stared up at him, "but you know . . . nurses talk."

Waldemar shifted in his seat and cleared his throat. He looked into her bright green eyes. "They do, do they?"

*

Waldemar studied the placement of the opponent's yellow stones. There were three of their stones in the house. It was the last play of the tenth end and it was up to him to him, the skip, to make a winning shot. He positioned his shoe against the hack, his eyes fixed at the end of the curling rink. He lined up his stone in front of his right shoe. He rose slightly from the hack and pulled the stone back to his toe. He lunged forward, pushing the stone down the rink. As he approached the hog line, he twisted the stone slightly and let it go. He stood up, following down the ice, on his gliding shoe, watching the rock.

"HARD!" he yelled to his teammates, "SWEEP HARD!"

His two sweepers brushed the ice furiously, guiding the stone to its destination, the closest yellow stone.

"HEAVY HARD!" Waldemar yelled, "SWEEP!"

Their red stone struck the first yellow stone, spiraling it away from the button.

"TURN, TURN, TURN!" Waldemar yelled.

The sweepers madly swept in the direction of the next stone, smoothing its path to the next yellow target. The second stone slid out of the way, causing the red stone to turn back toward the center of the button.

The red stone slowed and stopped. Half of the stone lay in the white center of the button and the other in the outer blue ring. Waldemar's team began to cheer. "YES! WE GOT IT!" They all leapt together in a celebratory hug. They had won the tournament. They were national champions.

"Good work!" Waldemar roared.

Everyone clapped each other on the back and cheered.

"WE DID IT! VICTORY FOR THE RCMP!"

After the game, the team sat around a table, eating a banquet feast, put on by the host of the Brier.

"What a good game," one of Waldemar's teammates, Wilson, stated happily.

Waldemar raised his glass. "Cheers. Cheers to a great team. To a great time with friends."

The men all raised their glasses and crashed them together at the center of the table. "CHEERS!"

Wilson looked at Waldemar. "What a good night. Thanks for driving all this way—just for our game. We really couldn't have done it without you."

His other teammates, Martin and Campbell, agreed, "Great to be here with you, Pete."

"Speaking of which," Waldemar looked at his watch. "I should be getting back to the detachment. I've got a bit of a drive ahead of me tonight."

Martin moaned, "Ah, stay the night. I'm sure your replacement won't mind. He can stay an extra night."

Waldemar laughed, "Well, that's the thing. I didn't get a replacement."

Campbell gasped, "What? They let you go without a replacement?"

Waldemar shrugged and grinned sheepishly, "Not exactly."

"Did you drive your car?"

"I don't have my own car." Waldemar answered.

Martin chuckled, "Don't tell me you drove the patrol car without permission."

Waldemar shrugged, saying nothing.

Wilson began to laugh. "Just like you, Peterson. Never a man to let the words of a superior influence you. You guys should hear this story from training."

"No really," Waldemar interrupted. "There's no need."

Wilson put his hand up, "Don't try to stop me." He laughed and took another swig of beer. "So we're in Regina—we're training for the last time before we are supposed to ship overseas with the Provost Company. We're training in the boxing ring and the sergeant tells Pete here that because he physically outmatched the other recruits, he isn't allowed to hit back."

"What?" Campbell shook his head. "That's ridiculous."

"You're telling me," Wilson continued. "So for a few rounds he's in the ring, avoiding punches . . . getting hit, but not hitting back. Then he looks at me and says, 'To hell with this.' Next thing you know he's wiping the blood from his lip and he starts to clobber his teammate."

Campbell and Martin laughed.

"Sergeant steps in and says 'Whoa, whoa, whoa . . . did I say you could hit?' and our Pete here," Wilson slapped the table, "he says, 'I'm not going to be a punching bag for anyone!' Next thing you know, Sergeant's telling him that it's his way or else he can report to Sergeant Major. Well Pete here . . . he doesn't care. He marches right out of the gym."

"And then what happened?" Martin asked.

Waldemar spoke slowly and softly, "I told the Sergeant Major what had happened. He agreed that it was unfair. We came to the agreement that I could train independently in the gym."

"Wowee." Campbell whistled. "You are quite the guy."

Waldemar stood up from the table and extended his hand to his teammates. "Well, men," he said as he shook each of their hands, "it's been a pleasure. And now, I must be off."

Before he left town, he went by his old detachment to pick up the mail. He opened the door to his familiar home with his key. All was quiet. He went to the desk where all of his mail was sitting. There was a letter from the farm and a postcard from Gus. He slipped them into his coat pocket. He got into the police cruiser and drove out of town.

Three hours later, back at his hotel in Slave Lake, he read the postcard from his brother Gus. He was in England in the thick of the war. Waldemar was always relieved to hear from him. He lay back on the bed and read the tiny cursive, packed onto the small piece of paper the military allowed for correspondence.

Dear Bro Waldy,

Here I am at last to let you know where I am and how I am. I am real swell only a bit of a cold that I brought with me from good old Winnipeg, just something to remember home by. Well, Bro, so far I have had quite a good experience one might say. Xmas and New Years I spent in the heart of England for two weeks; had a very nice time, met some nice girls. They sure go for the Canadians; I wish you were here, however, I think I will enjoy myself while I am here. The station is no 'hell' and I mean it but one has to put up with things like that. After all, this country has been at war for three years, it's really not bad. Truly something feels good within me, to get the ships ready and send them away hoping they will all return. They do at times. I hope to get my leave next month—I'll be on my way to London. I hope to tell you more about the places next time I write. However, I hope to hear from you before then; let me know how everything is going. Thank you very much for the wire I received on the party in Winnipeg. We had a swell time only wished you could have been there. The weather here is very damp, we feel the cold much more than we do in Canada. Well, Bro, hope this letter finds you in good health just the way in leaves me. Until I hear from you, I remain your Bro Gust. Cheers. Write soon please.

Waldemar didn't care where the RCMP sent him; he knew if it ever got too bad he could join the thousands of other Canadian men overseas. He closed his eyes and let himself drift into sleep, thinking of Gus swooning the English girls without him.

A few days later, Waldemar was looking over his messages when there was a knock at the detachment door.

"Hello?" Waldemar opened the door to find Sergeant Bringham, one of his superiors from Peace River, on his doorstep.

"Constable Peterson?"

"Yes, that's me." Waldemar looked the sergeant over, "Come in. How can I help you?"

"Inspector Adams sent me. I am here to investigate a claim made against you. I have some folks saying that you left your post, took the cruiser and went to an event in Peace River."

"Is that so?"

"What do you have to say about these claims?"

"Ah, I'm not sure." Waldemar began to feel sweat on the back of his neck.

"Please get me your diary from the time in question. I'd like to see what you were doing at the time."

Waldemar's muscles tensed as he reached for the diary. He could see the blank pages in his mind.

"I won't look at it now, Constable Peterson. I do, however, want you to know that you could be facing formal charges if these allegations are true. Taking a police cruiser to an unauthorized social call is not something we take lightly."

Waldemar held his breath.

"I'll report back to Inspector Adams. I'll take a look at your diary and I'm sure this will all blow over." Bringham smiled reassuringly at Waldemar as he left.

Waldemar shut the detachment door behind Bringham. He exhaled loudly as he said, "Oh shit."

*"For we are God's
workmanship, created in
Christ Jesus to do good
works, which God prepared
in advance for us to do."
Ephesians 2:10 NIV*

November 1944
Kinuso, Alberta

Ruth walked through the snow into the village, her medical bag clutched tightly in her gloved hand. The wind bit at her cheeks and stung her nose. Every morning she began her day by checking in at the hotel. Anyone in the area who needed a nurse would call or send a letter letting her know that her services were required. On any given day, she didn't know how far she'd have to walk or what she'd be working on.

Ruth was stationed in Kinuso, Alberta. It was her first district nursing job since graduating from school. Kinuso was a small village with a population of eighty-two. She had met nearly everyone who lived in the village: a shopkeeper, a hairdresser, the pub owner and the hotel manager. There was very little to do in her free time other than clean the cottage.

The summer had been bearable. Every morning she made a house call, plotting out someone's residence on a map that the last district nurse had given her. The area around the village was heavily wooded and it allowed for long, peaceful walks. She had done plenty of immunizations and checkups, followed one woman's pregnancy and even delivered the baby. Now winter had set in. The snow drifted up to the bottom of her cottage windows. This made travelling on foot very difficult.

She opened the door of the hotel and went inside. The owner's wife sat at the front desk.

"Hello, Miss Bohlman."

Ruth stamped the snow off her boots. "Hello, Ellen."

"How are you today?"

Ruth pulled off her foggy glasses. "I'm fine. And you?"

"Good."

"Any messages for me?"

"Just one." Ellen shoved a piece of paper across the front desk. Ruth walked over and picked it up.

"Oh, Mrs. Robson wants me to pay her a visit." Ruth shook her glasses back and forth, trying to clear the fog. "How far is she?"

Ellen thought for a moment. "I'd say forty minutes in this weather."

Ruth groaned. "Oh, it's so cold!"

"Why don't I see if Thomas can take you in the sleigh?"

"Would you?"

"Sure. I'd hate to find you frozen to death in a snow bank."

Ruth laughed.

Ellen raised her eyebrows. "I wasn't kidding. Young thing like you . . . walking in a winter storm . . . you could get disoriented. Next thing you know . . ." Ellen smirked, "Nurse popsicle."

Ruth laughed, "Okay I hope you're joking now!"

Ellen started to laugh with her. "Maybe just a little. I'll go get Thomas."

Ellen left the desk and went to look for her husband. They returned a short time later. Ellen was holding two large stones. "Take these for the cutter. They'll keep you warm. If you make it quick, they'll probably be warm for the trip back too."

"Thank you very much," Ruth said sincerely.

"Shall we then?" Thomas asked.

"Yes, away we go."

Ruth and Thomas went out the side door of the hotel and walked to the barn. It was bitterly cold, chilling Ruth to the core. She held her hot stone tightly, tucking it inside her coat.

"So," Thomas asked as they entered the barn, "You must be pretty new at this nursing business."

"Ah yes. I graduated last spring."

He went to the horse and led him out of his stall. He began to hook up his harness. "Have you had any emergencies yet?"

"Well no . . . just the delivery."

"Well any woman can deliver a baby, right?"

Ruth rolled her eyes behind his back. "I suppose. But it does take some skill if any complications should arise."

Thomas led the horse to the cutter, a small two-person sleigh. "In you go, Miss Bohlman."

Ruth climbed in and put her medical bag at her feet. Thomas led the horse, pulling the cutter, out into the lane. Once he had opened the gate and closed it behind them, he climbed in next to Ruth. He pulled a heavy fur over their knees.

"Off we go!" The cutter lurched forward.

Within twenty minutes, they had reached the Robson's secluded cabin. Ruth went up and knocked on the door.

A young woman opened the door.

"Hello, I'm Nurse Bohlman. You sent for me?"

The woman smiled broadly. "Hello, come in."

Thomas had already disappeared to the Robson barn to find shelter for his horse. Ruth came into the cabin and made herself comfortable at the kitchen table. Mrs. Robson sat across from her.

"What can I help you with?" she asked.

"I think I'm expecting," Mrs. Robson said shyly.

"That's fabulous!" Ruth exclaimed. "When do you figure the baby is due?"

"I don't know . . . I think I might be about four months."

"And this is your first, correct?"

"I had a miscarriage with my last." Mrs. Robson looked down at her hands. "It was so sad."

"I'm sorry. Miscarriage is quite common," she paused. "I know that doesn't make it any easier. How long did you carry that pregnancy?"

"It was the fourth month." Mrs. Robson dabbed her eyes. "I just want to make sure it doesn't happen again."

Ruth sighed, "Well I'm not sure if I can predict that. But I'll examine you and we'll see how things are going. I'll check if you are gaining weight and if your abdomen feels the right size for the timeline you are figuring."

"Thank you."

Ruth had Mrs. Robson lie down on her bed. She examined her from head to toe. She checked for lice, looked over the condition of her skin, her hair and nails. She felt her abdomen, estimating the size of the uterus. She checked her blood pressure and then pulled a device from her bag.

"What's that?" Mrs. Robson asked as Ruth pulled a fetoscope out onto the bed. It looked much like a stethoscope with one major difference: it had a resting place for Ruth's forehead and a bell-shaped listening end that would be pressed against the fetus' back. Two buds, the same as a stethoscope, went into her ears to hear.

"This," Ruth explained, "is a fetoscope. It's for hearing the baby's heartbeat. I think you're actually five months along given the size of the uterus. If we're lucky I'll be able to hear the heartbeat." Ruth put her finger to her lips as she bent down close to Mrs. Robson's abdomen. She listened carefully for a long time, slowly moving the fetoscope around. Finally, her eyes lit up. "I've got it!"

Ruth could hear the rapid beat of the baby's heart, clear and strong. She looked at Mrs. Robson, her face expectant and curious.

"Do you want to listen?"

Mrs. Robson nodded.

Ruth held the listening end steady with one hand and with the other hand she passed the ear buds to Mrs. Robson. It was awkward but with some adjustments Mrs. Robson was able to hear it.

"Wow," she breathed, "that's amazing!"

"Isn't it something?"

They both were silent for a while as Mrs. Robson listened. Finally, she handed the ear buds back to Ruth.

"Everything sounds great." Ruth said happily. "I think that you may be far enough along that you don't need to worry about a miscarriage. By this time things are usually well situated. The baby has a good, strong heartbeat."

"Thank you," Mrs. Robson wiped a tear from her eye. "Thank you for coming today. I feel much better after seeing you."

Ruth began to pack up her bag. "My pleasure. I'm glad you called.

*

The wind rattled the cottage windows. Ruth looked up at the vaulted ceiling and sighed. The dark night pressed in all around her. She got up and added more wood to the stove. "I should be sleeping," she said to herself. The wind howled in response. She picked up her watch. Two o'clock. "What a long night." She put on her robe and sat at the large kitchen table. She pulled out her bible for comfort. She flipped it open, looking for some encouragement.

She ran her fingers over the familiar pages. "How am I going to make it until spring comes in April?" she groaned. The wind shaking the cottage windows was making it hard to focus. Ruth went to the window and looked out into the inky night. She touched the frost on the window, melting it with her fingertips. She began to sing to ease her loneliness.

Suddenly, there was a loud banging on the cottage door, startling her. She rushed over and opened it. The wind blew in, bringing in the swirling snow. Two men, one of them in an RCMP uniform, stood outside holding a third man on a stretcher.

"Come in, come in!" Ruth motioned the men inside and shut the door behind them. "What's going on?"

The Mountie spoke first. "Evening, ma'am. Sorry to barge in on you. We've got a man from up north, from the sawmill. He's nearly severed his leg. He's been in and out of consciousness."

Ruth recognized the other man as a worker from the train station. "Hello, Mr. McKinnis."

"Evening." He stood quietly holding his end of the stretcher.

"We haven't got much time," the Mountie urged. "We brought him in on the train. We've only got about an hour before he needs to be back on the train to Edmonton. We knew if we didn't stop he'd die before we got there."

"You're right," Ruth agreed. "I'll get changed. Then we'll set up on the table and see what I can do." She went behind a small screen and hastily changed into her uniform. She went to her wash basin and scrubbed her hands. Next, she cleared off the kitchen table. She went to her cupboard and grabbed three crisp white sheets. She draped them over the tabletop. "Move him onto the table," she commanded.

The Mountie and Mr. McKinnis laid the stretcher on the tabletop. Ruth held one end of the stretcher while the Mountie gingerly shifted the man to the table. The man cried out as they moved him.

"You," she pointed at Mr. McKinnis, "keep the fire warm. I'll also need you to hold up the lamp over the leg so I can see what I'm doing." She went into her medical bag and pulled out a rag. She poured ether onto the rag. "Hold this over his mouth and nose," she instructed the Mountie.

He did as he was told. Ruth assessed the patient, cutting away his pant leg. The leg was only holding together by the fractured bones and a few small pieces of tissue. She put on a pair of gloves, rolled out her equipment and went to work.

Ruth checked the patient's pressure. She waited until he was unconscious. As soon as he was under, she began to look at each vein and artery. She carefully sewed each one back together. She used clean rags to soak up the blood, clearing the field so that she could see what she was doing. She thought of all of the times she had assisted in the operating room. With God's help, she could focus and get the job done quickly.

After an hour, she was stitching up the last of his leg and bandaging it up securely. Her work had been successful. Color returned to the foot of the injured leg. The Mountie and Mr. McKinnis bundled the man up with warm blankets for his trip back to the train. The patient now responded to pain as the anesthetic wore off but he had still not opened his eyes. Ruth looked at him briefly before he left. He was just a young man.

"God speed to you," Ruth said goodbye to the trio, "take care of him."

"Thank you very much, Nurse. Surely, you've saved his life." The Mountie took hold of the stretcher handles. Mr. McKinnis and the Mountie took the patient out into the cold night, in a hurry to get him on the train to Edmonton.

After they left, Ruth let out a big sigh. "Wow!" She looked around the cottage at all the blood-stained sheets and rags. Her equipment lay on the table, having served its purpose. She closed her eyes and prayed for the young man. She prayed that he would make it to the hospital in Edmonton and receive the care he needed.

The next day, she spent the afternoon washing sheets at the hotel. She had slept until noon and then bundled up the bloody sheets and walked into the village. Ellen had been willing to help out with the bleaching and washing of the sheets.

As they sat over the wash basins scrubbing the sheets, Ellen said, "The whole town has already heard what happened."

"It's really not a big deal. I'm just doing my job."

"You're such a young thing though. Fresh out of nursing school!"

Ruth blushed, "I had good training."

"Well I'll say. You're not only a nurse, you're a surgeon!"

"Oh no. God guided my hands. I can't take the credit."

Ellen laughed, "You're too modest, girl. Be proud of what you did! The Mountie's been boasting about you all morning. He said he wouldn't have believed it if he hadn't seen it for himself. We're lucky to have you in our village. God forbid anything happen to any of us—well at least we know we've got a fighting chance!"

"Well thank you. Thank you very much. I just had to do what was necessary to get him to Edmonton."

Thomas stuck his head into the laundry room. "Hello, ladies. There is a phone call for you, Miss Bohlman."

Ruth jumped up from her washing. "Thank you."

Thomas led her to the phone at the front desk. She picked it up and said, "Hello?"

"Nurse Bohlman, this is Dr. Goodwin from Edmonton. I've been treating your patient this morning, Mr. McIntyre."

"Oh! Fantastic! How is he?"

"He's doing just fine, no thanks to us. We didn't have to do a thing. Your work on his leg was completely thorough. We had a surgeon look it over. He said that he hasn't seen finer work."

"Thank you."

"I wanted to call and tell you myself what an amazing job you did on Mr. McIntyre's leg. Your skills are impressive. You have the hands of a surgeon. There is no infection and here at the hospital we can all agree that you have saved Mr. McIntyre's life."

"Thank you, Doctor. Surely God guided my hands." Ruth was pleased to hear the young man had made it to Edmonton and had suffered no complications.

"You have a gift, Nurse. You sound so young. How old are you, may I ask?"

"Twenty-three, Doctor."

"Incredible! You have the skill of someone twice your age. I must congratulate you. You should be very proud of yourself."

"Thank you, Doctor. Please, will you send Mr. McIntyre my regards?"

*"Now to him who is able to
do immeasurably more than
all we ask or imagine,
according to his power that
is at work within us, to
him be the glory in the
church and in Christ Jesus
throughout all generations,
for ever and ever! Amen."*
Ephesians 3: 20 & 21
NIV

February 1945
Saddle Lake Indian Reservation, Alberta

Ruth rolled over in her sleep, alone in her nurse's cottage on the Saddle
Lake Indian Reserve. She tucked the warm quilt tightly under her chin,
her nose chilled from the cool night air. The fire burned down low in the
wood stove.

Suddenly, there was a loud knock at the door, waking her.

"Nurse! Nurse! We need you!"

Without hesitation, she hurled back the warm blankets. She threw
her winter coat on over her nightgown. She ran to the door and pulled off
the latch.

A young Native man stood at the door, his face peeking out from the
fur trim on his parka.

"Hello," Ruth smoothed her ruffled hair. "What's going on?"

"My wife—baby is coming!" Behind him was a horse with a blanket over its back.

"Okay. What's your name?"

"Kisecawchuk."

She gestured him into the cottage, "Come in, come in. It's cold!"

"No," he waved his hand at her, "you come." He pointed at her bare feet and then at his own moccasins. "Be ready. Time to go."

"Okay," she gestured toward his horse, "you can go ahead, I'll catch up." She shut the door on him and hastily changed into her uniform, a long navy blue wool skirt with a white blouse. She did up the buttons on her coat as she jammed her feet into her winter boots. She grabbed a clean apron and her medical bag, and opened the door. Kisecawchuk was still standing in the swirling snow.

"Come. Hurry!" he barked.

Ruth replied, "Yes, I'm coming."

He turned his back to her and began to walk briskly to his horse. She went toward her car and began to brush the snow from the windshield. Kisecawchuk studied her quizzically.

"No car, Nurse. Horse." He pointed at her and then to his horse. He pointed at the snow-covered road. "Too slow."

"Good grief," she muttered. "I don't think so." She hated riding a horse without a saddle, especially in her skirt.

"Horse!"

"I'll get the car warmed up in a minute."

With one swift movement, Kisecawchuk grabbed her around the waist and hoisted her onto the horse's back. She grabbed the horse's mane tightly with her free hand as she tried to find her balance. She slowly exhaled into the icy night air, "Dear Lord . . ."

Kisecawchuk mounted the horse, put one hand around her waist and then clucked a familiar sound to the horse. Ruth held her breath as the horse lurched forward in the snow. Its hooves moved steadily over the icy ground.

The ride to the Kisecawchuk's cabin seemed endless. Every time the horse took a step, Ruth was certain that she would fall off and break her neck.

She could see the smoke from the chimney long before she could make out the details of the cabin. The light from inside shone in bright patches onto the snow-covered ground. As they neared the cabin, Kisecawchuk slid off the back of the horse, pulling her down with him. She gasped as her feet hit the snow.

"Wow! What a ride!"

He cocked his head to the side. "Baby. Help with baby."

Ruth nodded again. "Yes, I know."

She went to the front door and opened it. A rush of warm air came at her, filled with the sights and smells of childbirth. A young Native woman lay naked on the bed, her thighs stained with blood.

"Oh dear," Ruth approached the bed. "What's going on?"

An elderly Cree woman looked at Ruth and shook her head. She muttered something that Ruth did not understand.

"She says," the laboring woman gasped, "that the baby is sideways."

The elderly woman began to speak again, more rapidly and angrily this time.

"She also says," the young lady cringed as another labor pain hit her, "that she's not sure what *you're* going to do about it." She screamed in pain, drawing her legs up.

"Okay," Ruth soothed, "I'm sure we can figure this out. Where can I wash my hands?" The young woman translated and another elderly woman came forward with a basin. Ruth took a bar of soap from her bag and began to scrub her hands vigorously. The laboring mother carried on screaming as the contractions gripped her. Ruth pulled on a pair of thin rubber gloves.

"What's your name, love?" Ruth asked tenderly as she moved between the woman's legs.

"Tanis," she cried.

"I'm Ruth Bohlman." Ruth looked around the room and saw half dozen young children on a cot. "And this is not your first baby?"

"No, the seventh."

"Have you ever had this problem before?"

Tanis cried out again. "No."

Ruth probed the woman's abdomen, trying to feel the position of the baby. Tanis screamed as Ruth pushed down on her belly. "I'm sorry," Ruth said softly as she continued. "I want to save your baby."

The elderly women clucked loudly at Ruth, pointing disapprovingly.

"Are you the only one who can translate?" Ruth asked.

"No. My husband," she panted, "he can."

Ruth turned to one of the elderly women. "Go, get her husband."

Tanis rapidly translated.

The woman smiled a toothless grin and went to the door, calling out for Kisecawchuk. He came inside.

"Sir," Ruth looked at the nervous husband, "I need you to help me. Hold her leg back like this." She showed him how to support Tanis' leg. She pointed to one of the elderly women. "You need to be on the other side." Kisecawchuk translated.

Ruth kneeled up on the bed and began to lean down on Tanis. With one hand inside the woman, pushing up on the baby's back and the other on the outside, she began to manipulate the position of the baby. The uterus contracted vigorously, fighting Ruth's efforts. Tanis screamed in pain. The elderly woman yelled frantically in Cree at Kisecawchuk.

"Come on, little one . . ." Ruth whispered as she leaned into Tanis. "Come on!"

The voices in the room reached a fevered pitch. The children on the cot began to wake and cry.

Ruth turned to Kisecawchuk. "Listen. Tell everyone to be quiet!"

Kisecawchuk barked at the women.

"Now," she said, looking at Tanis, "let's take a big, deep breath. I'm going to give one more push after the contraction ends. I think this is what we need to get the baby head first."

With one last push, Ruth was able to manipulate the position of the baby. Suddenly, its head was down, and as Tanis pushed, it shot out into Ruth's waiting arms.

Ruth clutched the slippery baby tightly in her arms, holding it awkwardly against her chest. She pulled up her apron, drying the baby's face. She quickly grabbed a clamp from her bag and clamped off the umbilical cord. She turned the baby over and began to rub its back vigorously. The baby sputtered and then let out a loud wail. Tanis laid back and cried, finally relaxed. Kisecawchuk leaned in and wiped Tanis' sweaty hair from her brow. He spoke to her in Cree. She softly answered, tears falling down her face. The elderly women said nothing. One woman came to Ruth and put out her arms.

Ruth handed the baby to the woman. She reached in her medical bag for scissors to cut the cord. The woman wrapped up the baby and took her to a wash basin near the wood stove.

Ruth spent the next hour tending to Tanis, delivering her afterbirth and cleaning her up. When she was through, Ruth helped her into a nightgown and onto another cot where she could nurse the baby.

After all of the soiled bedding and tools were clean, Ruth looked around the room at all the smiling faces.

"Thank you, *Asheni*," Tanis said quietly.

"Bohlman," Ruth smiled, "Ruth Bohlman."

"*Asheni* means angel," Kisecawchuk explained.

Ruth flushed, "I'm not an angel."

"You," Tanis explained, "are so young and fair. Only an angel would know how to save my baby."

Ruth smiled and shook her head. "I'm not an angel. I am, however, an instrument of God. He guides my hands when there is a patient in need. I cannot take credit for his work."

"Regardless," Tanis replied, "we are grateful. Will you stay and eat with us? Celebrate the birth of our daughter."

"Of course. It would be my honor."

*

Waldemar got out of the truck, shut the door and turned back to the driver. "Thanks a lot, Stan. I'm not sure if I'll be staying here or at the hotel. I'll just go inside and ask. Will you wait for a minute?"

"Absolutely," Stan agreed. "Take your time."

Waldemar walked up the stairs of the St. Paul detachment. It was a new post for him, his first post since he had been transferred to his prison assignment in Edmonton. He had been working in the guardroom for nearly two years.

It was late. He was looking forward to finding out what his accommodations would be and getting out of his uniform. He opened the door hesitantly. It was dark but in the shadows he could make out a desk with a typewriter sitting on the top of it. Behind it was a large wooden chair. Waldemar reached past a large filing cabinet and flicked on the light switch. The electric lights hummed.

He set his bag by the door and walked around the detachment. He quickly found the prison cell as well as sleeping quarters and washroom. As he came back to the front desk, he saw a note. It read, 'Welcome to St. Paul. You can stay here or at the hotel.'

"Nice," Waldemar muttered, shaking his head. The phone rang, making Waldemar start. He walked to the desk and picked it up. "Ah, hello?"

An irritated voice on the other end of the line asked, "Is this the police?"

"Ah, yes. Constable Peterson here."

"There's a fire down on Main Street! You should get down here." The person slammed down the phone.

Waldemar studied the receiver for a minute and then sat it back in the cradle. He wasn't even sure where Main Street was. He picked up his bag and went back to Stan.

"Hey, Stan. Can you take me to Main Street?"

"Sure thing, Constable, but the hotel isn't on Main Street."

"Ah, I know. I just got a phone call saying that there's a fire." Waldemar climbed into the front seat. "Say, do you know how to reach any of the other officers that work in St. Paul?"

Stan shrugged. "Not a clue."

Waldemar tapped the dash. "Let's get going then."

The two sped off in the truck toward Main Street. As they approached, they could see the liquor store. Flames were coming out of the second-storey windows, and shattered glass littered the boardwalk out front. A large group of people stood around, watching the blaze.

"Stop," Waldemar ordered. "Let me out."

Stan put the truck in park. Waldemar flung the door open and then began to push through the bystanders. "Excuse me," he yelled, "out of the way."

Waldemar broke the glass in the front door and then reached inside to open the door. It was hot. The smoke stung his eyes and burned his lungs. He went straight to the sales counter and looked behind it. The safe for the store was there. On top of it were the ledgers that kept track of the inventory. He struggled to pull the safe loose. A man entered the smoky store.

"Give me a hand," Waldemar shouted.

The man came over and together they dragged the heavy safe out onto the street. Waldemar looked at the man. "Thank you. I need you to keep an eye on the safe and the ledgers for me until some of the other RCMP officers get here."

"Sure thing," the man agreed.

Waldemar saw Stan standing in the crowd. "Stan, give me a hand!"

Stan jogged over to Waldemar. "Do you think it's a good idea to go in there?"

"The province will lose a lot of money. Any cases we can pull out before the main floor goes . . ." his voice trailed off as the sound of the beams cracking filled the air. He grabbed Stan by the arm. "Come on!"

The two rushed in, dragging out case after case of liquor. Finally, the smoke was so thick Waldemar gave up and ran out of the building. As soon as he was on the street, the second floor collapsed.

"Damn!" Stan exclaimed, coughing. "That was close!"

Waldemar looked at the cases of liquor. He hadn't been counting but there seemed to be considerably less than he and Stan had pulled out. He looked at the bystanders. "Hey! Listen up! Did someone take cases of liquor?" Everyone looked away, avoiding his menacing gaze. "Did you think I wouldn't notice?"

No one answered.

Waldemar growled, "Stan, get these cases in your truck. I need to check the neighboring buildings for anyone who might be sleeping."

"Okay, I can do that." Stan immediately began to pick up cases of liquor and load them into his truck.

Waldemar walked past the safe and noticed that the ledgers were missing. He looked at the man he had assigned to watch the safe. "Hey," his frustration was mounting, "where are the ledgers?"

The man shrugged. "I didn't see any ledgers."

"What the hell!" Waldemar banged his fist on the top of the safe. "If this isn't here when I get back I'm holding you personally responsible!" Waldemar ran toward the neighboring bakery. It had already caught on fire on the second floor. He broke open the door. "Hello! Anyone in here?" He quickly searched the first floor. He called upstairs, "Is anyone there?" There was no response. As he was leaving, he found a young man grabbing loaves of bread. "What are you doing?" he bellowed. "Get out of here!"

The young man ran away, saying nothing.

Waldemar shook his head as he left the building. "This whole town's gone mad!" He went into all the neighboring buildings on the street to check for occupants. When he was done, he stood on the street and watched with all of the other bystanders. It was cold, even with the heat of the fire. Waldemar's fingers had all turned blue. He shoved them into his pockets. People were shouting and grabbing merchandise from the stores, openly stealing and running away. He looked around to see if there were any other RCMP officers. No one had come. He stood and watched for the next three hours as the buildings burned completely to the ground.

Stan and the truck were gone so Waldemar decided to walk back to the detachment. He hoped that there would be another officer there to help him unload the cases of liquor.

It was four o'clock. The night was finally quiet. He opened the door to the detachment, hoping to be greeted by someone. It was dark in the detachment, and only the safe and half a dozen cases of liquor greeted him.

Waldemar shook his head. He recalled seeing Stan's truck filled with at least forty cases. Did Stan think he wouldn't notice?

"Jeez." He sank down in the desk chair with a sigh. "What a night." He looked at the note on the desk. "Welcome to St. Paul indeed."

*"I can do everything
through him who gives me
strength."
Philippians 4:13 NIV*

February 1945
St. Paul, Alberta

Ruth had both hands on the steering wheel. The roads were slippery and she did not want to end up in the ditch. She was on her way from the Saddle Lake Reserve into St. Paul. She had a few letters to mail and a paycheck to cash. It was a sunny winter day and the reflection of the sun off the snow-packed road caused her to squint her eyes.

She was glad to be getting away from the reserve for the afternoon. Things had been quite challenging lately. She had discovered that the endless headaches on the reserve, and the requests for Aspirins, had not been completely legitimate. She realized after she had given out nearly five bottles of Aspirins in two weeks that some of her patients were mixing the Aspirins with Coca Cola to get a high. Since then, she had insisted that her patients take the Aspirins in her clinic if they were indeed inflicted with intolerable pain. This had caused quite a stir. Many of the Aspirin users had come by to yell at her and call her an idiot, threatening her and trying to intimidate her. To top it off, a Mountie from St. Paul had written her a letter warning her not to withhold medication from the residents of the reserve. She shook her head as she drove.

"Who does he think he is?" she muttered as she drove. "What does he know about anything?" She had promptly set him straight, sending him a scathing letter telling him to mind his own business. She had written that he didn't have a clue what he was talking about and that he should stick to policing the residents of St. Paul and leave her alone. She figured he wouldn't be telling her what to do after he read the letter.

Nurses and Mounties worked closely together in rural Alberta. Mounties not only policed the community, they helped the mentally ill, the elderly and the disadvantaged. Many nurses would chase after Mounties, romantically speaking. Jessie, Ruth's nursing friend, had seen one Mountie who was working in Slave Lake a couple of years ago. She had gone on and on about him. Jessie had accompanied a matron, a female inmate, with this Mountie and she couldn't stop talking about how she was going to marry him once his seven-year commitment with the RCMP was over. Ruth had met many kind Mounties for sure, but marriage was not a consideration for her.

All of her peers were searching for husbands or starting their families. Ruth didn't feel the same pressure. She was still in contact with Nick. They wrote letters back and forth. He became increasingly committed to her as she began to feel increasingly cool. She was enjoying her independence out on the reserve, and all he wanted was for her to settle down in Edmonton with him, once he was done serving in the war. When he got back, she would talk to him face to face and tell him that he was not the one for her.

Ruth parked the car across the street from the bank. She had her paycheck to cash before she could buy postage to mail her letters to her father and Artrude. Ruth took her papers off the passenger seat and went inside. After cashing her check, she came out of the bank and crossed the street to her car. The sun was shining, reflecting off the snow, the sky was blue and the air was crisp and clean. As she paused to open her car door, she saw, across the street, a Mountie coming out of the post office. He had his hat under his arm. In his hands were some letters. He was tall and had blonde wavy hair. His brown uniform showed from beneath his winter coat and his tall boots clung to his muscular legs. Ruth was frozen, watching him descend the post office steps. He smiled at someone he passed.

Her hand went instinctively to her chest. "Oh my," she muttered. She wondered if one of the letters in his hand was her letter, admonishing him for sticking his nose into her business at the reserve. She felt a pang of embarrassment and then pushed it aside, *At least I'll make an impression on him!* she thought.

"Miss," a passerby asked, "Are you alright? Is your key working?"

Ruth blushed and snapped back into reality, "Yes, I—I was lost in thought there for a minute."

The passerby chuckled, "It looks like you were studying St. Paul's newest Mountie," he paused, "Peterson's the name, I think."

"Peterson," Ruth considered the name for a minute. That was the Mountie Jessie had been going on and on about! Now she could see why.

Waldemar came out of the post office with two letters under his arm.

"Good afternoon," he said, smiling at a young lady he passed.

"Afternoon, Constable," she replied, returning his smile.

Waldemar ripped open the first letter as he walked down the street back to the detachment. His smile dissolved as he read the first few lines. When he was done reading it, he decided that he needed to get out to the Indian Reserve as soon as possible. He would have to speak to this Nurse Bohlman and explain his intentions.

"Ugh," he sighed as he shoved the letter back in the envelope. "What a mess."

He opened the second letter, hoping that would cheer him.

February 3, 1946

Dearest Waldemar,

How are you? I hope this letter finds you well. I will get straight to the point although I must admit I find this difficult to say.

I am writing to tell you that I no longer am interested in pursuing you romantically. My sweetheart from overseas has returned. We have concluded that we are not meant for one anther, as we had thought so many years ago. I regret to tell you that another man has captured my attention and I thought it only respectful and fair to tell you about it straight away.

He is a pilot and was kind enough to take me on a flight with him in his seaplane. Unfortunately, due to the shortage of fuel, we ran out of gas on our trip and ended up spending the night out on the lake. We had meaningful conversation and since then have realized we may be in love.

I hope that you are not upset by this formality of me telling you that I have found love elsewhere. I felt as though things between you and I have cooled in this last year. I wanted to be straightforward with you, because I do love you in so many ways. You have always been a good companion for me and perhaps if you were not in the Police Force we could have been a couple. The lifestyle just isn't favorable to us keeping as close as I would like. I am sorry.

I hope that we can remain in touch as friends; you have always been such a good friend to me, Waldemar. I love you dearly and wish only the best for you as you pursue your career.

Love Marie

"Well then," Waldemar said to himself as he folded up the letter and tucked it into his pocket next to the letter from the reservation nurse. "Today is not my day."

He pushed open the detachment door and went to his desk. His fellow officer, Harry Thompson, sat at his desk.

"Hey, Pete."

"Hi, Harry."

Harry took his hands off his typewriter and picked up his coffee. "You don't look too happy."

Waldemar sat down in his chair and began to sift through the papers on his desk. "I'm having trouble with a reservation nurse. The Aboriginals were complaining that she wouldn't give them any Aspirins. I simply wrote her a letter—hoping to clear up the matter, to say that she shouldn't hold back medication from her patients."

"I see," Harry put down his coffee cup. "So what's the problem?"

Waldemar smirked and raised an eyebrow. He reached into his coat pocket and selected the letter from the nurse. "Read this."

Harry skimmed over the letter quickly. He let out a low, long whistle. "Wow. She told you!"

They both began to laugh. Waldemar said, "I'm telling you . . . she makes a memorable fist impression!"

"Listen," Harry said, leaning forward, "I've heard a lot about this nurse. I was hoping that you could take me out to the reservation tonight."

"What for?" Waldemar asked, a puzzled expression on his face.

"A social visit."

"A social visit? Even after reading this?"

Harry laughed. "Hey, I've heard nothing but good things. Maybe she's right. Maybe you have no business sticking your nose into things you know nothing about."

Waldemar frowned and shook his head. "Thanks. Just what I need."

"What?"

"I'll take you on your social call. But you owe me one."

Harry smiled widely. "Thanks. And don't bring up the letter. If we're going, then we're going to have a good time."

Waldemar began to press down on his typewriter keys. "Sure thing, Harry. Sure thing."

Out at the Indian Reservation, Ruth sat with her friends, Harold and Annie. Harold was the Indian agent at the reserve. He and his wife lived in a large house there. Harold was an employee of the Canadian government and he dealt with relations between the Aboriginals and the government, both financially and socially. Ruth was drinking coffee and talking to Annie about the latest spring fashions when they heard a car pull up its tires, crunching through the snow.

Ruth got up and went to the window. She pulled the curtains aside and wrinkled her brow as she asked, "Are we expecting a police cruiser?" She looked at Annie. "Were we having trouble with someone?"

"No," Annie answered, "we didn't call for anyone."

"Perhaps they have some business of their own," Harold commented.

Ruth felt butterflies as she saw Constable Peterson step from the cruiser. She wondered if he was here to talk to her about her letter. She saw a second constable step out from the passenger side. *Oh boy, what is this about?* she wondered.

"I'm going to put another pot of coffee on," Ruth said nervously.

"Sure," Harold agreed. "I'll see what's going on."

Harold greeted the constables at the door as Ruth disappeared around the corner into the kitchen. "Evening, gentlemen, please come in."

"Evening, sir." Constable Thompson greeted Harold as he came in.

"What brings you by today, Officers?" Harold asked.

"We've come for a social call this evening, sir. I'm Constable Harry Thompson and this is Constable Waldemar Peterson."

Harold shook hands with each of them. "Pleasure to meet you."

Harry asked, "Is the nurse here this evening?"

Annie looked relieved, "Oh, of course! She's just in the kitchen. Let me get her!" Annie hurried off into the kitchen to get Ruth while the two constables sat down with Harold.

Ruth was making herself busy in the kitchen when Annie came in.

"Ruth, the constables are here for a social visit." She smiled and winked at Ruth. "They sure are handsome! You go and visit. I'll finish the coffee."

"Okay." Ruth wiped her hands on a tea towel and then smoothed her hair before she went into the living room. She took a deep breath before entering the room.

"Ah," Harold smiled, "here she is!"

"Evening, gentlemen," Ruth greeted the constables.

Harry and Waldemar rose to their feet. "Evening, Nurse." Harry stuck out his hand. "I'm Harry Thompson, pleasure to meet you."

"I'm Ruth Bohlman, it's a pleasure to meet you." She turned to the other constable and smiled.

"I'm Waldemar Peterson, pleasure to meet you Miss Bohlman."

"Evening, Constable Peterson."

The five of them talked for just under an hour. After all the coffee and desserts were gone, Waldemar started to get the sense that Harry was wanting some time alone with the nurse.

"Harold, could you show me the stables?" Waldemar asked. "I grew up on a farm and I'd like to see the horses you have."

"Sure, I'd love to show you around. I'll get my coat and we can go take a look." Harold winked at his wife.

"I have to go tidy up the dishes." Annie rose from the sofa and smiled at everyone. "If you'll excuse me, I'll go attend to that while you young people visit."

Ruth and Harry looked at each other. Harry grinned broadly. "All right then, Miss Bohlman and I will keep each other company."

Waldemar went outside with Harold and the two discussed the different kinds of horses that he kept on the reserve. The two men had a wonderful conversation while Waldemar admired the grand horses.

Meanwhile, inside the house, Ruth and Harry talked about matters on the reserve, issues in the town and politics of the war. While Harry talked, Ruth's mind began to wander. She wondered what Constable Peterson was doing with Harold.

"Miss Bohlman?" Harry interrupted her thoughts.

"Ah, yes?"

"I asked you what church you were attending."

"Oh," she laughed uncomfortably, "I—ah, I haven't found a church just yet."

"Perhaps then I could accompany you to a Sunday service?"

"What denomination?"

"Catholic. Are you Catholic?"

"Uh, no. I'm Baptist."

"Oh," Harry shrugged. "I suppose it doesn't matter. You could come to a service. There aren't any Baptist churches in St. Paul."

"Thank you for the invitation. That's kind of you. I think I will worship on my own for now."

Harry looked puzzled. "Have I offended you?"

She smiled reassuringly, "No, of course not."

Just then, Harold and Waldemar returned to the house. Annie came from the kitchen.

"It's been great fun having you out to visit," Annie remarked.

"Thank you for having us," Waldemar replied.

"Thank you very much for the splendid evening," Harry said.

Ruth looked at Waldemar and smiled.

Waldemar tipped his hat to Ruth. He smiled back at her and said, "I'll be in touch with you, Miss Bohlman."

"Yes, Constable," Ruth looked into his sparkling blue eyes, "I imagine you will."

*"Your beauty should not
come from outward
adornment, such as braided
hair and the wearing of gold
jewelry and fine clothes.
Instead, it should be that of
your inner self, the unfading
beauty of a gentle and quiet
spirit, which is of great
worth in God's sight."
1 Peter 3: 3 & 4 NIV*

March 1945
St. Paul, Alberta

"OUT OF THE WAY, PETERSON!" Ruth screeched as she gripped the steering wheel of her blue Ford Tudor. She was barreling down the snowy Reservation road taking care not to leave the rutted tracks. The snow was deep and if she swerved she would surely be stuck again. "OUT OF THE WAY!" she yelled as she honked the horn.

Constable Peterson's police cruiser was headed straight for her.

"Peterson," she hissed, "I'm not going to move." She stepped on the gas, accelerating toward him.

At the last minute, he jerked his car off the road and into the ditch, narrowly escaping a collision.

Ruth slowed the car down and brought it to a stop. She climbed out the driver-side door. She inspected the wheels, now sinking in the soft snow. "Oh hell. Now I'm going to be stuck again."

Constable Peterson came marching angrily down the road. "Nurse Bohlman," he shouted when he was still several yards away, "what in heaven's name are you doing?"

"I," she pointed angrily at her car, "was trying to get back to the cottage without getting stuck!"

"You were speeding!" he came right up to her and waved a finger in her face. "I should give you a ticket!"

She pulled her wool cap tightly over her ears and huffed. "Do you have any idea how many times this stupid car has been stuck today?"

He shook his head, still scowling.

"Six! Six times I have had to figure out how to get out of the snow and back on the road. Do you think I have time to get stuck again?" She leaned toward him, "Do you?"

"I understand—"

"I don't think you do," she interrupted. "I have people dying all over the Reservation. Typhoid fever—if I had to guess. I am very busy teaching hygiene to try to stop the spread. I also have to care for the sick and to top it off I'm collecting water samples to send to the lab in Edmonton. I've got fifteen places to get to today and," she pointed furiously at the sun, "the sun is already going down!"

"I can appreciate that you are very—"

"I don't know that you can. Do you have any idea how hard it is to get this stupid car around the reservation in the snow? And now—now you want to give me a ticket?"

Waldemar put up his hand. "Stop. Stop talking."

Ruth crossed her arms across her chest and scowled. "What?"

"Stop talking and listen for a minute."

She opened her mouth to say something.

"Stop. I mean it or I *will* write you a ticket. A big one."

Ruth clamped her lips together, frowning.

"I hear what you are saying. I can see that you are a very busy woman with a big job. What I want from you is a promise." He studied her for a moment. "I need you to slow down. If you hit someone on these roads, you're going to have a lot bigger problem on your hands. Let this be a warning to you. You and I are a team out here. We both want to keep people safe. No more speeding . . . understand?"

"Yes, sir."

"Good." Waldemar relaxed for a minute. "Now I'm going to help you get going. It's getting dark so perhaps you should head back to the house for the night. Tomorrow morning you can go back out and finish your work."

Ruth glared at Waldemar. "Are you finished?"

He looked puzzled. "What?"

"Are you finished telling me what to do?"

"I guess—" he stammered.

"I'll be on my way then." With that, she turned and got into her car, slamming the door behind her. The water samples on the seat all shook precariously. She looked in her rearview and saw the constable, his hands on the back of the car, ready to push. He made a signal for her to step on the gas. She did. With one mighty push from Waldemar, the car rolled down the road. She drove slowly and carefully in the direction of the Indian agent's home, watching the constable get smaller and smaller in the distance.

A few days later, Waldemar sat in the detachment going through the mail when the phone rang.

"Constable Peterson," he answered.

"Hi Constable, it's Ruth Bohlman, I'm the nurse from Saddle Lake."

"I know who you are," Waldemar grinned as he leaned back in his chair. "What can I do for you?"

"I wanted to see if you had freed your car from the woods the other day."

"Yes thank you," Waldemar said, "and what if I hadn't? You're only just calling now?"

"I'm sorry if I was abrupt. I called to apologize. I was rude. I have quite a lot on my plate right now with the fever."

Waldemar's eyebrows shot up. "It's okay."

"Yes," she paused, "I also wanted to say that it was nice meeting you the other night—ah, at the house. You and your fellow constable were very kind to come by."

"I assure you, it was my pleasure. It was nice to put a face to the name. I've heard a lot about you."

Ruth laughed nervously. "Ah—Harold said that you had a nice visit with him out in the barn."

"Yes, I grew up on a farm. I enjoy looking at the livestock. I was showing him how I am at guessing the weight of his horses."

"Hmmm, how does that work?" Ruth asked.

"Well, I take a good look and feel of the livestock, from all angles. I measure up the shoulder width, the backside and I have to say I'm quite accurate at guessing their weight within a few pounds."

"Really, and why would you do this?" Ruth wondered what purpose this skill would fill.

"Well, when we were young we would take our livestock to market. You had to know the weight of your livestock so that you could get fair value for money."

"I see, it sounds like you're quite the expert at sizing things up."

"Well yes," Waldemar chuckled, "I suppose I could size you up if I had the time to take a good look."

"Excuse me!" Ruth laughed despite herself.

"I'm just saying if I had a good look I bet I could guess your weight within five pounds."

Ruth grinned, "I don't think so, Constable."

"I'll make you a deal. I'll come to call on you and if I can't guess your weight within five pounds I'll buy you a box of chocolates. If I get it right then you'll buy me a box."

"I have to say you've caught me off guard." There was a long silence on the other end of the line. "Listen, I'll look forward to your visit but hear this: you can look but you can't touch—then we'll have a deal." She paused for a moment. "I'll look forward to my chocolates."

"Me too." Waldemar smiled and said goodbye, promising to come to the Reservation as soon as he could.

Waldemar took Ruth up on the bet and went out to visit her as soon as he had a free evening. He pulled up to the Indian agent's home and parked the police car.

Ruth waited at the window. She looked at herself in the hall mirror before answering the door.

"Evening, Constable," Ruth said softly as she opened the door.

"Evening, Miss Bohlman." Waldemar smiled and removed his hat. "How are you this evening?"

"I'm fine. Will you come in and have some coffee?"

"It's a mild night for March. If you have a warm coat I thought we might go for a walk. Would that be alright?"

Ruth shrugged. "Sure. I'll get my coat and boots and we can walk around the property."

The pair went out into the winter night and walked the well-worn path between the house and the barn, through the tall Spruce trees.

"So tell me about yourself, Miss Bohlman," Waldemar said. "Where are you from?"

"Well, I grew up in Leduc, with my father and step-mother. My father runs a hardware store there. He's been quite successful with it."

"And where have you been since you left home?"

"I went to nursing school in Edmonton for three years. Then I did some private nursing and some district nursing. After that I was told by a friend about working for Indian Affairs and thought it sounded like a challenge I might be up for."

"It is challenging, isn't it?" Waldemar said quietly. "How is the sickness? Did you find out if it's Typhoid?"

"Yes. I sent my water samples on the train to Edmonton. The lab there was able to confirm that we are infected."

"Oh dear."

"Now I have to go dump Lye down every toilet on the reservation. Hopefully the people will let me do that. It's the only way to stop the spread."

"That sounds like a big job."

"Not bigger than treating a whole reservation of sick folks."

"That's true." He looked at her, trekking through the snow next to him. He smiled.

"Let's stop in the barn," Ruth suggested. "We can warm up for a minute."

"Sure." Waldemar pulled the large barn door open. "After you."

Ruth and Waldemar entered the barn. Ruth pulled down a horse blanket and set it on a few bales of hay. The pair sat down and continued to get aquatinted.

"Tell me about yourself, Constable."

"Well, I grew up in Lac Du Bonnet, Manitoba, on a farm. I've got a large family, three brothers and five sisters."

"Wow, that must have been fun."

"Yes, I had a wonderful childhood. I was always busy on the farm. I loved the wildlife, the swimming and the land."

"What drew you to the RCMP?" Ruth asked.

"I knew an officer when I was a young boy. He was killed in the line of duty and it left such an impression on me that I decided that one day I would join the Force myself."

"Wow, and do you enjoy it?"

"Yes, it has its ups and downs, as does every job. But for the most part it is quite rewarding."

The two sat quietly lost in thought, listening to the rustle of the animals in the barn. Finally, Waldemar spoke up. "So for our bet, will you let me have a guess?"

Ruth laughed and blushed slightly. "I'm looking forward to my chocolates . . . so yes."

"Well I need to have a good look then." Waldemar smirked at Ruth.

Ruth stood up from the hay bales, unbuttoned her coat and then spun around, laughing.

He studied her admiringly, noticing every curve. Finally, he said, "Well, you look good. I think you'd fetch a good price at market . . . I'd say 132."

Ruth stood with her mouth open. "That's a little high, don't you think?"

"Well, am I right?" he laughed.

"Well you are, but it doesn't hurt to flatter a lady by guessing a little low!"

Waldemar smiled as Ruth buttoned her coat. "I just love chocolates that much. I guess you owe me a box."

"Yes . . . I guess we'll have to be seeing each other again." Ruth smiled at Waldemar. "Come on, farm boy, let's go back to the house and have some coffee so that we can warm up."

"Sure thing, Nurse, sure thing," he rubbed his gloved hands together to try to warm them.

The two walked back to the house laughing and talking as Waldemar shared childhood stories of swimming against the current while his mamma worried herself sick. After a cup of coffee inside the house, Waldemar left for the night. He made a promise to meet Ruth on Saturday night for dinner in town.

Ruth stood outside the restaurant with a box of chocolates in hand, waiting for Waldemar to arrive. She was anxious for their night together. She had her hair done that afternoon and she had put on her best dress. It was a tailored grey wool dress. A row of black buttons went down the left side of the dress, drawing attention to all the right places. She always tried to wear the latest fashions despite her limited budget.

Waldemar walked toward the restaurant, lost in thought. He smiled when he saw Ruth waiting with her box of chocolates in hand.

"Hello, Miss Bohlman," he greeted her.

"Hi, Constable." She waved back at him.

"Shall we?" he asked as he opened the restaurant door.

The two settled themselves at a quiet table. They ordered dinner. As they were waiting for their meal, Ruth noticed that Waldemar was unusually quiet.

"Is everything okay, Constable?"

"I—I had news from home," he paused, "—bad news."

Ruth waited quietly for him to explain.

"It's my sister, Alice, she has passed away."

"Oh, I'm so sorry." Ruth reached across the table and took his hands. She said a quiet prayer in her heart. "Are you going home for services?"

"No, it's too soon and the train is too costly. I've sent word home with my sympathies for the family."

"I'm sorry."

"Thank you."

They sat in silence for a while. The waitress brought dinner followed by coffee along with a slice of pie for Waldemar and a piece of rich chocolate cake for Ruth. They sipped their coffee, occasionally meeting one another's gaze.

Finally, Ruth said, "Why don't you tell me about her?"

Waldemar thought for a moment. "She was quiet. She had blonde hair . . . we all did when we were young . . . but she did even as a young woman. She was Mamma's right hand. Always helping on the farm. Mamma was always overprotective of Alice. Both Alice and Victor . . . they both had special treatment as children." He took a bite of pie. "I don't know why."

"Perhaps they had a health condition."

Waldemar considered this for a while. "Maybe. Alice loved the garden. And the younger children . . . she always took good care of the younger children. She was only thirty-two . . . so young."

Ruth rubbed Waldemar's hands reassuringly. "It is too young. Too young for us to understand."

The words caught in his throat, "I didn't even know she was sick."

They ate the rest of their dessert and had several rounds of coffee as the evening turned to night. The conversation drifted to matters of the reserve, St. Paul and the local social scene. Finally, after the waitress had wiped the last empty table clean, Waldemar said, "I guess we better leave before they throw us out."

Ruth chuckled, "Yes. I'd hate to be a troublemaker."

Waldemar raised his eyebrows and put an arm around her shoulder as they walked out of the restaurant. "I think you already are."

At the car, Ruth turned toward him, suddenly uncomfortably close. Waldemar looked down at her. She slipped her arm around his back and gave him a hug.

"Thank you for the evening, Constable Peterson. I had a nice time tonight."

"Me too. And you know . . . my friends call me Pete." Waldemar smiled at her. "I think we could say that we're friends now."

"I'd have to agree . . ." Ruth smiled, hesitating for a moment, " . . . Pete. And you can call me Ruth."

"Thank you for your company, Ruth." He ran a hand through his hair, smoothing it into place. "I hope we can do it again sometime."

"Definitely."

They hugged awkwardly.

"Goodnight, Ruth."

She got in her car and gave a little wave as she drove away.

Waldemar watched the car fade into the darkness. He thought about this pretty, young nurse that had captured his attention. They definitely had the potential to be good friends. It was nice to have a friend out here. He was determined to nurture that friendship as much as he could before he was sent somewhere else.

*"Defend the cause of the
weak and fatherless;
maintain the rights of the
poor and the oppressed."
Psalm 82: 3 NIV*

May 1945
St. Paul, Alberta

Ruth dumped Lye down nearly every toilet on the reserve, killing the Typhoid and purifying the water before it leeched back to the water table. Good health was returning to the community. Spring had turned into summer and traveling the reservation roads was easier, allowing her to visit more patients in a day.

Now that the fever was subsiding, there was a new concern. There was great fear among the families with young children. The Catholic school was coming through to register children for the following school year. Any child seven years of age or older would be sent away to Red Quill School. There they would be taught English and educated properly. *Properly*, Ruth scoffed inwardly. She felt it was hardly proper for a child to be taken from their home and culture. She didn't understand how it could be right to force a child to learn a new language and religion. When the Native mothers came to her, begging for help, she told them the only sensible thing she could—hide the children. This was a secret between her and the Native mothers; of course, there was no way that a woman in her position with Indian Affairs should be encouraging this blatant disregard for government rules. She had been to the school and she knew the children were better off at home, learning their own language and traditions, the way it had been for generations. She fumed when she thought of the injustices against the Cree people. The school had a wire fence surrounding the premises. Children who tried to escape were treated as prisoners. The school had purposefully been built twenty-six kilometers from the reserve so children only saw their families a few times a year—if they were lucky. Ruth realized that there were many injustices toward the Cree people. This mandatory schooling was one she disliked in particular.

Today was Victoria Day and Ruth was on her way to meet Waldemar. Their friendship was deepening. They worked together at least once a week. Every Saturday night they met in town for supper. They exchanged stories from their past and shared dreams for the future. Today Waldemar had promised Ruth that he was going to take her boating, fishing and swimming out on the nearby lake. Ruth didn't tell Waldemar that she couldn't swim but she agreed to go anyhow. It sounded like a good time and any excuse to be in a rowboat with him for an afternoon was okay with her.

Ruth pulled up to the restaurant where they usually met for supper. She saw Waldemar waiting outside. She parked the car and waved to him.

"Hi, Pete!" she called through the open window.

Waldemar walked over to the car and opened the door. "Hi, Ruth! Are you ready for our fishing trip?"

"I think so. I've never been fishing, so I'm as ready as I know how."

"Never been fishing?" Waldemar looked puzzled and wondered how anyone could get to their twenties without fishing.

"Where would I fish in Leduc?" she laughed as she stepped out of the car.

"I guess. Well I've got everything ready here. I'll throw the fishing gear in the back seat. Do you want me to drive?"

"Sure, it's your day."

The two drove off toward the lake with all of their fishing gear and the picnic basket in the back seat. The breeze was warm. The pair chatted as they drove to the lake.

"How are you doing?" Ruth asked.

"Pretty good." Waldemar's eyes were fixed on the road.

"Any luck with the chickens?"

Waldemar looked over at her and laughed. "Ah no. No luck at all. I've been trying to show the people on the reserve the idea behind farming but it doesn't seem to click."

Ruth smoothed her shorts. "What do you mean?"

"Well I've helped them purchase seeds, cows, chickens and horses . . . you know with the money they get from the government . . . but instead of using those things—cultivating—they use them up!"

"Oh dear."

"Yes. I tried to explain that the chicken will lay eggs if you feed it and care for it . . . then you can eat the eggs. But every time I come back the chicken is dead." Waldemar laughed, "Supper."

Ruth chuckled. "Their ways are not your ways."

"I'm realizing that. They sure respond well to me. They like my advice when I'm giving it but the moment I'm gone . . . well . . ."

Ruth laughed, "I know what you mean." She looked over at Waldemar fondly. "It's their rich traditions and culture that makes them such amazing people. Who are we to interfere?"

"Exactly. Just because I know what I'd do if I were receiving government provisions doesn't mean it's right for them. I'll keep trying though. I'd love to see at least one family keep a chicken long enough to lay an egg!"

Once they arrived at the lake, Waldemar found the boat they would be using. He loaded up the fishing gear. Ruth left the picnic basket in the backseat and closed up the car. She wore a light summer blouse and a pair of black shorts with sandals.

She headed toward the water, a little apprehensively, wishing she could swim, even just a little. She was sure that if the boat flipped in the lake, Waldemar would be able to manage to get her to shore one way or another. She hadn't been in such a small boat before. As Waldemar took her hand and helped her from the dock into the boat, she felt her nerves jolt. She realized how unsteady this tiny vessel was. She held her breath.

"Okay, Ruth, sit right there in the middle. I'll step in and push us from the dock." Waldemar stepped into the boat, being careful to keep the boat balanced. He untied it and pushed away with obvious skill.

Ruth watched his muscular arms row them into the middle of the lake. The sun was shining off his golden hair. He looked so relaxed, completely in his element. The oars broke into the glassy surface of the lake and propelled them forward. Her stomach fluttered as she watched him. She found so many things about him very appealing. She loved the way he handled the affairs on the Reservation, and the gentle nature he had with the Aboriginal people. She loved the way he respected her, yet stood up to her all in the same breath. She smiled as she thought of their conversation last week when she had told him that he needed to round up everyone for vaccinations. He had smiled and given her the firm answer 'no' that he would not force anyone to do anything. She had pleaded that it was in their best interest but he didn't want to get involved.

"What are you smiling about?" Waldemar broke into her thoughts.

"You."

"Really?" he stopped rowing.

"Yes, I was thinking about how you are too stubborn to help me with my vaccines."

"I'm not stubborn," he said defensively, "I just don't want to be in cahoots with you!" With that, he took an oar and splashed her with the lake water.

Ruth laughed, "How dare you!"

Waldemar laughed and continued to row. "I think we're at the perfect spot to fish. What do you say?"

Ruth wiped her face on her blouse. "Sounds good to me."

Waldemar put the oars in to the boat. He set up the fishing rods with lures. He showed Ruth how to lower the line into the water, deep enough to catch the larger fish and not too deep to get tangled on the bottom of the lake. Ruth thoroughly enjoyed his instruction, this special time they were having together under the morning sun. He spoke of Tom McLeod, his childhood mentor, and the hours they spent together fishing. He spoke of his brothers catching frogs in the stream out front of their house while their Mamma watched them dirty their pants and shoes.

After a few hours and several fish in the bucket, Waldemar rowed them back to shore. Ruth spread out the picnic blanket on a soft grassy area near the beach and set out their sandwiches. She poured the thermos of coffee into cups. They ate and laughed and talked about an upcoming event they had been invited to on the first weekend in July. They would be paying treaty to the Aboriginals, as they had done before, but they were invited to see a special ceremony and dance, something that not many white folks had been invited to. It was an honor. They were both looking forward to it.

"So how many more years until your commitment to the RCMP is over?" Ruth asked, trying to sound casual.

Waldemar looked up from his sandwich, surprised. With his mouth full he said, "You mean until I can get married?"

"Yes." She avoided his gaze and took a long drink of coffee.

"Ah . . . less than a year."

"So do you have plans? You know, to marry right away?"

Waldemar sat up, brushing the crumbs off his shirt. "I don't know . . . I haven't given it much thought."

"I see."

"And you?" He ran his finger down her arm.

Goosebumps rose up where he had touched her. "I don't know. People keep saying that if I don't marry soon, I'll surely be an old spinster."

Waldemar smiled, "Not you. Don't you have a sweetheart?"

Ruth blushed and smoothed out her shorts again. "No. I used to . . . but we've grown apart now. I haven't seen him in years. Sometimes you just know . . . when it's not meant to be."

"I know what you mean. I've had a few sweethearts myself . . . but," he cleared his throat, "there has always been something missing."

"God will find us each our mate . . . when the time is right."

The two caught each other's gaze, locking eyes for a moment.

Waldemar studied Ruth. She was such a fun companion. Headstrong, but fun all the same. He admired the way she held her own. She had her career and her purpose in life and wasn't simply looking for a man to latch onto. He loved the way she had an inner strength that coursed through her, radiating to those around her. He knew that whatever life would throw at her, she would handle it. Her faith was intriguing to him too; she was never shy about sharing her faith, and yet not pushy either. He certainly had a religious upbringing but her faith was so engaged, minute by minute she seemed connected to God. She never boasted about any of her accomplishments either. She always just gave the credit to God, stating that she was simply doing His work. He had never met anyone so reliant upon God, every minute of every day, someone that was so in tune with their own spirituality.

She smiled at him coyly. "What? What are you thinking about?"

"You," he said softly.

She blushed. Changing the subject, she said, "Did you hear about my present that some of the fellows left me on the fence last week?"

"No," Waldemar was puzzled, "what was it?"

"Apparently some of the men were unhappy with some of the advice I was giving to the women and so they left me a gift on the fence to let me know their feelings."

"What? What did they leave you?"

"I woke up in the morning and left the house to walk to the nurses' office only to find that strung along the picket fence were snakes," she paused for effect, "dead snakes."

"That's terrible!" Waldemar knew how Ruth felt about snakes.

"I was quite horrified at first, but didn't want anyone to know so I just went to work in the office, knowing that eventually someone would come for medication. Sure enough, within an hour, a gentleman came into the office. I asked him, 'Do you know anything about this?' and he replied, 'No, ma'am.' I asked him if he was a nice guy and after he agreed that he was, I told him to be a nice guy and go take all the snakes off the fence."

"What did he do?"

"He went out there and took all the snakes off the fence of course!" Ruth beamed. "I just went about my day and didn't say anything further on the matter. I didn't want word to get out that it bothered me, but I certainly don't want it to happen again!"

"I should see who's responsible."

"Don't bother, it's done. They didn't get the rise out of me they wanted so I'm sure that it won't happen again."

"You let me know if it does," Waldemar shook his head. "Good for you though, I'm glad you sent that fellow to take care of it."

"I certainly wasn't going anywhere! It was all I could do not to scream when I saw them all hanging there."

"Ugh. Disgusting."

The two finished up their lunch and stretched out on the picnic blanket, taking in the warm afternoon sun. The warm weather always felt terrific in the beginning of the summer. It was such a refreshing break from the eight months of cold and snow.

Waldemar drove them back to the restaurant where they got out of the car to part ways.

"It was nice today." Waldemar took Ruth's hand in his own. "I had a good time." He looked at her smile. The thought crossed his mind to kiss her.

"I had a nice time too," Ruth beamed up at him, "we'll have to do it again—you know, now that I am an experienced fisherman."

Waldemar laughed, "Experienced, eh? I don't know about that."

"I had a very good teacher."

Waldemar ran his hand through his hair. "Yes you did."

Ruth looked at her car and put her hand on the door handle. "Well I guess I better get going."

"Yes, for sure. Tell me, when will I see you again?"

"Wednesday? You could come help me round up people for vaccines."

Waldemar laughed, "You never give up, do you?"

Ruth looked at him and said softly, "Never."

"Let us not become weary
in doing good, for at the
proper time we will reap a
harvest if we do not give up.
Therefore, as we have
opportunity, let us do good
to all people, especially those
who belong to the family of
believers." Galatians
6: 9 & 10 NIV

July 1945
Near Lac La Biche, Alberta

Ruth bounced along in the back of her car. Waldemar was driving. Harold and Jack, the clerk, were also in the Ford Tudor. They were on their way to pay treaty to the Aboriginals near Lac La Biche. It was a beautiful summer morning. Ruth had a scarf over her hair as they drove. The windows were open and the wind whipped all around them. They were packed tightly into the car because Ruth had all of the medical supplies she would need for this weekend and an overnight bag for their stay.

Ruth gasped when they arrived at the site. "Have you ever seen . . ." Her sentence hung in mid-air.

Waldemar said softly, "Beautiful, isn't it?"

There was a large horseshoe of tepees and tents set up, with the lake in the background and fires burning in the foreground. People were milling about dressed in their best traditional clothing. Dogs were barking, children were laughing and playing games.

Waldemar got out of the car and asked one of the elders where they would be working. The elder showed Waldemar to three military style tents.

Waldemar looked back to the car where Ruth was getting her supplies organized.

"Ruth, over here," Waldemar called as he motioned to the clinic tent.

"Fantastic, isn't it?" she said as she walked toward him.

"Yes, it's quite something to see all these tribes together."

"How is this going to work? Do you know?"

"You'll be here in this first tent and then they'll move into my tent where we'll settle debts and let them know what they'll be receiving. Harold will be working next to us to pay treaty when they've seen us all." The two had entered the tent and Waldemar set the bags down. "Do you need help?"

"No, I'll be fine. I'll get my things organized and then I'll come and find you."

Waldemar grinned and left the tent to go and find Jack. Jack was bringing all of the logbooks from the trunk of the car. Waldemar could see he needed a hand.

"Hey, Jack, I'll help you!" Waldemar rushed over to take some books from Jack. The two walked over to their tent. They had a half-hour at best before people would begin to line up for their services.

Ruth was busy setting up an examination cot where she would be de-lousing, giving vaccines and checking general health. She had a checklist of things she was looking for and some educational information she wanted to give out as well. It was a great opportunity for her to have so many people come through at once, a chance for her to see people that were normally beyond her reach, people who might not see a nurse but had the incentive of getting money at the same time.

Before long, there were people starting to gather outside her tent in the warm morning air. She went to see if Harold, Waldemar and Jack were ready as well.

Ruth poked her head inside Waldemar's tent, which was adjoining hers. "Ready, Pete?"

Waldemar looked up from the logbooks that he and Jack were reading and answered, "Yes, are you?"

"Yes. Are you going to get things started, or am I supposed to?"

"I will," Waldemar went out to tell the people how they were to line up and to admit the first family into Ruth's tent.

The first family came into the tent. She put out her hand. "Ruth Bohlman. And you are?"

"John," the young man said softly. He pointed to his wife, "Adriel."

Ruth looked at the young child strapped to Adriel's back. Only a thick tuft of black hair was showing at the top of the cradleboard.

"How old is your baby?"

John looked at Adriel and said something quickly in Cree. She answered "Eight months."

"Okay. Let's start with you, John. Can you sit on the cot here? I'm going to examine you."

He sat on the cot, his large black eyes following Ruth's every move. She hummed softly as she went into her medical bag for a comb. She began to look through his hair for any signs of lice. She looked over his whole body, from his hair to the soles of his feet. When she was done, she showed him the needle for vaccination.

"This is going to keep you from getting sick. I'm going to inject it in your arm."

"No," he replied firmly.

Ruth sighed and looked at Adriel for support. She shrugged.

"It will keep you from getting very sick. Your wife, your baby, they need you."

He looked hesitantly at Adriel and then back to Ruth. "Fine."

Ruth quickly cleaned the area where the needle would go in with rubbing alcohol. Then she plunged the needle into his arm.

"Ow!" he exclaimed.

"Sorry," Ruth apologized. "It does hurt for a minute."

Ruth carried on examining Adriel and their infant son. She counseled, educated and treated everything she could.

The morning and the afternoon carried on this way, one family after the next. She treated each person, talking, laughing and hearing stories of loss and heartache. She vaccinated those who were willing, and even some that were not. She examined the little babies all tucked in on their mothers' backs in their moss-bags, some sleeping soundly until she poked and prodded them awake. The Aboriginal babies were so cute and stout with their jet-black hair standing up on end.

She loved this part of the job. She loved that she could impact so many lives in a positive way in such a short amount of time. She worked tirelessly to attend to each person who came to her. She prayed while she worked, that God would touch each of their lives.

Waldemar worked away next door asking and answering the same questions again and again.

"Name?" Jack asked.

"Whiskeyjack."

"Your debts include one wagon, ten chickens, a plow, three cows and seeds. You owe $374. What do you wish to pay at this time?" Jack asked.

The man stood there and shrugged his shoulders.

Waldemar leaned across the desk and said, "Pay one dollar, that is the minimum." Waldemar knew it was hopeless for most of these people ever to pay back what they owed the government. They were so poorly equipped to succeed after they had been stripped of their original way of life.

"One dollar," the man nodded at Waldemar. "Thank you."

"One dollar it is," Jack said as he recorded the information in his books. "We shall record it. Go forward and receive your treaty from the next desk."

The man nodded and went to where Harold paid out all but one dollar of the man's treaty, keeping it for debt re-payment.

The day went on like this, some choosing to pay back more than others, but Waldemar's advice remained the same. By nightfall, they had processed the last family. All four, Harold, Jack, Waldemar and Ruth, were exhausted from the day's work. They were looking forward to the upcoming feast and celebration. As Ruth cleaned up her clinic tent, Waldemar came in to offer his assistance.

"Can I help?" he asked.

She smiled wearily, "Of course. Can you fold up the cot for me and dump the wash basin out?"

"Sure can. How was your day today?"

"Busy, for sure, but it's great to see so many families at once."

Waldemar watched Ruth packing up her medical bags, carefully wrapping up needles, vials and other equipment she had. The setting sun came through a crack in the tent flaps and glistened off her strawberry-blonde hair. He stood there, admiring her, while holding the basin of water in his hands.

She looked up at him. "You okay?"

"Yes," Waldemar replied, caught in his act of admiration. "Can you open the flap for me?"

Ruth moved to the side of the tent and held it open while he went out behind the tent to dump the dirty water. Then they carried the bags back to the car.

"You two make a good pair," an Aboriginal man called out. He had been watching them dismantle their workspace.

Ruth smiled and thought, *yes we do.*

"Are you ready for the feast?" the man asked, walking toward them.

"Yes we are," Waldemar answered.

"Time to go then."

They ate delicious Aboriginal food and relished the different rich tastes of the dishes the women had made. The men prepared for the dance and singing by dressing in their most ornate, traditional celebration clothing, painting their faces as tradition dictated. The night was filled with dancing and singing. The singing was in a melodic rhythm that captivated Ruth and Waldemar. The leaders spoke, fires burned brightly and they told stories late into the night while wide-eyed children looked on.

Ruth was so enraptured with the ceremony and the beauty of the people that she was surprised when she looked at her watch. It was two o'clock. Waldemar sat next to her on a log bench. The moonlight shone down on them both. She looked at his handsome profile, the way he too was taken in by the magic of it all. There were a million stars overhead. Ruth felt the warmth of him next to her. She felt an excited chill go down her spine.

"Are you cold?" Waldemar asked.

Ruth shook her head no but he put his arm around her instinctively. Ruth felt warmth from the tip of her head to her toes. She knew there was nowhere else she'd rather be. He was the one. She knew that whatever happened in the future, he was the one that she wanted to be with. She wanted to feel the strength of his arms around her forever.

Into the morning hours, Ruth and Waldemar watched the dances until the fires burned low and people began to return to their tents. Many came by to thank Ruth and Waldemar for their work that day, for their care for the people.

Exhausted but happy, Jack, Harold, Waldemar and Ruth drove back to the hotel they were staying at in Lac La Biche.

Waldemar walked Ruth up to her room.

"Goodnight, Ruth," he said softly. He stood relaxed, his hands at his sides. He reached out for her hand.

"Goodnight." She smiled as he lingered. *Go on, kiss me.*

Waldemar waited nervously, knowing what he wanted to do, but not sure if it would be well received. He leaned in to hug her. The embrace lasted longer than usual.

What should I do? He wondered.

Go on, Ruth thought as he lingered with his hand on the small of her back. She closed her eyes and stood on her tiptoes to reach up for what she knew he was waiting for. He kissed her firmly, yet tenderly.

Ruth smiled as the kiss ended.

"See you in the morning," he whispered.

"See you," she said quietly. She hugged him again and then went into her room. She flopped down onto her bed with a sigh. "What a day."

*

A month later, back in her nurse's cottage on the Reservation, she looked at her bottles of medicine lined up neatly on the shelves behind her. The shelves had large glass doors so that she could secure the medicines at night. She opened the doors and began to examine her inventory, deciding what she needed to order.

The chimes on the door rang as a young Aboriginal woman came in with her daughter. Her face was tear-stained.

"Hello, Enola." Ruth came around her desk.

"Hello, Nurse." Enola shifted nervously. "I think you could help us."

"Of course, what is it?"

"Tehya here . . ." Enola looked around the cottage and paused.

"No one else is here. What is it?"

"She—she is of school age."

"Oh." Ruth knew immediately.

"She cannot go—they are asking me all the time and I hide her when they come but I am worried."

"I understand." Ruth thought about the situation and what she could do to help.

"If they come to you—will, will you tell them?"

"No, of course not! What are you telling them when they come?"

"That my son—two years old—that he is my oldest." She burst into tears. "What will I do when they come for him?"

Ruth wrapped her arm around the young mother. "We will trust God that he will help us when that day comes."

Enola cried softly. Her daughter clung to her, speaking softly in Cree. Enola stroked her daughter's hair and spoke words of reassurance back. Ruth thought of her own birth mother. She felt a tear come to her eye and brushed it aside, re-focusing her thoughts.

"Won't you get in trouble if they find out you are helping us?"

Ruth shook her head. "I've never been worried about things like that. We both know that Red Quill isn't the answer for the Cree children."

"I have heard terrible things."

Ruth rubbed Enola's arm. "I know. I have too. I respect your way of life. I don't think it should change."

"But aren't you trained as a Catholic nurse?"

"I went to a Catholic school—but I am not Catholic. I don't agree with what they are doing and I plan to do everything I can to help you. If they ask me, I will simply say that you only have one child. A son. And hopefully by the time he is school-aged, the school will be history."

Enola buried her face in her handkerchief. "I cannot bear it—to say goodbye for an entire school year!"

"It's ridiculous, that's what it is." Ruth touched Teyha's hair. "Don't worry, sweetheart."

Ruth reassured Enola again, hugged them both and sent them on their way, promising that their secret was safe with her.

*"Cast all your anxiety on
him because he cares for
you." 1 Peter 5:7 NIV*

December 1945
St. Paul, Alberta

Waldemar drove his Police car out to the Lomatski's farm. The soft snow slowed his progress on these unused roads. He had been investigating the Lomatski family over the last few weeks and he had confirmed that they were not Canadian citizens. Waldemar was on his way to search the farm, confiscate and store any weapons.

He rolled the car up the long drive to the dilapidated farmhouse. There was smoke coming from the chimney. Waldemar hoped that the whole family would be home. He walked up to the front door and knocked firmly.

"This is the police!"

The door opened and a young girl peeked out.

"Hi there," Waldemar spoke softy and took off his Mountie hat. "Is your father home?"

She nodded and opened the door all the way, "Daddy!" she hollered into the house. Footsteps came down the hall. An unshaven man in his undershirt and trousers came toward Waldemar.

"Afternoon, Mr. Lomatski. I'd like to talk if you have a minute."

"Ah—of course, will you come into the kitchen? I'll have my wife make some coffee."

"Thank you." Waldemar moved through the shabby living room into the small kitchen and sat on a wooden kitchen chair.

Mr. Lomatski pulled on a dress shirt and began to button it as he sat down with Waldemar. "Irina," he called, "come and make some coffee for the constable."

Waldemar began speaking as Irina came in and busied herself making coffee. "It has been brought to my attention that you do not have citizenship."

Mr. Lomatski shifted uncomfortably. "No, sir."

"I can help you with your papers if you'd like but for now I need to search the property." Waldemar waited for a reaction. Irina set down a cup of coffee in front of Waldemar. "Thank you." He smiled at her.

"Go ahead then, Constable, you can search."

"How are things on the farm? Are you having any success?"

"The chickens won't lay."

Waldemar talked with Mr. Lomatski for a while, giving suggestions for his livestock. They drank their coffee, discussing Mr. Lomatski's job at the auto body shop in town. Afterwards, Waldemar thanked Irina for the coffee and began to respectfully, but thoroughly, search the house, the outbuildings and small barn where they kept a cow and some chickens. He ended up taking a shotgun and rifle, which he placed in the trunk of his car. He arranged for Mr. Lomatski to come to the police station so that he could help him begin his paperwork for immigration.

*

Ruth left her office and headed to the main house. She was looking forward to dinner. Annie was a fabulous cook and Ruth was always anxious to sit down at the table with both Annie and Harold to talk about their day. She entered the house and stomped the snow from her boots. She sat down to undo her boots and take off her winter coat.

"Hi, Ruth!" Annie called from the kitchen. Ruth could hear the sounds of clinking pots and pans.

"Hi, Annie," Ruth called back.

"There's mail for you on the table, sweetheart, take a look and then come and join me in the kitchen."

"Thanks, I will." Ruth picked the four envelopes off the table and read the return addresses. One was from Artrude, one from her dad, one from Edith and one from the Government of Canada. She opened the one from the government first. She settled into the armchair and began to read.

November 17th, 1945

Nurse Bohlman,

We are writing to you regarding Enola Smallbear. We believe that she has a daughter who should be enrolled in Red Quill School. We are asking that you look into this matter and alert us if there is any such child who should be sent there. It is required by law that all children over the age of seven be enrolled in school. As you know, as a government employee, you are required to report any minor that is not attending. Please contact the Smallbear family as soon as possible to follow up. Thank you for your prompt attention to this matter.

Sincerely, Indian Affairs

Ruth set the letter aside. She knew there would be no need to return any information regarding Enola. She hastily tore open the letter from Edith wondering what it could be about.

November 18, 1945

Dear Ruth,

I wanted to inform you that I am coming to St. Paul to meet you for lunch. Your father will be unable to accompany me on this journey so I will ask that you meet me at the bus stop. I will arrive on December 15 at 11:30 in the morning. Please be on time.

Mother

What on earth? Ruth wondered. *What would Edith want to do in St. Paul? What on earth would interest her to come here?* She tore open her letter from her father. She loved his gentle cursive writing and felt closer to him just holding the letter.

November 19, 1945

Dearest Ruth,

I am sending my birthday wishes to you along with a cheque for you so that you might buy something nice for yourself. I cannot believe my little girl is another year older. I remember the first time I looked into your bright eyes. I knew that when your little hand reached out for me that we would be forever connected in a special way.

I hope things are going well for you in St. Paul. I think of you every day and I wonder how you are managing dealing with all of the trying situations that must come your way. I know you must handle it all with grace and fierce dependence on God. I pray for you daily that God will guide your healing hands. I am so proud of you.

Things here are going well. Business continues to grow. The store is busy keeping up with the growing population in Leduc. Lorne is doing well with his high school studies. It is hard to believe that all my children are growing up so fast. I miss you every day. I hope that your work will bring you back to Leduc someday.

I enjoy reading about all of your adventures. It sounds like you have a good friend in Constable Peterson. I can feel the fondness you hold for him in your letters. It is wonderful to have a good friend in an isolated town.

Mother is coming to see you and will send you a letter shortly with her travel plans. She insists that she would like to see how you are doing in person. I would like to come as well but sadly the store ties me to Leduc, especially as Christmas approaches.

Do you have plans for the holidays? Will you be spending time with the Constable? I am sure that your work never ceases, even for Christmas. We are busy at the church arranging a Christmas pageant. Do you remember the year the candles on the tree caught the tree on fire at the front of the church during the pageant? Every year I miss your singing voice when the children sing.

*Please write soon and call when you can, I love to hear
your voice.*

Love, Dad

Ruth thought about her father's words. She did indeed remember the
Christmas when the tree started on fire at the front of the church.

Ruth wondered about Edith as well. What was she up to? Ruth
supposed she would know soon enough, as the 15th was only a few weeks
away—a Saturday. She opened the last envelope from Artrude. It was
filled with all of Artrude's latest news and warm birthday greetings. Ruth
chuckled as she read Artrude's teasing about Pete. Artrude and Ruth were
like sisters. In their letters back and forth, no detail was left unsaid.

"Supper's ready," Annie called.

Ruth folded up her letters and headed to the kitchen. "Quite a day
for mail."

"Yes," Annie agreed. "Birthday wishes? It's only a few days away."

"Yes, everyone is sending their love."

"Speaking of love," Annie winked, "are you going to celebrate with
Constable Peterson?"

Ruth smirked, "Of course!"

Waldemar indeed had plans. It was a cold Thursday night. He had
paid a small fortune for winter flowers from a local shop. He was driving
out to the reserve to pick up Ruth and take her out for supper in town. He
was happy that he could spend her birthday with her, hopefully, making
it a special night. He had spent the last six months since their first kiss
falling in love, a little more each day. They worked side by side caring for
the Aboriginal people and gaining favor in St. Paul among the residents.

Waldemar pulled up to Harold and Annie's and he looked himself
over in the rear-view mirror before approaching the house.

Ruth heard knocking at the door as she was getting ready. She had
picked a special dress and curled and styled her hair for the night. She
heard Annie let Waldemar in. Annie exclaimed loudly over whatever he
had brought. Ruth hurried to grab her fur coat from the closet and rushed
down the stairs. She turned the hall corner and saw Waldemar standing
at the front door with flowers in his hands. His blue eyes sparkled, as he
looked her over.

"Oh, Pete! They're beautiful!" she cried.

"Not as beautiful as you," he said as he smiled at her. "Happy birthday. Are you ready to celebrate?"

"Yes, let me put these in water and then we'll go."

Ruth went to the kitchen. Annie agreed to arrange the flowers in a vase while she was out for supper.

Ruth and Waldemar headed out into the night. They talked as they drove to St. Paul. Ruth told Waldemar about her father's letter. They talked about how Leduc was growing and how her dad had become increasingly successful as the town grew.

The night flew by and as they ate dessert, Waldemar asked Ruth if she would be interested in going on a hunting trip with him.

"A hunting trip?"

"Yes, have you ever been hunting?"

Ruth laughed. "No, definitely not!"

"Do you want to?"

"Sure, I don't see why not." Ruth looked puzzled. "In the winter?"

"Yes, that's the best time. You can track the animals' footprints in the snow—if it's a mild day it can be quite a wonderful experience. When I was young I used to go out every day. I had a trap line I kept throughout the winter. I remember how excited I used to be at the first snowfall."

"What sort of animals did you catch?"

"Weasels, rabbits, sometimes foxes. I would sell the fur for extra money for the family."

"How did you know what to do?"

"Our good family friend, Tom McLeod, he taught me a lot about the wilderness and hunting. Everything you wanted to know about the earth, he could tell you."

"Oh yes, you told me about him when we were fishing. He sounds fascinating."

"Yes, he is such a kind person. He still looks out for our family. I appreciate everything he taught me, especially now that I'm an adult; looking back at all he invested in me, it means a lot."

"I had someone like that," Ruth paused thoughtfully.

"Who was it?"

"Mrs. Daum, she is Artrude's mother. She even cared for me for a while before Dad married Edith."

"How old were you when your dad re-married?"

"Four. I'll never forget when Mrs. Daum told me that I was going to get a new mother. She was so excited for me." Ruth added quietly, "Little did I know."

"What?" Waldemar asked.

"Little did I know that Edith and I wouldn't ever really connect."

"Why?" The restaurant clattered with noise around the pair as they ate.

"I don't know really. Looking back I guess I was always the apple of my father's eye and Edith could never compete."

"Did it have to be a competition?"

"No, it shouldn't have been." Ruth was quiet for a moment feeling all of the regrets from her childhood come rushing back.

"Are you okay?" Waldemar took Ruth's hands in his own.

"Yes. It's all in the past now but there are some things that still hurt."

"Did she treat you poorly?"

Ruth nodded but said nothing. Some things were better left unsaid.

"Let's change the subject," Waldemar suggested. "We're here to celebrate."

"Yes. Tell me, have you heard any news on your posting here? Do you think you'll be in St. Paul for awhile?"

"It's hard to say, it seems they just decide and the next day I am gone."

"I don't know how I'd live in St. Paul without you." Ruth smiled at Waldemar.

"We've become quite the pair." Waldemar winked. "Haven't we?"

"Be joyful always; pray continually; give thanks in all circumstances, for this is God's will for you in Christ Jesus." 1 Thessalonians 5:16-18 NIV

December 15, 1945
St. Paul, Alberta

Ruth waited nervously at the bus stop on December 15th. She adjusted her skirt, her boots, her coat and her hat while she waited. She wondered what Edith would criticize first.

The bus came into view and Ruth walked toward it hesitantly, looking for Edith through the frosted windows. Ruth held her breath as people began to exit the bus.

Edith stepped from the bus in her three-quarter-length tweed coat with a fashionable hat perched upon her head. She clutched a small overnight bag and looked around for Ruth.

"Hello, Mother," Ruth called and waved.

Edith smiled her tight-lipped smile and walked toward Ruth. "Hello. How are you?"

"I'm fine. How was your trip?"

"It was bumpy. The roads were snowy and one might even say that the driver was a bit reckless." Edith's arms were crossed over her chest.

"I'm sorry to hear that." Ruth looked toward the parking lot where the car was parked. "Are you ready for lunch? Are you hungry?"

"Yes, what do you have in mind?"

"There is a place I often go to—a diner, it's nice. It's just down the road."

"That will do."

Ruth looked at Edith. "Can I carry your bag?"

"Yes, please." Edith handed her bag to Ruth.

Ruth could feel the tension in the air. "The car is over here, let's go."

The two walked in silence to the car. Ruth opened the passenger door for Edith before placing her bag in the back seat.

"Do you know how to drive this?" Edith looked questioningly at Ruth as she slid into the driver's seat and put the keys in the ignition.

"Yes, Mother," Ruth sighed, "I can drive. I drive all over for work."

"I see." Edith clutched the door handle as Ruth began to back out of her parking spot and out of the parking lot into the street. "You should be careful. It's icy," Edith warned.

After a long silence, she asked, "How is Father?"

"He's busy with the store of course. He is very good at his business, you know."

"Yes, he's always had a mind for business. And how is Lorne?"

"Oh he's doing very well in school; you know Lorne, he's always been an outstanding student."

Ruth smiled. "Yes he is." She pulled into the diner parking lot and parked the car. "Shall we?"

Edith and Ruth went inside, sat at a table and ordered soups and sandwiches. Edith and Ruth continued their awkward conversation as they ate. Ruth was surprised when Waldemar came into the restaurant. He was in his plain clothes. She looked at him as he came in and shook her head in a subtle 'no.' He ignored Ruth as he walked by and found a table near the back of the restaurant away from Ruth and Edith. It was then that Edith's motives for her visit seemed to come to light.

"So it seems you have a special friend that you keep mentioning in your letters."

Ruth groaned inwardly, "Ah, who's that?"

"This constable you mention, Peterson, that sounds Scandinavian."

"Yes, it is." Ruth offered nothing more.

"How is Nick?" Edith probed.

"I'm not sure. I haven't talked to him in ages."

"He's a nice German boy, isn't he?"

"I suppose."

"Is this constable a Baptist?"

Ruth sighed, "No, no he's not, he's Anglican."

Edith's eyebrows raised, "Anglican?"

"Yes, Anglican."

"You're not Anglican."

"No, I'm not."

"Well . . ." Edith took a spoonful of soup and brought it to her lips.

She longed to change the subject. "So, do you and Dad have plans for Christmas?"

"The pageant at the church of course, and I'm involved with the ladies auxiliary. I'm very busy with that."

"Of course." The two talked on, Ruth avoiding the topic of the constable. She kept glancing over at Waldemar peacefully eating his lunch. She kept silently wishing he would leave. After they were all finished, she drove Edith around St. Paul, and then took her to her hotel. The visit was as unpredictable as Edith was. Ruth answered and evaded several lines of questioning regarding her love life, her work life and her future. It was good, however, to hear about how some of the families from Leduc were doing, to hear about Aunt Lilly and especially to hear about Father and how he was doing. She missed being around him.

Ruth dropped Edith off at the hotel for the night.

"Do you need a ride in the morning?"

Edith shook her head. "No, I can hire a driver."

"Okay." Ruth walked Edith to the front of the hotel. They stood in the lobby. "Well I should be getting back to the reserve, in case someone needs me."

"That's fine." Edith clutched her bag. "I hope the room is nice."

"Would you like me to come up with you?"

Edith shrugged. "I suppose. That would be nice."

Ruth went to the front desk and helped Edith check in. They went up to the third floor where Edith's room was. Ruth used the key to open the door. She motioned Edith to go in ahead.

Edith went in and set her bag down on the bed.

"Just one more thing, Ruth . . ."

Ruth exhaled, "What's that, Mother?"

"It's not a good idea to set your heart on a man who isn't compatible with you."

"Oh?"

"You know, someone who isn't German . . . someone who isn't Baptist. You've got a good boy . . . Nick, don't lose sight of that."

Ruth rolled her eyes. "Mother, I don't love Nick. I don't think I've ever loved Nick."

Edith clasped her hands together tightly. "It's not always about love."

"You didn't love Dad?"

Edith shifted uncomfortably. "That's irrelevant. Of course I did."

"Is it?"

"We're talking about you. And the constable."

"Ah, I see. You came here to persuade me to not get involved with the constable?"

Edith said nothing. She walked across the hotel room, over to the window. After a long silence, she said, "I'm only looking out for your best interest."

"Thank you. I have to go now." Ruth looked at the back of Edith who was still looking out the window. "Thank you for coming all this way for me."

Edith turned around. "Goodbye, Ruth."

Ruth let out a big sigh as she left the room.

*

Three months later, Ruth was bundled up against the cold and snow as she walked in Waldemar's deep footprints, reaching to match his long stride.

"Now," he said quietly, "don't touch anything, you don't want to leave your scent on anything. Keep an eye out for tracks in the bush as we go. Oh, and be quiet."

"Okay," Ruth whispered back. She smiled as she watched Waldemar, bundled in his warm Mountie coat ahead of her. He had a bag over his shoulder, holding their lunch and a thermos of coffee. He had a rifle in hand, ready to take out any game they might come across. Ruth was nervous and excited. She was unsure how she would react if they actually came nose to nose with an animal they would kill.

Waldemar's feet crunched through the snow. His keen eye looked all around for tracks. He was impressed that Ruth was keeping up, trudging through the snow eagerly behind him. She walked the talk—she wasn't the type of girl who just said that she would do something and then flaked out when the time came.

Ruth jumped every time a bird took flight and rustled the trees. Waldemar smiled each time.

"Tom taught me that when you set your traps you have to wear gloves soaked in balsam bark solution. If you leave your scent, you won't catch anything," Waldemar spoke softly as they walked.

Ruth followed patiently for over an hour, silently looking around. Finally, she whispered, "Pete, I'm hungry."

He smiled back at his hunting companion and spoke out loud, "Okay, we can stop and eat."

"Great! I need some coffee to warm up!"

Waldemar found a log they could sit on, brushed off the snow and patted the spot next to him for Ruth to sit down. She cozied up next to him. They shared the thermos of coffee. Ruth carefully pulled the wax paper off their sandwiches.

Waldemar pulled his gloves off and exposed his hands, blue from the cold.

"What's wrong with your hands?" Ruth asked, alarmed.

"They've always been like this, when I'm cold, I lose circulation."

Ruth peeled off her own mitts and took Waldemar's big cold hands into her small warm ones. "I'll warm them up."

Waldemar looked down at Ruth vigorously rubbing the warmth back into his hands. He leaned in for a kiss. She was happy to respond.

"I love you, Ruth." Waldemar drew her closer to him, embracing her. Her nose, a tiny bit pink, was chilled from the cold.

"I love you too, Pete,"

"I'm very glad we found each other."

"We didn't," Ruth said, looking up at him.

"What do you mean?"

"We didn't find each other. God found you for me and me for you." She paused before she continued, "Think of everything that happened in your life to bring you to me. We're not exactly young kids anymore and yet we both knew that we didn't want to settle for something that wasn't in God's design."

Waldemar hadn't really thought about God's design for his life. He hadn't really looked at life with such a broad perspective. He liked that about Ruth. Her faith was so real and immersed in everything she did. He thought about how many choices he could have made that would have set him on a different path from where he was. If he had been the type of kid just to settle into farm life, he could still be in Winnipeg, helping Victor on the farm. He could have been overseas with the Provost Company. He could still be in Slave Lake if he hadn't made the choice to take the cruiser to the curling match—he wouldn't have been shipped to Edmonton. There were so many things that had brought him to St. Paul and to Ruth. He hadn't really considered that God was laying out a plan for him. It gave him goosebumps to think about.

"Do you see a future with me, Ruth?" Waldemar asked.

She smiled and held his hands tightly, "Of course I do, I couldn't see a future without you."

"We have to talk about something," his voice turned serious.

Hesitantly she asked, "What?"

"I just had word that I'm leaving St. Paul in two weeks."

"What! Oh no!"

"I know; I've really settled into life here, more so than anywhere else. I always told myself that it wasn't wise to get too attached to any place or person given my job, but here I am feeling total dread at the possibility of leaving."

"Where?" Ruth was worried that it might be far.

"Evansburg, it's east of Edmonton, a little over an hour drive."

Ruth was slightly relieved. "I guess we could see each other on weekends, but it won't be the same—not working together on a regular basis."

"I know," he lamented. "I know—I don't want to go."

The couple watched the birds in the trees flutter from branch to branch, looking for winter berries. Neither one knew what to say.

They held each other, there on that log in the bush for what seemed like an eternity, not wanting to accept the change that would come.

"We should go," Waldemar said eventually. "You're going to get cold just sitting here."

"You're keeping me warm," she smiled, "but we can go."

"Maybe we'll see something on the way back. You can follow in my footprints again and we'll keep our eyes peeled. There has to be a rabbit or something out here!"

"Roger that," Ruth laughed.

The two trekked back through the woods to where Ruth's car was parked along a country road. Ruth was happy to see the car and think about the warmth it would offer from the wind. Waldemar sat in the driver's seat and started the car. The engine roared to life. He was quiet as he thought about how many more adventures he and Ruth would be able to have together before he had to go.

Ruth could see that Waldemar was troubled. "Don't worry, Pete, we'll find a way to make it work. God didn't bring us all this way to give up now.

After dropping Waldemar off at the detachment, Ruth drove back out to the reserve. She came into the house with a big sigh.

"Hi, Ruth!" Annie called from the kitchen.

"Hi," she called back unenthusiastically.

Annie came into the living room where Ruth had flopped down into the armchair. "What is it? What happened?" Annie asked.

"It's Pete."

"Is he okay?" Annie was alarmed.

"Oh yes, he's okay. It's just that he was posted out of St. Paul."

Understanding dawned on Annie as she sat down on the couch opposite Ruth.

Ruth continued, "He's going to be posted in Evansburg."

"So, what are you going to do about it?" she asked.

"What do you mean?"

"I mean are you going to sit there and pout or are you going to look for work in Edmonton?"

"Edmonton?"

"Yes," Annie insisted. "I am sure that you could commute between Edmonton and Evansburg."

"I know but is it right to be following him around?"

"Do you love him?

"Yes, I do."

"Do you think he is part of God's plan for your life?"

Ruth closed her eyes and leaned back in her chair. "I think he is. I want him to be." She looked at Annie. "How can you be sure?"

"You can pray about it and look for doors to open."

Ruth tried to feel the calm she had expressed to Waldemar but inside she was all knots. After finishing her conversation with Annie, she decided to write Artrude for guidance.

Dearest Artrude,

How are you? How is your family? I am doing well. Work is challenging. Every day I see so many injustices to the families I work with on the reserve. The government and the church have meddled with things they have no right to. It saddens me but I try to support my own beliefs and the people in the best way I can.

As you know, Pete and I are head over heels. He is such an amazing man and I find myself feeling like he could be the one. The trouble is that he has just been assigned to Evansburg. Annie suggested I go and find work in Edmonton; perhaps the Miz would take me back—wouldn't that be a laugh to go and work with Sister Saint Christine again? I've always led my own life though; it seems strange to alter course for the sake of a man. I guess I will just have to pray about it and see where God will lead me.

I think in some ways I am ready to be closer to home—I miss Dad terribly. I love the work out here but it is draining. I feel like I have learned a lot and grown; perhaps I am ready for something new.

Let me know what you think. I love hearing from you.

Love, Ruth

Ruth went to lie on her bed after writing and sent heavenward all of the thoughts on her heart.

*"I have not stopped giving
thanks for you,
remembering you in my
prayers."
Ephesians 1:16 NIV*

June 1946
Edmonton, Alberta

Ruth had all her worldly possessions in the back of her Ford. She bounced along the highway singing along to one of her favorite songs. She had made up her mind to move to Edmonton about a month ago. Indian Affairs had been supportive, suggesting that she apply for the new hospital in Edmonton, the Charles Camsell. The hospital would be treating Aboriginals who were suffering from tuberculosis. She was looking forward to being closer to Leduc and to her dad. She wasn't too disappointed that she would only be an hour from Waldemar either. He had been in Evansburg since March. Each week had dragged by until she had finally set in motion her plan to move. She had spent endless hours on the phone with him, talking several times a week, but it wasn't the same as being together in person. God had helped her find peace with her choice to follow Waldemar to Edmonton. She knew that she wasn't losing who she was by following him but instead *finding* who she was, and especially, who she could be with Waldemar in her life.

She had been driving for about three hours. She was glad that the lonely trip was almost over. The war in Europe was over and people everywhere were in good spirits. Edmonton was crawling with soldiers looking for homes, jobs and re-connecting with old sweethearts. Speaking of old war sweethearts, Nick had written her and asked her to meet with her on the first weekend in July. Ruth was glad that she would finally have the opportunity to meet with him in person and finally put things to rest. She even hoped that he would be breaking the news to her first that he had his own girl, or even fiancée, that he had come to be with. She felt a twinge of guilt that she hadn't just written him months ago and said that things were over, but it always seemed like a conversation that would be better served face to face.

Ruth had trouble finding an apartment in Edmonton with the boom of population so she had arranged to stay with a fellow nurse, Megan, who was working at the Royal Alexandra Hospital. Ruth had to give up her government-issued car at the end of the week, now that her job at the reserve was over. She would be reliant on the bus to take her to the outskirts of the city where the new hospital was being built.

Finally, Edmonton came into view. Ruth focused on her driving in the bustling city. She looked at her street map and navigated her way to her new apartment. She saw what she thought was the apartment building. She checked the number and name against the handwritten notes she had made.

"This is it," she said wistfully. She got out of the car and went to the trunk. She started to pull out some of her things. Suddenly, there was a hand on her back. She jumped.

"Sorry to scare you," a familiar voice said.

Ruth whirled around. "Pete!" She threw herself into his arms. He held her tightly. She looked up into his face. "It's great to see you!"

She laughed and cried all at the same time as he kissed her. "I've missed you." He looked into her eyes. "I really have."

"I missed you too! It's been too long!"

"You look great."

"Saddle Lake has become empty and intolerable without my constable to call on." She hugged him again, laying her head on his chest and feeling the warmth of his body.

"Well, enough sadness," he joked, kissing the top of her head. "We're here now, let's get your things and get you settled."

She let go of him and pointed at the trunk. "Everything is in the car. Let's go up and talk to Megan and then we can bring everything in."

Waldemar and Ruth walked hand in hand up the three flights of stairs to Megan's apartment, talking about how they were going to spend the weekend. After chatting with Megan and getting Ruth's things into her room, the pair went out for supper. As they ate, they talked about her upcoming trip to Leduc to see her parents.

"Are you ready for *me* to meet your parents?" Waldemar asked.

"I don't know if you'll ever be ready to meet Mother." Ruth made a sour face.

"Come on," Waldemar said calmly, "how bad can it be?"

"Mother can be a bit rough around the edges. She will figure out that we are more than just friends and she won't hesitate to let you know your shortcomings."

"I can handle it." Waldemar grinned. "I can handle *you,* can't I?"

Ruth laughed, "Oh I'm nothing compared to Mother."

"Well, when the time comes I'm sure I'll be fine."

"How are things at home for you?" Ruth asked, changing the subject. "Have you had a letter from your mamma lately?"

"Yes, she says that Victor is doing well on the farm. Mary has been thinking about opening a rooming house for the elderly in Vancouver, and she and Stanley have been quite busy with plans to relocate."

"And Sing and Marg?"

"Sing is busy with the kids and Marg is working."

"Wonderful. So everyone is well?"

"Yes."

"Now that you are going to be meeting my family, I'd love to meet yours. Perhaps we should plan a trip to Lac Du Bonnet."

"We'd have to find someone to chaperone. Who do you think would want to come on a long trip like that?"

Ruth laughed. "Maybe you're right."

Ruth and Waldemar talked into the night, finishing their supper. After that they went for a walk. Even though it was eight o'clock, the sun shone brightly in the sky. They held hands and soaked up one another's company until nearly midnight when the summer sun finally began to set.

Waldemar drove Ruth back to her apartment in her car. When it was time for them to go, he kissed her goodnight. "It was great to see you again, Ruth. I've missed you."

"I've missed you too, Pete. It feels fantastic to be in Edmonton and know that you're only an hour away. Hopefully, your work will bring you into the city from time to time over the next few weeks."

"I'm sure I can find a way." Waldemar grinned. "I have a few tricks up my sleeve."

Ruth smiled and reached up to touch his cheek. "If not, I won't see you for couple weeks."

Waldemar pulled Ruth close and hugged her. "Don't spend any time worrying about that. Do you hear me?"

"I'll try, it's just . . ."

"Just nothing. Well it's getting late. I'd better be heading back. Don't worry, we'll be together soon enough . . . I'll find a way."

Waldemar gave Ruth another kiss. Then Ruth disappeared into her apartment. He smiled as he watched her walk away. He knew that her trip to Leduc would be memorable—he was counting on it. He patted the package in his pocket and walked to the bus stop with a satisfied smile on his face. Life was good, really good.

*

Dr. Chism stood over the dead man and shook his head. He wiped the sweat off his brow. He wasn't sure what had happened, perhaps a stroke, heart attack . . . he didn't know. The man lay on his living room floor with his eyes closed not showing any sign of what led him to this moment. Constable Peterson was waiting outside with his patrol car, keeping nosy neighbors at bay. Dr. Chism didn't think it was foul play, but he and the constable would figure that out together.

"Come on in, Peterson," Dr. Chism called out the front door.

Waldemar entered the house. It didn't smell good even though the man hadn't been dead for long. "What have we got here?"

"I'm not sure, stoke, heart attack, foul play?"

"Who called it in?"

"His boss . . . he hasn't shown up for work for two days, which isn't typical."

Waldemar shook his head and looked around. His eyes swept the room. Nothing looked particularly out of the ordinary. His mind went to Ruth. "Perhaps we need an autopsy?"

Dr. Chism considered the matter. "Yes, that may not be a bad idea. I don't think anything is amiss here but I'm sure it wouldn't hurt. The only issue is that I don't want him sitting in my morgue for a week while we wait for transport to come and pick him up."

Waldemar tried not to smile. "I can take him to Edmonton for the autopsy."

Dr. Chism looked at Waldemar skeptically. "That's nice of you, and just how would you do that?"

"In the back of the patrol car."

"Really?" He looked at Waldemar, wondering what the young man was thinking. "I hope you have a blanket."

"Yes, sir."

"Any reason why you want to go to Edmonton?"

"No, sir."

"Really?" he asked skeptically.

"Just to get the job done."

Dr. Chism's eyebrows rose as high as they could go. "If you want to, I don't see why not. I'll do a preliminary exam, you go over the scene and then we'll prepare him for transport."

"Yes, doctor." Waldemar smiled and began to take notes on the condition of the room. Before long, he had processed the room and taken the necessary notes in case this turned into a crime scene.

"Are you getting lonely in that large barrack of yours, Peterson?" Dr. Chism asked.

Waldemar had been staying by himself in a nine-bedroom log building that the RCMP had assigned him to. He had to bring in his own water and there was no electricity, just simple coal oil lamps. "I don't mind it, Doctor, it's easy to do the housecleaning." Waldemar smiled.

"Is that so?"

"When my room gets too dirty, I just pick up my bedding and move to another room!"

The two men laughed, "That's one way to do it!" Dr. Chism patted his friend on the arm. "I think I'm finished here. You take our victim here and head to Edmonton where you can see your friend Ruth. Have a good time, okay?"

"Yes, sir," Waldemar chuckled.

As he headed into Edmonton with his deceased passenger, Waldemar could hardly contain himself. He couldn't wait to see the look on Ruth's face when he surprised her.

Ruth was scrubbing hospital beds at the Camsell and thinking of her nursing days at the Miz. Today there would be no Sister Saint Christine to check her work, thank goodness. As she worked, she thought of next week. She was looking forward to spending a week in Leduc visiting and catching up. It would be nice to spend time with her father. He had been working so hard lately. She hoped that he could take some time this week to visit and re-connect.

The Camsell had been an easy place to work so far. They only had a handful of patients who had been brought in from various reservations in northern and central Alberta. The hospital would officially open this summer but patients had begun to trickle in as the need arose. So far, the patients were all tuberculosis patients, which is what the hospital was geared for. It would function for other areas of Aboriginal care but the hospital's main ambition was to take tuberculosis patients off the reservations and prevent the spread of disease.

Tonight she had no plans. Perhaps she would read at the apartment. She missed Waldemar terribly even though they had just seen each other last weekend. She longed for their St. Paul days where they saw one another more often. There was something so comforting about his nearness. She missed him terribly.

She finished scrubbing the last bed and threw the rag into the bucket of bleach water. "Done," she said to herself. "Done for the day. Time to go home."

Waldemar dropped his passenger off at the morgue and was heading to Ruth's apartment. When he arrived, he parked the patrol car. He took the stairs two at a time up to the third floor. He knocked on the door of her apartment with an armful of red roses.

Ruth opened the door. Her jaw dropped as she saw Waldemar standing there with a big grin on his face. "Pete!"

"I told you I'd find a way to come and see you." He reached out for a hug.

Ruth took the flowers and wrapped her arms around him. "How long will you be here for?"

"Just tonight, I have to be back tomorrow for work but we can go for supper and maybe a walk in the river valley."

"That would be great! Let me get ready. Come in and sit down. I'll get you some coffee while you wait for me."

Waldemar came in and sat at the small kitchen table while Ruth fixed him his drink. "So what brought you to Edmonton?"

"A passenger I had to accompany."

"An inmate?"

"No . . . not exactly."

"A citizen? For court?"

"Ah, no."

"What then? Was he a troublemaker?"

"No . . . he was pretty quiet." Waldemar grimaced.

Ruth looked at him quizzically. "Well, that's good I suppose."

"So," Waldemar said, changing the subject, "how is the hospital?"

"It's definitely a change of pace . . . not as busy." Ruth handed him a cup of coffee and then excused herself to go get ready for their night out.

As they strolled through the trails down by the river that night, they held hands. They listened to the breeze rustle the large trees that grew along the north Saskatchewan riverbank, just enjoying one another's company. Ruth tried to soak in every moment of his nearness, knowing that the next few weeks would be lonely without him.

At the end of the night, they said goodbye outside her apartment.

"It's going to be a long time before I see you again," Ruth lamented.

"Don't worry," he said comfortingly.

"But I have my trip to Leduc and I'll be there for a couple weeks."

"I said I would come down . . . didn't I?"

"I know. But who knows when."

He took her chin in his hand. "Cheer up. I'll find a day. I'll make an excuse to come to Leduc. Then I can meet your parents."

Ruth laughed. "Okay. I'm sorry. I always used to tease my friends who were so lovesick. Now I'm one of them!"

"It's okay." Waldemar hugged her tightly. "I feel the same way."

*"Above all, love each other
deeply, because love covers
over a multitude of sins."*
1 Peter 4:8 NIV

June 1946
Leduc, Alberta

"What a gorgeous day." Ruth walked arm in arm with her dad around the pond. This morning, she had arrived in Leduc and gone straight to the store to see him. He decided to take the rest of the day off. Rather than head straight home, they went for a walk so that they could have some time to catch up in private.

"It's beautiful. I'm going to try to do some gardening this afternoon." He looked at her fondly and asked, "Do you want to help?"

"I'd love to."

"So tell me more about how things are going. I can tell that you are in a time of transition."

"Yes," Ruth agreed, "I am. I think I am done with district nursing for a while. The Camsell is a good fit for now. Not too intense."

"Good. And housing? Your roommate is suitable?"

"Yes, Megan is great. She's a nice girl. We get along fine."

"And the constable? Tell me about your constable."

Ruth looked ahead on the grassy path. She watched a duck waddle into the pond. "He is good," she answered at last. "We are good friends."

"*Nur gut befreundet?*" Herman said skeptically, his eyebrows rising.

Ruth looked at him, her cheeks blushing. "Yes, we're just friends."

"You speak highly of him in your letters. It seems like the time you worked together brought you a lot of joy."

"It did. I miss our St. Paul days. Since he's been out in Evansburg, it's been hard."

"Do you see him very often?" Herman asked softly.

"He finds a reason to come into town on business. Then he'll stop by and see me. I never know when I'm going to see him next." Herman was silent for a long time, walking in step with her. Finally, he said, "I know the look in your eye when you talk about him, Ruth. I think you are more than friends."

"Dad," she moaned. "I don't want to talk about it."

He stopped walking and turned to face her. "Why don't you have him come to the house . . . for dinner?"

"I don't know. What will Mother say?"

"Well I would like to meet him. Let's just worry about that."

"Okay, okay. I will ask him next time I see him." Changing the subject she said, "And you? How are things for you?"

Herman smiled as they started walking again. "Just fine. The store is thriving. I am on the Board of Deacons at the church. My garden is blooming and my favorite daughter is here to visit me. What more do I need?"

Ruth laughed. "Your only daughter . . ."

"Favorite all the same," he chuckled.

"It's good to be back. I'm looking forward to this week here with you."

"Me too," he agreed. "I've missed you terribly."

She put an arm around his shoulder, hugging him.

"Shall we go back to the house?" he asked. "We can have lunch with your mother."

"Sure. But before we go, there's one thing I wanted to ask you."

He looked at her and smiled. "Anything, *Schatzi* . . ."

Ruth paused, hesitating on the words that were running through her mind. In German, she asked, "How did you know that you wanted to marry my *Mutter*," she took a deep breath before she whispered the name, " . . . Ruth?"

Herman's body stiffened. His eyes were fixed straight ahead.

"I'm sorry," Ruth whispered. "I shouldn't have asked."

Herman shook his head. "It's fine." He looked her in the eyes. His voice cracked as he replied in German. "You know because when you imagine a future without her . . . it is empty . . . It is the blackest void you could imagine . . . a life hardly worth living." A tear slipped from his eye. He ran his hand over his wrinkled cheek, hastily wiping it away.

Ruth swallowed the large lump in her throat. "*Es tut mir leid*, I'm sorry . . ."

Back at the house, everyone sat down at the table for lunch.

"It's nice to have you back, Ruth," Edith said as she passed the plate of ham around the table."

"It's nice to be here. Thank you for the wonderful meal."

"Well you are looking a little thin."

Ruth rolled her eyes. "I am, am I?"

Edith busied herself scooping out the mashed potatoes. "I'm just saying that if a girl wants to get married then she might need to accentuate her curves."

"So," Herman burst into the conversation, "how was the Social Committee today, Edith?"

Edith glared at Herman. "It was fine." She turned her attention back to Ruth. "Do you have plans to meet up with Nick?"

"Actually," Ruth said as she served herself some peas, "I do."

"Fantastic!" Edith turned her head and smiled knowingly at Herman.

"The first day when I get back to Edmonton, in fact. I plan to tell him that I no longer have feelings for him."

Edith nearly spit out her food. "What? Why?"

"Mother, really—"

"But he's such a nice German boy!"

Ruth shrugged. "Maybe so, but he's simply not for me."

Herman looked at the two women desperately. With fake happiness, he burst in saying, "My forget-me-nots are growing like crazy this season."

Ruth ignored her father's diversion. "Frankly, Mother, it's none of your business what I do in my personal life. Is it?"

Edith stabbed her fork into her ham. "Well as your mother, I would say it is my business."

Herman got up from the table suddenly, nearly spilling the water glasses on the table. "Anyone need some coffee?"

Ruth looked up at her father, her furrowed eyebrows softening. "Yes please, Dad. That would be nice."

"Tea for me please, Herman," Edith replied.

"Ruth," Edith carried on as Herman disappeared into the kitchen. "You have to face the facts that you aren't getting any younger. It's high time you settled down and found a man . . . had children and all the rest of it. You're going to be twenty-five in December—"

"Thank you, I know."

"What I'm trying to say is that sometimes the best option is the simplest one. Do you want to be a spinster?"

Herman called out from the kitchen. "Ruth, can you give me a hand?"

Ruth surrendered. "Thank you for the advice, Mother. Let's leave it at that." Ruth got up from her chair and went into the kitchen. Herman looked at her piercingly. Loudly he said, "Can you get the last cup of coffee? And the cream?" He came up close to her and whispered, "Read the phone message."

She answered, "Sure, Dad, I can get the cream."

He walked out of the kitchen and began to serve Edith her tea. Ruth took a quick glance at the notepad by the telephone. "Constable, coming at 2:30," and underlined was the word, "today."

Ruth's heart skipped a beat. She quickly grabbed the last cup of coffee and the cream from the icebox.

Edith glared at Ruth as she came into the dining room. "What took you so long? Lunch is getting cold!"

"Ah, I couldn't find the cream." She exchanged a look with her dad.

Ruth inhaled her lunch and then excused herself from the table. "I'm going to get settled into my room," she explained as she hastily cleared her dishes from the table. "Maybe freshen up a bit."

Herman went out in the backyard to tend to his garden while Edith washed the lunch dishes. Ruth went up to her childhood bedroom and opened her bag. She looked around the room, noting that little had changed since she left. Her bed had the same worn quilt. The rocker stood in the corner of the room, moving gently in the summer breeze. Her large windows faced the street where an occasional car went by. She opened the wardrobe door and was pleased to find Rosalie sitting on the top shelf, faithfully smiling at her. Ruth picked up the doll and embraced her. "Hello, old friend. It's been a long time, hasn't it?" Ruth carefully set Rosalie on the bed, straightening the doll's dress.

"What should I wear tonight?" she asked as she pulled out her dresses and laid them on the bed. After some consideration, Ruth slipped on a summer floral dress and admired herself in the mirror. "This should do." She began to brush her hair and pin it up. She applied a soft layer of make-up. She finished by wiping her glasses clean.

Ruth slipped out of the house wordlessly, past Edith, and went around to the backyard to see her dad. She decided that she would try to intercept Waldemar before he came into the house.

She found her dad kneeling in the grass, pulling out weeds in his flowerbed.

"Hi, *Vati.*"

"Hello, child."

"Your roses are looking beautiful."

"Yes, it's only a little over a month of growth and already they're going wild." He sighed, looking up at her. "I love being outside in the summer months. I guess you won't be joining me this afternoon."

"No, I'm sorry. I wish I could. Tomorrow perhaps."

"That's fine. Do you know where you and your friend are off to?"

"No, it's not like Pete to surprise me. I can't imagine what he's up to."

Just then, Ruth heard a car pulling up. "That must be him." Ruth leaned down to kiss her father, gave a little wave and then ran around to greet Waldemar.

"Have fun!" Herman smiled after his daughter.

Edith listened to Herman and Ruth from the window. She squeezed out her dishrag angrily as she watched him return to his gardening. She wiped her hands on a kitchen towel, planning to go out front to greet this fellow at the front door.

Ruth rushed to the car and jumped in before Waldemar had a chance to get out.

"Well hello," he laughed, "what's the rush?"

"Let's just go." Ruth leaned over and kissed him on the cheek. "Come on, go."

"Okay, okay. Did you rob a bank? Anything I should know about?" He pushed his foot on the accelerator and took off down the street.

Ruth looked in her side-view mirror to see Edith opening the front door. She breathed a sigh of relief.

"What's going on with you?" Waldemar asked.

"Nothing . . ."

He gave her a funny look. "If you say so."

Once they were on their way, Ruth asked, "Whose car is this?"

"Oh, I borrowed it from a friend in Evansburg."

"That's nice of your friend. So, where are we off to?"

"I thought we could go visit Annie and Harold."

"That's a good idea! What prompted this?"

"I had a business trip to Edmonton and I was missing you. I thought I'd just come down here and find you."

"Well it's a pleasant surprise!" Ruth was happy that they were on their way to see Annie and Harold. The couple had moved out to a reservation just outside of Lacombe shortly after she had left Saddle Lake. They hadn't had any contact since. After living together on the reserve for so long, Ruth missed Annie.

They spent the evening eating supper and visiting over coffee. Ruth was worn out by the time they started their drive back to Leduc. It had been a long day starting with her drive from Edmonton this morning. She was glad to be heading home to bed. She started to doze as they drove along the dark highway with only their headlights piercing through the night.

Suddenly, Waldemar pulled off the highway onto a bumpy farm road.

"What's wrong?" Ruth asked as she jolted awake.

"Nothing." Waldemar brought the car to a stop and turned to face a rather alarmed-looking Ruth. He started to laugh. "It's okay, really."

"Is something wrong with the car? Flat tire? Engine troubles?"

"No, nothing is wrong with the car."

"Are you okay? Feeling sick? Do you need me to drive?"

"I'm fine, stop for a minute and let me talk."

Ruth looked at him curiously. "If you're not feeling well I can drive."

He put a finger to her lips. "Shhhhh. Just listen."

Ruth clamped her lips together. "Okay."

"You know I love you, right?" He placed the car into park and turned toward her, taking her hands.

"Yes." Goosebumps pricked up along her spine.

"You know that my job makes my life unpredictable. I never know what's coming next."

"Yes." Ruth's heart began to pound.

"You know work has always been my first priority, and it probably will dictate most everything I do until I retire."

"Okay."

"I didn't really want to get too attached to anyone. I knew that my career was going to take me from place to place . . ."

"Oh no! You're being transferred far away!"

"No . . ."

"Overseas? You're leaving the RCMP! You're getting a new job?"

Waldemar shook his head and started to laugh. "Please, Ruth, just let me continue!"

She smiled. "Sorry. Please, continue."

"As I was saying I've always tried not to get too attached to anyone. Because . . . well you know . . . I never know where the RCMP is going to take me next. I never wanted to be in the situation where I had to say goodbye to someone I cared about. Well, since I've met you," his voice cracked, "all that has changed."

Ruth nodded and said nothing, a lump forming in her throat.

Waldemar sighed and said, "What I'm trying to say is . . ."

"You don't want to see me anymore?" Ruth asked, tears springing to her eyes.

Waldemar started to laugh as tears began to stream down her cheeks.

"No, I'm trying to say . . ." he hesitated. "Will you marry me?"

"Oh yes!" She breathed a big sigh of relief. She wiped the tears away, laughing. "Of course!"

Waldemar leaned over and gave her a big kiss, which she returned enthusiastically. He reached into his pocket and pulled out a small velvet box. He opened it and showed her the engagement ring he had chosen.

"Oh, Pete, it's beautiful! Thank you!" He pulled the ring out of the box and slipped it on her finger. They both held hands and looked at one another.

"I can't believe it. I didn't know what you were getting at! My mind was jumping from one dreadful conclusion to the next!"

"You need to slow your mind down and just listen," he laughed.

After a few minutes, she asked, "When were you thinking?"

"It doesn't matter, what are you thinking?"

"Soon, perhaps this fall." She laughed, "We're not getting any younger,"

Waldemar looked serious again. "It won't be easy, Ruth, with my job and yours . . . I'm not German or Baptist . . ."

"You know that doesn't matter to me!" she interrupted. "And, Pete, nothing ever is easy, we're old enough to know that by now. But one thing I do know is that without you everything feels impossible. When we're together, I know we can conquer whatever comes our way."

"I've always felt that way about you too. I always knew that you were the kind of woman I could marry . . . that you could take on any challenge."

"Thank you." She leaned in to kiss him again. The two sat in the moonlit car holding each other and thinking about the future. Thinking about the fact that they would never have to face anything without one another.

Finally, he said, "We should go. I don't want to make a poor first impression on your dad before we've even met."

"It is getting very late." She giggled. "I don't know if I can sleep though!" She twirled the ring on her finger, admiring the way it sparkled in the moonlight.

The two drove home, discussing which date would be best for the wedding day and where they would have the ceremony. Waldemar dropped Ruth off in front of the house and said goodnight, kissing her one last time before he left. "I'll head back to Edmonton tonight. I'll try to come back on Sunday to meet your family."

"That sounds perfect." Ruth fingered her new ring. "I love you."

"I love you too."

"He who finds a wife finds
what is good and receives
favor from the LORD."
Proverbs 18:22 NIV

June 26, 1946
Leduc, Alberta

Ruth came down for breakfast the next morning to find Edith busy baking bread. She was kneading dough, quite focused on her job. Ruth came into the kitchen humming a light-hearted tune with her left hand tucked into her pocket.

"Good morning, Mother," Ruth greeted Edith cheerily.

Edith continued to knead. "Good morning. What time did you get in last night?"

Herman came into the kitchen, interrupting the exchange, "Good morning, ladies."

"Good morning, Dad." Ruth smiled at her father. "Can I get you a cup of coffee?"

"Sure, sweetheart, that would be lovely."

Edith scowled into her dough as she continued to knead more and more aggressively. "You didn't answer my question, Ruth."

"Oh yes . . . I got in around midnight, I think."

"Don't you think that is a bit late to be out with a gentleman friend?"

"I suppose, I had good reason though." Ruth grinned broadly despite herself. She poured her father a cup of coffee and stood at the counter next to Edith.

"Where did you go?" Herman asked.

"We went out to see Harold and Annie at their new place; it's a bit of a drive."

"No reason for not getting home at a decent hour," Edith interjected.

"Well we stopped on the way home . . ." Ruth paused and looked at her father, "and . . ." Ruth pulled her hand from her pocket and waved her ringed finger in front of Edith.

Edith stood with her fists mid-knead. She looked at Ruth with her mouth open. "I knew it, I knew it!" She gripped the counter with as much dramatics as she could muster. "I feel faint."

Herman jumped up, ignoring Edith's reaction, nearly knocking over his chair to give Ruth a hug. "That's fantastic! Congratulations! Edith, isn't that wonderful?"

"Do you think this is appropriate?" Edith continued to grip the edge of the counter. She fanned herself with a tea towel. "We haven't even met him!"

"Well the distance hasn't been terribly favorable to meeting just yet. He can try to come for lunch on Sunday if that's suitable for you." Ruth looked at her dad with a twinkle in her eye.

"That would be fine," Herman piped up. "I can't wait to meet him! Oh I am so happy for you!"

Herman and Ruth talked excitedly all morning about the wedding date, the size of the wedding and where it would be held. Edith worked at the kitchen counter feverishly, stopping only momentarily to add her two cents to the conversation between father and daughter. Soon it was time for Herman to leave for work. Ruth decided it would be a good time to go and visit Aunt Lilly and Uncle Fred. She didn't want to pursue the wedding conversation any further with Edith.

She drove out to Lilly and Fred's farm with the window down, feeling the fresh morning air. Ruth was excited about the engagement and prospects of the upcoming wedding. Now that Waldemar had proposed, Ruth realized how ready she was for this step in her life. She knew that her wedding would be the talk of Leduc. Her dad mentioned this morning that this would be the first RCMP wedding Leduc had ever hosted. It was sure to draw a lot of attention. She could already picture Waldemar in his red serge at the front of the church.

Ruth pulled up the long dirt driveway to the farmhouse. She was eager to share the news with Aunt Lilly. She knew that her aunt would be thrilled for her. She parked the car and walked around the side of the house to find Lilly hanging the wash in the yard.

"Well mercy me!" Lilly gasped as Ruth approached.

"Hi!"

"I heard you were coming to town but I didn't know when I might see you!"

"Today! Are you free?"

"Of course, I'm always free for you! Let me finish hanging my washing and then we'll sit on the porch."

"I can help." Ruth helped to hang the bed sheets on the line. "So, I have news . . ."

"What?" Her aunt smiled broadly and stopped hanging for a minute to look at her. "You're in love, aren't you?"

"Yes, and he proposed!"

"Oh you are kidding me! That's wonderful! When's the big day?"

"Well we just got engaged last night so we aren't completely sure but we were thinking November."

"Is it the constable you've been talking about in your letters?"

"Yes," Ruth smiled, "the one and only."

"Oh a winter wedding will be so beautiful! Leduc will be abuzz with the excitement of the first RCMP wedding! Oooo I can hardly wait!"

"I hadn't even thought of that until this morning, but it will be exciting, won't it?"

"Oh yes! How did your mother take the news?" Lilly asked.

"Not too well . . . you know how she is."

"Don't let it get to you, she just can't handle change."

"I know but it's not like I live with them or it will really affect her in any way. I'm twenty-five, for goodness sake."

"Even so, she never could cope with anything she wasn't in control of."

"I'm not going to let it get me down. You only get to do this once. I plan to enjoy it."

"And children? When will you have children?"

"One thing at a time, Aunt Lilly," Ruth laughed. "We're not even married, last time I checked it takes at least nine months!"

Lilly laughed and said, "You know they say the first baby can come any time and only the *next* one takes nine months!"

The two chuckled as they finished hanging the wash. Afterwards they sat on the porch and sipped lemonade. Ruth thoroughly enjoyed Lilly's company and enthusiasm. Ruth told her all the stories about Waldemar, what he was like, his childhood, his career and the highlights of their time in St. Paul together. Lilly was like the mix of a best friend and a mother to Ruth. They spent the day together until just before dinner when Ruth decided she had better head home. Her dad would be home from work soon and she wanted to spend the evening visiting with him.

"Thank you very much for the fun day, Aunt Lilly; I had such a wonderful time with you."

Lilly hugged Ruth, "I'm glad you came! I am also happy to know that you are nice and close by in Edmonton so that we can see you a lot more frequently. We've missed seeing you as often as we used to."

"I know, I am glad to be back in Edmonton and closer to home. Letters are wonderful but it is so nice to have the frequent face-to-face visits."

"Well come around anytime. How long are you in Leduc for?"

"About a week, I'm sure we'll be seeing a lot of each other as we plan for the wedding."

"Goodbye, dear!" Lilly waved as Ruth drove away, smiling broadly.

The following Sunday, Herman, Edith and Ruth were finishing up their lunch at the dining room table. As they pushed back their plates, there was a knock at the door.

Ruth jumped up. "That must be Pete." She hurried to open the door, straightening her skirt and smoothing her blouse. She took a deep breath and opened the door. "Hi!"

"Hey," he said fondly, "it's good to see you."

"Come on in." Ruth smiled shyly. "We just finished lunch."

"Sorry, I tried to make it for lunch but work held me up this morning."

"It's not a problem. There are plenty of leftovers. Come in and meet my parents." Ruth took another deep breath. She led Waldemar to the dining room where Herman and Edith were drinking coffee.

Herman stood up and put out his hand. "Hello, Mr. Peterson! It's wonderful to meet you!"

"It's a pleasure to meet you, Mr. and Mrs. Bohlman." Waldemar shook Herman's hand. "I've been looking forward to this for some time." Edith rose and shook hands with Waldemar.

Herman grinned. "Ruth has told us all about you."

"All good things I hope," Waldemar laughed.

"Yes, yes of course . . . have a seat at the table. Ruth can get you a plate for lunch if you'd like."

"That would be wonderful. I was just telling Ruth, when I came in, that I was hoping to be here a little sooner but work held me back this morning."

"Duty calls," Herman said thoughtfully, "and a man must answer."

"Yes I suppose," Waldemar chuckled, "although it isn't always terribly convenient."

"Well," Edith said suddenly, "I need to excuse myself so that I can start the dishes."

"Of course," Ruth said, "I'll come with you to get a plate."

As they went into the kitchen, Edith whispered to Ruth, "He missed lunch."

"I know. He had work to do this morning." Ruth turned around with a plate in hand before Edith could say anything else. She returned to the dining room and gave Waldemar his plate. "Help yourself to the bread, and anything else you need."

"Thanks," Waldemar replied. He picked up several pieces of bread and pulled the small dish of jam toward his plate.

"Waldemar was just telling me a little bit about his life in Evansburg," Herman said as he sipped his coffee.

"Yes, I've been coaching a ladies softball team and having a great time with it. It looks like I might turn them into local champions."

Herman and Waldemar continued to talk. All Ruth could focus on was how much bread Waldemar was eating and how again and again he dipped his bread into the small dish of jam, eventually wiping it clean.

When he was done, Herman suggested that they move into the living room to continue to get to know each other. Edith joined them. She subtly interrogated Waldemar on various hot topics such as religion, war and politics. While they talked, Ruth took the jam bowl and washed it in the sink before Edith had a chance to notice the missing contents.

After the visit, Ruth suggested they go for a walk around Leduc so that Ruth could show Waldemar some of the highlights.

"What did you think?" Waldemar asked once they were outside. "I thought that went well; your mother wasn't too bad. She seemed to like me."

"I can't believe you!" Ruth exclaimed. She walked quickly with Waldemar keeping pace behind her.

"What?" Waldemar threw his hands up in the air.

"You ate the whole bowl!" She stopped and faced him with her hands on her hips.

"Of what?"

"Jam!"

"What are you talking about?"

"You ate all the jam, you wiped the bowl clean!"

Waldemar started to laugh. "That was jam? I thought it was a bowl of fruit, you know, for dessert!"

"It's practically an unforgivable sin to eat all the jam in one sitting!" Ruth shrieked.

"Boy, I really need to brush up on the Baptist rules, I had no idea!" Waldemar laughed and grabbed Ruth in a big hug. "Don't worry so much!"

"The whole time you were talking, I couldn't even focus on the conversation. I couldn't believe you were eating the whole bowl." She looked up at him with her arms wrapped around his waist.

Waldemar laughed. "I thought you were just nervous about me meeting your parents. Why didn't you say something?"

"I didn't want to be rude." She smiled meekly.

"So you let me be rude instead?" Waldemar shook his head. "Back home jam isn't a rare commodity. You can eat all you want. In fact, we had so much fruit we'd usually have a whole bowl with cream for dessert every night."

Ruth giggled, "Oh, Pete, sometimes we are worlds apart."

"That's okay, I'll learn." He leaned down to kiss her. "What did they think about the engagement?"

The two began to walk again and Ruth answered, "Dad was excited."

"And your mother?"

"She wasn't terribly impressed; she nearly collapsed in the bread she was kneading."

"That happy, huh?"

"I don't know. She is such a mystery to me."

"Have you made any decisions this week on the wedding?"

"Well, Mother and Dad thought that it should be a large wedding. I think that sixty people would be enough, so they conceded for it to be small. We'll have it in the church, Temple Baptist, since it's just a few minutes from the house."

"That sounds good."

"And the reception I think we should have in Edmonton, at the Hotel Macdonald. Mother and Dad will come back to Edmonton with me and talk to the people at the hotel. We'll see if I can secure the weekend we're after."

"It sounds like you've got a lot of things accomplished in the last few days."

"It's been nice to be off work and to be able to just sit and think about everything."

"Are you driving back on Tuesday?"

"Yes, I'm working on Wednesday so I thought I'd come up Tuesday morning and we can all go by the hotel in the afternoon."

They talked while they walked around Leduc. Ruth showed Waldemar where certain neighbors lived or had once lived. They enjoyed each other's company for over an hour until Waldemar decided he should get back to Evansburg.

"Have you sent in your application for marriage?" Ruth asked.

"Yes, they'll be in contact with you and your references fairly soon I imagine."

Waldemar had to submit an application for marriage with the RCMP. It required a background check on Ruth and evidence that Waldemar could support them with his income. It was a bit of a laugh since Waldemar had no money. He did, however, have a friend who was a loans manager at the Imperial Bank who was willing to put $500 in Waldemar's account and then write a letter indicating that he had the funds. Everything was falling into place as Waldemar prepared his application. He had a friend in Entwistle, which was a town that neighbored Evansburg, who was a kind Swedish man. He had agreed to rent his house to Waldemar. Waldemar had to show the RCMP that he could provide married accommodation. He had set into motion plans to convert the house to include an office and a cell. His Swedish friend wasn't thrilled about the modifications, but because of his fondness for Waldemar, he had agreed.

"Why do I need a reference?" Ruth asked.

"The Force wants to know if you have any value to them." Waldemar smiled broadly, knowing how Ruth would respond.

"What?" She put a hand on her hip and wrinkled her brow.

"You know, if you're a nurse it's in our favor, or a teacher is beneficial. In these remote rural areas, they want to know if my wife will be a support to the community."

"Hmmm." Ruth thought this over.

Waldemar stopped and looked at Ruth. "You're pretty valuable to me you know."

"Yes, you're pretty lucky to have such a smart, talented, beautiful woman who's willing to marry you." She winked at him.

"I sure am." Waldemar gave Ruth a kiss.

*"Why, you do not even
know what will happen
tomorrow. What is your
life? You are a mist that
appears for a little while
and then vanishes. Instead,
you ought to say, "If it is
the Lord's will, we will live
and do this or that.""*
James 4: 14 & 15 NIV

June 1946
Leduc, Alberta

Ruth was getting ready to head back to work and was looking forward to their afternoon meeting at the Hotel Macdonald tomorrow. Her week had been lovely, visiting with friends and family. Aunt Bertha, Edith's older sister, from Saskatchewan had been over all day. The pair of sisters were out in the backyard hanging laundry together. Ruth loved the dynamic between the pair. Bertha was so matter-of-fact about everything and had such a wonderful older-sister way of putting Edith in her place when needed. Ruth was about to join the ladies in the backyard when she heard them talking about her. She paused at the door and listened.

" . . . she just shouldn't be rushing into this!" Edith exclaimed. "Look at this. A letter from a nice German boy who would marry her in a heartbeat!"

"Leave the girl alone, Edith," Bertha chided, "she knows what she is doing."

Ruth let the door shut loudly so that the sisters would know she was joining them.

"Hello. Can I help?" Ruth asked as she crossed the yard.

"No, dear," Bertha said warmly. "Sit down and relax, we're almost through."

Ruth found a place to sit. She watched Edith and Bertha stretch out the last sheet on the line.

"Have you made any wedding plans, sweetheart?" Bertha asked Ruth.

"Well we'll have the ceremony next door. Nothing too large, about sixty people."

"The community is already a buzz about your engagement and the possibility of hosting its first RCMP wedding. You're practically a local celebrity!"

Ruth laughed, "Well hardly, but we did decide to have the reception up in Edmonton at the Hotel Macdonald. Mother, Dad and I are going tomorrow to make the arrangements."

"Well that's unusual, isn't it? A hotel reception? What made you decide that?"

"It seemed like the easiest thing for everyone."

Bertha came to Ruth and hugged her. "Well I am just delighted!"

Edith sat down next to Ruth. With measured emotion, she said, "I'm happy for you too, Ruth."

"Thanks, Mother," Ruth smiled at her warmly.

"Did I hear you say you have a letter?"

"Ah, yes." Edith exchanged a glance with Bertha.

"Well give it to her, E."

Edith begrudgingly handed the letter to Ruth.

Ruth ripped it open and read it quickly.

"What does it say?" Edith asked.

"It says that he'll pick me up at the apartment at eleven o'clock. He says he has a surprise for me."

"And you're going to tell him about your engagement?"

"Of course, Mother. I've just been waiting for the right time."

"I'm sure he'll understand," Bertha said reassuringly, "he probably has a nice gal of his own."

Ruth shrugged. "I hope so."

"Should we head inside?" Edith asked.

"Yes, let's do that." Bertha linked arms with Ruth as they walked inside. "Tell me about your dress, Ruth."

"I have my graduation dress from nursing school. It's white and I think it would be suitable."

"That sounds lovely." Bertha smiled at Ruth. "It sounds like you are getting everything into place quickly."

"We're hoping for the first weekend in November. It doesn't leave much time. Besides, I've had enough years to think about this day!"

"You've been busy doing a noble cause; your nursing certainly kept you on the go. Besides, it looks like God was keeping you waiting for the perfect man for you. The best things are worth the wait!"

*

Ruth waited anxiously for Nick under the oak tree in front of her apartment. Finally, a silver car pulled into the parking lot, its tires crunching over the gravel. She saw his familiar outline. He parked the car. As he stepped out of the car, she felt ill for a moment. *Why didn't I just tell him a long time ago?* He looked so happy as he strode toward her. He had always treated her kindly. Something had always been missing though—that thing she had with Waldemar. She had taken her engagement ring off so that she could tell him before he saw the ring.

Nick quickened his pace as he drew near to Ruth. He could not suppress his grin as he came up and gave her a big hug. "*Ruth! Ich habe dich vermisst,* I've missed you!"

Ruth returned the hug and smiled, "Hi, Nick, it's nice to see you too."

He held her shoulders and stepped back, looking into her eyes. "God, it's been too long, I've been dreaming about this moment for so long. You look amazing."

Ruth shifted uncomfortably. Her stomach flipped. "So where are we going?"

"I'm going to take you for a drive. I have something to show you! Let's go and you'll see." His grin didn't falter as he took her hand and walked her to his car. He opened the front door for Ruth and helped her in.

Ruth smoothed her skirt and cleared her throat. She said a silent prayer, *Oh God, what can I say? Protect his heart, make this easy.*

"So tell me about your work. What are you doing now?" he asked. "What's keeping you busy?" He put the car into drive and began to pull away from the apartment building.

"I'm working at the Camsell, a new hospital for Aboriginals. It is geared toward treating tuberculosis. How about you? What are you doing now?"

"Well I have been building up my life here in Edmonton; I have found a good job and a place to live."

"Oh good for you, where's your new place?"

Nick looked over at her and winked, "I'll show you."

Ruth's stomach knotted further. "That would be nice."

Nick pulled up to a small bi-level home in the Highlands area of Edmonton. It was a nice new neighborhood. He turned off the ignition and turned to Ruth. "Do you want to see inside? My dad and I have been building it together."

"Sure." Ruth's knees began to feel weak. She sent another prayer upward. *God, let me get through this.*

Nick walked proudly up to the front door, unlocked it and motioned her inside. "Well?" He smiled and then took Ruth's hands in his own. "What do you think of our new home?"

Ruth felt unsteady. *Oh no, oh no, oh no.*

"I know, it's a lot to take in, but isn't it great? I wanted to ask you the big question once I showed you our new place!"

"Oh, Nick," Ruth looked down at her shoes.

"Don't say anything." He got down on one knee, right there in the middle of the empty living room. "Ruth will you—"

Ruth touched his arm and pulled him to his feet. "No, Nick. Please . . . *nein.*"

"What is it? Are you surprised?" His smile dissolved. He began to look puzzled.

"This," Ruth gestured around her, "this is unbelievable—and wow, I am so surprised and thankful. And—you, you've been such a good friend—and you've been a sweetheart too—but, but I . . ." Ruth looked at Nick in the eyes. "I've changed, I thought you had too. Wow, this is really *schwierig,* difficult."

Nick's expression began to go from puzzled to upset as he realized the dream he had envisioned was not coming to pass. "I know we haven't talked too much in the last few years, but I thought that you still felt the same."

"I know. I'm sorry."

"You never really said otherwise."

"I know, I guess I just thought you had moved on too."

"What do you mean, moved on? Did you think I had found someone else?" He took his hands away from Ruth and shoved them in his pockets. His eyes began to mist.

"Well . . ."

"Why, have you?"

Ruth paused and took a deep breath.

"You have, haven't you?" He slammed his fist against the fireplace mantle. "I can't believe this!"

Ruth wished over and over that she had said something a long, long time ago. "I didn't know you felt so strongly."

"Well I do. I guess not anymore! I always thought that when the war was over and I was back in Alberta that we would reconnect. *Ich liebe dich.*"

"*Danke* for this," she motioned around the house, "I am so sorry, I—I'm engaged . . ."

Nick threw up his hands. "What?"

"I'm sorry, it was just last month."

"I should have come to see you sooner." He turned around and walked away from Ruth to the back of the house where the simple little kitchen had been laid out and built with love.

"*Es tut mir leid,*" Ruth whispered.

She stood in the front room and let Nick take in the news. She didn't know what to say. She felt terrible about what had happened. She tried to rationalize it in her mind. He hadn't even been in touch. He hadn't said he was thinking of marriage. He hadn't done anything to make her think that he was going to propose. She stood watching his back, sensing his frustration and feeling the tension as he digested the information.

He turned around and walked toward the front door. He opened the door and motioned her out, saying nothing. Ruth walked out the door and toward the car. She opened the door for herself and got in wordlessly. Nick went around, got in and slammed the door. He put the keys in and took off down the street.

"Nick, I'm sorry."

"Don't . . . just don't . . ." he exhaled loudly. "I don't understand! Why didn't you say that you had a boyfriend?"

"I didn't think we were still an item. I just thought we were friends. Besides, I wanted to tell you face to face. I'm sorry, I misjudged."

"Misjudged?" he scoffed. "Misjudged?" Nick slammed his fist on the steering wheel, clearly hurt, more than words could say. The pair drove in silence back to Ruth's apartment. The drive felt long. When Nick stopped the car, Ruth looked at him one more time. "I'm sorry, the house, it's beautiful and I really appreciate the gesture."

"Goodbye, Ruth. Good luck with everything." He kept his gaze facing forward. Ruth got out of the car and shut the door behind her. He didn't look at her as he drove away. As she watched the back of his car disappear, she moaned. She went into her apartment building, up the three flights of stairs and into her room. She went to her bed and laid down, thinking of how she hadn't meant for things to go so sour. She cried into her pillow.

Two months had passed. It was the fall of 1946; the trees had turned from green to amber. The wedding preparations were in full swing. Ruth was working hard at the Camsell and keeping busy with trips to Leduc to visit with family and finalize wedding arrangements.

She was back in Leduc for a few days, enjoying her morning cup of coffee at the kitchen table when the reality of Nick came crashing at her like a freight train. The headline glared out at her, challenging her to forget . . . to deny what had happened back in July. She read the article and tried to suffocate any sense of responsibility. After all, they didn't know why it had happened.

She hadn't told anyone what had happened with Nick. She felt that if she said it out loud it would make it even worse. She hadn't even told Artrude. She just tried to push it out of her mind whenever it came into her thoughts. She had heard from people in Leduc that he had gone out to Vancouver to be with his sister. She wondered what would become of that little house in Highlands.

Herman walked into the kitchen, joining his daughter. He immediately noticed her expression. "Ruth, are you okay? What are you reading?"

Ruth shoved the paper toward him, saying nothing.

Herman read the headline out loud, "Local War Hero Drowns in Horseshoe Bay." He scanned the article. "Oh, Nick Schellenburg." He looked at Ruth.

Ruth choked back tears, "Yes."

"I'm sorry." Quietly he said, "This will be so difficult for the Schellenburgs."

"Yes."

"It says here his boat capsized, that he was alone," Herman scanned the article, "I wonder what he was doing out there all alone. It says here that the owner of the Bay, Mr. Woodbridge, warns against people going out alone on the Bay in a small vessel . . . that the ocean can be unforgiving."

"Why was he out there?"

"Yes, I wonder why he was out there on his own. Maybe fishing?"

Many dark thoughts ran through Ruth's mind.

Herman read on. "It says that his family is perplexed. Only that he was going through a difficult time and perhaps seeking solace on the ocean."

Ruth felt ill.

"Maybe the war." Herman shook his head. "Such a shame. These good young men go off to war and they come back all muddled. Memories of the war can plague a young man. And," Herman carried on, "he must have seen some terrible things as a medic."

Ruth nodded, saying nothing.

"Didn't you just see him lately?" Herman asked.

"Ah, yes. In July."

"And how was he then? Down?"

Ruth could barely speak. "He seemed happy . . . at first. And then . . . I don't know. I don't know how he was. We didn't visit for very long."

Ruth drank her coffee in silence. Her dad began to talk about other articles in the paper as he drank his coffee. Finally, she excused herself. She walked in a daze to her bedroom. *Oh, Nick, what were you doing?*

*"For this reason a man will
leave his father and mother
and be united to his wife,
and they will become one
flesh." Genesis 2:24 NIV*

November 6, 1946
Leduc, Alberta

Ruth looked herself over in the mirror again. She couldn't believe the day was finally here. Her gown was beautiful, a lovely, unexpected surprise from her father. Two days ago he had whisked her up to Edmonton to a bridal shop where he had chosen a wedding gown for her. He had stated that 'No daughter of mine is wearing a graduation dress on her wedding day.' When she had tried on the gown in the shop, she knew that he was right on. Edith had even been swept up in the excitement when Ruth twirled in the gown. It was white satin with accordion pleats accentuating the neckline. The bodice fastened down the back with small covered buttons. It had long lily-point sleeves and a sweetheart neckline. It fit perfectly. Ruth felt like the Queen of England when she put it on. She looked out her bedroom window. The skies were blue and the whole world seemed to be celebrating with her. She sighed, "I am getting married today!"

Meanwhile, Herman sat in his bedroom holding the ring in his hands. *Was now the time? Was this the right time to tell her? Was she ready to hear about her mother or would it spoil the day? Should he tell her of her young mother's love? Give her the ring?* Herman prayed. In his heart, he felt the time was right but he could not bring himself to walk to her room and actually say the words. It was as if he relived the past he might die inside all over again. As he fingered the ring, he could almost hear her sweet laughter. This object had once been on her finger, touching her. He held the ring tightly. It was a symbol of their lifetime commitment. The day he placed it on her finger he never expected that her lifetime would be so short.

He rose to the door of his room, feeling like it was miles to his daughter, and no words could explain appropriately without being a betrayal to Edith. His heart and his mind could not find peace. He paced across the floor of his bedroom and slipped the ring back into his breast pocket.

Ruth had spent yesterday with Waldemar's sister Margaret. She had come from Winnipeg a day ahead of time to get to know Ruth. Ruth had thoroughly enjoyed her company. She loved getting to know Waldemar's sister and feeling a connection to his family. Margaret entertained Ruth with endless stories of her big brother and all his antics as a young boy. Margaret was the maid of honor, Rachel from nursing school was a bridesmaid, as well as Lilly and Fred's daughter Joyce. The girls had picked their own dresses, all in white, to go with the groomsmen's red serges. Sadly Ruth's dearest friend Artrude was in Seattle and was unable to attend. She had sent her endless love and congratulations in a telegram that morning.

Margaret, Rachel and Joyce had met at the local hotel a few hours before the wedding to do their hair, make-up and get their gowns on. The room was abuzz with excitement. All the businesses in Leduc had shut down for the day. The whole town was excited for the big event. Rachel fastened a fine gold necklace around Ruth's neck and handed her a bouquet of red roses and baby chrysanthemums. They were all being driven over to Temple Baptist shortly, the wedding party in one car and Ruth in another with her father.

"Can you believe it, Ruth?" Rachel asked.

"I can't! It's stupendous! I'm excited to share this with all of our family and friends. I am so glad that you could be a part of it!"

"I wouldn't miss it for the world," Rachel said excitedly.

"I am happy to be here too," Margaret agreed. "This is such an honor to be a part of your big day."

Joyce nodded in agreement, looking lovely in her white gown with a bandeau of flowers in her hair. "You look stunning, Ruth, just stunning."

"Are we ready then?" Ruth asked, smiling from ear to ear.

Waldemar and his two groomsmen prepared for the wedding at a friend's house. All three were in uniform looking rather impressive. Waldemar wished his Mamma could see him now. He knew that her health was failing though and travel was impossible. Nonetheless, he wished his whole family could join in on this special day. He was happy that Margaret was able to be a part of it, as well as Stanley, Mary's husband, who had come from Winnipeg. His family had sent telegrams earlier that day. Waldemar read them over before they left for the ceremony. The first one was from Gus and Annie:

> *Constable and Mrs. WW Peterson*
> *Congratulations on this, your wedding day. May*
> *God's richest blessings abide with you in love—Gust*
> *and Annie*

Waldemar read the next three with a smile on his face.

> *Constable and Mrs. WW Peterson*
> *Let all the joy and happiness brought to you today be*
> *the kind that lasts. Good luck, God bless you both.*
> *Love, Sister Mary*

> *Constable and Mrs. WW Peterson*
> *Congratulations, may God give you both a long and happy*
> *life together.*
> *Love, Mother, Dad, Victor and Douglas*

> *Constable and Mrs. WW Peterson*
> *Congratulations, Ruth and Waldemar, from the*
> *bottom of our hearts we wish you lots of good luck*
> *and happiness—Singhild and Nick*

He knew that today his Mamma would be sitting in her chair by the window, thinking of him and praying for his union.

It was time for the ceremony to begin. Herman and Ruth stood outside the swinging doors to the church. Just as they were about to walk in, he stopped. Ruth looked over at her dad, looking handsome and yet so troubled.

"Child, are you sure this is what you want to do?" Herman placed his hand over his breast pocket and felt the ring there, thinking of the heartbreak that such a love could cause.

Ruth smiled and laughed light-heartedly, unaware of his inner conflict. "For goodness sake, Dad, just open the door!"

Herman opened the door to the church. The scene was breathtaking. Beverly Klass began the bridal march on the organ. Ruth paused to take in the scene. The church was decorated with white chrysanthemums and ferns perfect for a winter wedding. The guests were all turned with their eyes on her. At the front of the church stood her three bridesmaids and Waldemar with his groomsmen. Waldemar wore his red serge adorned with gold buttons down the front, his black formal pants with the yellow stripe down the side. He looked at her and their eyes connected. Herman walked Ruth down the isle to the front of the church. She looked around the church and saw Edith smiling proudly in the front row. Lorne, next to her, was looking handsome and proud. Ruth's good friend Iris beamed at her. Reverend Huber stood at the front of the church with his bible in hand, ready to unite these two friends.

Walter and Rose Lessing sat in the second row, behind Edith and Lorne. Ruth nodded at them as she walked by. As Walter watched Ruth move up the isle on Herman's arm, it reminded him of the day, when his sister, looking much like her daughter did today, had wed Herman.

After Herman ceremoniously gave his only daughter over to Waldemar, he sat down next to Edith to enjoy the occasion. Reverend Huber began the ceremony, which was a mix of Baptist and Anglican traditions.

"Dearly beloved: We have come together in the presence of God to witness and bless the joining together of this man and this woman in Holy Matrimony. The bond and covenant of marriage was established by God in creation, and our Lord Jesus Christ adorned this manner of life by his presence and first miracle at a wedding in Cana of Galilee. It signifies to us the mystery of the union between Christ and his Church, and Holy Scripture commends it to be honored among all people. The union of husband and wife in heart, body and mind is intended by God for their mutual joy; for the help and comfort given one another in prosperity and adversity; and, when it is God's will, for the procreation of children and their nurture in the knowledge and love of the Lord. Therefore, marriage is not to be entered into unadvisedly or lightly, but reverently, deliberately and in accordance with the purposes for which it was instituted by God."

He continued on as Ruth and Waldemar stood hand in hand at the front of the church, listening solemnly. Waldemar's heart was pounding.

"Into this holy union Waldemar Peterson and Ruth Bohlman now come to be joined. If any of you can show just cause why they may not lawfully be married, speak now or else forever hold your peace."

The packed church was quiet. Ruth held her breath, waiting for Reverend Huber to continue.

"I require and charge you both, here in the presence of God, that if either of you know any reason why you may not be united in marriage lawfully, and in accordance with God's Word, you do now confess it."

Ruth and Waldemar smiled at one another as Reverend Huber turned to Ruth. "Ruth Bohlman, will you have this man to be you husband, to live together in the covenant of marriage? Will you love him, comfort him, honor and keep him, in sickness and in health, and, forsaking all others, be faithful to him as long as you both shall live?"

Ruth spoke the simple words that meant a lifetime of commitment regardless of what life would bring, "I will."

Reverend Huber turned to Waldemar. "Waldemar Peterson, will you have this woman to be your wife, to live together in the covenant of marriage? Will you love her, comfort her, honor and keep her, in sickness and in health, and, forsaking all others, be faithful to her as long as you both shall live?"

Waldemar looked at Ruth and knew there was no other promise he'd rather make, "I will."

Reverend Huber continued as he prepared for Ruth to receive her ring. "Bless, O Lord, this ring to be a sign of the vows by which this man and this woman have bound themselves to each other; through Jesus Christ our Lord. Amen."

Herman brought his handkerchief to his eyes as he watched his daughter commit herself to marriage.

Waldemar began to speak, "I give you this ring as a symbol of my vow, and with all that I am, and all that I have, I honor you, in the name of the Father, and of the Son and of the Holy Spirit."

"Now that Waldemar and Ruth have given themselves to each other by solemn vows, with the joining of hands and the giving and receiving of a ring, I pronounce that they are husband and wife, in the name of the Father, and of the Son and of the Holy Spirit. Those whom God has joined together let no one put asunder."

A chorus of "Amen" came up from the guests in the church.

As Waldemar and Ruth moved to sign the register, Iris came to the front of the church and sang "O Perfect Love." Not a single eye in the church was dry. The newlywed couple beamed at one another as they found themselves in the final moments of the ceremony.

Reverend Huber ended the ceremony with a prayer for the couple, each word sent from God as a foreshadowing of their life ahead.

"Eternal God, creator and preserver of all life, author of salvation and giver of all grace: Look with favor upon the world you have made, and for which your Son gave his life, and especially upon this man and this woman whom you make one flesh in Holy Matrimony.

Give them wisdom and devotion in the ordering of their common life, that each may be to the other a strength in need, a counselor in perplexity, a comfort in sorrow and a companion in joy.

"Grant that their wills may be so knit together in your will, and their spirits in your Spirit, that they may grow in love and peace with you and one another all the days of their life.

"Give them grace, when they hurt each other, to recognize and acknowledge their fault, and to seek each other's forgiveness and yours. Make their life together a sign of Christ's love to this sinful and broken world, that unity may overcome estrangement, forgiveness heal guilt and joy conquer despair.

"Bestow on them, if it is your will, the gift and heritage of children, and the grace to bring them up to know you, to love you and to serve you.

"Give them such fulfillment of their mutual affection that they may reach out in love and concern for others.

"Grant that all married persons who have witnessed these vows may find their lives strengthened and their loyalties confirmed.

"Grant that the bonds of our common humanity, by which all your children are united one to another, and the living to the dead, may be so transformed by your grace, that your will may be done on earth as it is in heaven; where, O Father, with your Son and the Holy Spirit, you live and reign in perfect unity, now and forever. Amen."

Ruth and Waldemar both had tears in their eyes as they looked at one another, feeling the weight and the wonder of all that those words meant.

Waldemar squeezed Ruth's hands silently, promising that he would be all of those things to her: a strength in need, a counselor in perplexity, a comfort in sorrow and a companion in joy. His blue eyes looked into her heart and silently promised her that he would forever be everything to her that she needed. He knew that she would also be to him all of those things, in perfect unity.

After a kiss and a cheer from the crowd, Ruth and Waldemar walked down the isle and opened wide the doors of the church. The sun was setting and the snow had begun to gently fall.

The couple paused to look at one another, now as husband and wife. "I love you, Waldemar Peterson."

"I love you too, Ruth . . . forever."

Lorne, just sixteen, was proud to be driving the car carrying Ruth and Waldemar to the reception in Edmonton. He carefully navigated the snowy gravel road. Ruth and Waldemar sat in the back seat. The guests from the wedding followed Lorne through the snow and wind, with only a few cars veering off the road into the ditch. Lorne gripped the wheel nervously, his knuckles turning white.

"You're doing fine, Lorne," Waldemar assured his new brother-in-law.

"Thanks, Pete. It sure is slippery."

"Just keep it nice and slow, and we'll get there." Waldemar turned to Ruth and asked, "Well, Mrs. Peterson, what do you say?"

"I'd say I'm the luckiest girl in Canada." Ruth held Waldemar's hand tightly. She snuggled up close to him. "The luckiest girl in the world."

Nine days later, November 15th, Waldemar and Ruth waited to board their flight. They were headed to Calgary, a short trip, but extravagant all the same. The tickets had cost $18.50 each. Ruth wore a brown gabardine dressmaker suit with a muskrat topcoat. Winter was fully upon them and her suitcase was full of warm clothes for their adventures.

"Are you excited about your first plane ride?" Waldemar asked.

"Yes, it should be fun. It's too bad you have to work in the middle of our trip though."

"I know, it won't be for long." Waldemar had been called to testify in a court case a few days after their trip began. It was regarding a traffic fatality. He was required to be a witness. The Force would be bussing him from Calgary up to Edmonton for the day and then returning him back that same night. They found out about the case just a few days before the wedding, after the details of the trip had already been worked out. With all of the costs of getting married, a new apartment, travel and new furnishings, it was a mighty stretch to find enough money to afford the bus ride. The Force would pay them back but in the meantime they had to find the available cash to get Waldemar where he needed to be. He had also found out after securing married housing in Entwistle that he was being moved to St. Albert, a small town just north of Edmonton. After that he would be moved to plain clothes in Edmonton. This was quite a disappointment to his Swedish friend, who had so kindly agreed to let him convert the house they were going to be renting. Now the house would go to another Mountie while Waldemar began his search to find housing in Edmonton. Thankfully, Ruth's friend Nora had been able to get them connected with someone who was renting the first floor of a house, right near the Legislative Grounds, for $45 per month. Housing in Edmonton was scarce following the war, and they were happy to find a place where they could be in walking distance of the Miseracordia, where Ruth was going to be working.

The pair boarded the plane and sat next to each other, holding hands and looking out the small window. It was quite a luxury to fly. Both of them were looking forward to their time together, away from work.

"What do we have planned for tonight?" Ruth asked.

"I was thinking that we should go for dinner and then to a show. What do you think?"

"That sounds fun. What shows are playing?"

Waldemar spoke over the roar of the plane engines as they started their ascent into the sky. "There's a new movie out, 'The Song of the South.' I think we'll go see that."

Ruth smiled and sat back in her seat, holding Pete's hand as they pulled up through the winter clouds. It was bumpy. Ruth gripped his hand tightly. The pair chatted about the friends they had seen at the wedding and the upcoming party at the Bohlman house after they returned. Edith was hosting a party for friends and family to come by, view the wedding gifts and to share the top layer of the wedding cake. They had so many wonderful things to look forward to, a lifetime of adventure and excitement with one another and it was all just beginning.

*"Before I formed you in the
womb I knew you, before
you were born I set you
apart . . ."*
Jeremiah 1:5 NIV

<u>December 1948</u>
<u>Edmonton, Alberta</u>

It had been a little over two years since their wedding day. Ruth and
Waldemar were happily settled into their life together. Ruth was expecting
their first child. She was already two weeks past due and every day seemed
to stretch on endlessly.

Waldemar was still in the plain-clothes division while Ruth had been
busy with nursing, up until the last month. She had been working at the
Miseracordia briefly after the wedding and had then transferred over to
the University Hospital, into administration. Waldemar took the streetcar
to work every day. Every morning, he kissed his wife goodbye, hoping
that today he would get the message to come home early because the baby
had come.

Christmas was a few days away. Ruth had been decorating their small
apartment and trying to take her mind off the impending birth.

She had broken her tailbone shortly after the wedding. Because of this
she was worried that she may have some difficulties with delivery. She had
suggested to her doctor, who was also her colleague, that she should have
a caesarian section. He assured her over and over, however, that nature
would have its way, and even though she carried on past her intended time
of delivery that eventually the baby would come.

Ruth had already felt the sting of a disappointing end to a pregnancy. Just before her current pregnancy, she had experienced a miscarriage. She was about three months into the pregnancy when it had ended, and although she knew miscarriage to be a common occurrence, it didn't ease the sting of losing a potential life. It was all in God's hands, however, and she felt blessed when this latest pregnancy developed and had so far gone smoothly. She had some sickness in the early months but since then had felt fine. She was planning to cook the Christmas meal in their home this year. Herman, Edith and Lorne were going to drive up for the day. Aunt Lily and Uncle Fred were also planning to join them. Ruth had assured everyone she could handle the meal preparations. Secretly, she was hoping that the effort of the event might send her into labor.

Ruth moved around the apartment dusting and cleaning. She loved the smell of the pine boughs that decorated the living room. She had made a wreath for the door, decorated it with red ribbon and bright Christmas balls. Waldemar had cut down a tree from the river valley. Together they decorated it and made it the centerpiece of the living room.

The couple had been busy converting a small bedroom in their apartment into a nursery. They had purchased a crib and a carriage for the new baby. Ruth bought a few baby blankets and some little white sleepers. She purchased a large length of flannel to make diapers. Everything was ready to go, should the baby finally decide that it was time.

Ruth felt the baby kick. "I know you're ready so come on out," she said. She rubbed her belly affectionately in response to the baby's movements. She thought again about the delivery. She desperately wanted her doctor to order her a caesarian section so that the delivery could be over and done with. About a month ago, she had been in Leduc visiting her dad at the store when the local doctor had come by and offered his opinion on the matter.

"When are you due?" he asked as she stood behind the counter with her father.

"December ninth." Ruth had responded.

Herman scowled as he checked out the doctor's goods, "Will that be all?"

"Yes, thank you. How is your tailbone healing?"

"It rarely gives me pain anymore but as the baby grows it does ache." The doctor had been the one to see her after she had fallen down the stairs at the Bohlman house and broken her tailbone.

"You know a broken tailbone can cause a lot of problems during childbirth,"

Herman passed the doctor his bag, "Thank you, Doctor, she has plenty of good care in Edmonton."

The doctor scowled at Herman, "I'm just saying that she shouldn't deliver naturally, she should be given a c-section."

Herman came out from behind the counter and began to usher the doctor to the door of the store, "Thank you for the advice, no need to worry the girl."

"Think it over, Mrs. Peterson," the doctor called as he left.

"What's wrong, Dad?" Ruth asked her clearly agitated father.

Herman said, "Don't let it worry you. You have far better care in Edmonton. He's just a small-town doctor. Leave these things to the specialists in Edmonton." Concern furrowed Herman's face as he looked at his bulging daughter.

"It's alright, Dad, don't worry, it's in God's hands. I don't completely disagree either; I've heard that it can cause complications."

"Well you can talk it over with your doctor in Edmonton—but I wouldn't hold too much weight in this doctor's words."

Ruth wasn't sure what bothered her dad so much about that doctor. She had talked it over with Waldemar and with the doctor at her hospital. He insisted on a natural birth. Ruth and Waldemar had decided to follow his advice since he had more experience in these matters. So here she was, nearly two weeks past her date and still waiting.

At his detachment, Waldemar sat at his desk, looking over a file he had been working on. His mind wandered instead of reading.

Just after the wedding, Waldemar had been posted in St. Albert, a small town north of Edmonton. He had very limited resources and no police car. He spent the days sitting in his small office, off of which were his living quarters, big enough only for a bed and a washstand. He patrolled St. Albert on foot and often he would receive a phone call from Edmonton, which he could do nothing about. One time there was a stolen car that the police in Edmonton thought might be coming through St. Albert. Waldemar could do nothing but watch the car drive through town and then call Edmonton back to let them know that indeed the vehicle was headed north.

After that, Waldemar had been moved to Edmonton, on plain-clothes duty. It had been a big adjustment from the type of police work he had been doing. It wasn't what he had expected. He tried to get through it one day at a time. In the beginning, he found himself occupying his time by driving around senior officers to the club or on their personal errands. It was tiresome and meaningless, but he and his younger co-workers had a joke that no matter what they were doing, it all counted toward their pension. He was happy when he was transferred out of that department.

Alberta was under a lot of pressure following the war. So many young men had returned, permanently affected by what they had seen, some injured physically and some mentally altered. There were no jobs, no housing and some had lost sweethearts who had given up on waiting. Men were desperate. Money was scarce. There were so few cars, even for the Police Force, that crime was often local. The City of Edmonton Police shared resources with the RCMP, each rotating when they would use a car.

Now that he was a detective in Edmonton, he saw first-hand how the economy had influenced crime. His focus was breaking, entering and theft cases, B.E. & T, which he investigated on quite a few instances already. Many of the rural merchants didn't have access to a bank, so they simply locked their money in a store safe for the night, leaving them vulnerable to criminal activity. B.E. & T was not his only focus, however, he would take any case that came across his desk, helping out in whatever way the department needed assistance. He enjoyed the variety and liked to keep busy. Just like his childhood days, he liked to live life at a running pace.

He was looking forward to Christmas Day and celebrating with Ruth's family. It would be a nice break from work. He thought of Ruth while he worked, wondering how she would manage when the baby came. He was glad she was so close to the hospital.

Christmas morning dawned. Ruth rose early, feeling every muscle strain under the weight and pressure of the baby.

Perhaps today would be the day, a Christmas baby, she thought, as she went to the kitchen to make some oatmeal for both of them.

Waldemar came to the table in his blue striped pajamas. Once Ruth had prepared the coffee and the oatmeal, she brought everything to the table. She sat down next to him.

"Do you need help with anything today?" he asked.

"I'm making a casserole for supper. We need to get the turkey in the oven right away. Perhaps you can lift it for me when I have it ready." Waldemar nodded in agreement as Ruth continued, "Mother and Aunt

Lilly are bringing the vegetables and side dishes so it shouldn't be too much work for me."

"What time are they arriving?"

"In the early afternoon."

"Did you send your family a telegram?" Ruth asked.

"Yesterday. Sing and Nick brought Pappa from the farm to visit so I'm sure Mamma is pleased."

"I wonder how your mamma is feeling."

"I think she downplays it, but Sing seems worried in her letters."

"That seems like a trend with the Petersons," Ruth said, "always overly calm about everything."

"She never likes to worry us children, even though we're not children anymore. I am glad she's living with Sing now in Winnipeg, at least I know she's well taken care of."

"Do you think your pappa misses her on the farm?" Ruth asked.

"Perhaps, but I'm sure he's good company for Victor."

"Sing is such a saint to care for your mamma."

"Mamma always did an awful lot for us; she gave everything for us. I'm sure Sing sees it as a blessing to be able to give back to her."

The couple finished their breakfast. Ruth began to prepare the casserole and the turkey. Waldemar watched her as she moved around the kitchen, her body big and awkward. He helped her lift the turkey into the oven and then they sat down to rest until the family arrived.

The afternoon went by and before long there was knocking at the door. Waldemar rose to answer it, pulling Ruth to her feet as he went. Herman, Edith, Lorne, Lilly, Fred and their children Joyce and Jean stood in the cold. Their arms were laden with gifts and food.

"Hello!" Waldemar and Ruth greeted their guests.

"Hello," they all responded warmly, coming into the apartment and stomping the snow off their boots.

"Well look at you, girlie, you look ready to have this baby!" Aunt Lilly laughed as she rubbed Ruth's belly.

"I am ready! I just wish my body would co-operate!" Ruth smiled and took the dishes of food from Edith and Lilly and carried them into the kitchen.

"It smells wonderful, Ruth," Edith commented as she laid her parcels down on the dining room table.

"Thank you, Mother, I've got a casserole in the oven and the turkey, of course."

Herman came over and gave Ruth a big hug. "How are you, child?" he asked.

"I'm doing well, Dad. How was the drive up?"

"It was fine, the roads were clear. How are you feeling?"

"I'm well; I'm more than ready to meet this little one."

"I am looking forward to meeting the little guy."

"Little guy, huh? What do you know that I don't?" Ruth laughed.

"I know either way I'm going to be a Grandpa very soon!" Herman smiled broadly.

Ruth rubbed her father's arm affectionately. "And a very good one at that, I'm sure."

The rest of the afternoon passed by quickly and soon it was time for dinner. Ruth had everyone sit at the dining room table. It was covered with a red tablecloth. Lilly joined Ruth in the kitchen to help her carry out the food.

Ruth pulled the casserole out of the oven, and as she did it slipped from her hands and smashed into a million pieces on the floor. Cheese, carrots and sauce splattered across the cupboards and across Ruth's skirt. Ruth looked at the mess and started to cry.

Aunt Lilly rushed over to Ruth and helped her to her feet, "Just leave it, girl, I can get it." She started to scoop up the broken glass and hot food into a tea towel.

Ruth felt the tears rush down her face, All the frustrations flowed out. "Oh, Aunt Lilly," she sobbed, "now what will I do? Dinner is ruined."

"Never mind that, it's not the end of the world. Get a can of corn from the cupboard and warm it on the stove. It only takes a few minutes." She tossed the casserole and the broken dish into the trash can and quickly wiped up the splatter from the cupboards and the floor. "Go and get changed and no one will know."

Ruth wiped her face on her apron. She nodded as she moved to the cupboard for the corn and proceeded to heat it up. After that, she quickly excused herself to change. By the time she returned to the kitchen, Lilly had everything under control, as though it had never happened.

"Aunt Lilly, you're an angel." Ruth smiled at her aunt as she looked around the kitchen.

"No matter, sweetheart, let's get this dinner on the table!" Lilly smiled reassuringly. She picked up the large turkey and headed to the table.

Herman thanked the Lord for the meal. They had wonderful conversation for hours, relaxing around the table. When the night was over, everyone said goodbye, wishing Ruth good luck with her upcoming delivery.

After they left, Waldemar and Ruth settled onto the sofa. "Well, Mrs. Peterson, Merry Christmas."

"And to you, Mr. Peterson." Ruth took his hand in her own. "I have something for you."

"You do?" his eyebrow raised. "A kiss perhaps?"

Ruth laughed, "I always have a kiss for you, but I also got you a gift!"

She took the last gift from under the tree and passed it to him. He opened it to find a handsome pair of leather gloves and a scarf to go with it.

"Thank you!" Waldemar slipped the gloves and scarf on, modeling them. "It just so happens I have something for you as well," he smiled at her and reached into his pocket.

"Oh!" Ruth exclaimed as he passed her a long narrow velvet box. Inside was a beautiful necklace. "Thank you, Pete! I love it!"

She turned her back to him and he fastened the necklace around her neck. She looked at him, fingering the delicate chain. "How does it look?"

"Beautiful," he smiled, "just like you."

*"He has made everything
beautiful in its time. He
has also set eternity in the
hearts of men; yet they
cannot fathom what God
has done from beginning to
end."*
Ecclesiastes 3:11 NIV

January 1949
Edmonton, Alberta

Ruth had woken to contractions about an hour ago. It was January 15th and it seemed that finally, more than a month overdue, the baby had decided to leave the comfort of the womb. The pain was intense and getting stronger and steadier as the hours went on. It was a cold Alberta night. Ruth had been pacing the apartment, waiting for the contractions to intensify so that she could head over to the hospital. Waldemar slept peacefully while Ruth paced. She hadn't wanted to wake him until it was time for her to go. She breathed slowly and steadily as the next contraction gripped her body. She looked at the clock—four minutes since the last one. Her nursing instincts told her it was time.

"Pete," Ruth shook Waldemar's sleeping frame, "Pete, it's time."

Waldemar woke up and rubbed his eyes, "It is?" He was sleepy and disoriented. "Time for the baby?"

Ruth smiled and then frowned as another contraction hit. "Yes, time for the baby," she said through clenched teeth.

"Okay, what do I do?" He had risen from the bed and began to dress as quickly as he could. He ran a hand through his hair to smooth it down.

"How about you help me get my coat and drive me to the hospital. And then you wait. The hospital will call you when all the hard work is done. Ahhhh . . ."

Waldemar began to get more excited and nervous as he watched the pain cross Ruth's face. "Okay, let's go!"

He assisted her into her coat and lovingly helped her slide on her boots. He held her arm firmly as they walked over the icy sidewalk and then helped her into the car. Ruth tried to breathe and focus through the pain as she had told so many of her patients to do. *Easier said than done apparently*, she thought as the pain made her grasp the door handle.

Waldemar drove carefully down the snowy streets to the hospital. Before long, he was in front of the hospital putting the car into park and pushing on the brake. Ruth focused all of her mental strength on managing the pain. Waldemar came around and opened her door, pulling her to her feet. He wrapped his arm around her waist and took her weight as he helped her up the front steps of the Miseracordia Hospital.

They were greeted warmly by the nursing staff. Ruth was a familiar face to some and to those who didn't know her, the way she described her symptoms, they realized she was a nurse. They wheeled her up to a delivery room.

"Okay, so is that everything you need, Ruth?" Waldemar set Ruth's overnight bag on a chair next to her hospital bed.

"Yes," Ruth groaned again as another contraction hit. "They'll call you once the baby comes and you can come back. Just wait by the phone. I'll be fine."

Waldemar felt weak. Something didn't feel right. "Are you sure you're okay?"

"I'm fine," Ruth said softly, "I'm in good hands here."

"I know," Waldemar paused, unsure of what to say, not being someone typically prone to worry. "Alright, I'll head home and wait." He smoothed the blanket over Ruth's legs. "I love you, Ruth."

"I love you too, Pete." Ruth could see the helplessness in his eyes. "Women do this every day, I can do it too."

"I know you can," he replied. "You're the strongest woman I know." He felt a pain in his own abdomen at the same time that she gripped his hand. Another contraction had come for her. It was time for him to go.

He went to the door and turned back one more time. She was rosy-cheeked and focused on what needed to happen. He felt ill as he turned down the hallway of the hospital. He saw a Sister going toward her room to care for her.

Waldemar got back into the car that was still sitting out front of the hospital. He drove slowly back to their apartment. Once home, he made himself some coffee and oatmeal, trying to make the day feel normal. Again he felt weak and ill. Pain shot through his abdomen. *Maybe I'm just nervous*, he thought. He sat down at the table and ate, not feeling much of an appetite. He wondered how Ruth was doing. Perhaps he would lie down on the sofa for a while and wait for the phone call. How long could it possibly take?

As time wore on, Ruth had a lot of reasons to believe things were going poorly. She felt it. She felt it with every fiber of her being that this was not progressing as it should. She had delivered babies before and she knew the familiar tension that hung in the air when things started to get complicated. When she tried to push, the pain was overwhelming. Even though the nurse was encouraging, Ruth was completely worn out. The hours stretched on and she knew instinctively that this was simply taking too long.

After a nurse came to check on her, she heard the nurse and doctor talking about mechonium, a baby's first bowel movement, that had happened pre-delivery. She knew that the baby was now at risk for infection. If she hadn't known it before, she knew it now—this tender life was in trouble.

January 16th dawned. Waldemar paced the apartment, feeling miserable. He was wondering why he hadn't heard from the hospital. It had been over thirty hours since he had left Ruth and he had been feeling awful the entire time. He felt sick to his stomach, weak and feverish and the pain in his abdomen would not let up. He was not accustomed to feeling this way. He kept dismissing his body, thinking that nervousness for Ruth had got the best of him. He had tried to read the newspaper, read the Bible and prayed endlessly for Ruth's health and safety. He had called Herman the afternoon before to let him know that Ruth was in the hospital and that labor had begun. He had promised another phone call once the baby had arrived.

Every few hours, he would pick up the telephone and check it for a dial tone, wondering if something was wrong with the phone itself. Every time it whined back in his ear, mocking his impatience.

Herman prayed for his daughter as the hours stretched on. Why hadn't Waldemar called yet? Had he simply forgotten in the excitement? Was something wrong with Ruth? *That couldn't be*, he thought, *she was in the best care possible at the Miseracordia, with competent doctors. This wasn't 1921 and women didn't die in childbirth, very often at least.* He wrung his hands and prayed for peace as he thought of his sweet daughter, not knowing how she was. He struggled to push away images from that cold December night so long ago, memories he'd rather forget. *Oh God, be there, be there for her.*

Finally, the phone rang, awaking Waldemar from a fitful sleep. He pounced on it, "Hello?"

"Mr. Peterson?" a male voice questioned.

"Yes, this is he." Waldemar waited.

"This is one of Mrs. Peterson's doctors. I'm afraid we've run into some difficulties."

Waldemar felt the room spin. He gripped the armrest of the sofa. "What is it?"

"We need you to decide, who we should save . . ." he paused, his tone even and steady. Waldemar felt his world spinning wildly out of control as the doctor said five of the most difficult words Waldemar had ever heard, "the mother or the child?"

*"I learned to say, 'When I
am afraid I will trust
You.'"*
—*Ruth Peterson*

January 16, 1949
Edmonton, Alberta

She couldn't die here; this wasn't how her story was going to end. Her father would never survive the pain—and her husband, what would he do if she did not get up out of this bed and come home to him? She thought of him waiting by the phone, waiting to hear the good news of the baby arriving and yet the hours went on and on and nothing was right. Everything was wrong.

The pain was like nothing she had ever experienced. Possibly more horrific than any of the births she had attended as a nurse. She could not carry on. She begged for the doctor to do something, but the baby had come too far now. She had to make it happen with her own strength. The room seemed to spin. Her fellow nurses encouraged her onward, telling her that she could do this. That she had to continue.

Her nursing school headmistress, Sister Saint Christine, had gathered every available nurse in the hospital to the chapel to pray for Ruth and Baby Peterson.

"Keep pushing, Mrs. Peterson," Nurse Jenkins encouraged.

"I can't," Ruth gasped. "It's bad," she moaned. "The pain . . ."

Her broken tailbone was causing Ruth insurmountable agony. She felt as though with each push she would lose consciousness. Sister Saint Christine had taught her enough about the human body to know that there was only so much a person could take. She could feel her blood pressure dropping. The edges of the room went fuzzy during each contraction. She knew the baby was in grave danger. She also knew that if it didn't come soon that there might not be a baby to bring home in her arms.

The doctor re-entered the room, commented to the nurse and turned to Ruth saying, "We need to get this done with, Mrs. Peterson. The next contraction I need you to give it everything you've got." Ruth laid her head back against the pillow in agony.

"Take a deep breath now," he said.

The words rang over and over in Waldemar's head. He wasn't sure how he had answered and hung up the phone. He said it again, out loud, in the emptiness of the apartment. "The mother. Who do you want us to save, the mother or the child?" Who was that? The mother? She was not a mother, not yet, she was just Ruth, his Ruth. He couldn't lose her. Four years ago she had told him that God had brought them together. God could not take her away, not yet. The pain shot through his abdomen again. He crumpled to the floor. He tried to push his six-foot muscular frame to his hands and knees but he found himself momentarily unable to move. What was wrong? *What is happening to me?* He pulled himself to the kitchen where he vomited in the kitchen sink. He rinsed it down and then decided that he should call on his upstairs neighbor. Something wasn't right.

He dragged himself up the flight of stairs to his neighbor's house. He knocked loudly as he let out a moan. Henry's eyes were wide as he opened the door. "God! Pete, what happened to you?"

"I don't know, something is wrong," he gasped. "Can you drive me to the hospital?"

Henry swiftly grabbed his coat and boots. "Let's go. I'll drive your car, okay?"

Waldemar nodded weakly and found his way down the icy stairs with Henry holding him steady. They drove to the hospital in silence, through the cold January evening, with only the odd moan from Waldemar. When they arrived at the hospital, Henry asked, "Where's Ruth?"

"She's here," Waldemar moaned. "She's having the baby—they're not sure she's going to make it."

"Oh no," Henry said solemnly. He aided Waldemar into the hospital where he turned him over to the care of the nurses.

The baby was finally out but it didn't make a sound. Ruth waited for the cry, the cry of life, the cry that signified that everything was going to be okay—and there was none. She saw the nurses huddled around the small infant, a boy, they had said. She could see them rubbing him vigorously and suctioning his airway, willing him to live. The doctor was focused on her, delivering her afterbirth and trying to control the bleeding. She surrendered herself to shut her eyes and then willed them open again to try to catch a glimpse of the infant. Every tick of the clock signified another minute the baby hadn't taken a breath. *Please God, please God,* she thought. Ruth focused all her strength on counting the minutes, each an eternity, five, then seven and ten until . . .

"Waaaaaaaa . . ." the blue little boy cried out from where the nurses were working.

"Thank God," Ruth whispered. "Thank God." The sound was music to her ears. It meant that he was alive. She laid back and let herself give into unconsciousness.

Seeing that Ruth had blacked out, the doctor barked, "She needs a transfusion! She's a mess! Someone get some blood for this woman or she's not going to make it!" He worked furiously to save her.

Waldemar laid on the gurney as they pushed him into surgery. "Appendicitis, Mr. Peterson, we're going to take it out before it ruptures."

"My wife," he moaned again, "my wife."

"We'll call your wife when you're all through," one of the nurses reassured him.

"No, she's—she's here. She's having a baby."

"Well, doesn't that beat all," one of the nurses said, smiling.

"No—it's not good, she may not survive." The tone in the room turned serious. The doctor told Waldemar to count backwards from ten as the medicine took him away. He heard hushed whispers regarding Ruth. He struggled to hold on and hear what they were saying . . . and then there was blackness.

The days and nights mixed together. Ruth didn't know how long it had been since she had delivered the baby. She hadn't seen Waldemar either. That bothered her immensely. There were many things she didn't know right now. What day was it? How was the baby? Where was Waldemar?

What was her state of health? All of the confusion swirled in her mind. What she did know was that she had more than one transfusion already and she felt incredibly weak. It was an effort just to raise her arms off the bed. Every single muscle in her body ached terribly. She knew that the prayers and support of the staff at the hospital surrounded her. She knew that God was here, in this room, keeping her alive. *But what about the baby?*

A nurse entered the room. Ruth wanted to ask her many of the questions on her mind. "Excuse me," Ruth croaked. She raised a finger off the bed.

"Oh, hello, Mrs. Peterson. I didn't realize you were awake."

"I'm thirsty."

"Certainly, let me get you some water." The nurse poured Ruth a glass of water from the jug that sat on the table next to her bed. "Here you are."

Ruth took a long sip and let the cool water linger in her dry mouth. "Have you seen my husband?" Ruth asked.

"Yes, he's doing fine."

Ruth was puzzled. Of course he was fine. Why wouldn't he be? "How many days has it been? Since the birth?"

"Three, today is the nineteenth. Now that you seem a bit more alert perhaps we could discuss a few things. I'll have Sister Saint Christine come down and talk to you."

Ruth felt a quiver in her stomach and shut her eyes for a moment. Scenes from the delivery flashed in front of her. Did this mean the baby was gone?

"Mrs. Peterson?" the nurse came over and placed a hand on Ruth's forehead, "are you alright?"

"Yes, I just feel confused."

"Of course you do, dear. You've been very ill. Not to worry, Sister will help you. She can answer your questions, alright?"

The nurse left the room. Ruth took a deep breath, feeling like she might cry. She must not though, for fear that Sister may withhold information that could cause her further distress. She too had been on the other end of giving a fragile patient bad news. It was never easy. What was her bad news? *God, let it be good. Let my fears be for nothing. Let my fear be untrue. Let the baby be healthy. Let him be alive.* The prayer came silently in her mind. Tears came to the corner of her eyes. She repeated a comforting bible verse from Isaiah. In the stillness of her room, she spoke a verse that she had memorized as a small child. It had seen her through her darkest valleys, of which there had been many.

"So do not fear for I am with you; do not be dismayed for I am your God. I will strengthen you and help you; I will uphold you with my righteous right hand."

Hearing her own shaky voice utter the words allowed her to breathe more evenly. She heard a knock at the door. She hastily wiped her eyes with the bed sheet. In came Sister Saint Christine pushing none other than Waldemar, looking pale and gray, in a wheelchair, clearly, also a patient.

Ruth gasped, "What happened?"

"He's fine, Mrs. Peterson," Sister Saint Christine assured Ruth as she wheeled Waldemar next to Ruth's bed. "Your husband didn't want to be outdone by you so he decided he'd like to deliver his appendix while you were having your baby."

Ruth looked at Waldemar. She held her hand off the bed toward him. He weakly reached up his hand to hers and held it tightly. "Sweetheart, I'm sorry. I was worried about you." Waldemar reached up to stroke Ruth's hair away from her pale face. "I kept asking but they wouldn't tell me what was going on, until today."

"Oh, Pete, it was awful." Ruth began to cry. "Have you seen the baby?"

Sister Saint Christine interjected, "I will bring him to you, but you need to stay calm. I know that this has all been very overwhelming."

Waldemar turned to look at Sister Saint Christine and asked the question neither wanted to utter, "He is alive then?"

Sister nodded, her expression grim. "He is. However, we feared for several days that one of you, mother or child, might not survive. It is only by God's grace that you have turned a corner today." She paused, looking at the couple intently. "It is not over for you either of you. Mrs. Peterson, you have a long road of recovery ahead. Your blood pressure is low. You are very weak and it will not be an easy recovery. I do want to show you the baby though. Before I do, you must know that he—he is very fragile."

The room was silent as Sister Saint Christine decided how to phrase the news of Baby Peterson's health. "Your son, he didn't breathe for a long time. He is quite bruised from the birth and is still very unstable."

Ruth felt her body trembling. Waldemar gripped her hand tightly. Sister continued, "His health was so poor that we decided to have him baptized. We committed him to God, fearing that he may not have the opportunity later on." Sister paused, waiting for Ruth's reaction. "I'm sorry, I know it isn't what you would have chosen but you were in no condition to make a choice. It was what we thought was best."

Ruth said nothing but Waldemar spoke up, "That is fine, Sister, thank you." Ruth was not offended; in fact, she was grateful.

Sister went on, "I will bring him to you but I wanted you to know about the bruising, and the fragile state of his health so that you will not be alarmed by his appearance. I know you have nursing experience, Ruth. But when it is your own child, it can be difficult."

"Thank you," Ruth whispered. Her entire body trembled. Her stomach lurched as she looked at Sister Saint Christine.

"I'll be back shortly with the baby. You two can take a minute to prepare yourselves."

With that, she turned and left the room. Waldemar and Ruth were left to look at each other and soak in the events of the last few days. The baby was here, finally, but his life was still in God's hands—whether he was going to live or die was still unknown and the thought of it threatened to overwhelm the couple completely. They both sat quietly, each sending up their own deeply personal prayers to God, searching for answers.

Waldemar brought Ruth's hand to his lips and kissed it tenderly. "Ruth, whatever happens, I'll always be here."

She nodded. She felt a lump in her throat. All she could say as they heard a knock at the door was, "I love you."

Sister wheeled the bassinet over to the couple and took a minute to adjust Ruth in her bed. Sister propped her slightly upright so that she could hold the baby, with support. Once Ruth was ready with a pillow under her left arm and several behind her back, Sister Saint Christine brought the baby to Ruth and placed him in her arms.

"I'll leave you for a minute but he should get back to the nursery shortly. We don't want to cause him any undue stress."

Ruth felt it odd that being in his mother's arms could cause him stress but said nothing. She took in the sight of this lovely little boy. Waldemar was breathless as his eyes settled upon the baby.

Only his head peeked out from the tightly swaddled blanket. A small knitted cap came down to his little wrinkled brow. He was as cute as anything. Even though he had dark bruising on his face, they could see the apples of his cheeks and his delicate little red lips. He slept peacefully in Ruth's arms while Waldemar looked on, soaking it all in.

This child was a beautiful mix of both Ruth and Waldemar, a symbol of their love for one another. He was an incredible force of life that was certainly none other than a gift from God. Ruth tentatively stroked his brow.

"What will we call him?" Waldemar asked.

Ruth suggested a few names until they settled on Gerald. Gerald Frederick. It was a strong name that matched his show of extraordinary perseverance thus far. His middle name they decided should be Frederick, after her dad, Herman Fredrick.

"Hello, little Gerry." Waldemar placed his hand on the sleeping baby, his large hand spanning from the tip of Gerry's toes to his tiny chin. "I love you already."

Ruth looked at Waldemar and said, "We did it, Pete. We're more than just a couple. We're a family." She had tears in her eyes as she watched Gerry take every breath. He seemed like he would be okay. He looked peaceful in her arms. How could he not be okay? "Thank you, God. Thank you for our son."